William Sharp

Children of Tomorrow

William Sharp

Children of Tomorrow

ISBN/EAN: 9783337049423

Printed in Europe, USA, Canada, Australia, Japan

Cover: Foto ©Andreas Hilbeck / pixelio.de

More available books at **www.hansebooks.com**

CHILDREN OF TO-MORROW

A ROMANCE

BY

WILLIAM SHARP

"How leapt we into this Labyrinth of Love?"
GIOV. FLORIO, *Seconde Frutes.*

"We, who live more intensely and suffer more acutely than others, are the Children of To-Morrow, for in us the new forces of the future are already astir or even dominant."
H. P. SIWÄARMILL.

London
CHATTO & WINDUS, PICCADILLY
1889

𝔅𝔞𝔩𝔩𝔞𝔫𝔱𝔶𝔫𝔢 𝔓𝔯𝔢𝔰𝔰
BALLANTYNE, HANSON AND CO.
EDINBURGH AND LONDON

DEDICATED

IN FRIENDSHIP AND ESTEEM

TO

JAMES SUTHERLAND COTTON, M.A.,

FELLOW AND LECTURER OF QUEEN'S COLLEGE, OXFORD,

AUTHOR OF "INDIA,"

ETC., ETC.

CHILDREN OF TO-MORROW

CHAPTER I.

THE twilight of a raw evening early in May dimly pervaded Felix Dane's studio, sombre with the drawn blue-black window-screens. The fire smouldered in the grate, although every now and again the flame spurted upward and cast fantastic flickerings athwart the walls, or ruddy gleams upon the figures, carven in marble or wrought in clay, which occupied so much of the underspace of the lofty apartment. The shadows were so deep that neither the size of the room nor what it contained would have been obvious to any intruder—to whom little would have been visible but the partial outlines of various sculptures, a white mass upon the floor, and a man, with bent body and face shrouded in his hands, seated in an arm-chair, a few yards from the fire. By the side of the chair, to the right, was a low table, whereon stood a cup of untasted coffee,

A

several unopened letters, a copy of a weekly paper, and a slim parchment-covered volume, with the printed contents downward, as though the reader had been interrupted, and had so placed the book for easier resumption.

Had any of Felix Dane's friends observed him at this moment he or she would have concluded that the sculptor was asleep. It could . scarcely have been imagined that he was in any strait of wretchedness. Successful men are not supposed to suffer from any profound sense of despair—the lot, by common consent, of the ill-equipped, the baffled, the already doomed. And that he was, in a sense, greatly successful, not even his rivals and detractors could deny. Was he not still young—only in his thirty-fifth year? Had he not achieved almost phenomenal success as a sculptor? Had he not in Lydia Dane a wife as handsome as she was distinguished; blessed, moreover, with several hundreds a year in her own right, and. with influential family connections? To be dissatisfied in the face of such weal would surely be iniquitous; to sit in an arm-chair in the dusk, with hands shrouding drawn features, and a dull sense of despair and self-contempt aching at the heart, would be folly as weak as that of the Oriental king who, after having engraved *There is no reality but Allah* upon his palace-wall, fled from his harem and vast wealth to dwell solitary in waste places.

Yet the silent occupant of the studio was not asleep or physically exhausted. He, Felix Dane, the most successful, and at one time the most promising, of English sculptors, the friend of the leading painters, poets, and novelists of the day, was so sick at heart, there in his well-known Hampstead studio, the Sycamores, that he would fain, in deepest earnest and without affectation of renunciation, have forfeited position, comparative wealth, and the still more cherished things of his life, if only the old impulse, the old insight, the old passion, might be his again, and the hope and dream of his soul be once more no idle fantasy.

He was suddenly startled from his attitude of dejection by the abrupt entry of some evidently unexpected visitor. The room was so enveloped in shadow that the new-comer did not see the look of chagrin and momentary anger that changed Dane's expression.

"Are you there, Felix? Why, what are you sitting here for in this gloom? The fire is almost out, and it is wretchedly cold."

"That's just it: the fire *is* almost out," Dane muttered as he rose and advanced towards his wife.

"What is all this on the floor, Felix? Has there been an accident?"

"Nothing that you need trouble about, Lydia. Let us go into the house: you should not come along that cold passage or into this place."

"No; light the lamp."

Without a word, Dane turned and lit a large chain-lamp which swung from the ceiling, and thereafter the candles on the projecting shelf of the fireplace. As he did so, his face was reflected in the antique Italian mirror which hung above it, and Mrs. Dane found herself curiously regarding it —as one might look for the first time at a stranger in whom one was more than ordinarily interested and had heard much discussed.

The face was that of a man who while still young in years and energy had yet lived rapidly. The features were fairly regular, the nose slightly aquiline, the complexion pale, the forehead broad rather than high, the eyes large and lustrous, but of such an indeterminate hue that they at different times appeared as dark-grey, purple-black, or gipsy-brown. The hair that clustered about the forehead was of a deep brown, every here and there just threaded with grey. The general impression given by the features was of mingled sensitiveness and strength—as of one whose nerves were very mortal indeed, but whose will was potent and beyond the sway of other minds. A characteristic poise of the head—backward thrown, half-interrogatively, half-defiantly—added to the effect of keen mental alertness which his personality had upon most people. Tall, and powerfully built, he appeared more robust than he actually was.

As his wife looked at his mirrored face she noticed that some recent powerful emotion had left its traces. She was too well accustomed to signs of weariness upon these handsome features not to know that the strained lines about the forehead and mouth betokened no ordinary ennui.

Nor was it to be wondered at that casual acquaintances and strangers regarded the twain as a couple blessed by the gods. Mrs. Dane was what many people called beautiful. She was certainly unusually handsome, and had an air of distinction, of hereditary refinement, which in itself was full of charm. With the advent of her thirtieth year she had lost little of that which makes early womanhood so exquisite, for she had never been youthful save in years; and those who remembered her on her twentieth birthday, when as Miss Lydia Falconer she was presented at Court by her worldly old aunt, Lady Margaret Trevor, could see little change, save that of the inevitable, however slow, growth towards maturity, in the Mrs. Felix Dane of thirty. Somewhat above the average height of her sex, she had the further advantage of a good figure : her features were regular, and her hazel eyes could do everything but glow with tenderness. The pale-brown hair, which she habitually wore coiled in broad plaits, exactly suited her complexion, which was of almost waxen delicacy; but composed and dignified as she was with the stagnation of a sterile spiritual nature, her voice betrayed that gentleness was not her most dominant trait. It was firm, almost bell-like, in ordinary utterance; at other times it was apt to be hard and metallic.

When Dane turned from the fireplace and looked at his wife, the ghost of a mocking smile played for a moment about his mouth. She was staring now at him, now at what lay in a heap upon the floor—a mass of shapeless clay, yet in parts showing some human curve or contour, a fragment of an arm, a divided torso.

"I thought that something was the matter. Was that due to an accident?" and Mrs. Dane's voice was almost tender, for she could understand what a blow it would be to a sculptor to have his best year's work suddenly brought to ruin; almost as tragical, to her, as the loss of valuable jewellery or the failure of one of those monetary speculations wherewith she delighted to stimulate her sluggish excitement.

"No, Lydia, it's my own doing."

"Your own doing! What foolery is this, Felix? You are no longer the moonstruck boy who used to vapour about ideal life and all that kind of thing: you do not mean to tell me that you have been so insane as to destroy that 'Hertha' over which you have already wasted so much time?"

"Do not excite yourself, my dear Lydia. It is my affair, and not yours. The wretched thing is destroyed, and there's an end of it."

"But it *is* my affair. You have done almost nothing for months save to work away at 'Hertha:' it was to be a great feature at next year's Academy, and to bring you increased prosperity and influence, and in all probability would have assured you the next R.A.-ship."

"That is an honour I can very well dispense with, *ma chère.* I know too many Academicians to be in the least degree desirous of official association with them. I admit, however, that if I had not demolished 'Hertha' she would probably have brought about my election. She was so deadly commonplace that she would have enraptured the academical mind."

"I have no patience with you, Felix. You throw away all your best chances; indeed, it is a wonder to me how you have gained your present reputation. I suppose some of your precious poets or fledgling artists have been persuading you to be truer to yourself, whatever that may mean. I see you have the *Metropolitan* there : I noticed that some scribbler, who had much better have attended to his own business, said you might have done, and even yet might do, this, that, and the other thing, but that, like many another man in art and literature, you had sold your genius for excess of gold. And you allow yourself to be influenced by that kind of folly! You pay attention to the patronising nonsense of an art critic who would only too thankfully sell *his* genius for what he calls excess of gold, and "———

"Permit me to interrupt your eloquent denunciations, Lydia, to inform you that the article in the *Metropolitan* is written by Harold Field, whom you as well as I know to be sincere as a man, loyal as a friend, and one of the truest and keenest critics we have."

"I do not call a man a friend who could write that article, and I shall tell Mr. Field so when next I see him."

"He wrote it *because* he is my friend, and because he believes in me notwithstanding all the poor work I have turned out."

Lydia looked contemptuously at her husband,

as she daintily picked her way through the *débris* of what was once Hertha, the Earth-Goddess, and stood between the fire and the low table.

"I hate mock modesty."

Dane made no reply, but looked quietly at his wife, with such a curious mocking light in his eyes that she felt uncomfortable.

"And now, Lydia, perhaps you will allow me to escort you to the drawing-room. This is the night of Sarasate's concert, is it not? I understand that Adama Acosta, the 'amateur-genius' of one society chronicler, the 'mad Jew' of another, will for the first time play in public—persuaded thereto by Sarasate, it is said."

Lydia listened with sullen disdain, and partly to show her indifference, partly from that craving of jealous curiosity which consumes such natures as hers, lifted the slim down-turned volume which lay upon the little table. As she did so, one of the letters fell to the floor, to be immediately picked up and opened by her husband.

The latter was interrupted in perusal by an abrupt exclamation.

"Sanpriel? Who is Sanpriel?"

"I know no more than you do; for I see that you have read the inscription on the fly-leaf."

"What impertinence!—'*To Felix Dane, in admiration of his earlier work.*'" As she scornfully commented on the inscription she glanced at the first page, which bore the curious title, " *White Nights—* by Sanpriel—Printed for the Author," followed by the printers' name and the date.

" Ah, some budding poet or soulful maiden who is in mortal fear of the critics, or in dread, perhaps, of what 'papa' would say ! I congratulate. you upon your new admirer, Felix."

Dane was too familiar with his wife's habit of sneering at all the things he most cared for, to pay, as a rule, any attention to her scornful remarks, but for some reason he was deeply annoyed at what she had just said.

" Give me that book, if you please, Lydia. There are things you should not interfere with, and this is one of them."

" Ah, here is a clue to the mystery ! A poem called 'Hertha,' and turned down at a certain page. . . . So, it is this young person's rhymed nonsense that has made you dissatisfied with *your* 'Hertha' ? "

" I did not mean to tell you, for I knew that you could not, or would not, understand ; but as you have discovered what you call the clue, I may assure you that you have at last gained the information you want. In that poem of 'Hertha,' Sanpriel, whoever he. or she may be, has a finer conception than ever mine was. I was vaguely dissatisfied with my work from the outset, and latterly came to despise both it and myself; and when this afternoon I gave up in despair, and having glanced at that book, which had been sent to me, found there a higher conception of ' Hertha,' I had the good taste as well as the strong impulse to destroy my handiwork. Henceforth I'll do nothing in ideal sculpture that I do not *know* to be good; and if I cannot succeed, why, then, I'll restrict myself to portrait-sculpture."

" I do not think our marriage has brought us much happiness, Felix. You have disappointed me. I thought you would make a great name for yourself, though I always did consider you were foolish to discard painting for sculpture. Why couldn't you have kept up both, for that matter ? And now you are going to throw away all the chances you— and I—have so laboriously won. And for what ? For an ideal that does not exist, for a phantom of your imagination ! If you would be like other men, you would be much happier, much more respected, much wealthier and more influential, and would make *me* much more content with my life."

" How tenderly considerate of you, Lydia ! But you see, as I told you even before I married you, I love my art above everything else—and not even to please *you* can I discredit such talent as I may possess. But as I have already said, let us leave this cold room; and don't you think, my dear, that we might as well bury the tomahawk? We have long ago threshed out this subject of loyalty to artistic ideals, and as we shall never agree, we but waste our breath in vain assertions and denials."

While he was speaking, his wife glanced through the sextains on the pages which had wrought him to such wrath with his own work:—

All things before her were laid bare,
All knowledge and all power she had;
She knew no sorrow, felt no care,
Had perfect vision, and was glad:
    Even as in a glass she saw
    The evolution of one law.

She watched the life of nations grow,
She heard the sound of puny wars,
Each mockery of triumph blow
Beneath the same unchanging stars:
    She heard the sound of prayers rise,
    Felt the old stillness 'midst the skies.

Within her brain each thought that passed
Within the minds of men was held;
Her gaze on each new dream was cast,
To her the mists were all dispelled;
    She saw in flawless nakedness
    Each truth that man would curse or bless.

She had strange dreams, she felt the throb
Of the great world-heart pulse and swing;
She heard the low continuous sob
Which universal death did wring
    Amidst the loud discordant strife
    For ever echoing from life.

To her all passions were as things
Of little heed, like leaves that fall,
Dead leaves the wind takes up and flings
Aside: o'er her they had no thrall—
    She knew their heights and depths, but wise,
    She looked through each with cold calm eyes.

How little seemed each living thing
How puny life of man—brute—flower:
And yet, how wonderful the Spring
That with regenerative power
    Swept round the earth—how vast, how great,
    Humanity confederate!

This Hertha saw, and was content:
What mattered each small life was vain
When all in one great whole were blent,
When all were links in one vast chain
    That rose from earth's remotest sod
    And passed the stars and reached to God!

"They may be fine and may be poor: to me they are simply meaningless."

"Lydia, did you hear me ask for that book? Be so good as to return it to me."

With a sudden passionate gesture Mrs. Dane threw it backward on to the smouldering fire. Whether by the momentary draught thus caused, or accidentally, a red tongue of flame spurted forth, hungrily licked the leaves, and before Felix was able to snatch it away it was ablaze.

To Mrs. Dane's surprise—an agreeable surprise, for she had expected bitter reproaches for what she could not but realise was malicious folly—her husband took her action very quietly. He had tried to rescue the slim booklet from destruction, but had only succeeded in tearing away the outer cover and the fly-leaf: the former he threw back upon the coals, evanescently aflame again, and the latter, curled at the edges with heat and partially browned, he leisurely folded and placed in his breast-pocket. He then lifted his letters, and crossed the studio to the door, which he opened and stood beside till his wife should pass out.

"If you have anything to say to me, Felix, I should prefer it to this solemn silence ? "

"I have nothing to say to you, except to remark that I forbid you on any pretext whatever, unless invited by myself, to enter my studio again. I must emphasise this command by the further condition, that if you pay no attention to it I shall work elsewhere."

Without a word, husband and wife walked along the tiled and covered passage which connected the studio and the house. . When they entered the latter they walked across the hall—beautiful with a falling fountain and a mass of greenery, and, on pedestals, various replicas of famous sculptures— and upstairs to the drawing-room, a large and handsome apartment, which, notwithstanding the refinement and taste displayed in its decoration, had yet not the appearance of a room habitually lived in by occupants who felt at home.

"Some of Dane's marble has got into his drawing-room," a friend once remarked to Arlo Spence, the famous impressionist and wit, who had at 'once replied, "Yes, his 'Lydia' is there."

There was a pause for some minutes after entrance. Lydia reclined on a couch, and played idly with a paper-knife; Felix stood by the fire and read his hitherto unopened letters. When he had finished he glanced at his wife, and was half-bewildered, half-amused to find himself admiring her.

The subdued light, roseate in hue, from the huge lamp on the book-table threw a warm gleam upon her face; the firelight shone and cast flickering shadows upon her graceful figure; and as she lay there, Lydia Dane appeared the embodiment of re-fined grace and beauty.

As Felix looked at her he realised, all the more vividly on account of the gulf which separated them, how fair to look upon his wife was; and how, though it never had appealed, though it did not now strongly appeal to him, her beauty was of a nature that fascinated many men.

"There are two kinds of women," he caught himself repeating under his breath—"there are two kinds of women—so says the Persian poet: those who are made of fire, and those who are made of water.   Those created from fire know how to love, and as a reward their hearts become as molten gold, and they enjoy the second life : those created from water are but semblances of women—their hearts grow colder and colder till they become blocks of ice—and when the wind of Death comes they melt into nothingness, like the rime of frost before the sun."

"Felix."

"Well ? "

"Was it not Gabriel Ford who commissioned that 'Hertha' ? "

"Yes.   Why do you ask ? "

"Because I presume that he will hold you to your bargain.   You cannot substitute some other work, whether inferior or superior, for it.   Moreover, he is to dine with us to-night, and accompany us to the concert; so it might be as well if you were prepared with your answer in case he should ask to see or inquire about 'Hertha.'"

"You need not be uneasy.   Ford commissioned it, it is true, but only conditionally on my part.

I said that if I sold it at all, he should have the option of purchase. I warned him that I might not sell it at all, or that I might never go on with it. Moreover, I am not anxious for any of my work to go to Ford; nor do I imagine that his wish to 'patronise' me is wholly disinterested."

There was no sneer in Dane's concluding words, and he did not even look at his wife as he spoke; yet she flushed, and a swift look of passing anger came into her eyes. He knew that her fair skin had reddened, and that her eyes were momentarily alight; and, though his gaze was averted, she too knew that he knew it.

For though never a hint of the matter had crossed the lips of either, both were aware that Gabriel Ford entertained a more than merely friendly admiration for Lydia. Felix himself was indifferent, partly because his wife had alienated herself from his sympathies, partly because he felt assured that no breath of passion could do more than ruffle for a moment the frozen calm of her nature. Ford, the handsome and accomplished but reputedly unscrupulous son of the millionaire banker who controlled the great house of Fioravante & Co., was not a man for whom he cared, though the extreme interest which the history of Israel and most things Judaic had for Felix Dane had prompted him to familiarity with Gabriel Ford, who was quite unaware of the kind of interest he excited, and, indeed, would have resented it, for he never voluntarily admitted anything more than a business relationship with the Hebrew merchant-princes and bankers. In truth, Dane's apprehension of the facts was based rather upon vague surmise than upon actual knowledge. Not that Ford was an ordinary Jew. Neither he nor his father, Sir Lewis, belonged to the Jewish community in London; nor did either give in adherence to any religion, save such as might be implied in a greater largess to the Church of England than to other ecclesiastical institutions. But racially both were Jews, and none the less so though in features they were Caucasian rather than Semitic. The Fords, the Montagues, the Despards, and a few other wealthy families occupied a strange position. They were not Christian, nor were they Jewish, in faith; yet they never intermarried save with the sons and daughters of Israel. The orthodox Semites regarded them jealously, hating them because they mixed mainly in Christian society, and made their wives and children cease from attendance at the synagogue, but eager not to offend them on account of their paramount influence and also, to no slight extent, because of their reputed earnest though disguised sympathies with Judaic federation.

The silence which had ensued upon Dane's words was broken by the entry of a servant, who announced Mr. Gabriel Ford.

A tall, fair-haired man, slender of build, smooth of face, and of a complexion that was almost girlishly olive - toned, bowed as he approached and took Mrs. Dane's hand in his own. Though handsome, he would not have been a noteworthy man but for his eyes, which were impenetrably dark — black as night, though ʼthe deep night of the South, not that of the North, blankly nigrescent.

In the interval which elapsed before Felix—who had left the room as soon as he had greeted the visitor—returned in evening-dress, Lydia alluded to the " Hertha " incident.

Ford listened, with a curious smile on his face —a smile that somehow displeased his listener, for she suddenly became more reserved.

Then, as if he had not apprehended what she had said, and without preamble, he looked at her intently as he uttered a remark whose abrupt irre-levancy startled her.

" I do not understand ? "

" I repeat : it is just ten years ago, Lydia, since you and I first met. You had not then encoun-

tered Dane. Your excellent aunt yearned after the
Fioravante coffers, but mistrusted the keeper's in-
tentions. Eh? Has it ever occurred to—to—*you*
that as your aunt dropped a goodly flavouring of
gall into your pot of honey, you should discard the
mixture and select a new jar for yourself?"

"You are as fond of enigmas as ever, Gabriel.
All that I concern myself about is—that the past
is the past. You and I might have—but why
talk of 'mights'? There is now a depth between
us which is bridgeless. But even in our friendship you must be more careful. I know that my
husband suspects your attitude towards me. By
the way, Gabriel, do you know what he told me, I
suppose in some fit of prejudice? He said you
were a Jew."

"What then?"

"What then? Why, of course, I contradicted
him; and with that arrogant gravity of his, he went
on to state that though you and Sir Lewis were
what is called 'enfranchised Jews,' you were racially
so exclusive that neither you nor any of your set
would, in any possible circumstances, marry a
Christian."

"Well?"

"You are very laconic, my good Gabriel. Of
course it is not true?"

"It is not true."

“ What is not true ? ” asked Felix, who at this moment entered the room.

“ That I am about to conduct the Paris house of Fioravante & Co.,” Ford answered with quiet readiness ; “ for though London has more drawbacks than any other great city, it is yet the best place to live in.”

“ The best for *us*, Ford, perhaps ; but not for the three million or so of people of limited means and of *no* means.   A great city is a great ulcer.”

“ Heine says our civilisation is cancerous, you know.”

“ Heine’s own ‘ cancer of life ’ made him say many such things.   Lydia, did you reply to the Walfords that it would be impossible for me to accept their invitation just now ; and have you made up your mind as to whether you are going or not ? ”

“ Yes ; I am to join them in Dorset to-morrow. I told them you could not accompany me.   Are you going to the Cranes’ ?   You promised Sir Arthur, that day you introduced him to me at the Grosvenor Gallery, that you would spend a few days at Forest Manor.   Mr. Ford is going ; you might journey to-morrow in company.”

“ No.   I do not feel inclined to go anywhere at present.   I have too much to do.”

“ So it would seem,” Lydia replied, in a low sar-

castic tone.   " Ah, there's the gong ; let us go down
to dinner."

So emphatic had Felix been in his determination
not to pay his promised visit to Sir Arthur Crane,
that Lydia was very considerably surprised when,
later, during the homeward drive, her husband
informed her that he too would leave home on
the morrow for a few days, and accompany
Gabriel Ford to the Cranes' place near Grantley.

CHAPTER II.

Through most of the concert Felix Dane sat in mental and physical apathy. Not even the magic of Sarasate's violin-playing roused him from his despondency, almost over-sensitive as he generally was to music; and, with curious introspection, he caught himself watching, with a scrutiny at once observant and indifferent, his wife and Gabriel Ford, as they sat two or three rows ahead of him. He had been glad when he learned that the three seats were not together, and only too willingly obtained isolation at the expense of Lydia's company. While the chords and sharp minors vibrated stridently or through infinite delicacies of melody, he pondered deeply on all manner of trifles—upon the texture of an Oriental shawl a few yards away from him, upon where the violets which lay enmassed against yonder girl's bosom had grown, upon what fate was in store for the tea-rose that nestled in the dusky hair of the brunette just in front of him. Often he would look at Lydia; sometimes in unconscious admiration of her sculpturesque beauty, again in vague wonder at the fact that that woman, so remote, so alien, so all unknown to him, should be his wife. Nothing of that familiarity of deep love, which is as the dew upon flowers, had ever existed between them. Love is not love when its buoyancy has vanished; and never in the love, in the affection which at first had mildly existed in the heart of either for the other, had there been one buoyant moment. At Ford also he looked as though upon one of whom he was ignorant and to whom he was indifferent: perhaps a sensation of repulsion, physical in part, rendered his indifference less fundamentally real.

Of his fallen aspirations, his slackening cunning of mind and hand, even of his ruined " Hertha," he thought nothing, or next to nothing. It was all a blank, a sense of malfortune, a weariness, a shadow whence there was no escape.

The sudden cessation of the song that had followed Sarasate's last fantasia, the loud applause that was sweeter in the ears of the singer than her own notes, and a silence, filled as it were with the palpitation of expectancy, stirred him to partial attention. Ere he could relapse into apathy again, his gaze was attracted by the strange figure which appeared before the footlights.

Rumour had long wagged her tireless tongue concerning Adama Acosta, the Jewish violinist, whose genius, it was said, Sarasate himself revered. Little was known of him, scarce more than that he was the child of the mad Dutch organist, Salathiel Acosta, and a Spanish Countess, who in the fervour of her passion for " the angel ·Salathiel "—as he was often called on account of his extraordinary beauty—had given up position, kindred, nation, and religion for love's sake, in the days when the hereditary taint in the Acostas had not shown itself; that, at an early age, their child Adama had shown unmistakable genius, but was subject to periods of melancholia, if not of actual insanity— an idiosyncrasy, however, which had not prevented his marriage with a very beautiful Englishwoman, of whom nothing was ever known save that she had spent most of her life in Mexico and was possessed of considerable fortune.

Adama was reputed to be the father of a son— of a daughter—of several children, all of whom were mad, all of whom were musicians, all of whom were beautiful, all of whom were deformed —and so forth.

Only a few knew that his wife had died in childbirth, and that the sole offspring of the marriage was a girl, who was neither mad nor a musician, but certainly rarely beautiful. His one intimate friend, Sir Arthur Crane, knew that " the divine amateur " had shown traces of his hereditary malady not long after his wife's death, and that at intervals a shadow gloomed the imagery of the brain and veiled the outer world in folds none the less impenetrable because phantasmal.   Sir Arthur knew, also, of the strange fate which marked out the Acostas.   For several generations each head of the family had suffered from intermittent insanity, but in no instance had any daughter of the line showed even the faintest trace of the hereditary taint—neither she nor her children, nor her children's children.   Adama had once told his friend that six generations back an Acosta, a married girl, had fled with a Christian; that she had been recaptured and literally starved to death as the penalty of a sin worse in the eyes of Israel than murder itself; but that ere death had relieved her from her shame and sufferings, she had cursed the men of her blood unto the seventh generation, setting upon them the bane of madness, and upon the women of her kindred, one in every seven, the lust of alien beauty.   And thus had it been.   Unto each Acosta there had been born but one son, and to him madness in some form or other, temporally or intransiently, had sooner or later come; and though not once did any of the women of the house betray aught of the mysterious malady, every now and again one—so Adama declared— had committed, or attempted to commit, the unforgivable sin. It was this secret curse, with its uncertain visitations, much more than his possession of ample means, that made the public appearance of " the seventh and last Acosta "—as he sometimes, to his friend Crane, called himself—so intermittent, and latterly so rare. Of his genius there was no question, though in magic of touch he was surpassed not only by his pupil Sarasate, but by one or two other famous violinists who daily gave to their art hours of manual labour, a mechanical but necessary task of which he felt himself incapable.

Dane was not prepared to find in Adama Acosta so striking a personality, nor, indeed, a man apparently so advanced in years.

Tall, but very sparely built, with bent shoulders ; with long grey-white hair hanging from a head which would have been remarkable for its massive dignity had it not been for the face, so painful in its intensity, death-pale, cadaverous, baleful, save when the eyes lit up with soft emotion. · As soon, however, as the bow moved across the strings of the violin, the whole expression and attitude of the man changed. With head poised like a hawk's, with limbs trembling from nervous excitement, and with eager, almost radiant glances across the sea of unknown faces, he began his famous

"By the Waters of Babylon." The wailing cadences, the passionate sorrow, the undertone of exultant fervour, electrified the audience—and with them, Felix Dane.

As the last chords resounded through the hall, Dane's gaze was suddenly attracted by a face so beautiful that a thrill, subtler than any caused by the violin music, stirred every nerve in his body. The girl, apparently about twenty, or perhaps a year or two more, sat at the end of the row to his left. He could see only her profile, but the poise of the head, the mass of lustrous bronze-hued hair, the mobile features and noble contours of the face, the complexion pale and delicate as the most transparent white amber, and the expression, rapt and wonderful under the influence of Acosta's strains—all came upon him as a revelation. Often, how often ! he had dreamed of this ideal beauty ; and though in London, in Paris, in Rome, in Venice, in the Greek isles, he had encountered women of rare loveliness of face and figure, never had his eyes rested on one like unto the girl upon whom he now gazed as though fascinated.

From the cessation of applause and the moving to and fro of members of the audience he was vaguely aware that the first part of the concert was over. With an impatient exclamation he turned to answer some remark from his right-hand neighbour, but when he turned again he noticed, with a pang of disappointment, whose bitterness almost made him smile at his folly, that the girl had gone.

Starting to his feet, he caught a glimpse of a tall, lithe figure passing down the sideway, and by the movement and the gleam of the hair rather than by the back-turned looks and whispered questions of those past whom she walked, he knew that his vision had been no phantom. With eager haste, and heedless of the salutes and occasional friendly summons from acquaintances, he gained the entrance-door, but too late to encounter the object of his pursuit.

Baffled, he sought the doorkeeper, who, to his delight, was able to give him the information he asked, though he moved away in impatient chagrin when he learned that "Miss Acosta" would not return to her seat, as she had driven home with her father, who was not to play again that evening. No, the man had added in reply to a final question, he did not know where Mr. Acosta lived.

On his way back to his seat he met Ford, who had been conveying a message from Mrs. Dane to some friends she had descried.

"By the way, Ford, am I right in thinking

that you said Adama Acosta and his daughter were to be at the Cranes'?"

"Yes, I said so.   They are going down to Yorkshire by the midnight mail—on account of some whim of Acosta's as to travelling by night. But how do you know there is a daughter?   I don't believe there are three people in this room who have met her?"

"Do *you* know her?"

"Yes—intimately," Ford replied, with a ghost of a smile, and with a look in his eyes that made Felix vaguely uncomfortable.   "Ah, there's Signora Alba coming forward; we must be seated. One moment; have you made up your mind not to go to the Cranes'?"

"No, I feel I need a change after all; so I'll run down to-morrow for a couple of days or so. We shall meet at King's Cross, I suppose?"

Throughout the rest of the concert Felix sat in a dream.   All manner of fantasies beset him. He fancied that he had lived through many earthly existences, and that in each he had met and loved the beautiful girl whom he now knew to be the daughter of Adama Acosta; that they had endured many perils together, but that love had guided them aright; that they had rejoiced in Greece, that they had laughed in Pagan Rome, that they had intrigued in Medicean Florence, that they had played desperate hazards for passion's sake in the Venice of the Doges, and so forth in a strange medley of all lands and epochs. A new life began to animate his being; the blood coursed more swiftly; his latent energy bestirred itself. Hopes, aspirations, determinations that had long lain dormant haunted the chambers of his brain; and when the closing music of the trio of stringed instruments was at an end, he rose to join his wife with a feeling to which he had long been strange, a sense of physical exhilaration, of mental elation even, almost of triumph.

But when Ford had bidden good-night, and the carriage had started, the old weariness flowed in upon him again like a tide. At all times magnetically sensitive, he was almost invariably conscious of the drain upon his inner self in Lydia's presence, of her malign influence upon his artistic nature, of her cold, calm, sponge-like absorption of his mental and spiritual vigour. Her silence was not less exigent than her questioning: it was her personality, antipathetic to the last degree, that rendered life in her company mere existence.

In common with most highly-strung natures, Felix experienced similar sensations, in more or less acute form, with several people with whom he was closely related, or whom he affectionately regarded. With his mother, for instance, whom he certainly loved genuinely if with no depth of emotion, he could not remain for any length of time, for Mrs. Erskine (for she had married again shortly before Felix had wedded Lydia) was but the passive counterpart of her daughter-in-law. But, on most occasions, he could control or disguise his sense of resilient energy—his feeling, as he once put it to Harold Field, of being plucked feather by feather, and left naked and void of motive-power. Too often, however, he found himself quite unable to subdue the sense of revolt with which Lydia inspired him, struggle against it as he might.   In vain he conjured up all her good qualities, some genuine, some imaginary; in vain he placed himself in the wrong; in vain, in despair, he leant as it were against the very frail bulwark of his affection; for over and above all crept the cold, resistless tide of Lydia's spiritual impassivity.   Thus when alone with her he generally took refuge in silence, or in the utterance of such commonplaces as occurred to him in what he vaguely felt to be some happy fortuitous way.

In the long drive Hampstead-ward husband and wife spoke little.   As the carriage rattled along the thoroughfares and sped through quiet byroads, Lydia seemed absorbed in her own thoughts; as for Felix, he was possessed of an intolerable restlessness, which made him long to be out and afoot, to walk swiftly onward, anywhere, with the scents of the white lilac and the hawthorn blooms filling the air, and the nocturnal fluting of the moon-awakened thrushes rising and falling in prolonged vibrations through the May night.

Something restrained him, however, from leaving the carriage at Haverstock Hill. How was it he found it so difficult to tell Mrs. Dane that on the morrow he purposed to go to the Cranes' after all? When at last he did announce the fact Lydia was surprised, but said nothing.

A little later Hurst Road was entered, and then the short avenue of The Sycamores; and with a cold kiss and a polite good-night, husband and wife went their separate ways.

CHAPTER III.

When Felix was just about to enter the York express at King's Cross in the conviction that Gabriel Ford had missed the train, he was saluted by a young man with the inquiry as to whether he were Mr. Felix Dane.

" I thought so, sir, from the description given me by Mr. Ford.   I was sent to tell you not to expect him, as he finds he cannot leave town until to-morrow.   He said he would telegraph to his cousin."

" His cousin !   Who is his cousin ? "

" I presume he meant Sir Arthur Crane, sir, but those were his words."

A few minutes later and the express was beyond the dreary suburban districts and speeding towards the Cambridgeshire flats.   As the sole occupant of the carriage sat in the right-hand corner and looked out upon the landscape, vividly green on account of the rain that had fallen over-night, and agleam every here and there with orchard-blooms

and a widespread surf of blackthorn and other
blossoms of field and hedgerow, he kept wondering
at his folly in feeling any manner of annoyance in
the fact that Ford was a cousin of Adama Acosta,
or perhaps of Miss Acosta.   What could it matter
to him?   He was not so ignorant of human
nature, or of his own heart, as to be oblivious of
the truth that in a sense he loved this unknown
girl, of whose very name he was unaware.   It was
ridiculous, no doubt; but gunpowder will leap into
flame at the sudden accidental concentring of solar
rays through the most insignificant magnifying-glass.
If it should happen, he admitted to himself, if it
should so chance that he should never see her again
—and it was possible that the concert-attendant had
been mistaken—or if he should find that she was
married, or absolutely indifferent to him, still, he
had enjoyed his vision of love, and henceforth his
ideal would be a truer one, an imperishable possession, an enduring stimulus to utmost effort.

For there are natures so alert to the magic
of beauty, so sensitive to its instantaneous appeal that their spiritual insight triumphs over
all ordinary limitations.   In the briefest interview,
nay, in the apprehension of a passing remark, of
the inflection of a voice, in the revelation of a
glance, they know everything essential that is to be

known. Naturally this faculty is rare—so rare that it is laughed at and disbelieved in by many, particularly by those who could not become spiritually *en rapport* with others though their souls' salvation depended thereupon ; but snow is rare in Australia, for instance, yet is an occurrence credible even by the North Queenslander.

A man must love a woman sensuously, or his passion is apt to be of the intangible sort that has the radiant tints but also the evanescence of dew. But beyond bodily desire, remote even from the communion of intimate friendship, there is the phantom-lover, more beautiful than the physical environment, rainbow-hued, immortal. When love's flame intensifies to the white heat of passion—as it does perhaps once in ten thousand instances—the phantom-ideal and the loved one are identical, but even then the former is imperishable and unchangeable, while the latter is in sad sooth subject to the ebb as well as to the flow of all mortal tides.

But fortunate are they who thus love dually, for whatsoever time or change may bring, neither can affect the ideal which has its abode in the heart of the lover. There are men who have been passionately in love, nay, who have even known ecstasies of communion, who have never pressed their lips against those of their beloved, never felt their own heart beating against that of the woman who is "all in all."

Thus was it with Felix Dane. Passion, save in a vaguely ideal way, he had never felt, though he was well aware of the potentialities of his nature. He was not ignorant of its lower phase, for he was no alien from the common lot, the unavoidable heritage ; but his essentially pure mind and poetic temperament kept him almost as ascetic in this respect as any priest engirt with the armour of voluntary sanctity. For his wife he had at no time felt more than an admiring affection, which, in his inexperience, he had confused with more strenuous and vital emotion ; but the marriage had scarce been consummated ere he had learned how blind he had been, and what a Nemesis would thenceforth dog his footsteps. Perforce, therefore, the repressed passion of his nature exercised itself in visionary life, till it came to pass that, practical and worldly-wise as he was, he really lived only in his studio, where he could work at what he loved, and where in spirit he was free from all trammels of circumstance.

Startling indeed was it, therefore, when at the Sarasate concert he had caught a glimpse of that haunting, ever-evanishing face of his ideal. Heretofore he had seen it but as through a veil, as a light

in a filmy cloud : now and henceforth it was real
to him—for had he not, at a London concert, amid
the most ordinary surroundings, in the glare of
gas and the vitiated atmosphere of the hall, seen
her whom he had loved and wooed in the spirit ?
The face in itself, indeed, he had not actually
visioned formerly, but what of the accidents of feature when the animating loveliness was none other
than that which, as in the uncertain light of dusk, he
had long worshipped ? How his heart had beat, how
every nerve had thrilled, when there—but a score
of yards away—the ideal of whom he had dreamt,
the woman for whom he had, half-unconsciously,
longed, was visible to his bewildered gaze ! Well,
come what might, he had won something from life
of which no god that ever presided over human
destinies could deprive him. Henceforth his soul
knew its beloved—and no indifference or cruelty of
circumstance could stand between him and that
which he had inalienably won.

These, and such as these, were the thoughts
which thrilled him as the train swept northward.
A swift intoxicating elation—perhaps in part due
to the very motion of the " Flying Scotsman,"
for in all things and at all times we complex
creatures are subject to all physical as well as
spiritual influences—occasionally lifted him to a

state of serene trust in himself and 'fate to which he had long been strange ; but for the most part he was restless, eager, perturbed by all manner of uncertainties in the tragi-comedy in which he dimly foresaw his participation.

Was it the excitement of anticipation, or the mere change of scene and almost rhythmic movement of the train, the reaction after the " Hertha " incident, or the relief in escape from Lydia's numbing personality, coupled with the unselfish satisfaction that she too was travelling at the moment towards enjoyment—mayhap it was not one but all of these which secretly unclosed again the portals of the chamber wherein slept his long-dormant artistic imagination.

With a sigh of weariness, almost of disgust, at what he recalled of his recent work, with a bitter smile at the well-deserved fate of his " Hertha," and yet another at the squandered certainty of that R.A.-ship upon which Lydia, for no other than that of commercial and social reasons, had set her heart, he gave himself up to idea after idea, revelling in the imaginary accomplishment of sculpture which should excel all modern art, excited as beautiful possibility after possibility came shadowily stealing forth or leapt fully created from the inner sanctuaries of his brain.

Life, whose splendours had recently appeared so tawdry, whose apparel of miseries had seemed so sordid, was now as though touched with the magic of the spring which laughed and burgeoned around. In place of avenues of dull outlook there stretched perspectives irradiated with a glow that was not of the common earth. Not since the days of his youth had he experienced such a vital surge of hope and energy. For the last ten years of his manhood he had slowly but surely passed toward the shadowed way of life, and had feared, nay, had felt, the advent of that autumn from which many serene souls are saved even to the end of their fourscore years—the autumn of youth.

But now, again, he, by friendly and hostile critics once hailed, gladly or deprecatingly, as the typical romanticist, looked forth and beheld all things in that light whereby alone genius can reach the heights whereto it strives. Yes, he would not again fall away. Realist and romanticist—words constantly in foolish application—he would be, he was, both : henceforth he should not work at all unless in harmony with the truths both of nature and of imagination.

Genius, particularly since the great arising of the tide of scientific knowledge and inquiry, has complexities of which few observers seem to be aware. It is so often asserted that with the passing away of the old faiths there would be nothing left for the poet, the idealist, but to bewail the golden past, to cry out that all the poetry and romance of life have been banished to an exile from which there may be no return. This may be true of the third-rate poets, the third-rate artists, and all whose vision is narrowly circumscribed; it is not true of those, whether they work with pencil or brush or have no creative faculty, whose intellectual scope is not bounded by immediate horizons. It is no new thing, this hesitant outlook, this partial eclipse of hope. It is a phase that has come to humanity again and again, and whose recurrence is more frequent as our race grows older and, mayhap for a season, a little wearier. There will be, as of yore, new perspectives—all in good time. Science will bring us to a goal whose far shining we do not even descry as yet ; but Nature—and we are only the spoilt children of Nature—abhors abrupt transitions, and will not help us to perceive clear horizons till we have learned how to accommodate our eyesight to a serener atmosphere. Meanwhile it is folly to lament the inevitable. One of the most obvious lessons of human history is, that with growth in the main comes partial retrogression somewhere, that we cannot have our "New Days"

without intermediate glooms and dawns.   Not in
the golden age itself was there ever a time more
wonderful, more romantic, than the present.   Now,
however, we have to search for the accidents of the
true, and as the old limitations to our knowledge of
the world we inhabit recede farther and farther—
till this little earth shall no longer have a mystery
to baffle the curious—to seek in the infinite possi-
bilities beyond our present sphere, and above all in
the imperishable youth and variety of the . human
heart, that which the old legends of ignorance and
surmise wrought for our joy and wonder.   When
we cease to wonder we cease to live, in any
other sense than that of mere existence.   Those
who have the faculty of vision perceive that the
closer and more profound the study of nature be,
the more unprejudiced the acceptation of its hints
of beauty and horror, hope and despair, pitifulness
and irresponsible brutalities, the likelier that one's
insight will be more penetrative, one's apprehension more acute, one's outlook more serene.   Felix
Dane was no third-rate artist, though each work
of his had ever fallen far short of his concept;
but as he was a man of genius—most abused
word!—and not merely of talent, he was also a
deep and fearless student of life.   The frightful
banalities, the cruelties, the heedless brutalities

of nature did not cloud his vision of what was interblent therewith and lay beyond.

The hours passed, and Felix looked with amaze
at his watch when the train drew up just outside
York.　But the hour there recorded, as well as the
sight of the familiar Ouse, along whose waters he
had often rowed in boyhood, and the massive front
of the Minster, convinced him that he had indeed
fleeted the time right royally.

At York he had to change in order to resume
his journey to Grantley by a local line, and in
less than an hour was again speeding on, though
now eastward.　The ensuing two hours were weari-
some; but at last the small deserted-looking station
was reached.

As he stepped across the platform and took
his seat in the dogcart from Forest Manor which
had been sent to meet him, he was conscious first
of a peculiar crispness in the air, and then of the
unmistakable briny smell of the sea.　Yet even when
Grantley Rise was reached he could not descry the
German Ocean; all that he saw in the near distance
was a great crescent of apparently narrow forest.

In reply to his inquiry the groom told him
that the Manor lay in a small park on the verge of
the forest, and within sound of the sea—whose deep
resonant boom was indeed already faintly audible.

As the cart rattled down a birch-margined slope, where the white foam of the elder and the black-thorn and a perfect maze of the blooms of the dog-rose made the floating fragrance almost intoxicating, the groom remarked that they were passing through West Dingle, and that from the rise just beyond both the sea and Forest Manor would be visible.

It was with a thrill of gladness that Felix all at once caught a glimpse of leagues of ocean, deep blue in the May afternoon. The sea ever held him in thraldom, and beside it he was wont, as he asserted, to live twice as keenly as usual. To be within sound of its voice, within sight of its calm or turbulent life, was a joy all the more precious in that it was often productive of a mood that, for lack of a better word, he called inspirational.

Suddenly the dogcart swerved to the left, and though the now loud and insistent boom of the sea seemed to be close by, it was no longer visible, on account of a gorse-tufted ridge—among whose golden blooms flitted innumerable yellowhammers and stonechats—which curved northward. Again to the left, and an elm-avenue was entered; then an ivied undercliff was passed, and, on higher ground, a grove of curiously distorted and evidently very ancient yews; and then the many-gabled weather-stained old Manor came into immediate view, not more than fivescore yards from the sea-wind haunted oaks which formed the outlying eastern flank of the once vast Grantley Forest.

With eager eyes he scanned the balconied stairway in front of the Manor, the lawns and gardens that lay to the left, and the French windows of the house itself; but nowhere did he see the figure upon which he longed to look once more. From the groom he had learned that Mr. and Miss Acosta had arrived shortly after ten that morning.

As he dismounted at the lowest step an elderly gentleman, clad in rough tweeds of a somewhat pronounced pattern, descended with outstretched hands and a hearty welcome.

"Delighted to see you, Mr. Dane; most kind of you to come to us quiet folk out of your busy London. Nothing like keeping promises, and I was determined not to let you off your visit. Sorry Ford couldn't come down with you, but he'll be here to-morrow, I expect. Meanwhile we'll do our best to amuse you, and you'll be interested to meet my old friend Adama Acosta, who is here with his daughter on one of his sudden visits. Perhaps you've met him in London?"

"I heard him playing at St. James's Hall last night. What a marvellous musician he is! And if all accounts be true, Sir Arthur, he has experienced strange vicissitudes."

"Yes; he's had some rough buffetings from fate. Ah, here is Lady Crane. My dear, this is our very welcome guest, Mr. Felix Dane."

Felix shook hands with a largely-built, stout woman of fifty, comely of feature, but with an obvious hardness of expression and prideful demeanour indicative of a certain lack of good-breeding. Her eyes were bright black, but of an unchanging beady glitter; her broad fair face was expressionless; and though she moved with ease and even dignity, and spoke with fluent suavity, her intonation and some occult or not easily definable mannerism testified against her constantly implied claim to be a woman of natural culture and hereditary refinement. Possibly her Semitic origin might not have been suspected by most people, though to some it was obvious apart from definite knowledge; on the other hand, her husband was as absolutely the English type as though he could trace his ancestry back through squires and merchants and yeomen till the days long before any son of Israel set foot in Britain. Tall, robust, somewhat cumbrously but not coarsely framed, his rubicund face was refined by the white whiskers and moustache trimmed Kaiser-fashion, and by the curly grey hair which age had not thinned; while his blue eyes were still alert with energy, when not heavy with a dull content.

"I am charmed to see you again, Mr. Dane, and I hope that you have left all your tiresome work behind you—I mean, that you are not going to allow yourself to do or think of anything but rest and enjoyment. Do you recollect our having met before—it was at one of the Despards' musical evenings, I think?"

"Of course I remember, Lady Crane. Gabriel Ford did me the honour of introduction to you, and I bored you for full twenty minutes with my enthusiasm for Sarasate, whom you had not then heard."

"Ah, but I have done so since, and entirely agree with you. No, this way; you must be dying for a cup of tea. There is nothing like it after a journey. You are not one of those tiresome people with nerves, are you, Mr. Dane?"

"I'm afraid I must plead guilty. But as to tea, no nerveless individual could be a greater slave to it than I am."

"Well, you shall have some such as "——

"Now, Olivia, don't say such as can't be got elsewhere in this country," interrupted her husband; "you're always repeating that fiction. Take my word for it, Mr. Dane—ah, excuse me, here's Robert with a message from our friends. Well, Robert?"

"Miss Acosta sent word to say, Sir Arthur, as neither she nor Mr. Acosta would be in to tea. They've gone a walk to Wolf's Crag."

"Very good. And now Mr. Dane, as soon as you've finished your tea, I want you to come and give me some advice about my pictures and sculptures, which I am rearranging. Your own 'Javelin-thrower'—which I bought at Montague's sale —is already the occupant of the best place."

"Ah, you have the 'Thrower,' have you? I'm glad of that. It is one of the best things I've done."

"So Miss Acosta says, and she seems to know everything you've done."

Felix felt as though the heavens had opened and dazzled him with excess of light. That she—*she* —should like his "Javelin-thrower," should know everything of his, it was too good to be true, absurd almost, incredible! His fear had been that she might not give a second thought to him; that she might never have heard of him; but if she knew his work so well, and had the judgment to pick out his little-known "Javelin-thrower" as his best achievement in sculpture, she must have artistic instincts and interests. Here then, was a bond of sympathy—a bond that Felix welcomed as he might a way of ‚escape from some sore strait of life. Strange, that this new tide of inspiration which had come to him should have been propelled by two women, both unknown to him : Sanpriel, the author of " White Nights," and the beautiful daughter of Adama Acosta.

" Is—is—Miss Acosta "——

" Oh yes, she is staying with us also. By the way, they have a quaint old house not very far from where you live : a place called Dreamthorpe, almost on the heath at Hampstead."

" Dreamthorpe—Dreamthorpe," repeated Felix amazedly ; " why, of course I know the dear old house. Arthur Graham has it ; I know him well."

" Yes, just so ; but he sublet it for this year to Acosta. He and his daughter have been there since January, off and on."

" Good God, and I never knew it ! What a "——

" What do you say, Mr. Dane ? You seem disturbed ? "

" Oh, nothing, Sir Arthur. Your mention of Graham put me in mind of something I had forgotten."

" Your *own* mention of him, I presume ; but

never mind, here we are.　Now do tell me what kind of general arrangement I should adopt."

He accompanied his host in a kind of waking dream.　He answered yea or nay as the spirit moved him, but luckily did not betray his complete absorption in his own thoughts ; nor did he make any palpable error in direction, for which, in his ingratitude, he craved no benison upon the gods.

It was with a sense of relief that he found himself at last in his bedroom, and alone.

Through the open window came all manner of sweet fragrances from the garden-plots underneath, with confused but exquisite odours from the forest ; on the narrow lawns the blackbirds hopped to and fro, with piercing flute-like cries, and in the woodland a thrush sang its vesper-song in such an ecstasy of abandonment that Felix almost imagined himself again in the garden of Dante's villa at Verona, where once he had heard a nightingale sing till it fluttered earthward, killed by the excess of its own passion.　Below, and through all, came the deep, hollow boom of the sea, now rising, now falling, but ever insistent.　To the enthralled listener there was something ominous in that relentless, that for ever inquiescent undertone.

CHAPTER IV.

He was aroused at last from his reverie by the sound of the dressing-bell, an interruption he would almost have resented were it not for the fact that ere long now he should surely meet Miss Acosta.

In his impatience he dressed in half the usual time, and with a swift step, and eyes alert with an eagerness which made his pulse quicken, he descended to the drawing-room, which was on the ground-floor—a long, narrow room, with French windows, and at its sinister or western end a curious curve, so complete that it almost formed an ante-room.

The door was ajar, and moved back noiselessly at his touch. For a moment he hesitated, and then entered. There was no one visible. He was conscious of a sense of disappointment, strangely commingled with one of relief, as he slowly advanced across the thick carpet, and halted, in an attitude of indecision, by the side of a table whereon stood a huge Japanese bowl filled with the carmine and cream-colour blooms of magnificent roses, surrounded by a medley of books, some obviously foreign, but none, whether by accident or discrimination, out of harmony with the dominant tones.

Suddenly he gave a slight start, and was conscious of a curious sensation of surprise, almost of bewilderment, as he noticed among the books a slim parchment-covered volume with, above, " White-Nights," and below Sanpriel, in the familiar bronze-gold lettering.

How strange it would be, he thought, if this unknown " Sanpriel " should indirectly prove a potent influence in his life as well as in his art ! If Miss Acosta, for example, should have been as much impressed by the book as he was, it would be another bond between them——a bond all the subtler from the surety that Sanpriel's poems could of necessity be only of limited appeal.

He lifted the little volume and instinctively glanced at the fly-leaf, whereon was an inscription. Yes ; the handwriting was identical with that on the copy which Lydia had contemptuously thrown on the fire——a year, some months, no, but a single day ago. He recognised it in a moment. Ah, she was a friend, then, of the Cranes; that accounted for the presence of "White-Nights" in such an unlikely place. There it was writ unmistakably, in that small, firm, yet womanly penmanship: "To Sir Arthur and Lady Crane, from their affectionate Sanpriel."

Just as he was about to turn over the leaves he became aware, in some vague way, that he was not alone. He looked about him, but could see no one, till suddenly he perceived the slight movement of a shadow on the carpet near the western window.

Four or five steps brought him to a standstill, thrilled as by an electric shock.

There, facing the splendour of the sunset, and herself irradiated by the golden glow, stood, clad in a straight simple gown of softest and whitest material, the beautiful vision of the previous night. The sun-rays burned in her hair, till its waves and curves of bronze shone like flame; her neck and arms, bare and delicately white, gleamed like antique ivory in candle-light; and in her attitude, the pose of head and bust and body, there was such repose, such beauty, that the sculptor who looked upon her trembled as every sensitive nerve answered to the magic.

Slowly, and as if drawn rather by some occult

magnetic influence than of her own conscious will, Miss Acosta, after a long sigh, half of pain, half of exquisite enjoyment, turned and looked upon Felix Dane.

There are moments when speech is as impossible as it is unnecessary; nay, when utterance would mean the violation of a charm that might never again be as potent. Such a moment had arrived, as simultaneously as incalculably, for the man and woman who now confronted each other.

Felix gazed with such a rapt intentness that, for a brief interval, all thought either of himself or his companion lay dormant. Beautiful as he had thought Miss Acosta from the glimpse he had obtained at the concert, he found her even lovelier than his passionate after-dream : then he had seen but the features ; now he looked into eyes such as never before had stirred him to his depths.

They were large, and had the softness and duskiness of twilight, so deep that to him they seemed as the midsummer darkness itself, purple-black, dewy-soft, luminous though without moon or star. Depth within depth lay the shadows cast by the thoughts of an ardent and imaginative mind ; yet they were depths inscrutable, and for ever inviolate of shallow or irreverent questioning.

She was taller, too, than he had fancied, and

though not less lithe or graceful, somewhat less girlish in the contours of her figure.

Her gaze answered his, steadfast, serene; but she was the first to become conscious of something strained—something so strained, indeed, as to be perilously near the verge of absurdity.

With a smile and a slight flush, she advanced a step or two with outstretched hand,—" Mr. Felix Dane, I am sure ?   I consider myself half-hostess here, so you must permit me to introduce myself— though, if I mistake not, here are Lady Crane and my father."

As she spoke, and her voice was of rare delicacy and charm, she moved forward towards her father, as if instinctively, Felix noticed.

As soon as the introductions were over, he realised how strong was the likeness between Adama Acosta and his daughter, though the re-semblance was that which death bears to life.   Mr. Acosta, too, impressed him even more than on the previous night.   There was something noble and dignified, as well as dominant and eccentric, in his whole physiognomy ; though at first the attention was unduly arrested by the deathly pallor of the face, set off by the long white hair that fell negli-gently about it, and the sombre gleam of the large, dark eyes.

" I am very glad to meet you, Mr. Dane. I know your work well, and if you will allow an old man—or one who feels as though he were an old man—to express his opinion, I should like to add that you seem to me one of the very few sculptors from whom much may be expected. But we'll talk of this afterwards. Sculpture is a hobby of mine, and I probably know as much about it as any layman."

" I'm pleased to hear it, Mr. Acosta. But I often wonder if there will ever again be a widespread love, a widespread appreciation even, of sculpture. I hope for, but I hardly dare say I expect to see it."

" That is what Sanpriel says ; she "——

" What *who* says ? " interrupted Felix, in amazement.

Mr. Acosta stared at his companion, who had spoken with quite tragic emphasis ; and then, with a momentary laugh, replied, " I suppose the name puzzles you. Sanpriel is certainly a rare name anywhere, and absolutely unique in this country in all probability."

" Yes, but *who* is Sanpriel ? I have a particular reason for wishing to know."

" What is your reason, Mr. Dane ? "

" Oh, well—ah—she, or he, published a remarkable little volume recently—and "——

" Dear me, have *you* seen ' White-Nights ' ? Well, since you admire it, you must let me introduce you to the author.   Sanpriel, my dear, step forward and make your best bow."

To Felix's astonishment and confusion, and almost to his dismay, Miss Acosta, smilingly and with the ghost of a blush on her fair face, advanced and made a curtsey of mock gravity.

" Oh, if only you were a reviewer, Mr. Dane, what an awkward position you would have placed yourself in !   You would be bound to maintain what you said in private, and yet would yearn to be critical—and so it would happen that the last case of poor ' White-Nights ' would be very much worse than the first.   But you are only a sculptor, and so I shall not listen to anything you say to me about my booklet."

At this moment Sir Arthur entered, in company with a stout elderly ecclesiastic who was Rector of Grantley ; and in the partial dispersion thus caused, Felix and Miss Acosta were left standing beside each other.   Under a sudden impulse the former turned and looked meaningly at Sanpriel as he spoke :

" It will, I hope, please the author of ' White-Nights ' to hear that I have taken her lesson to heart.   The book came to me in the nick of time.

I was engaged on the sorriest piece of work I had ever done. If I had gone on with it, I should have been elected to the Academy, and probably have never done anything in sculpture worth a second thought.   It was *your* Hertha that killed *my* Hertha."

"What do you mean, Mr. Dane?   Were you at work upon a Hertha?   Surely you did not "——

"Yes, I destroyed it.   Ah, there is the dinner-gong.   We shall talk of this again, Miss Acosta. I must now go and offer Lady Crane my arm."

Seldom had Felix ever better enjoyed a dinner-party.   True he found his hostess extremely difficult to converse with, for her interests were very narrow, and except the Fords and the Despards they seemed to have no acquaintances in common.   What amused him was her obvious tone of condescension when she found that he did not know the Monterolis and the Barons Stock-meyer, and other financial princes of Israel.   Yet, notwithstanding this drawback, and the distance between himself and Sanpriel, he managed to obtain keen pleasure and stimulus from his sur-roundings.

During the last course he was challenged by Sir Arthur.

"What is this I hear from Acosta, Mr. Dane? He says that you are one of the romanticists?"

"And if so, what then, Sir Arthur?"

"What then? Why, as I am always telling that foolish enthusiast here, Sanpriel, no good either in art or literature—I won't speak of music, with my good friend Acosta at hand to overwhelm me with his eloquent wrath—can come out of your new-fangled romanticism. Classical art and literature have withstood the test of time, and they have a dignity and repose which all your romanticism never achieves."

Felix was on the point of reply when he noticed that Miss Acosta was about to speak.

"Before you two engulf yourselves in an endless argument," she began, somewhat hesitatingly at first, till she became conscious of the deference as well as courtesy with which both men awaited what she had to say, "would it not be as well to see if you don't both mean the same thing, though you apply a different *ism* to each? I have so often heard this subject discussed at my father's house, and have considered it so impartially, that I have come to believe there are only two ways of looking at art—and of course I use the word in the most comprehensive sense—namely, the point of view of those who see in it mere representation, and the point of view of those who use it and look to it for interpretation.   Most of the former call themselves classicists, most of the latter romanticists.   Among the latter, however, there are of course many who prefer classic to so-called romantic art and literature —but it generally amounts to little more than a dislike for or indifference to contemporary work. The wider one's sympathies, the truer one's culture, the surer is one's insight into what is real, whether it be antique, or mediæval, or modern, or contemporary.   As I have heard my father say, every creative artist is of necessity a romanticist."

"Yes," interposed Adama Ácosta ; "I have said so often, and I am convinced of its truth.   Whenever the dominant taste of the day is towards what is misleadingly called classicism it will be found that the artistic productions of the period are critical and illustrative merely, or when nominally original are derivative and third-rate in every respect save valuable but often exaggerated attention to technique.   Look at the fashionable poetry of the day : —polished and graceful verse for the most part, but without a breath of real life in it.   The excessive laudation of the prosaic eighteenth century literature (and not so much for its few splendid achievements as its polished mediocrity) is significant."

"Yes," resumed Sanpriel; "and it is further significant that these minor writers—whom my father wickedly calls tertiary scribes, for he won't even admit them as secondary—almost invariably despair about, and very often despise, our own time. Nothing is so good now as it was then: everything is now crude, or in bad taste, or too vehement, or too dramatic, or too little *en regle*—in fact, too everything except commonplace. Enthusiasm of any kind is their special abhorrence. Look at their particular newspapers. In this week's 'Critical Review,' for instance, there are three consecutive articles which are deplorable in their narrowness. One is an emphatic puff of an exceedingly poor book, and praises just those things in it which are at once derivative and indifferent—but it is written by one of the set, who will expect similar kind of treatment when his own turn comes; another is a general article upon American poets and novelists, betraying almost as much impertinence as ignorance; and the third is a paper upon the poetry of the Victorian age, mainly occupied with a lament for the halcyon days of Pope and Gray and Collins. Praise of these three great writers, and others of the time, is of course right; but when the writer says that the Victorian epoch has produced no poetry to compare with theirs, either in matter or manner, he simply stultifies himself in his office as critic."

"I see you are no amateur in regard to periodical literature, or some of it, Miss Acosta," Felix remarked with a smile. "Wait till you publish another book, and not privately, and then you will know to the full the tender mercies of the 'Critical Review' gentry."

"Well, all this is very reasonable, no doubt," broke in the host, "but I still maintain that classicism is synonymous with sterling and romanticism with spurious art."

"What of Shakespeare, Chatterton, Coleridge, Keats, Scott, Tennyson, William Morris, Rossetti —to mention but a few of the older and modern great names which occur to me? Each of those I specified may be considered in the truest sense of the word a romanticist."

"I never heard of either Morris or Rossetti, Mr. Dane, or at any rate have never read anything of theirs; and of the others, indeed I am acquainted but slightly even with Tennyson and Scott — though Shakespeare I do know pretty thoroughly. I should have thought both Shakespeare and Scott classical."

"Would you think so if they were living, Sir Arthur?"

"Eh, what ? Well, upon my soul I can't say. By Jove, d'ye know, Dane, I don't believe I should ! "

Every one laughed at Sir Arthur's half-rueful, half-humorous discomfiture ; but Sanpriel gave a glance of quick and eager sympathy towards Felix, as though expectant of further utterance which should express her own convictions.

"The whole question, Sir Arthur, lies in the *spirit.* As long as people confuse the spirit with the letter, so long will there be confusion and misapprehension. I am a Romanticist, as I am glad to find are Miss and Mr. Acosta, but I have nothing to do with, and care nothing for what I think you mean by, romanticism. These *isms* are abominable. None of us wants romanticism ; we want, and look for, and try to intensify the romantic spirit—a very different thing. Romanticism of the stereotyped kind is a mere phase ; the romantic spirit can never die as long as the creative impulse is potent. It is apt to be blurred, to be misled, to be distorted—though it sounds paradoxical to use these words for so abstract a thing."

"Now I see that my wife is anxious to rise, and I fear that we have been boring both her and Mr. Carter with our arguments."

"Not at all, not at all, my dear Sir Arthur," hurriedly exclaimed the Rector, as he gulped down the port he had been sipping; "on the contrary, charming, most charming, I assure you. So—eh, ah, such cultivated talk is eh, h'm, ah, delightful. Our yound friend Sanpriel, too "——

But here Lady Crane broke in with some remark of local interest for her husband, and Felix was amused to see the look of quiet disdain which Miss Acosta cast upon the inane and foolish cleric, whose condescending manner and perpetual banalities were almost the only disagreeable things she had to undergo at Forest Manor.

With mock seriousness Sir Arthur turned towards Felix, and told him that he must now utter his final word upon romanticism, as thenceforth the subject was to be tabooed; for he, Sir Arthur, could never do battle with three such doughty antagonists.

"So now, Dane, out with it; have you anything more to say about your Romantic Spirit ? "

"I have nothing to say about *my* romantic spirit," Felix replied laughingly; "but as you are so insistent, here are my *urbana dicta*. It should never, of course, be taken for granted that the romantic spirit must in its manifestations be restricted to art or literature that is obviously romantic. It must, of course, manifest itself variously—but its mere aspects are of secondary import. We have experienced within the last decade or two the curious contradiction of a strong wave of romanticism (its comparative futility due, it seems to me, to its emphasis on archaic methods), and a commonplace acceptation thereof as a mere phenomenon. It has been a gross blunder—that of the abrupt division of the Romantic and the Realistic sentiment. There is no vital reason why a man in a railway carriage should not look upon life through the romantic atmosphere just as sincerely as did Æschylus (the greatest ancient romanticist) when looking through the ilex-boughs upon the hillsides of Hellas, as Chaucer when he walked in the Islington meadows, as Blake when he saw the elm-branches become wings of angels, as Ossian, even, when he brooded by his melancholy sea. I can descry no new motor in civilisation, in science, or in nature that must tend to eradicate the romantic spirit : it is but a change of outlook. The world is as wonderful now as it ever was, and the potentialities of life not one whit less marvellous and fascinating essentially than in the olden days. Believe me, Mr. Acosta's ' tertiary scribes ' existed in some guise or other in the golden age itself ; there must have been shepherds then who lamented the prehistoric grace in the handling of the crook, swains who sang dolefully of the lost lyric art.   We are really all divided into the number of those who have the beautiful, artistic, spiritual faculty of wonder, or into the number of those who have it not; and in some ages the wonder-eyed prevail, and then we have our Homers and Shakespeares, our Coleridges and Keatses, our Titians and Leonardos and Turners, our Beethovens and Chopins and Wagners; while at other periods we have the indifferentists, optimists and pessimists alike.   But, as in everything in Nature, there is in humanity an endless ebb and flow.   There are souls that grow and grow, and there are souls which are slowly perishing.   Perhaps in neither case is the motive-force what we call good or evil.   Nature has far deeper roots than our human parochialism has cognisance of.   But there, I am straying from the subject and becoming metaphysical.   You have had my *finis*, Sir Arthur.   So henceforth let romanticism and classicism join politics, and keep out of our way."

Hereupon the ladies rose and left the room.   As she passed, Sanpriel glanced at Felix.   He could not flatter himself that there was any special significance in the look, yet it thrilled him with keen elation.

CHAPTER V.

The evening was one long memorable to Felix Dane. Everything helped to produce a sense of delicious repose, a languor without apathy. The flowers in the drawing-room, particularly some great clusters of white lilacs, emitted fragrances poignant enough to have been overpowering, had it not been for the open window at the farther end of the apartment, whence came softly at intervals a breath of air laden with forest odours and bearing with it the undertone of the sea. Sir Arthur and the Rector had left the room for an hour or so to attend to some pressing local matter, and Lady Crane had become so absorbed in her novel that she had closed her eyes so as to more fully realise the persons and scenes depicted, and had become unconscious of all extraneous matters. The music of violin and piano soothed her, though had she had any idea of the labyrinth of love wherein Felix and Sanpriel had already begun to wander unwittingly, she would have been as alert as any wary barn-fowl when a kestrel hangs poised in air.

Adama Acosta was restless. The sea-sound disturbed him, and the gradually deepening stagnancy of the atmosphere affected his nerves. Occasionally he played, sometimes a fragmentary melody, again in impromptu accompaniment to Sanpriel.

How beautiful the latter seemed, Felix thought, as he watched her sitting beyond the black ebony piano, whereon lay a cluster of blood-red poppies ; her soft white dress, her delicate arms and neck, and those large dusky eyes filled with vague reverie and the dreamy pleasure of the music which she loved almost as well as did her father.

There was but little conversation, yet each felt as though some bond had drawn them close. The graciousness of familiarity was already a solvent among the inevitable conventionalities, the familiarity of spirits akin, not that of vulgar indiscriminacy, the bane of so much contemporary social life.

The last sense of strangeness departed when Lady Crane, after an abrupt return to a consciousness of her surroundings, and the announcement of a bad headache, bade her guests good-night and left the room.

Felix was amused to note the instinctive expression of relief upon Acosta's face, and Sanpriel in turn smiled as she perceived the identity of sentiment in both her companions.

Suddenly Acosta walked up to Felix and looked at him earnestly for a few moments ere he spoke.

"I like you, Felix Dane. Will you come and see us informally in Hampstead? You are the first man of your race whom I have asked to visit us at the promptings of inclination and heedless of the usual formalities. In other words, will you look in upon us whensoever you care?"

"I take your kindness as a great compliment, Mr. Acosta. Although you may be surprised to hear it, I am somewhat lonely in my life; and as I grow older I care less and less for people with whom I have little in common, and more and more for those with whom I can feel myself in sympathy."

"You know we are Jews, do you not?"

"I—I—understood so, from our host," Felix answered rather hesitatingly, with an apprehensive glance at Sanpriel, for he was uncertain how she would regard either her father's question or his answer. "Fortunately I am in keen sympathy with what may be called the new cause of Israel, as possibly he may have told you."

"Yes, he did tell me so. We are, however, ourselves outcasts to a certain extent from our own people, for we are of the league of the 'Children of To-morrow.'"

"May I ask who and what are the 'Children of To-morrow'?"

"Yes; but let us go out into the open air. Sanpriel and I have often spent the hour before rest talking and playing in the yew-grove which you probably noticed as you drove up the avenue."

Felix gladly acceded, and as soon as Miss Acosta had procured a light shawl, and the gentlemen their hats (while Adama brought also his violin), the three crossed the south lawn and strolled slowly towards the yews.

The stars hung like drops of white fire, but owing to the vaporous breath of earth without palpitation or sparkle. The white spaces of lilac and thorn, interspersed with laurels, and, farther back, oaks and scattered firs, seemed alive with birds; everywhere there was a commingled sound of twittering, faint warbles, and rustling of nervous flight. From the parklands beyond came the occasional lowing of cattle and the stamping of the horses that had been turned out to grass, and here and there, indeed, their misshapen shadows caught the eye. Between two great walnuts the bats

flittered untiringly ; and across the pastures came
the rasping, strangulating cry of the goatsucker as
it hawked the beetles and moths which flitted by on
bristling shards.   Beyond the avenue, deep within
a great beech, a nightingale sang intermittently,
now giving forth its preliminary *tcheug-tcheug-
tcheug*, anon uttering piercing minors, but oftenest
reiterating certain tremulous notes—all the prelude
to the rapture which ere long would break forth
into uncontrollable song.   Among the firs still the
cushats crooned monotonously, and from where
the oaks rose in ridges came the cries of the
curlews and plovers which perpetually haunted the
margin of the land, whereon the sea broke heavily
as with the sound of distant thunder.

"Is not this a perfect night ? " Sanpriel remarked in a voice into which the dreamy languor
of the evening had passed; "the sounds that we
hear make the silence only the more impressive.
I love this place beyond words, if only for the sea
that lies yonder.   Death is not death in such a
place as this ; here he is but the kindly, mysterious,
merciful spirit of the dusk."

"What makes you think of death, Miss Acosta,
unless it be the exquisite reposefulness, the sense
of absolute human quiescence, which environs us
just now ? "

" You may well ask her that question, Dane ! Every time—from the first visit we ever paid here —that we have come this way by night, Sanpriel has invariably recurred to the subject of death. She is not morbid, and elsewhere I am sure she feels as full of hope and energy as she looks—but here it is always the beauty, or the poignancy, or the brutality, or the heedlessness, or the something else of death. I do not understand it; and I think, Sanpriel, *carina*, that this place cannot be good for you. I'll have to take you south when we next want a sudden holiday. You will be becoming as foolish as I am sometimes, and believe that the wave which is to drown you has already left its far-off seas."

" Do you believe that?" Sanpriel asked with startling vehemence. " For I too, father, have sometimes felt the same thing overwhelmingly. Only a little ago I had, in a moment, and without any predisposition to such thoughts, an irresistible conviction that the last sound I should hear would be the boom of the sea yonder—*that* sea, yonder shore, no other."

" What do you think, Dane ? Had I not better remove this young woman out of the reach of temptation ? "

Felix laughed lightly, but uneasily ; and after a few moments replied hesitatingly—

"It is strange, but I suppose it goes to prove what a subtle thing magnetism is, thought-transference rather. The idea of death, of death *here*, within sound of yonder sea, seems to have occurred to all three of us simultaneously, or very nearly so. Perhaps it is to be so, for all we know. Perhaps we three may unveil the darkness, if any veil there be, at one and the same time."

"Don't, Mr. Dane! I do not know why, but what you say seems, in some absurd fashion, to be so probable that I am already deep in despondency."

"Oh, Miss Acosta, you must be well aware that these moods signify nothing. Their value is in their possible inspiration of a 'Melancholia' or of a poem like Shelley's 'Stanzas written in Dejection,' or, if you will permit me to say so, your own lines entitled 'In Una Silva Oscura.'"

"Ah, now you are swinging round too far: you know as well as I do that such moods are not mere vagrant irresponsible dreams. But here we are: are not these wonderful old yews? There is a superstition that whoever walks among them three nights following is foredoomed to sudden and early death—or, if he or she be not young, at any rate to sudden death ere long."

"Now, Sanpriel, there you are again talking about death. I believe you are as fond of thinking about it in your own way as Gabriel is as a chemist."

"Yes," resumed Acosta in reply to an interruption from Felix, "I do mean Ford. Of course he is not a chemist save as an amateur, and then only in a special direction; but he has long made a secret study of poisons. I understand that he hopes to discover some poison so strong that it will arrest all the ordinary processes of decay, and enable one to lie as though dead for any reasonable number of years, and then to come to life again."

"To what end?"

"Oh, I do not know. He will never discover it, nor does he in his heart of hearts think he will. He is as fond of playing with some impossible theory as a boy is with a ball. But he is beyond question a curious and deep student in toxicology. I remember that he told me, some months ago, he had discovered the nature and constituents of the *poudre d'or* of the Borgias—a poison so subtle and in its traces so untraceable, that even the alert eyes and wits of the gentry of mediæval Italy could not discover anything about it—though there was no lack of victims, it is said. But to revert to what I began to tell you. I told you that we were in a sense outcasts from our people; but of course I mean only from the orthodox majority, and then only in point of faith, the rigours of Judaic faith, and not in point of race. We 'Children of To-Morrow' are Jews in all verity, though perhaps we have no right to adopt a name which our Dutch compatriot Siwäarmill has bestowed in no exclusive sense."

" May I ask what Siwäarmill's words are ? "

" They are in Dutch, but they run thus: 'We, who live more intensely and suffer more acutely than others, are the Children of To-morrow, because in us the new forces of the future are already astir or even dominant.' Siwäarmill does not allude to Jews or to any other religious nationalities, but to those of all peoples who, as he says, live more intensely and suffer more acutely than others. He sees, as do so many of us, that the old conventionalities, the old moralities even, are in process of rapid evolution, if not of dissolution ; and he perceives that now, as always heretofore, the future is foreshadowed in the present, the To-morrow is foretold in certain vivid moments of To-day."

" In what sense, then, are you Jews and yet not orthodox ? In what sense are you Children of To-Morrow ? "

Acosta was about to reply, but with impetuous eagerness his daughter answered for him.

"We are Jews in that we are proud of our race, proud of our history, proud of our victories over our long national agony of nigh upon two thousand years, proud of our enduring martyrdom, proud of our great poets, philosophers, leaders, heroes, patriots, artists, and musicians, proud of our slow but sure emergence from the rank and file of modern peoples, proud of our previsioned destinies, proud of our inevitable triumph."

Felix stood for a few moments bewildered by the heightened beauty of Sanpriel, and by the passion that animated her words, which she had uttered with a rapid and almost tragic intensity. He had never realised that the incorruptible Jewish pride of which he had read could be a vital force in the present day, had not dreamt that a new Banner of Israel had been uplifted, that a new impetus had commenced to stir the ancient and long-suffering clan of the Semites.

A look of abstract passion, of reverie in which there was something of ecstasy, had come into Sanpriel's face, and it was evident to both her companions that, in the exaltation into which her impetuous outburst had swept her, she had become momentarily oblivious of her surroundings.

Acosta looked at his daughter with elate

and happy eyes, and muttered some words in Hebrew.

"Yes, my friend, my daughter speaks as becomes a daughter of Israel who has devoted herself to a great and noble cause. She and I both have our artistic aims to fulfil, but over and above all we work for the glory of Israel. Every day, every hour, we move, or hope we move, nearer to our goal. Either of us would gladly give up life if we could thereby accelerate the redemption of our people; either of us would die rather than by any act of ours retard the consummation of our national hope. I tell you, Felix Dane, that I too have had my sacrifice. I, Adama Acosta, the last of our accursed family, a family doomed by the blight of an anathema which God heard and permitted, I, Adama Acosta, the Jew, not only loved but was beloved by a beautiful woman, a Christian and of noble rank. To give her up, to assuage my passion with the bitterness of renunciation, was torture; but I should no more have defiled myself by marriage with her than I should have cursed Jehovah in the Holy of Holies at Jerusalem. Yet we loved each other—my God! how we loved each other! She would have followed me, but I feared the spell of her beauty; in her voice I dreaded the persuasion of the siren; and so—I slew her."

"What!" cried Felix, horrified; "you *slew* her?"

"Yes, though not with any weapon forged of man. I forbade her to follow me. When, in all the recklessness of loving sacrifice, she did so, I refused to see her——though I lay upon the floor of my chamber, grovelling in my agony of mind and body, and with my heart in fierce revolt and clamouring for its beloved. Then she came in unto me and stood before me, and prayed that she might at least be allowed to join my people; but the Lord gave me strength to resist the terrible temptation, and led me to see as in a flash that if she remained I should be won over by her and go forth for ever from Israel; and so, with face averted that I might not be overcome by the terror and the glory of her eyes, I bade her depart from me and return not. Thereupon she stood a long while silent, but in the end laughed bitterly, and said to me that my curse would be to desire her for evermore, and that in the fulness of time my pride of Israel would be humbled to the dust. Then she went forth, and in the morning they found her body among the sedges in the river."

A deep silence followed this avowal. Scarce a sound now palpitated distinctly, save the troublous voice of the sea, calling, calling, calling with its ancient monotony of reiteration. The moonlight irradiated the upper branches of the yews, but made them look even more distorted and vaguely human than their wont, and when suddenly a nightjar swept by with its muffled whirr all started as though conscious they were upon haunted ground and had seen the unlaid ghost glide by.

Then, with a low voice, in which his hearers detected something strained and painfully vibrant, Acosta spoke again.

"And verily, she spoke not wholly in vain. I have wrought for my people; I have renounced and forsworn many temptations; I have come nearer and nearer to the goal to which I have striven—but from my heart, from the depths of my being, from my inmost soul, I crave still and yearn unspeakably for my lost love. Yea, indeed, is the undying desire of her become part of me. Yet not wholly hath she prevailed, for my daughter Sanpriel is even as I am, and would let no lust of the flesh overcome the passion of the spirit. Yet "—and here, for the first time, Felix saw some indication of that abnormal insanity in Adama Acosta of which he had heard, for the man's whole manner and appearance changed, and he spoke as one distraught, with savagery of expression, gleaming eyes, and words strident and metallic—"Yet, in case she should, let me again lay upon her the blight of unfulfilled hopes and the curse of untimely death ; yea, if ever she wed with one not of our people, with other than a Semite, may "——

" Stop, father, stop ! " cried Sanpriel imploringly, as she laid her hands on his upraised arm ; "you know not what you are saying when you add yet another curse to those that haunt our lives. You have sworn that *you* will never curse man or woman, and yet you are about to speak the irrevocable word ! Fear not for me, father. Surely you know that Sanpriel Acosta is not likely to betray her trust, to desert the cause to which she is wedded."

Acosta hesitated, and stood looking now at Sanpriel, now at Felix, now vaguely at the yew-boughs and the stars which seemed to hang upon the outer branches. An owl veered past with a scream that seemed to two at least who heard it to have an echo of derision, and with a louder swell than usual came the hollow and indifferent voice of the sea, a listless chime dully surcharged with the echo of things irrevocable and irrecoverable, and weighty with inarticulate prophecies.

Then the madness which ever lurked in the inner chambers of his brain came forth laughing and regnant.

"Take off your hands, woman; what have I to do with you or this man? Go your own ways, and leave me to mine. Your time is short; I saw Azrael fly overhead but a moment ago, and his shadow fell upon you both. I see love in your eyes: love then, poor fools, while ye may. It is the last dream, the last madness of humanity. Why do you not take her in your arms, man? She loves you—look at the light in her eyes, see the flame in her cheeks! Why do you not run to his breast, fair maid, who art so like one who was dear to me long, long ago—my Sanpriel, who died, ah, God knows when! Why do you not run to him? See, he perisheth for love of thee—his eyes betray him—I can hear his heart beating louder than the fall of the seas yonder. Nay, speak not, implore not; I am no judge. If ye have not sinned, go hence in the peace of righteousness; if ye have sinned, go hence in the peace of doom. No, I know you not, save that we three have all lain drowned in yonder sea—have felt the waves roll over and about us, and the tide-sand fill our mouths and hollow eyes—and that now we are here again. Nay, I am a Judge of Israel; I am Moses Ben Ezra; I am the law-giver, Salathiel; I pronounce you both man and wife—may Jehovah Himself not come between you—in life and death may body and soul of each of you be one with the other!"

Then, ere Sanpriel could speak again, the mad musician seized his violin, and immediately the night air throbbed and thrilled with a music as wild and rare as ever swept from the lute of Israfel.

Felix felt as though he were in a dream. Beside him stood Sanpriel, scarce whiter in her vestments than in her colour, with clasped hands and eyes dark and ominous from tearless suffering; a few feet away was Adama Acosta, erect, with white hair about his deathly pale face and eyes gleaming with excitement, his violin against his left shoulder, and with bow that seemed animated by some demon of fantasy; around were the ancient yews, here black and weary as with great age, there white in the moonshine, and filled with what seemed appealing arms, and limbs contorted in a medley of tortured creatures; beyond all, the night, hushed, aromatic, seductive, and the perpetual booming undertone of the sea, now moaning and sibillant, anon harsh and resonant as with swift-following thunders.

So wild and fantastic had Acosta's gestures been when he first upraised his violin that Felix had mechanically stepped forward to intervene against he knew not what sudden violence of frenzy, but Sanpriel had arrested his impulsive advance and whispered to him to be still.

" Hush ! It is the one thing that will make him well again. He is never long distraught when he has his violin. He does not see or hear us now, and if he be not interrupted, he will play away all his frenzy."

But for all her forced calmness she was trembling, and erewhile she would have fallen had her companion not caught her and gently moved her back a step or two till she could lean against a forked branch which gave her ample support. Yet, wittingly or unwittingly, her hand lay long in that of Felix, who was as one rapt in a dream of assured beatitudes ; indeed, throughout all the time that Acosta played he was electrified by that small hand he held in his, like a white roseleaf within a shell. It touched him, it thrilled him, it gave him a wild desire to kiss it passionately, and then—why then, there was the sea beyond, the sea that each had foreseen as a grave, the sea with its wave-music for requiem, its windless depths for peace, and its long, inalienable silence.

Now fitfully, again with prolonged chords as of despair, and yet again with a sad pitifulness that brought tears to the eyes of his listeners, Adama played on till all his frenzy had expended itself. Then, exhausted by the physical and mental strain, he threw himself upon the ground and sobbed like a wearied child.

Sanpriel stole to his side and gently soothed him, and with tender caresses wrought him again to his manliness. At last he recovered, and, with a long sigh, looked at his companions, and then, having taken his daughter's arm, slowly walked away.

The latter gave Felix a glance. It was but a sudden light turned upon him, but he knew that it bade him follow, and in silence. He picked up the violin, and kept a few paces behind the musician and his daughter, the former of whom seemed to have become feeble and stricken in years.

Not a word was spoken till the house was reached, and then Sanpriel gave her hand to Dane, took the violin, and with a smile which had in it more of infinite pathos than aught else, passed out of his sight by a side-door.

As he crossed the hall he was met by the butler, who informed him that Sir Arthur had some urgent correspondence to attend to, and begged to be excused reappearance, and, as he already knew, Lady Crane had gone to her bed some time previously. Only too thankfully he found himself free to go at once to his own room.

Was it possible, he thought, as he sat by his open window and inhaled the sweet scents which stole upward upon the soft night-wind, was it possible that but a day had elapsed since he had seen Sanpriel at the concert ?   Was it conceivable that less than thirty hours ago he had realised his artistic decline, had been reinspired by some stray verses in a poem by an unknown writer, and had destroyed his long-worked-at "Hertha"?   Could it be that in so short a time ago he had experienced one of the too familiar disagreements with Lydia ?

Lydia !   How strange the very name sounded to him !   It was as though it belonged to some distant relative, some friend's wife, some woman of whom he had heard particulars which had scarce interested him.   For the first time in his married life, moreover, he saw her in mental vision exactly as she was—every plait of her hair, every calm line in her features, every curve of her neck, each poise and mould of limb, just as if she or her phantasm stood or lay before him.   In love one's eyes are veiled, and even in the unruffled placidities of affection one's vision is, in absence, apt to be blurred ; it is only when we are indifferent, when no echo of passion, no whisper of affectionate heed even, stirs the heart, that in absence we see clearly every feature, every expression, of those near to us—as we might image forth a casual friend or any ordinary acquaintance.   Deep love is like deep water that runs darkly in shadow; in vain we peer into its depths for the beloved face, in vain we strain our ears to catch the thrilling tones, for at most only a fugitive gleam of eyes or a haunting gesture is revealed to us, at most we hear only an uncertain, a too tantalising echo.   Love sees not clearly; when the blue mist lifts from the avenues and perspectives of the land wherein he would fain linger, he shrinks and cowers, and all-affrighted and distraught evanishes to other undiscovered Edens.

Lydia : how the name galled him ! How true it was of *her !* Yet why he knew not.   Names may help to mould characters, but they do not affect physique or one's inherent individuality.   To Felix Dane, however, it seemed as though no other name in the world was so weighted with dull apathy, so significant of lifelessness, of soullessness, of negations manifold.   Yet he was not unaware of his having yielded to that last vanity of human egotism, and found in accidental nomenclature the secret clues of nature.   Lydia—what if she had been called Leonora, or Lavinia, or Lucretia, and if *she*—Sanpriel—had been Lydia ?   That Felix laughed with mocking incredulity at this idea was proof to him, if proof he needed, that the passion of an overwhelming love had usurped his heart, proud and elate in its consciousness of inevitable tyranny.

What Acosta and Sanpriel had said about their Judaic loyalty, still more what the latter had led him to infer by her enthusiastic ardour in the cause of New Israel, of which he knew but little, perturbed him strangely; yet over and above all was the happy fact that Adama himself had welcomed him as a friend, had sought his intimacy, had shown him that he had touched the musician's heart as no other man had done for long. Even in his madness would Acosta have allotted Sanpriel and himself to each other, have wedded them as a Judge of Israel, with Jehovah called upon as witness? No, surely not, Felix thought, and as he so convinced himself his heart swiftlier pulsed at the memory of that strange betrothal, that weird wedding.

Now at last he no longer disguised from himself that the passion which had lain dormant from the dawn of adolescence had come—like one of those brilliant ocean flowers which rise to the surface only when in all the fulness of their beauty—all-unexpectedly upon him. Right or wrong, for weal or woe, a new life was his. He was as one who, suspended in mid-air, had severed the rope beneath his grasp, so that he had no option but to climb farther or fall into the abyss.

The thought brought him a keen exultation. He loved, even though Sanpriel might never love him. No sense of loyalty to his wife forced him to surrender something of his vautage; he could not be disloyal, he argued, where there had never been loyalty. Neither had ever loved the other; in mind if not in deed each had turned elsewhere for what of life-glamour had been denied them. He knew not how much foundation there was for his suspicions of Lydia and Ford; for one thing, he believed in his wife's chastity in the conviction that she could not do more than dally haughtily with the thin ghost of a phantasmal passion. Ford he neither liked nor trusted; but what then? What right had *he* to interfere? He wished no subterfuge, no intrigue; but if they cared to force upon him a divorce, he would only too willingly stand aloof and permit them to do as seemed to them best. It might be immoral, it might be wrong, but the truth remained; and he had no desire to wrap himself in sophistications, and go on his way crying out " All is well," when in deep verity all should be ill.

But as for definite action of any kind, no idea thereof crossed his mind. His reflections about

Lydia were as vague as they were brief; and when he thought of Sanpriel it was as one dreams of Paradise, with ecstasy poignant indeed, but touched with a sense of infinite remoteness. Then below all his fluctuating hopes, regrets, and visionary dreams was the, to him, exquisite conviction that his genius had been reborn, had been dipped in rainbow-gold, had been touched with the magic chrism that the Spirit of Beauty carrieth but none hath seen.

Wearied at last with stress of emotion, he undressed and lay down. For some time he could not sleep: the vagrant odours which came in at the open window intoxicated rather than soothed him, and the intermittent booming and resilient sough of the sea charmed his unwilling ears. But erewhile slumber settled upon him, and then from the dominion of day-dreams he passed to those of night.

Through all the visions that held him in thrall, sometimes strangely real and coherent, oftenest inchoate, he was haunted always by the face of Sanpriel. But through each was a sense of mockery, over all an unexpressed prophecy of doom. Again and again he and she were about to go forth to some unpermitted Eden, but ever something terrible intervened; again and again he was rewedded by Adama Acosta, and then banned with an anathema too terrible to endure. Through each and every dream brooded this latent curse; it pulsed, it clamoured, it sobbed with dread unvarying reiteration.

For, out beyond, the sea moaned and sobbed, with the night-wind, now astir and ready for tempestuous flight, wrestling with the inward tide: moaned and sobbed, and sobbed and moaned, with ever, below all, its old, brooding, monotonous boom, the dull chime of oblivion.

CHAPTER VI.

It was late when he opened his eyes next morning.
His first impression was one of chill, and almost
immediately he was aware of the swish of rain and
the loud vehemence of wind.

Over his dressing-table lay a number of wet
blossoms, blooms which had been torn from the
roses that clustered close up to his window, and
among them, but newly dead, a delicate sulphur
butterfly.   The tablecover and white curtains were
soaked, and a letter which lay on the floor seemed
but a white sop.   Mechanically he lifted the latter,
and as soon as he had glanced at it, recognised it
as one that Lydia's maid had brought him just ere
he had left home.   He had thrust it in his pocket
with intention of perusal in the hansom that conveyed him to King's Cross, but had failed of remembrance ; it must, he realised, have escaped
from the breast-pocket of his coat when he had
thrown the latter on the chair by the window.
The gum of the flap had softened, but the enclosed

missive had thus been more affected by the damp. Still, it was possible to make out portions of it; that it was only legible here and there was just as well, Felix admitted with a grim smile, when he perceived that some mistake had occurred. For the letter began "Dear Gabriel." It was probable that in her haste she had enclosed the written message she had meant for her husband to Gabriel Ford, since it was quite clear that the communication intended for the latter had gone awkwardly astray.

Felix's first instinct was to do his utmost to decipher the epistle; his second, to destroy it unread, as it was not meant for him.

"I've certainly no right to read it," he muttered hesitatingly. "It would be a low thing to do; and yet—and yet—no, I know what I shall do," and as he spoke he refolded it and placed it in his coat-pocket again.

Neither Sanpriel nor her father were at breakfast; the latter, indeed, was unwell, and—as Felix heard with chagrin—talked of a speedy return to London.

The forenoon was spent somewhat listlessly. Having no letters to attend to and nothing to do, Dane lit his cigar and strolled forth to have a look at the sea. For some reason he did not attempt to define, he avoided the yew-grove where in the bygone night-tide he had witnessed such a strange scene, where he had been wedded to Sanpriel by the father who would have slain her rather than see her married to another than one of her own people.

A short distance from the lawns and flower-gardens to the east of the house ran vagrantly the first undergrowth and scattered arborage of the forest. A few yards farther on and the scattered oaks, bushes, and ashes grew denser, and then the ancient oak forest itself opened up in endless avenues and groves.

It was with delight that he walked through the woodlands. The dark rugged boles of the oaks, the huge branches which threw vast masses of shadow across the mossed ground, the wind-flowers, violets, and wild hyacinths that clustered among the gnarled roots which lay like uncouth limbs of strange creatures, or stretched in shimmering spaces where the sunbeams leapt and danced and gleamed in fantastic revelry, all were as a feast to his eyes. How gladsome, also, sounded the cries of the thrushes and finches, the woodlark and hedge-sparrow, the sweet bubbling music of the black-cap, and, with startling alterations of distance and direction, the bell-like voice of the cuckoo. So complete was the suggestion of forest depths that it was with a start of surprise he heard, suddenly, as he crossed a hyacinth-covered hollow, the sea-sound, of which he had been vaguely conscious from the first, become suddenly loud and urgent. When he reached the eastward end of the short slope and stood among some of the hugest oaks he had ever seen, he beheld the sea breaking upon the sands but a few feet away. The day was stormy, and the rain-clouds still swept by, though the sunlight flashed forth in a dozen places, and made the ocean seem in parts as though resplendent with liquid topaz and chrysoprase and sapphire. The marvellous jubilation of the sea in a clearing gale was ever a joy to charm him, who loved ocean as few do, loved it because he knew it in all its phases, had sailed much upon it, and found in it at all times a wonder and significance and mystery which no other aspect of nature afforded in like degree.

It was with keen delight, therefore, that he walked along the grassy dunes which fringed the forest, and watched the endless variety of the sea, —heard the crying of the gulls and oyster-openers and sanderlings blent with the surge and resilience of the waves, the sibillant hiss of foamy waters running swiftly into myriads of hollow shells and

all manner of little nooks and crannies among
the tiny rock-citadels scattered along the sands,
with, under all, the deep booming undertone of
ocean itself.

He did not dwell much upon memories of Sanpriel; neither did Lydia, nor the minor circumstances of his life, nor even his work, much occupy
his thoughts. But when he turned back to Forest
Manor it was with the knowledge that he had
gained a new energy, that he had been as it were
reborn. Love had overwhelmed him; for the
surest token of its mastery is the impetus of high
resolve, which it stimulates and supports.

Yet—so inconsequent and frail is high-strung
emotion—he was conscious of something of relapse,
of the return of the shadow, mayhap, of his late indifference, when, on his return to the house, he
learned that Gabriel Ford had arrived.

The butler could not tell him where Mr. Ford
was; he had seen him last in the drawing-room
with Miss Acosta, but they had gone out together
—possibly, however, they had returned.

With swift step, and with an expression into
which something of a native imperiousness, almost
arrogance, had entered, Felix entered the drawing-
room, but a glance satisfied him that no one was
present.

He advanced to the open French window at the far end, where on the previous afternoon he had seen Sanpriel irradiated by the glory of the setting sun. For a moment or two the memory took possession of him, and his heart beat the quicker; but even while his eye softened he caught sight of two figures slowly advancing along one of the box-hedged avenues which engirt the west garden.

One was Sanpriel; the other was—not Adama Acosta, as he hoped, but—Gabriel Ford.

Felix stepped on to the lawn and walked towards the twain, whose faces, however, were averted, for they had turned into a side avenue. They did not see him, and so absorbed were they in their conversation that they did not hear his approach along the soft turf till he was close upon them. Sanpriel was speaking as he drew near, but he only caught the closing words of her remarks.

"Why do you object to the name, Mr. Ford? It seems to me that you are but half-hearted in our cause."

"No, Sanpriel, I am not half-hearted; but I think we should work without ostentation and exert our influence as secretly as possible."

"I do not agree with you."

"But you ought to agree with me. I have more experience than you, and I see that the cause

is often retarded by such frankness as you delight
in.   But to change the subject for a moment, why
is it that you have gone back to calling me ' Mr.
Ford '?   You have done so each time you have
addressed me by name."

" It really is a matter of no importance, but you
know my dislike to unnecessary informalities."

" Dear me, Sanpriel, you have suddenly changed
your   character !   May I inquire if Mr. Felix
Dane "——

But at this moment Felix's footsteps were overheard, and the conversation came to an abrupt close.

Miss Acosta's face slightly flushed as she caught
Dane's gaze fixed earnestly upon her, and Ford
frowned and bit his lip ere he greeted the new-
comer with anything but cordial welcome.

After a few incidental remarks, which served but
little to remove the sense of strain experienced by
each, the walk was resumed.

There was an embarrassing silence, until Sanpriel broke it by calmly taking up the thread of
the conversation in which she had been engaged
ere Felix had appeared.

" We were discussing some aspects of the question which is so dear to us, Mr. Dane—the subject
which my father broached last night.   Mr. Ford
here, who of course is one of us "——

But here Ford interrupted the speaker with a remark uttered in a tone which could not disguise his chagrin.

"I think, Miss Acosta, we had better not discuss this subject further at present. It can have no interest for Mr. Dane; and, moreover, as it is a matter in which he can have no possible concern, I am sure he would prefer that we should talk on some theme in which we can take a common interest."

Felix experienced a desire to say something bitter, for his dislike and mistrust of Ford had suddenly turned from the passive to the active stage; but he controlled himself, and replied quietly that he already knew about the aspirations and aims of the Redemption movement among the Jews; that he himself might in some measure be enlisted among those, whether Judaic or not, who called themselves Children of To-morrow; and that his interests were keenly awakened in what he had heard of the new movement.

"In a sense, Mr. Dane is one of us, you will now be glad to hear," Sanpriel remarked in a tone wherein the irony was not wholly disguised.

Ford shot a quick glance from one to the other, and it was clear that he was far from pleased.

"For myself at any rate, I decline to discuss

a question which is, or should be, so private to *us.*"

" Then you *are* a Jew, Ford ? " asked Felix.

" Yes.　Why do you ask ? "

" Because we certainly inferred—my wife and I —that you were not."

" I cannot help your inferences.　I do not see "——

" That ' we inferred' was only a polite way of saying that you certainly, on one occasion, told us that though you intimately knew the Monterolis and Cranes, and others, you were absolutely un- related to them except in business."

This was a home-thrust that pierced Gabriel Ford in his weakest part.　It suited him to adopt two *rôles :* in secret, and among his kindred, that of the Jewish emancipator ; in public, that of the wealthy, art-loving, unprejudiced Gentile.

Sanpriel looked at him fixedly while Felix was speaking, and was convinced that he had indeed misled his friends as to his nationality—a short- coming which in her eyes was as impolitic as it was despicable.

" That is not the case."

" Excuse me, Ford, I am not in the habit of uttering untruths.　Did you not, also, tell my wife, two nights ago, that you were *not* a Jew ?

She unquestionably informed me of the circumstance. By the way, that reminds me of the fact that I have a letter for you, from her."

Skilled as he was in physiognomic control, Ford was unable to repress a start and an apprehensive glance at the speaker. In another moment, however, he had regained his self-possession, and took the missive which Felix handed to him, without the slightest trace either of eagerness or reluctance.

"Ah, from Mrs. Dane?   I suppose it is about that newly discovered fugue by Bach which I promised to lend her.   In the hurry of departure I came away without having sent it off, but I'll write to my man by the afternoon mail."

Then, without glancing at the letter, he put it in his pocket, and with an ease of demeanour that did him credit commenced some chit-chat about the Sarasate concert, Adama Acosta's performance, and other matters musical.

A restraint, however, lay upon his two companions that was not altogether the result of what all three felt to have been an untimely and disagreeable rencontre. It would have been strange if after the events of the past night Felix and Sanpriel could have walked side by side as new acquaintances merely ; each felt a magnetic current flowing from the other; both were conscious that the hand of destiny, of circumstance, of chance, had wrought certain vital threads of their being into a woof that bound them each to each.

Now and again a slight touch, a meré hint of contact, sent a thrill along Felix's nerves, and though Sanpriel seemed to studiously avoid his swift and searching, glances, he knew that in her eyes there was a strange and fugitive light that was not native to their fathomless serenity.

How personal the conversation — or Gabriel Ford's monologue rather—had become! he vaguely reflected once or twice; nor was it till a certain accent of quite unnecessary emphasis in the repetition of "your wife" aroused him that he understood, for the first time, how he had given Ford cause for resentment.

Ford was jealous—of Sanpriel! Could he, then, thought Felix, have any real love for Lydia? Or was he playing a double game, with self-interest and possibly passion of a kind on the one side, and self-indulgence and mere desire on the other?

This insistent reminding of him, and Sanpriel, that there was a Mrs. Dane in the background, witnessed, clearly enough, to an intention to prejudice him in Miss Acosta's eyes—or, rather, to

render any growth of love, perhaps even of friendship, between her and himself impossible.

How much right of interference had he? Felix
wondered. Was he a kinsman? Was he a guardian?
Was he a lover? Was he, even, a suitor accepted
of Adama Acosta? This, of course, he would find
out as soon as opportunity favoured him.

But as for Sanpriel herself, how did she look
upon him, if, indeed, he had not mistaken a quick
and almost passionate sympathy for the conscious
or unwitting birth of a more potent emotion? If,
he argued, she had felt something of that electric
flash which had thrilled him to his inmost being
when he first confronted her at the sunset window
in Forest Manor, then she must be aware that
love, unquestioning, imperious, irresistible love,
had come to them like lightning out of heaven.
And if she were so aware, how looked she upon
the front of circumstance? That he had pre-
sumably loved before, that at any rate he was
married, and that in all likelihood he knew not
the peril of his blind venture; that, again, she
might not give way openly to the summons of
love, that marriage with him was a thing banned
and impossible, that a higher cause than that of a
woman's heart refused enfranchisement from bonds
which were not altogether of her own making,

—these, and such ponderings as these, occupied Felix's mind even while his outer senses were alert to his surroundings, and his brief answers and remarks sufficiently coherent.

Erewhile Miss Acosta complained of weariness, and so all three turned towards the house. Soon after they had entered the drawing-room through the open window, Sanpriel left in order to join her father; and, at the same time, Ford, having remarked he had letters to write, went to the library.

A dull listlessness overcame Felix, and he knew not how to combat it. After some loitering by the book-covered table, and an indifferent glance through an illustrated paper which he had duly looked through some days previously, he turned to the escritoire and sat down to write a brief letter to Lydia.

Thrice he finished a note, and each time impatiently tore it up in fragments. Finally he selected a telegram form, and wrote simply a message to the effect that he was glad of the rest and change at Forest Manor, and should remain for some days.

As he inscribed his signature Lady Crane entered, and then ensued a period of dull gossip about matters of no moment to either till Felix felt as though one of the silent evenings at The Sycamores, with Lydia alone for company, would by comparison be delightful.

With unutterable relief he heard the luncheon-gong sound, though, to his surprise in one instance, and chagrin in the other, neither Ford nor Sanpriel was present at the table.

After lunch his host suggested a long ride inland to see a friend of his, whom Felix also knew, and as the latter was a good horseman, and riding his favourite exercise, he gladly enough agreed to the proposal.

It was late in the afternoon before they reached Forest Manor again, so late that there was but time in which to dress for dinner.

Once again life became other than mere existence, when he saw Sanpriel standing near the piano, talking with Sir Arthur. She looked so beautiful, and welcomed him with such simple dignity, and yet with a friendliness that had in it something of no mere conventional cordiality, that his ennui suddenly vanished.

It certainly did not detract from his satisfaction when he learned that Lady Crane had gone to Crevil Court to witness an archery tournament, and that she had persuaded—more likely, Felix thought, had imperatively required — Ford to accompany her. She had left word that dinner was not to be delayed on her account, and thus it was that, as soon as Adama Acosta, looking pale and worn, but calm and almost stately in a certain pathetic dignity of demeanour that was as a kind of instinctive protest, had joined them, and the gong had sounded, Felix was asked by Sir Arthur to take Miss Acosta in to dinner, "while we two old fogies will follow, and attend to our gross appetites; for no doubt you, Dane, will be quite as enthusiastic as my friend Sanpriel in the discussion of poetry, art, romance, and all the rest of it, to the exclusion of all such base matters as fish, flesh, and fowl."

It was certainly a delightful dinner, and none the less so because Sir Arthur's laughing suggestion was borne out by no undue abstinence on the part of his younger guests. Even when Felix thought it all over, later on, he scarce realised how wide had been the reach of their topics, how relatively profound had been their diving into speculative depths, how mentally alert and how swift in sympathy each had been with the other. In that hour, disturbed as it was by endless minor interruptions, how close he had drawn to the beautiful woman for whom his whole heart and soul now yearned! how akin he found himself in all matters of art ! how stimulated to worthier endeavour than he had ever been before !   Felix Dane was passionately in love, and thus the common vanity which we all share in degree was in his case sublimated to an emotion wherein the .personal argument exercised no dominion.   He tortured himself with no calculations as to whether so beautiful and rare a creature as Sanpriel could love him, whether there were anything in his appearance or manner or nature that could, for her, afford attraction or fascination ; he *knew* that his life and hers had touched, and that though her will might be enthroned serene above the mischances of circumstance, all else of her turned towards him with the same unwitting yearning as, with an inevitableness that seems not void of conscious desire, the golden-lily of Brazil grows towards its male counterpart. Perhaps—he pondered, nay, he believed—that to such an one as Sanpriel love was so absolute, so royal a· thing that no thought was given to the fugitive minor attendants which are commonly so obvious, like the daws and magpies and sparrow-hawks that flutter vehemently after the first skyward circles of the eagle.

There was but that one drop of dubious bitter in his cup of joy : Sanpriel's fervour, her passion for the cause of her people which she had so deeply to heart. Could love enter in at gates so guarded? Could any flag of surrender ever wave from battlements which were thus inviolable? This dread would haunt him again and again, though he strove to overcome it; but at last as a phantom constrained to obedience, it veiled its presence, though it departed not.

After dinner there was an interval of music, though Acosta declined to play on account of the mingled weariness and despondency which still held him in thrall. But even the early departure of father and daughter was compensated for by the promise of both to spend a few days in June on Felix's house-boat——one or two idle days upon the Thames on its remoter reaches.

Not long after Mr. and Miss Acosta had left the room, the sound of carriage-wheels was heard, and Sir Arthur, having first bidden his guest to go out into the grounds and smoke, if he felt so inclined, hurried off to meet his wife.

An hour later, as Felix was strolling through the yews, endeavouring to create in fancy the scene that had been enacted there when last he stood among the gaunt, contorted branches of the ancient trees, he was startled at the abrupt appearance of a figure from out of the deep shadow of one of them, scarce ten yards away.

The next moment he recognised Gabriel Ford. As the latter cleared the reach of shadow, the moonlight shone full upon his face, which was white and set.

"I have come out to meet you, Felix Dane. I suppose you can guess my errand."

"No, I cannot."

"That letter you handed to me—the letter from Mrs. Dane?"

"Well?"

"That letter was *open*, although it was a private note addressed to me."

"Well?"

"Well? By God, you take it coolly! Are you in the habit of opening other people's letters?"

"Not as a regular thing."

"Look here, Dane, drop that tone, and answer me frankly. Did you open Mrs. Dane's letter to me?"

"I did."

Ford stepped a little nearer, and the lines in his face hardened.

"Your reason for so forgetting yourself?"

"I omitted to tell you what you will yourself have noticed, that the writing on the envelope was blurred, though not then, as now, indecipherable. Just as I was about to leave home two mornings ago, the servant handed me a note from Mrs. Dane. I had not time to glance at it at the moment, and put it in my pocket with intention to read it in the hansom; however, I forgot all about it. Last night or early this morning there was a rising of wind and rain, and as I had left the window open, everything near the latter was soaked. The letter meant for you fell out of my breast-pocket, and was no doubt soon pretty thoroughly damped. When I picked it up I could just make out my own name on the envelope, and recognised the letter as that which my servant had handed to me."

"What? Do you mean to say that it was *addressed to you?*"

"Yes. In her haste my wife must have enclosed the note meant for me in an envelope addressed to you, or to some one else."

A look of mingled surprise, chagrin, and suspicion came into Ford's face, though he could not but believe that Dane spoke the truth.

"And the sequel? You read the letter?"

"No. I saw that it began 'Dear Gabriel.' It was news to me that my wife and you were so intimate as to call each other 'Gabriel' and 'Lydia,' but it is, of course, no affair of mine. I did not read your letter—which I dare say was no easy task for you, as much of it seemed indecipherable through the damp."

" That is all you know of the letter ? "

" Yes."

" On your word of honour ? "

" My word is sufficient for those who are themselves men of honour."

Ford took no notice of the implied rebuke, but shifted restlessly.

" I have been too hasty," he said at last in a constrained voice, "and beg your pardon. It so happened that there was something private in the letter; something about—about—a mutual friend, and of course I "——

" There is no necessity to explain," Felix interrupted coldly ; " I have nothing to do with my wife's private correspondence. And now I think I'll stroll back ; it is becoming chilly."

The two men walked side by side for some time without speaking, but at last Felix broke the constraint.

" Are you going to make any stay here ? "

Ford shot a quick glance at his companion, and was about to make a not over-courteous reply, but he controlled himself.

" I do not know ; it depends on circumstances. Are *you* ? "

"In my case also it depends on circumstances."

"Such as the stay or departure of Miss Acosta?"

Ford spoke with a distinct sneer, but though Felix was conscious of it, he showed no sign of having apprehended its significance.

"Undoubtedly Miss Acosta is the chief attraction here," he replied quietly, "and she and I have many interests in common. Her father, also, I find a most interesting man."

"What would Mrs. Dane say to it?"

The sarcastic laugh that accompanied the remark made the latter offensive, but still Felix maintained his attitude of calm and somewhat contemptuous indifference.

"That question is not in your usual good taste, Ford. But let us change the subject. I want to hear more about the aims and hopes of those who call themselves emancipated Jews."

"Oh, damn the Jews!"

"Certainly do so if it afford any relief to your feelings. I have myself known some whom I could damn most heartily."

"I want to speak to you about a personal matter, Dane."

"Well!"

" Probably you do not know that I intend to marry Miss Acosta ? "

A furious surge of blood made Felix's heart throb as though it were about to burst, and a choking sensation came into his throat, but with a powerful effort he controlled himself. It was not merely that the announcement gave him a shock ; he resented the arrogant tone in which the remark had been made, and the " I intend to marry," with its implication as to Sanpriel's consent being a secondary matter.

" I was *not* aware of your intention."

" It is not intention, merely ; Adama Acosta knows of and approves my suit."

" And Miss Acosta ? "

" Miss Acosta will do as she thinks right. She sees that her father wishes it, and that the cause of—of "———

" The Jews ? "

" That the cause which she has so much to heart may thereby be materially helped. Therefore, even if she were indifferent to me, which she is not, she would not hesitate to do what is her manifest duty."

" So far as I can judge she does not seem to have the staunchest or most enthusiastic ally in you : the cause of Israel is not so important with you as the cause of Gabriel Ford, eh, *mon ami?*" Felix remarked, with a short cynical laugh.

"You do not know what you are talking about, and Miss Acosta is, to say the least of it, indiscreet in her zeal. The best way to nip a revolution or a reform is to chatter freely about it ere the time of fruition is at hand."

"Dear me, I had no idea you were of the reformers of any kind. How interested Mrs. Dane —Lydia, I should say—will be to hear about your Jewish *bund!* It is true that she has a stupid prejudice against your people—a prejudice so strong that the word seems euphemistic; but no doubt *your* persuasive powers will modify or even convert her opinions."

He saw that his shaft had gone home, and that the poison was rankling, and it was with cruel pleasure that he made the wound deeper.

"And in any case she will be most interested to hear about Miss Acosta. I shall write to her about it to-night. *Sanpriel Acosta:* she cannot but admire the name at any rate. I must tell Lydia how much in love you are, and how beautiful Miss Sanpriel is."

Twice Ford essayed to speak, but each time his hesitation overcame him. At last, and it was curious what a metallic ring had come into his voice, he replied that he did not think either matter could have any special interest for Mrs. Dane.

Silence again ensued, and both men walked up the avenue with slightly quickened step.

The rare beauty of the cloud-drift caught Felix's attention, and with his characteristically swift responsiveness to any extraneous object either beautiful or strange or unusual, he became absorbed, almost to obliviousness, of his companion.

The moon seemed as though poised, like a cresset of primrose-fire, on the summit of the highest among the yews; but she threw upward such a flood of light that the dappled curds of cloud, quiescent surf of the storm that had drifted inland, were fringed with faint yellow. Elsewhere, white as snow and soft as lambswool, stretched long peninsulas of irradiate vapour, save towards the south-west, where the accumulated drift was as softly grey as the breast of a cushat, but, at its hither extremities, fibrous, and frayed by little circling eddies of wind.

Some wild-fowl, flying in a vast wedge-wise figure, as they crossed the great space where the amber radiances prevailed, no longer blurred and dusky as when clearing their way through the farther glooms, grew as black and as clearly defined as rooks in the first afterglow.

So absorbed was Felix in observation and in vague trains of surmise, that he was unconscious of Ford's having left him, till, suddenly looking round with an abrupt sense of isolation, he discovered that he was alone.

Instead of entering the house when he reached the broad stone balcony that extended to right and left of the triple stairway, he turned, descended the few steps at the drawing-room gable, and strolled into what was called the Labyrinth, though its flower-haunted, box-bordered ways, devious as they were, had little of the intricacies of the old-fashioned maze.

One of those happy mischances which as often lead us to the golden as their contraries to the iron gates of experience had conducted him thither; for as he stopped to inhale the over-sweet pungent odour of the blossoms of a ceringa, he caught sight of a tall white figure standing among some late-flowering almonds, in whose profuse beauty he had been lost in admiration that forenoon, when walking in the Labyrinth with Sanpriel and Ford. Although half-lost in shadow, there was no doubt as to whose it was.

With eager eyes he hastened forward, and as

he saw Sanpriel come towards him, he felt an almost irresistible temptation to take her in his arms, and by the passion of his kisses declare the love that consumed him. A line from one of the Elizabethan poets came into his mind, and almost as he reached Sanpriel he muttered Florio's complaint, "How leapt we into this labyrinth of love ?"

"Are you composing a poem, Mr. Dane," asked Miss Acosta, with a low laugh. "No ? I suppose that, like myself, you have come here to obtain a breath of sweet garden-air before going to bed. But now I must hasten in ; I promised my father not to be away many minutes. But do not let me take you in ; I will say good-night now."

"I am so sorry you cannot remain out a little longer, Miss Acosta ; the night is glorious, and the air delightful after the morning's storm. But if you *must* go in, let me accompany you."

As they slowly walked towards the house, Felix made some further arrangements about the projected house-boat holiday, but when he added that he should call very shortly at Dreamthorpe, he fancied he detected something of hesitation in his companion's manner.

The idea that she perhaps regretted her father's open invitation to him, or that possibly Ford had prejudiced her against too frank a friendship, determined him to broach the subject which was causing such an ache at his heart.

"Miss Acosta, we have known each other but a few hours in point of time, though circumstances have done for us what weeks of casual intercourse might not have accomplished; and on this ground I am emboldened to ask you a question · of a private nature."

Impressed as much by something in his voice as by his words, Sanpriel gave a startled glance at his face, and then, in a low voice, assented.

"If you consider that I am taking an undue liberty, forgive me; but—but—is it the case that you are engaged to be married to Gabriel Ford? I understand so from the latter."

He could not see her face, which she had averted as soon as he had commenced speaking, and though he fancied that she trembled for a moment, like a doe at the distant bark of a hound, he could not tell how his question had affected her.

But a chill came into his heart when she walked onward without reply, and still with face averted.

Was it, then, true? *Could* she, willingly or

otherwise, be betrothed to a man with whom, despite his racial relationship and general culture, she had really so little in common?

A huge moth flew by with a harsh bristling crackle of its shards, and from the lawns beyond the Manor came the scream, at once wailing and strident, of a peacock; but scarce another sound broke the stillness, save the faint susurrus of the wind upon the wet grass and the crish-crash of the gravel upon which they walked.

So, Sanpriel resented his question, and was going to leave him without a word; and then his house of sand would collapse, and his next tide of life know it no more! As they both abruptly stopped at a side entrance, which led into the hall through one of the conservatories, he held out his hand in an impulse of combined hope and despair.

Sanpriel did not at first take it, but she turned and looked upon him, and he saw that in her eyes there was nothing of resentment.

"Good-night, Mr. Dane. I am not angry at your question, though it has made me think, —and wonder. But what you assert is not true."

Felix eagerly leaned forward and caught the hand that was outstretched to him, but he retained it as, in a low impassioned voice, he again spoke.

"He assured me that it was true; tell me again that it is not so,—San——Miss Acosta!"

He felt an instantaneous quiver thrill the hand he held, and even in the half-light where she stood, he could see that a flush had come and ebbed upon her face.

"It is not true. I am not engaged to him,—nor in any circumstances that I can foresee is such a thing possible between Mr. Ford and myself."

As Sanpriel spoke she disengaged her hand, and then, almost ere he realised her absence, he found himself standing alone.

But it was with a new life at his heart that he entered the house; the regnant feeling that had upborne him of late had returned, and his pulse beat as though under some potent stimulus.

When he entered the drawing-room he found no one there save Sir Arthur and Lady Crane, but so elated was he by what he had just learned, that he could have been amiable and entertaining even to the Rector of Grantley, to whom, on the previous evening, he had felt contemptuously hostile.

Half-an-hour or so passed in disconnected chat,

and then Ford entered. He seemed preoccupied, and far from cheerful; and once a baleful light came into his eyes when he heard that Dane had met Miss Acosta in the Labyrinth, and noticed how alert and almost joyous were his expression and voice.

Lady Crane, wont to retire at an early hour, remained in the room till late, and made a sufficient number of malappropriate remarks to have set her two guests wrangling had not each been on his guard, though for different reasons.

At last, to every one's relief, she said good-night and departed.   Soon afterwards Felix followed suit, but was startled, as he passed along the corridor leading to his apartment, to hear strains of wild and discordant music coming from Adama Acosta's room.

So strident, so savagely inchoate were they, that he feared the musician had again been overtaken by one of his brief attacks of frenzy; but though his heart was sore for Sanpriel, he could not venture to intrude. For some minutes, however, he lingered in the corridor, till the fitful strains of the violin abruptly ceased; and then, satisfied that Acosta had charmed away his distemper, he went to his own room.

But, till slumber became profound, his dreams were perturbed by imaginary and real echoes of sound, now of a music wild and barbaric, shrill and clamorous, now of swelling, resonant tones, borne inward, across dune and woodland, from leagues of violent sea.

CHAPTER VII.

Dane woke with a start next morning when he heard a voice by his bedside.

"It is a note, sir, from Mr. Ford; he is waiting for an answer."

Felix opened it with a strong feeling of curiosity, and with some misgivings, which proved unfounded.

Dear Dane,—I should much like to talk over and explain some remarks we made to each other yesterday. It is a glorious day, and as Sir Arthur is busy, he has asked me to ride with you, a pleasure I would have tried to ensure in any case. As it is late, I presume you will soon be out, so will order your horse to be in readiness. If you cannot come at once, will you ride round by the seaward side of the forest for about two miles, then turn to the left, and turn eastward again at the first road to the right: thus we may meet and ride homeward together. Please send me word by bearer.—Yours,

"Gabriel Ford."

He by no means felt anxious for Ford's company, but he could not without discourtesy refuse the proposed arrangement. He sent word, accordingly, that he had slept late, and so was not ready to go out at once, but that in half-an-hour he should be ready, and would follow in the course indicated.

Having had his bath and dressed, he strolled down to the breakfast-room, but found no one there. Norgate, the butler, notable for his reticence and monosyllabic utterances, vouchsafed no remarks, and as Felix was absorbed in some correspondence that had arrived over-night, he learned nothing of the movements of the other inmates of Forest Manor.

Ere he had begun his breakfast he was informed that his horse was at the door, so that by the time he had satisfied his hunger he did not delay to bid his host or hostess good-morning, but, having lit a cigar, mounted the handsome chestnut mare which had been placed at his disposal, and rode away.

As he crossed the avenue, just before the bend

which shrouded the yew-grove from view, he turned and looked at the house, in the hope that Sanpriel might be at one of the windows, but, to his disappointment, there was no sign of her in either her own or her father's room. For a moment, however, he reined in his horse as he fancied he caught sight, at the library window, of Gabriel Ford; but when he looked again there was no figure there. He smiled at the absurdity of his fancy, and then rode on.

The morning was blithe and fresh, and movement itself a very joy. Everywhere the birds were in a state of rapturous energy, though here and there a thrush, more lovelorn than its fellows, or an ecstatic little blue tit, poured forth a sweet, swift, lilting music that was simply intoxicating. Scents from the grass, the cowslips, and marguerites, from the trailing hedges of wild rose and honeysuckle, from the clumps of gold-flowered gorse through whose spiky branches flitted stonechats and yellowhammers innumerable, and from the forest beyond, with its violet-covered glades and dells haunted of the late-flowering primrose, mixed with the more pungent odours from the sand-dunes and the sea. Everywhere there was a sense of joy—in the blue sky, fretted with flying shreds of white cloud, in the wandering voice of the cuckoo passing over the woods and uplands, in the bubbling, trilling, omnipresent songs of the larks, poised, decrescent, or spirally ascending over the meadows, wherein the cattle stood or lay contentedly, with scarce a gadfly in that crisp and buoyant air to whisk from their sunlit flanks.

As he rode onward and crossed the dunes, he felt joyous with the long-forgotten gaiety of youth; so blithe was he that he would fain have raced the sea-gull or the deceptive, ever onward-sweeping curve of the foam-line.

Filled with glad thoughts and dreams bright in rainbow gold, he reached the grassy promontory that cut off the sands, two miles north-eastward of Forest Manor, without having given a second thought to Gabriel Ford—till suddenly he caught sight of the cart-road to the left which he had been directed to follow. With a sigh of regret at having to go inland, he turned and rode away from the sea, which was all in turmoil with the surge of the incoming tide.

Scarce fifty yards beyond the high sand-ridge which hid the sea from the mainland he came upon the track that led to the right, along which he mechanically rode, absorbed in thought.

He must have advanced close upon a mile when the stillness and sombre aspect of the locality

suddenly fascinated his attention. What a change
to the scenery through which he had ridden since
he left Forest Manor! Here all was barrenness,
and owing to the absence of birds, and apparently
of all other living creatures, the sterility had
nothing of beauty in it. There are moods in
most of us when the desolation of nature may be
our exhilaration, in the same way as, for some inscrutable reason, we are sometimes stimulated to
keen elation by the most commonplace or even
disagreeable environment—a sleety day in a locality
void of novelty or any particular charm, for example. But wherever there be desolation without,
apparently, the humblest agencies of nature at
work—save the two greatest, air and water—*there*
is no stimulus or help for any creature. The
most sordid hovels may be redeemed by a child's
laugh, nay, by a drunkard's oath even, so precious
is the breath of life; the most barren and un-
attractive waste may be pleasurable because of the
brown moth that flickers above the sand, the
carrion-fly, or the grey lizard darting among the
stones.

Felix—subject as he was to every atmospheric
change and apt to yield to the most extraneous
of influences upon physical mood—was at once
conscious of a sense of despondency. The place

was so gloomy, so lifeless; not even a dotterel or redshank flitted along the ground, and if a gull wheeled overhead, it was to pass swiftly away with a discordant scream. His mare also seemed to resent the soil; she stamped her feet and grew restless, and sniffed the air as if apprehensively. Along the flat clay-like stones which cropped up here and there, and by the margins of the rank sea-grass that grew in sickly patches, he noticed a white powdery substance, like the salt residue of the surf of primeval seas. *Salt:* why, of course, he muttered, he must be among the salt-marshes, perhaps in those of Ratho, of which he remembered having heard dire accounts. What a strange place to have been appointed as a rendezvous! And how was it possible for Ford to meet him in the salt-marsh when it stretched for leagues eastward till it met the sea? The reflection perturbed him, and a frown came upon his face. Under a sharp touch of the whip the mare bounded forward, then reared, and would have swung round; but, angry at he knew not what, he forced her onward.

Suddenly she gave a leap and nearly threw her rider, but before he could recover from his surprise she had again plunged wildly forward, and seemed in nervous distress, for her nostrils palpitated like valves of a machine, her eyes were strained and bloodshot, and down her neck the sweat poured in thick dark runlets.

What could this frantic labouring mean, Felix wondered; but he understood when in another moment he realised that, with all her plunging and other efforts, the mare was not advancing a yard.

He had ridden into the marsh of Ratho, that fatal quicksand where for centuries many an inadvertent wayfarer has encountered death. He remembered it all now, and in that extraordinary inconsequence of thought which comes to some of us at times of great peril or distress, he was conscious of speculating as to whether it was a man or woman who had last perished among these salt-morasses.

A swift glance around him showed close at hand a patch of tufty grasses, sufficient perhaps to afford firm footing—a grannock, as the fen-men call such places.

Half-slipping, half-swinging from his horse, he found, to his relief, that he was only at the beginning of the quaking morass, and that though he might sink over his ankles here and there, he would have no difficulty in leaping from grannock to grannock till he gained the rime-whitened sands beyond. But what about the mare? In vain he strove with encouraging words and tautened bridle, and at last with swishing lashes of the whip, to assist her: the poor beast had become distraught with fear, and was rapidly exhausting herself in her ceaseless struggles, which, misdirected as they were, only made her chances worse. From the appearance of the soil Felix felt certain that they were only upon the verge of the quicksand, and that, though the mare might sink a few feet, she would touch solid footing ere long, and then become quieted. He recollected having caught a glimpse of a hovel not far beyond the juncture of the marsh and the inland roads, and he determined to run thither in the hope of obtaining assistance.

It was not, however, without some awkward slips and plunges—in each of which he was conscious of something treacherous in the loose soil—that he regained firm ground, and then, with a backward glance and encouraging cry to the mare, who, either through exhaustion or having touched a solid foundation, was almost quiet, he ran rapidly along the edge of the salt-marsh.

In about ten minutes he had reached the hovel, only to find that it was, and had plainly long been, unoccupied and ruinous. From where he stood he could see no other habitation or sign of human being: nothing anywhere but the sand-ridge to the south, the bare uplands and distant forest to the

I

west, and east and northward the barren leagues
of the Sands of Ratho.

Setting his foot on a jutting stone at a corner
of the wall, he climbed on to the roof, and from
the vantage of the long smokeless chimney looked
eagerly around.   Still nothing visible save what
he had already seen : no sign of human life, and,
so far as he could make out, no road even, for it
seemed as though half-a-mile farther on the cart-
path meandered vaguely into a heath-clad sandy
waste and there lost itself.

And what of Gabriel Ford ?   Where was *he ?*
In what direction could he be coming ?   According
to the lie of the land, it could scarcely be from any
other quarter than from the north-west, where the
Forest of Grantley lay dark in the strong sunlight
—but in the intervening space there was not even
a crow in sight.

With an impatient exclamation Felix hastened
back to the marsh, not without hope that the mare
might have recovered herself, or at least might be
quiescent enough to let him help in her deliverance.
But as he approached the place where he had left
her he saw that she was inextricably in the toils.
She must have floundered madly after he had left,
for she was at least twenty yards farther into the
quicksand, but already she had sunk to her belly,

which heaved wildly against the enclosing grit, loose as snow-powder, yet irresistible as a vice.

He could not even venture to go near her. A single attempt sufficed to show him the folly of such a venture, for it was with difficulty that he regained the grannock from which he had stepped into the quicksand. It was not easy to judge what was safe ground and what was not, for on the surface there was little or no sign of the treacherous turmoil underneath, save here and there a serpentine motion as of drifting dust, or an occasional momentary undulation.

At last the mare had ceased struggling, except spasmodically. Her eyes were greatly distended, but were glazed, and with the froth that fell from her mouth ran a continuous thin stream of watery blood. The sight was a piteous one, and his heart bled for the suffering of his fellow-creature, but he could do nothing. If only he had had a gun or revolver with him, he muttered, he would soon have put an end to her agony.

Slowly but surely she sank deeper and deeper, and at last even the saddle became swallowed up in the quicksand. He could not leave, though he would fain have spared himself the pain of his useless witness of the mare's end. In a brief while longer she had sunk to her neck, to her head, and then her ears filled. Suddenly she gave a shrill, human-like cry; her ears quivered among the enveloping sand; her nostrils, wildly panting, emitted foam and blood, and then the sands engulfed her and left no trace, save for a few moments a little drift of blood-stained froth.

Sick at heart, and with rage at he scarce knew what or whom throbbing in his pulses, Felix leapt from grannock to grannock till he gained the path, and then strode rapidly homeward.

What did it all mean? Why had Ford not met him? Why had he sent him on this fool's errand? Could he——was it possible that the man could have been such a villain as to have endeavoured to compass his death?

But no, he thought, Ford could not have calculated upon such an outcome of the ride towards the Marsh of Ratho, for he must have known that in all probability he, Felix, would notice the danger in time. And yet——and yet——he may have thought the game a safe one, and always with the *chance* of success; or perhaps Ford had really meant to meet him at the verge of the quicksand, there force a quarrel upon him, and somehow or other ensure his death in the morass. If so, why had he not kept his appointment? The whole affair seemed wrapped in mystery, and the more he reflected upon its various aspects the more puzzled he became.

It was a long walk back by the shore, and it was not rendered pleasant by the weather, which had changed with true East Anglian abruptness.

The white fibrous clouds of the morning had drawn closelier to each other, and had thickened into grey densities, and across the sea there impended a slate-hued gloom, ominous of downpour. Landward, a thin drizzling rain had commenced to fall, and what had been so blithe and beautiful seemed somewhat sombre and dreary.

In ordinary circumstances the walk would have been nothing, but Felix was tired by his exertions, and, moreover, worried and impatient. But at last he came upon the extreme limit of Grantley Forest, passed through the yew-grove, and so up the avenue to the Manor.

As he walked across the terrace to the door he saw Norgate regarding him with as much curiosity as that individual ever manifested ; and for the first time he realised that his appearance did not betoken a pleasant ride, for not only was he horseless, but his boots and trousers were soiled with clay and sand and the mud from the hovel-roof. He was glad that Norgate and no other was there, for the man was as discreet as he was respectful.

" Has Mr. Ford returned, Norgate ? I missed him somehow, and rode into an infernal quicksand some two or three miles along the shore. I had rather a narrow escape from it myself, and the poor mare came to grief."

" I am glad to see you safe, sir. But it was extraordinary that you ventured on to Ratho Sands when the notice warned wayfarers that they must go no farther in that direction."

" Notice ?   I saw no notice."

" That's strange, sir, for after the gale yesterday morning Sir Arthur sent one of the men round to see if it had not been blown down, and it was reported all right. Sir Arthur has a horror of the place, for several deaths have occurred there within the last few years ; and he has had notice-boards stuck up at each quarter."

" H'm ; that makes it stranger still. But has Mr. Ford come back from his ride."

" From his ride, sir ? "

" Dear me, Norgate, don't you understand what I say ? Mr. Ford was to meet me either along the shore or at Ratho Morass, but I saw no sign of him. Perhaps he miscalculated the time and rode back by a different way."

"Mr. Ford went no ride since breakfast, sir. About an hour ago he drove to the station with Mr. and Miss Acosta, and went to London with them."

"*What!* Miss Acosta—and—and—her father *gone to London?* I heard no word of this either last night or this morning?"

"Mr. Acosta was taken ill last night, sir; and this morning he and Miss Sanpriel thought they had better return to London at once. Everything was hurriedly arranged. Both Mr. and Miss Acosta wanted to see you before they left, but though they were in the library with Mr. Ford at the time you left, no one saw you going away."

A flash of remembrance came into Felix's mind, and he saw again Gabriel's face looking out at him from the window; his fancy had not been false after all. With a flush of anger upon his face, he was about to say something concerning Ford, when he checked himself.

"Did you say that Miss Acosta asked to see me?"

"Yes; and Mr. Ford told her that you had gone off for a ride somewhere, most likely to join them at the station and say good-bye."

"Curse him!"

"Sir?"

" Nothing.   When is the next train to London ? "

" There is no other to York, sir, till the slow train at two o'clock.   It gets in shortly before four, and in time to catch the south mail which gets into London at eight."

" Then will you see to my things, Norgate, and have a trap ready to take me to Grantley in time for the two o'clock train ?   Where is Sir Arthur ? "

" In his study, sir ; first room beyond the library."

Felix immediately went to the latter, and was relieved to find his host in and disengaged.

As succinctly as he could he narrated his experiences, but said nothing about either Ford or the Acostas.   He wished to leave without giving offence to Sir Arthur or Lady Crane, and he knew that he could scarce do so at once when he had heard from the former of the abrupt departure of the other guests ; so he made as much of the " shock " he had received as he well could, and asserted that, as he did not feel well, he would prefer to go home and pay the rest of his visit later on.   Moreover, he said he wished at once to purchase a handsome chestnut mare which a friend wanted to dispose of, wherewith to replace Lady Crane's horse, which, through his carelessness, had come to such a tragic end.

Sir Arthur would not hear of the latter excuse, and protested that the fault was his for not having warned his guest about the fatal quicksands; but added how amazed he was at the absence of any notice-board, as such had certainly existed the previous day, and as there had been no storm since that could have blown it down.

"Ratho is most deadly after a gale, especially if from the east or south-east; and on such occasions I always send a man to see to the warning-boards, for fear any poor tramp, seaman, or other stranger should inadvertently flounder into the quicksand. It is so well known all along this northern coast that only strangers could fall a victim to it."

While Sir Arthur was speaking a startling idea had flashed across Felix, but he determined to test it himself.

His host, he was thankful to find, took his suggestion of departure in good part, though he laughingly asserted that there had been a carefully concocted conspiracy among his guests to deprive him and Lady Crane of any company save that of each other. Felix smiled uneasily, and with a hypocritical suavity that surprised himself, pretended much surprise at the news of the sudden departure of the Acostas.

Having expressed a wish to write one or two notes and telegrams, he went into the library. As soon as he had hurriedly written upon a form and finished a short business letter, he made as though to rise from the desk, but suddenly his attention was attracted by a clear impress upon the white blotting-paper. With conscious curiosity, he held it up to the light, and there, to his amazement, he saw his own name legibly written. The next moment he recognised the writing as identical with that on the fly-leaf of "White-Nights." He still had the fly-leaf in his pocket-book, and in a few seconds he had compared the two "Felix Danes." They were identical, so that Sanpriel had written to him ere she left! Where, then, was her letter?

He looked eagerly about, but could not descry a letter anywhere. Finally he rang the bell, and when Norgate appeared, asked him with an eagerness he could not altogether control if Miss Acosta had left a note for him.

" No, sir, she did not. But just about the time you rode away she was sitting at that table writing a note. As there were no envelopes in the case, she asked me to fetch her one, which I did. She then addressed but did not stamp it."

" Did she return to the library after having gone

out into the hall when the carriage was at the door ?"

"No. Why, let me see; yes, Mr. Dane, I believe she did—for a scarf, or glove, or something."

"Did Mr. Ford come back ?"

"Not that I know of, sir."

Felix was so far satisfied at what he had learned from Norgate, though, if he had seen the momentary smile on the butler's face as he closed the door after him, he might have been rendered suspicious.

Having looked at his watch, and found that he had close upon half-an-hour to spare ere early lunch, he passed out of the library, crossed the hall and the terrace, and went round to the stables. There he sought out the head-groom, and asked him to speak to him for a few minutes. He told him about the loss of the mare, whereat Smith seemed somewhat perplexed, but reiterated what Norgate and Sir Arthur had already asserted about the notice-board.

"And not only that, sir, but Mr. Ford was round that way for a ride early this morning, and as he knows every inch of the ground, and 'ow pertickler Sir Arthur is, he'd certainly 'ave told me or some one if the board had been blowed down or any scamp interfered with it."

So his suspicions were not unfounded, and an angry light came into Felix's eyes as he asked Smith if he were sure that Mr. Ford had ridden Ratho-way early that morning.

" Certainly, sir. He was up early, and Brown saddled his horse for him. He mentioned that he had just heard that Mr. Acosta was going back to town by the mornin' train, and that he was goin' too, but wanted a breath o' sea-air first. When he came back I asked him if he had gone far, an' he said he had gone to the joint-roads ; but he must 'ave been thinking o' summut, for he went a bit farther nor that."

" How do you know ? "

" Because I noticed in his horses' hoofs bits of a blackish clay that is found nowhere hereabouts but in the morass round about and beyond Ratho Quicksand. He must have ridden to the edge of the latter, I expect, and then turned."

Felix gave the man a sovereign, heedless whether the amount of the tip might not make Smith suspiciously reflective, and then walked slowly back to the house. So, it was true : Gabriel Ford had played with him. Even if he had not intercepted a letter from Sanpriel, he had deceived him about the meeting, had given him directions that in the instance of a stranger were perilously inadvertent, and, it would seem, had even gone the length of riding eastward toward Ratho Morass in order to remove the warning notice which Sir Arthur had erected at that dangerous locality.

Yet everything had been done so naturally, and with so little room for proof of guilty intention. So clever a man as Ford could well afford to laugh at any accusations based on such slender grounds, nor would he have any difficulty in explaining his contradictory messages and actions.

Felix recognised this, and his tide of anger against his rival—rival in a double sense—became more strenuous as he realised his astuteness and *sang-froid*. If he had only kept the note which Ford had sent to him, it would always have been something, though it would have proved nothing.

Throughout lunch he had to make himself as agreeable as possible, and anything distraught or apparently heedless in his manner was attributed by his hosts to his regret at the death of the mare and the shock which his nervous system seemed to have sustained.

A little later, after a definite promise to return and spend some weeks in the early autumn—a promise all the more readily made when he learned that the Acostas were going to spend August at Forest Manor—he bade farewell to Lady Crane, and, accompanied by Sir Arthur, drove to Grantley.

As the dogcart mounted the rise of Oakdene, Sir Arthur reined in the horse and pointed backward with his whip.

"There, Dane, that's the last glimpse of the sea you'll have till you come north again. But now, listen : you hear the boom of it quite distinctly ? Yes ? Well, a few yards away, as soon as we're round yon boulder, you won't hear a sound, strain your ears as you may."

It was as Sir Arthur said. Not a sound, not a vibration of the ocean, was audible, though in the air the brine still made a crispness. But the sudden cessation of the undertone to which he had grown so accustomed, which seemed to him, he scarce knew how, so interblent with the life of Sanpriel, with the lives of Sanpriel and himself, added in some mysterious fashion to his despondency.

Nor did his dejection leave him when at last he found himself in the train. The latter stopped at every little station, and the time appeared endless ere the engine puffed into York. He had about quarter of an hour to wait, so solaced himself with some strong tea, and then strode up and down, still thinking,

thinking, thinking, in a weary round of speculation and hesitancy.

He was roused by the inward rush of the Edinburgh express, and mechanically went forward to take a seat in a carriage, oblivious of the fact that he was about to enter the wrong train, when he was greeted by the familiar voice of his friend, Harold Field.

"Hillo, Dane, where are you off to? Coming north?"

"Ah, how do you do, old fellow? I didn't notice you. No, I'm going back to London."

"Then you're trying a very roundabout way, for *this* train is bound for Edinburgh!"

"By Jove! so it is. What an ass I am! But the south mail hasn't come into the station yet, and I had a vague idea this must be it."

"Well, we'll have time for a cigarette and a chat. Your train won't start for five minutes yet. Ours is a special express, and I'm here as the 'art special' of the *Metropolitan*. However, you'll see all about this in the papers shortly; and so now tell me about yourself. You finished your 'Hertha' before you left town, I suppose?"

"Look here, Harold, we're old friends, and I want you to answer me frankly. What do you honestly think about my 'Hertha'?"

Field looked somewhat embarrassed, and hesitated in reply.

"Well, old chap, you know, artists and critics often look at things very differently, and I have no doubt that the artists are oftenest right. Now, what do *you* think of 'Hertha'?"

Felix laughed at the kindly but too obvious subterfuge.

"My dear boy, I see what's in your mind as clearly as though it were written in large Roman capitals! You don't want to hurt my feelings, but you think my 'Hertha' would be poor as the first ambitious work of a youngster, and is execrable as the production of Felix Dane!"

"No, no, Dane, I don't go that length—but—but "——

"Yes, I quite understand; and what's more, I entirely agree with you. You will be pleased to hear that I smashed it up before I left London."

"*What?*"

"True enough; I smashed the poor feeble thing to pieces. Henceforth I'll do *good* work—or none at all."

Harold Field was one of Dane's most intimate friends, and he had also a great admiration for his genius, though he had lamented, both privately and publicly, the decadence of his conceptive powers.

Knowing Felix as he did, he rejoiced at the news he had just heard, for he believed that the latter had capacities which could carry him far beyond all rivalry.

With a swift movement he seized his friend's hand and gave it a strong, affectionate grip.

"You were right, Dane. The thing was poor; far below the kind of work *you* ought to be doing. But now you'll prosper. Some new force has come into your life, I see. As I have often said, no poet or artist can be great till, æsthetically speaking, he be born again. Most of us reach our fifties still *un*learning: happy are the few whose eyes the gods unveil while yet they can rejoice in outlook and are in their full vigour. But now, old fellow, we must part; yonder's your train, and it will start in a couple of minutes. By the way, I travelled up from Dorset yesterday with your wife."

"With Lydia? Why, I did not know she had left the Walfords'. Were *you* there?"

"Yes. She received a letter yesterday which she said necessitated her return to town. I understood her to say that she had to meet *you*. But now be off, or you'll miss your train; there's your porter beckoning you. Good-bye! I'll look you up soon at The Sycamores!"

K

Field's last words still further complicated the maze of Felix's thoughts.

There were three other passengers in his carriage, and his opposite neighbour was of an inquiring and communicative turn of mind, and whenever he dared to look up from his newspaper to glance through the window he was assailed with some unwelcome remark.

He wanted to think the whole matter out, and to discover what relevancy, if any, Lydia's prevarication had to Ford's action, but he simply could not concentrate his thoughts owing to the nervous perturbation caused him by his talkative neighbour, and even more by the glassy stare of a bookless and newspaperless spinster who sat at the far corner and transfixed him ever and again with her maddening, empty, relentless gaze.

"How on earth do people travel for hours and grudge themselves even a penny paper?" he muttered to himself in exasperation. "And why in Heaven's name does that woman not sleep, or look out of the window, or do anything but stare fixedly at me when I'm not looking? Thank God! there's Doncaster. I'll get some illustrated papers there, and choke her and this fellow off."

But when he stepped on to the platform he noticed that the next carriage was empty, for its two recent occupants had alighted.   With an eagerness which made the unoccupied spinster stare more absorbedly than ever, he gathered up his things and joyfully installed himself in the vacant compartment.

But even when by himself his thoughts were fantastically uncontrollable, and he could think of nothing long, nor of the sum of things in their due relation.

How different, he realised, the journey southward to what its counterpart had been a few days ago. It was not that his life was not fuller and richer, but that a cloud which had not then risen above the horizon now cast a gloom whence he could not escape.   He could not even make up his mind what to do when he reached London.   It often happens that when we are advancing towards some momentous decision we leave the gathering of the clues to chance, and only make up our minds when the two shadowy portals of choice suddenly confront us : and thus was it with Felix Dane. Finally, by that strange contrariety for which it is so difficult to account, he became immersed in some journalistic details which had no real interest for him, and gradually grew indifferent to the tyranny of his inmost thoughts, almost content, indeed, in the peace of his negative quiescence.

But when, after four hours that seemed daylong, he found himself standing on the platform at King's Cross, all hesitancy suddenly left him, and he was again as alert as of yore. Having deposited himself and his slight baggage in a hansom, he was soon bowling along Hampstead-ward, and in rather over half-an-hour recognised the houses of the lower end of Hurst Road.

The house below his own, which was separated from the latter by a large garden, was called Elleray, and it was here that he had instructed the cabman to stop.

Having paid the fare and taken up his Gladstone-bag, he stood at the door of Elleray till the man had driven away; then he walked onward a few yards till he came to a small oaken door marked " Studio. Private."

This door, which he unfastened with a latchkey, opened into a covered passage which led to the studio, wherein a minute or two later he stumbled through the darkness towards the fireplace, on the mantel of which he knew he should find a candle and matches.

How gloomy and deserted, he thought, the large apartment seemed in the flickering candle-light ! How gaunt everything was ! nay, how it seemed as though there were that pathetic and yet repellent negligence which death often invites in places once haunted of life ! Upon the floor still lay the shapeless mass of what had been his "Hertha," and as he looked upon it something humanly piteous in the ruin affected him, and he turned impatiently away. What a chill there was ! what a sense of lifelessness ! Could he ever have worked and dreamed in this room ? Could he ever again dream and work herein ? he wondered, as the sensation of he knew not what vital estrangement grew upon him.

All at once he knew in part what had occurred. He was indeed in the room where a dead man had once worked, for he, the old Felix Dane, no longer lived, would never work or dream here again. He himself, the Felix Dane who now stood like a stranger come to look upon an alien inheritance, had surely little in common with that other of his name, who, it seemed to him, had lived dully a commonplace life, without hope or strenuous endeavour.

"Yes, my old self died with ' Hertha,' " he muttered ; "and now that I am come again, it is as a stranger, with new aims, new energies, new hopes. What will be the end of it all ? But now, my God ! I have to simulate the dead man and live with *her*, who never loved me *then*, and will love

me less now, an alien.   An alien ! ay, so I feel
in all truth——a foreigner who may speak a tongue
familiar to both, but who has naught else in
common."

"Why did I not go and see Ford first of all,"
he resumed, speaking in an undertone, as was his
wont when alone ; "it might have been better,
and have saved further misunderstandings.   But
no ; since Lydia *has* come home so suddenly, and
in order to meet me, as she asserted, it is best to
see her first."

The smile on his face was a hard and unpleasant one as he passed along the corridor that
connected the studio with the house, but when he
entered the hall none who might have met him
would have perceived any trace of hurry or
curiosity.

There was, however, no one visible, and he
walked leisurely upstairs to the drawing-room.
The door was ajar, and by the dim light from the
solitary lamp he could see that no one was present.

For a moment he hesitated, and then walked
onward towards the room which Lydia called her
boudoir, though as a matter of fact she used it
but seldom, save occasionally in the evenings when
he was from home, or at work in his studio, as
occasionally happened.

As he approached, he could distinctly hear two voices, and almost immediately he recognised one of them as that of the man whom he had come to seek.

"So, they are together," he thought. "Well, I shall confound them by my sudden appearance, and it will not be difficult to gather in how far my suspicions of Gabriel Ford are just."

With a firm but noiseless grasp he turned the handle, but simultaneously he realised that the door was locked. An ugly look came into his eyes, but he made no sound. Suddenly an idea occurred to him, and he walked softly a few steps farther along. Lydia's bedroom lay beyond her boudoir, and a heavy *portière* was all that divided them; and Felix thought it possible that the bedroom-door might not be fastened.

His surmise was correct, and a few moments later, having quietly closed the door, he stood close to the *portière*. It was not an action which he would have permitted himself, if it had not been for the boudoir-door having been locked,— not even then, perhaps, but for the untruth of which Lydia had been guilty when she had informed her friends that she had to return to meet her husband.

Although Lydia and Ford spoke in subdued

tones, he could hear what was said as clearly as though he were sitting beside them.

For the first few moments, as he stood by the heavy plush curtain, there was a silence so deep and thrilling that he felt as though he were in a dream.

"Yes, I do love you, Gabriel. I have done so all along, as you know. And I am tired, tired, of all this empty bondage to *him*. But"——

Could that voice be Lydia's? Felix wondered. For the first time he heard in it a vibration that he had never discovered therein before,—for the first time its metallic clarity had become strangely softened. It was not a beautiful nor a moving voice, even now, to his ears, but how distinct from that he knew so well, which sometimes haunted him in dreams till he fancied he should go mad with its lifeless, persistent utterance!

"Do not utter any 'buts,' Lydia dearest. Surely the time is now past when there should be any barrier between us. You have been cruel to my love for you, but hitherto you have been loyal to a man who dislikes you; now, however, you need be so no longer, since he loves another, and would fain unite his life with hers."

"Gabriel, swear to me that you know this

thing to be true, that you know my husband to be in love with this Sanpriel Acosta—that you know him to be actually unfaithful to me!"

Felix smiled bitterly as he at last recognised *his* Lydia; there could be no mistaking that hard, icy voice.

"I swear it. But now, darling, kiss me and say good-night, for though it is not likely, it is just possible that Dane may have returned to London—and if so, he could soon be here."

"We should hear him if he arrived."

"Supposing he did come, could I get away from the house without his or any one else seeing me?"

"Yes; you could go downstairs by the passage at the end of this corridor, which would lead you to the studio. You could go through it and out by the private passage beyond; the doors all open from the inside. Oh, stay, Gabriel, stay: I am at once so miserable and so happy. I love you, I love you!"

The unmistakable yearning in his wife's voice touched Dane deeply, so deeply that all resentment died away from him, and a feeling of infinite pity conflicted with the strange inextricable maze of emotion in which his soul laboured.

As he heard the rustling of garments and the

sound of a passionate kiss, the old line which had occurred to him when he came upon Sanpriel in the garden rose to his lips, and inaudibly he muttered it over and over again—" How leapt we into this labyrinth of love ? "

Suddenly hot tears rose to his eyes, and he almost cried out ; but the next moment, all unangered and unresentful, and with a strange quiescence at his heart, he passed from the bedroom and out into the corridor, and so down into the chill darkness of the studio. He groped towards the arm-chair where a few days ago he had sat with bent head, in a greater agony but not in such blank numbness as now ; and there, again, he sat silent, bowed, and with his face in his hands. Verily, indeed, was the old Felix Dane dead, and here was his burial-place.

CHAPTER VIII.

For a long time he sat, overcome by a numb pain, a dull curiosity at he knew not what. Such slaves of association are we that not even can we be enfranchised from a loathed serfdom without some half-instinctive yearning for the old bondage. It is said that the Russian serfs were wont to miss the tyranny which for generations had held them in thrall, and literally to kiss the hand that had thrashed them; and true it is that new-won liberty often seems more lawless than regenerative. There are many of us, bondagers indeed, who have known the passionate yearning for freedom, and when freedom has come or has been gained, have found ourselves pitiably linked to our own past. The strong man is he who has no past—who yearly, daily, hourly burns his ships behind him.

"It all seems piteous and despicable somehow," Felix muttered at last, as with a weary sigh he sat back in the chair and pressed his hands to his hot forehead.

"It is inconceivable to me, this inability to cut myself adrift from—from—Lydia. *This* bondage is worse than the old one. I suppose it is that, now I know she does indeed love another, all my old resentment against her has passed away. Blame her? Good God! why should *I* blame her? She is but doing what I am doing, and the day is past when there is any distinction between what is right or wrong for a man and right or wrong for a woman. The new wave of a more natural morality is upon us, but we who are on its fringe, who are its flying spin-drift rather, must suffer. Those who come after us will laugh at our pitiable barterings of love,—at our marriage markets, which might so often be truly called slaughter-houses, for there innocence of soul, and spiritual purity, and true manliness and womanliness are continuously being slain outright. Perhaps the day is not so far distant when marriage as we now know it will exist only in barbarous and semi-civilised lands—the day when men will be unable to buy and women to sell that which nature loves to see in surrender, but loathes to behold in barter. But as for *us :* we, Lydia and I, have found our separate ways. I am glad, glad beyond words, if love has really come to her. Yet is it possible? Can Lydia know love as men and women know it who have hot blood in their veins? If only she could have surrendered herself to Gabriel Ford without the spur of jealous rage! She is proud with that insane pride of the narrow-minded, and though she does not love me, she is bitter against me for my love of another: *this* it is that has caused her to listen to her lover. God forgive me, it is my fault; whatever Lydia may be, she would have held herself apart but for the madness of jealousy. But no—there was real passion in her voice to-night; for the first time the ice about her heart gave way. And she knows what I never withheld from her, that I am of those who look upon love as no subject to the tyranny of human laws. Again and again she has heard me say that no human tie can come between two natures craving for each other. Yet Heaven knows what self-sophistication, what pitfalls, what snares beleaguer us. It cannot be well to do what may cause incommensurable hurt to others—and yet, and yet, ah! God knows it is all a mystery, a weary, interminable maze.

"Ay, we who feel thus and suffer thus are indeed the Children of To-morrow—though in us the new forces of the future are spirits of torment, driving us blindly forward, sometimes crying for the new heights we vaguely descry, oftenest clinging to familiar objects, or looking back longingly to ways that we may never again traverse. With Sanpriel—ah! my darling, my darling, how dark the way is before *us!*—we may well cry :—

> *'Forlorn the way, yet with strange gleams of gladness;*
> *Sad beyond words the voices far behind,*
> *Yet we, perplext with our diviner madness,*
> *Must heed them not—the Goal is still to find!*
> *What though beset by pain, and fear, and sorrow,*
> *We must not fail, we Children of To-morrow.'*

'We must not fail'—but nature, alas! pays no heed to human 'must nots.' Well, so let it be: Lydia must go her way, and I mine."

A cold draught struck upon him, and he rose to shut the door which he supposed he had left unfastened. It was, however, shut, and he then found that when he had first entered the studio he had left the outer-passage door ajar. This he closed, and again sat down, and ere long had once more assumed his former attitude of profound despondency.

What a home-coming! he thought bitterly, and yet without any self-commiseration, for he was not the man to bewail hardships which he had himself induced or furthered.

Then his thoughts wandered to Sanpriel, and

he wondered what the next few weeks would bring forth ; and then at last, out of sheer weariness, his thoughts passed into incoherent visions, till these again merged into sleep.

How long he slept he never realised, for the events that followed his awakening drove thought of time from his mind.

His dreams were curiously close to circum-stance, for his vision fashioned forth his studio as it then was, with he himself sitting, face in hands, in the arm-chair. Then it seemed to him as if the inner door softly opened, and as if a figure, the figure of a man, quietly entered, and, carefully stepping among the *débris* of " Hertha," crossed the room.

He did not recognise the dream-figure, for its face was averted or in a deep shadow, and it passed from his vision almost as soon as he had seen it. Then he fancied that the intruder had come up behind him and had touched him, lightly but firmly, while simultaneously there was a crunching of hard clay under the stranger's feet. Already he was half-awake, influenced no doubt either by the imaginary touch or sound ; but when he felt, or fancied he felt, a warm breath upon his neck, his consciousness suddenly swept back in one vivid wave.

Still, for a few moments he did not stir; and though he had a conviction that some living thing had been close to him, he wished to assure himself that he was not dreaming. The mind awakes before the body, and the latter often delays obedience to volition; so that even when, a moment or two after he had been conscious of a warm breath, he wished to spring to his feet, he found that movement did not follow will.

But when, with a distinctness unmistakable in the intense silence that prevailed, there came the click of a turned lock, the spell was broken.

Felix sprang to his feet and stared about him; but in the deep obscurity of the room, so deep that only large and light-hued objects loomed from the shadow, he could see no one. Had he been dreaming after all? No; he felt assured he had heard *that.* Surely it had been close to him, and therefore must have come from the door of the outer passage, the same which he had secured a short time before.

He stepped swiftly towards it, and at a glance saw that it was ajar. A slit of dull light, conveyed through the glass roofing of the corridor, betrayed the fact even before he had grasped the handle. The next moment he had thrown the door open, and was looking eagerly along the passage.

Almost simultaneously he saw the street-door open and swiftly close again—but in the interval he had caught a glimpse of a slim shadowy figure passing forth from the corridor. It was Gabriel Ford; he did not see his face, but he recognised him none the less.

For some seconds Felix hesitated, and he had almost made up his mind to remain where he was, when suddenly a passion of anger overcame him as he thought of the double game that Ford was playing with Sanpriel and Lydia, and of what mischief he had already tried to wreak upon him. If Lydia loved Ford, and he honestly loved her, Felix felt that he had not the wish nor, with his views, the right to interfere; but if Ford were scoundrel enough to betray both women—for betrayal of Sanpriel it would be if he married her to serve his private ends, and betrayal of Lydia if her surrender were only to form the basis of a *liaison*—he should find that he had as determined a man as himself to reckon with.

Hastily snatching the hat he had thrown on a sofa when he had first entered the studio, he ran along the passage and swung back the oaken street-door.

As he sprang out on to the pavement a hansom drove past, northward-bound, and for a moment delayed him ; but a second or two later he was in the middle of the road, eagerly scanning the footway farther down.

He was just in time. A figure, which he felt sure was that of Ford, was rapidly turning into Beech Road, a byway which branched to the right about a hundred yards below The Sycamores.

He was about to pursue, though to what end he did not clearly know, when he stopped short as he heard the hansom draw up at the house just beyond his own. An idea had occurred to him, and he hoped that the cabman would be amenable.

He watched the passenger get down, pay his fare, and enter at his gateway, and then the driver stand in his high box as he brought the horse round for the return journey.

Hurriedly walking towards the hansom, he hailed the man, and asked him if he could drive double-quick to Albemarle Street.

"Right you are, sir; my horse is pretty fresh, and it's going home for me. What number ?"

Felix gave him the number of Ford's house, or rather of the large mansion where he had his rooms, and then promised the man extra-fare if he managed the distance in twenty minutes—adding that he was to go by the Swiss Cottage and not by Beech Road.

The next minute he was being whirled along towards his goal, where it was his one wish to arrive before the man whom he had long instinctively disliked, and now hated.

His mind was in a ferment with conflicting ideas, and even the cool night-air and the rapid motion did not disperse the thronging thoughts that environed his central purpose. Just as the hansom swung round the corner of Orchard Street into Oxford Street he wondered what hour it was : that it was far advanced he could see by the deserted aspect of the great thoroughfare. He looked at his watch, but discovered that it must have stopped during the forenoon of the past day ; and it was in vain that he kept eyes and ears alert for any public clock.

Down South Moulton Street—and as he drew near his goal he thought no more of time, but only of the man whom he had come to intercept, and of that which stood between them.

How his head swam, and how difficult it was to think of any one thing long ! he muttered, with a vague feeling that mind and body were over-strained, and that he must take care.

Albemarle Street ! What had he come here for ? Ah, of course, to see Gabriel Ford ; and with a confused sensation, which puzzled rather than annoyed him, he paid and discharged the cabman.

A wide-arched passage led to a flight of stairs, and it was on the first landing that Ford had his rooms. Felix had been there once before; he had gone with Lydia one Sunday to see a new picture by Ford, for the latter was an artist, and, though an amateur, able to hold his own with most of his contemporaries.

He rang the bell, and after the lapse of some minutes without answer he did so again and yet again. At last he heard some one fumbling along the passage, and then the door was opened, and an elderly man—more like a goat than a human being, Felix thought—looked forth with anything but a cordial aspect.

"Has Mr. Ford returned yet?"

"Returned? Were you expecting him?"

"Yes. You know me, don't you? My name is Felix Dane."

"Oh yes, I remember you, Mr. Dane. But I don't know nothink about Mr. Ford's movements. He comes an' goes without notice. I am not allowed to fasten up the door at any time, as he comes in wi' his latchkey whenever he likes."

"Well, he'll be here shortly, I know; so I'll go in and await his arrival."

" Excuse me, Mr. Dane, but it's agin "——

Felix, however, took no notice of the protest, but passed on and, thrusting aside the *portière* that hung outside the studio, walked in.

The old man closed the door with a bang, muttered something viciously about fools making calls "just afore cock-crow," and then in surly silence struck a match and lit a single gas-jet in the studio.

" If you're expectin' Mr. Ford, no doubt he'll be 'ere soon.   He'll let hisself in, so if you don't want nothink else I'll go back to my bed."

He received no answer, so, grumbling more viciously than before, returned to his own room.

Felix had forgotten about old Samson, all about his expected interview with Ford—for, in the indifferent light, he had just caught a glimpse of a portrait which enthralled him.   It was Sanpriel ; a far-off, uninspired, almost lifeless portrait—but yet beyond doubt she and no other.   The sight sent the blood coursing more swiftly through his veins again, and the confused sensations in his head almost disappeared.

As soon as Samson had roughly drawn-to the *portière* again, he took a slip of paper and lit the other jets.   He remembered the room well, and there seemed to be but little alteration in it save for three new canvases on separate easels, which he had not seen before.   The studio was dark and gloomy, with its tapestried walls, and its lack of all ornamentation save weapons of many lands and old armour, a few brilliant Japanese fans, and some large blue Chinese jars.

On the easel next the fireplace was the portrait of Sanpriel—a half-length life-size likeness, full face, and with the large eyes looking dreamily forth. In her hair were two blood-red poppies ; blood-red poppies also clustered at her neck, and both hands toyed with a mass of them in her lap.   The effect was unpleasant : the canvas seemed as though stained with blood.   It was unfinished, and in a blank space in the right corner Felix descried some words scrawled in charcoal.   They were not easy to decipher, but at last he made out, " The blood of Miriam Acosta shall be as the poppies of the field."   Miriam : was not that the name of the un-fortunate woman who had laid upon the members of her family a curse that should work itself out through seven generations ?   What made Ford commemorate that anathema in this fashion ?   In his dull resentment Felix felt inclined to destroy the portrait as it stood ; but, half-mechanically, he passed on to the other easels.

At the first of the two he looked in astonish-ment.   It was almost the exact replica of the well-known "Lilith" of a great painter, but the beautiful woman who sat in luxurious abandonment while she combed out the tresses of her long hair was no other than—Lydia. On the frame were inscribed the words from Rossetti's Lilith-sonnet:

> " And still she sits, young while the earth is old,
>   And, subtly of herself contemplative,
>   Draws men to watch the bright web she can weave,
> Till heart and body and life are in its hold."

There was no mistaking the surer hand and surer artistic insight of the painter here; and Dane knew intuitively from the two portraits that whatever intent Ford might have in regard to marriage with Sanpriel, he loved Lydia. That he did not really know the former, that he had no insight into her nature, required no further proof. The third canvas, though it was a subject-picture, arrested his attention none the less. It was an unpleasant picture, representing as it did one of the long stone or slate slabs in a dissecting-room, with recumbent upon it the naked figure of a man. No one was visible, and the rest of the apartment was undisclosed by the pale yellow flame of a candle, whose whole light was concentrated upon the corpse. By the side of the latter, tied by a string to the left arm, was a small square placard, on which, beneath some indecipherable letters and figures, was roughly printed, *Found Dead: cause not ascertained.* What gave the picture an evil fascination for Felix was the unmistakable likeness of the features of the dead man to his own ; and the longer he looked at them the more obvious was the resemblance.

With a shudder, partly at the cold-blooded horror of the painting, partly from some occult feeling of superstitious dread, keen though transient, he turned away, and walked across to Sanpriel's portrait again, at which he looked long and earnestly.

Suddenly an intense inclination overcame him to accomplish what Ford had failed to do—not from any spirit of rivalry, but from an overmastering desire to represent the true Sanpriel.

He was an expert painter, though of late years he had wrought but little with the brush, and then only for his own pleasure. When he found that he could paint well only in rare moods, he had wisely concluded to restrict himself professionally to the chisel ; yet the few portraits he had made of friends were valued not only for their fidelity, but for their artistic worth.

Heedless of what Ford might with justice hold him guilty, he seized the palette and brushes which lay on a low table, among tubes of all shapes and sizes, and after a few moments' hesitation, with alternate use of brush and knife made an essential difference in the portrait. He had but touched the eyes, and here and there a line about the lips and mouth—yet it was Sanpriel herself, not yet her truest self indeed, but much more so than before.

So absorbed was he in contemplation of the features he knew so well and yet evaded his eager memory when he tried to create a mental likeness which would surpass that upon the canvas before him, that he did not hear the sound made by the opening and shutting of the hall-door; nor, situated as he was with his face to the *portière*, did he notice the pale face and startled expression of Gabriel Ford, who had silently entered the studio.

Ford made no sound, but stood rooted to the ground. His lips were ashy pale, and a look, half of fear and half of amaze, was in his eyes.

How came it that he saw Felix Dane sitting there in his studio, at work upon the portrait of Sanpriel Acosta, when, scarce more than an hour ago, he had left him, asleep and apparently overcome by profound weariness, in his own studio at The Sycamores? True, it was *possible* that Dane might have awaked, and have driven to Albemarle Street. There was actually time for him to have done so, for he, Ford, had walked all the way; but it was unlikely.

It was for the second time a wave of dread enthralled him. When, cautiously and silently, he had passed through the dark studio of The Sycamores, he had been startled by the sound of low breathing, and when, in the gloom that was almost darkness, he had discerned Felix, his heart had almost stood still. He had had strange thoughts that evening; among others, again and again that of a man struggling wildly among the quicksands of Ratho—and to see *that* man, and after all that had just occurred, sitting silently in the darkness and chill of his own studio, had been overmuch for his nerves. Gabriel Ford prided himself upon being a materialist, and on his freedom from superstition, but, like most materialists, he could not stem the tide of hereditary sentiment stronger than any personal idiosyncrasy. It was only by a great effort that he had overcome his sudden fear, and had convinced himself by touch, light as a feather, yet tangible, of Dane's actual presence; then, with a new apprehension, he had swiftly and quietly made good his escape.

He had not seen Dane's figure at the end of the passage as he had slipped forth from the outer door, nor had he seen him in Hurst Road; and he had concluded, naturally, that he had been unobserved.

He had intended to take a hansom homeward, but too many emotions excited him, and he preferred to walk and think over in motion the complexities in which he had involved himself. So, Dane had not perished in the quicksand; but what did this abrupt return to London portend? If he had come by the midnight mail, he might have naturally enough gone to his studio so as not to disturb Lydia or the household, and have there fallen asleep through sheer weariness; if, on the other hand, he had arrived earlier, why had he not gone into the house?—what had he suspected?—what had he, perhaps, seen or overheard?

When Ford had reached his rooms and quietly let himself in, he had at once perceived that there was a light in his studio. He did not imagine that this was due to any other cause than carelessness on the part of his old servant, Samson, but with his wonted caution he had made no sound in entrance.

His last thoughts, as he had walked down Albemarle Street, had been of the true portent of his vision of Dane. Had he, after all, been mistaken, and imagined a reality where none had been? No, he felt assured, he could not have been mistaken.

Had Dane, then, succumbed to anything other than sleep?—in other words, had he been tempted to put an end to himself—was he even then dead, or dying? Surely he had heard his low breathing—though *that* might have been fancy.

It was, therefore, with a shock that drove the blood from his lips and face that, as soon as he was inside of the *portière*, he had seen Felix Dane seated before *his* easel. Again, and more strongly than before, a supernatural dread took possession of him, and he would have been relieved rather than surprised if his enemy had suddenly become visibly fantasmal and then disappeared.

Did it mean that the latter *had* fallen a victim to the quicksand, and that he had returned in spirit to haunt the man who had been the cause of his death? But the very thought brought with it, to a man like Ford, its antidote; he did not believe in spirits, but he was absolutely convinced that if apparitions did exist, they were harmless.

The next moment reason triumphed altogether, when he saw the painter's brush leave a distinct impression on the canvas. An apparition might take on a semblance beyond visual detection, but it could not transfer material pigment to material canvas.

But the intensity of his gaze had magnetically

affected Dane, who suddenly laid down the brush and glanced round.

Both men looked at each other fixedly without speaking.

Ford was still ashy pale, and there was a furtive gleam in his eyes; but he was no coward, and here, in his own rooms, was conscious of a defiance which he would not have felt had he and Dane encountered in the studio of The Sycamores.

"Considering the hour and the circumstances, this is a pleasure I could not have anticipated," he remarked at last, dryly, with a sarcastic bow.

"With which of these two women are you in love?" demanded Felix, heedless of what had just been said, as with a wave of his arm he indicated the portraits of Sanpriel and Lydia.

In a flash Ford realised that a crucial moment had arrived. He had perforce to judge Dane from his own standpoint, and he knew that in similar circumstances he would have been prepared with the final argument. There was a look in his antagonist's eyes that he could not fathom, but he surmised that it signified—murder.

There is no man so ignorant of the real springs of human action as the so-called man of the world —and a man of the world Gabriel Ford was, and prided himself upon being. Doubly wronged as Dane was, and evidently roused to the extreme of endurance, what else had he come there for but to take the life of his enemy—or, at least, to force upon him a life-and-death struggle? So Ford argued, or so, rather, flashed his intuition through his brain, and the apprehension which had lain dormant in his heart ever since he knew that Dane had escaped the quicksand prompted him to resort to subterfuge. With that understanding of the almost irresistible appeal of seeming candour which characterises the incandid, he determined to declare himself frankly—and falsely.

"I love neither, Dane, in the sense that you mean. But I feel I owe you an apology concerning a foolish statement I made to you at Forest Manor. I am not, and never was, engaged to Sanpriel Acosta; nor, though we are very old friends, has there ever been, or is there likely to be, any question of a marriage between us."

"In a word, you lied to me?"

"Oh, come, my dear fellow, don't put it so offensively. You know how weak we all are when it comes to a question of jealousy."

"Then you were merely jealous as a friend?" Felix dryly interrupted.

"Merely as a friend. I have known the Acostas

for a long time, and have always looked upon Sanpriel as something of a sister, and I resented her obvious preference for your company. I admit it frankly, I was jealous; it is my nature, and I cannot help it; but it meant nothing. If you had asked Sanpriel——though, of course, it is not a question you could have had any right to ask her——she would have told you that nothing of the kind existed between us."

A momentary smile crossed Felix's face. Ford saw and understood it, and an angry gleam came into his eyes, but almost simultaneously passed away.

"I have no right to ask you, Dane, if you are in love with Miss Acosta. You are a married man, and, moreover, there are racial reasons which would stand imperatively in the way of marriage with her, were you free. I simply wish to assure you that, if circumstances permitted, you would find me a friend and not a rival."

So frank was Ford in this avowal that Felix believed him, and the dark cloud of which he had been conscious seemed to have greatly lifted. Still, he thought he would put Ford's genuineness to a severe test.

"If that is so, will you let me have this portrait of Miss Acosta? You will remember that you

promised me one of your paintings in exchange
for that little ' Dionysos ' of mine which you particularly wished and I refused to let you have save
in a friendly way in exchange for a picture by
you?   I see that you have done this portrait
from memory—and, as you have observed, I have
thoughtlessly taken the liberty of touching it up,
as I felt that I could catch just that peculiar expression which had escaped you."

Ford hesitated, but would have definitely declined had he not at the. moment happened to
glance at the neighbouring portrait of Lydia.
If he refused that of Sanpriel, he could hardly
retain Lydia's, and, for more than one good
reason, he did not wish the latter to leave his
possession.   Moreover, he did not know Lydia if
he were not sure that he could persuade her to
be a thorn in her husband's flesh on account of
the portrait of her rival.

With a graciousness that did him credit, considering the chagrin and jealous anger that moved
him, he acceded.

"I hesitated for a moment or two, Dane, because
I had thought of giving it as a present to my
old friend Adama Acosta.   But, as you hint I
have failed to make a good portrait of it, if you
care to have it, it is yours."

" You give it to me freely, to do what I like with ? "

" Certainly."

Without a word, Felix lifted a curved Malay blade which lay on the paint-table, and slashed the canvas into long strips, till nothing remained save a few long trailing shreds.

At first Ford had made a savage exclamation, and his face had become livid with fury ; but thereafter he looked on with sullen silence.

" It is better thus," Felix remarked simply, as he laid the knife down again and faced his companion.

" Have you anything more to say—or do ? "

" Ford, do you love my wife ? "

" I decline to answer any such question."

" If you play falsely either by Sanpriel on the one hand or by Lydia on the other, you shall answer for it—to me."

" How could I be false to your wife ? "

" *You* know. Beware, Gabriel Ford ; you are playing a difficult game. A man who is false to a woman who gives up everything for him is kin to a murderer—and should be treated as such."

" This moral lesson comes well from *you*, Dane ; in the circumstances, I think it would be more seemly if you kept your diatribes to yourself."

M

Suddenly Felix staggered, grew deathly pale, and then without a word of warning fell prone.

Ford sprang forward and, having lifted him by the shoulders, poised his inert figure against a couch that stood near.

Was he in a swoon, or dead? The suddenness of the collapse seemed to indicate some heart weakness; but, on the other hand, despite the white and drawn features, there was no lividness about the lips or hollows of the eyes.

It took but a few seconds to unfasten the waistcoat and shirt, and then, with his hand over the insensible man's heart, he realised that death was not imminent, and that Felix was only in a swoon.

He had some vague recollection of having heard of Dane's having in early manhood been subject to severe fainting attacks, a complaint inherited from his father and grandfather, who yet had been strong men, and had lived to advanced years; probably this, he thought, was some such attack, unpleasant but not dangerous.

As Ford looked down at his fallen rival a curious look came into his face. He even grew a little paler, as, having shot a searching glance round the studio, and particularly at the *portière*, he stepped towards a cabinet at the other end of the room.

As he let down the desk-leaf of it there was disclosed a mirror; in this he could see both the *portière* and the unconscious man who leaned in death-like fashion against the couch near the easel on which stood Sanpriel's ruined portrait.

He pulled out a drawer beneath the mirror, and touched a spring which revealed an inner hollow. In this was an old-fashioned silver snuff-box. He opened this, and glanced at the soft white dust within it, and then looked again and again, in the mirror, at the heavy curtain and at the recumbent figure.

He seemed to be in a strangely hesitant mood. At last he muttered "Why not?" and rose.

But as he turned he caught sight of the ragged remains of what had been Sanpriel's portrait. They altered his decision, whatever it was, for he closed the snuff-box with an abrupt snap. The sound, slight as it was, startled him, and he looked round apprehensively, but almost simultaneously regained composure. With a swift movement he stepped towards the easel whereon stood the picture called "Found Dead." The likeness between the corpse and the man who lay unconscious a few feet away, which had been unmistakable before, was now startlingly close—so close that the artist shuddered.

"No—no—it would never do," he muttered; "what madness to dream of it! That torn canvas, this picture, his death happening here, the hour and circumstances—what a fool, what a fool I am!"—and as he spoke, so softly that not the most strained ears could have heard him, he turned to the cabinet again and, having replaced the antique snuff-box, closed the lid.

He then stepped to an oaken piece of furniture that was part bookcase and part sideboard, and took thence a decanter of brandy, from which he poured a large glassful into a tumbler.

This he forced down Felix's throat, and ere long had the satisfaction of seeing him opening his eyes and coming swiftly back to consciousness. Ere the latter had quite returned, however, Ford had summoned Samson.

"Samson," he said sternly as the man entered, "you see what comes of breaking my rules. Mr. Dane here has unfortunately been drinking—and see what he has done to my picture there!"

"I saw 'ee was drunk, sir, when 'ee came in. But 'ee was so quiet I thought he'd sleep it off—and I knew 'ee was a friend o' yours."

The man was disrespectful, and had an unpleasant leer upon his face, but Ford contented himself with telling him sharply to go out and hail a cab.

A little later, Felix, feeling well again save for a sense of great prostration, was driven home, and arrived in time to astonish the not very early-rising housemaid.

CHAPTER IX.

THE month that followed Dane's abrupt return home was one wherein he lived a dual life. At The Sycamores, when with Lydia, at the houses of friends, and in ordinary social intercourse he seemed to himself as though he were in a dream. Often he found himself in the attitude of a spectator; the guests at his table appeared real only with the reality of dreams, always with that vague uncertainty which accompanies visionary figures; and their voices often struck him as coming from far away, or as being mere hollow echoes.

But in his studio, when alone with his work and his thoughts, and, above all, when at Dreamthorpe, in the company of Sanpriel and Adama Acosta, he was conscious of the pulse of life. Day and night he thought of Sanpriel; for even in sleep she dominated his imagination, and her fantasm became at last to him even as his own soul. Never had such a summer made the earth glorious, he thought ; never had the skies been so blue, the flowers so numerous, the birds so jubilant, the earth-joy so intoxicating. He had always loved Hampstead Heath, with its magnificent outlook across leagues of rolling country, but now he had come to look upon it as a Promised Land, the Land of the Sunset, the Land of Rest. Never in all his sojournings abroad had he seen such magic landscape, for here every gorse-bush glowed with the ardour of love, every pine-branch breathed forth a windy music, poignant, haunting, sweet beyond words.

He had gone to Dreamthorpe the very afternoon of the day on which, faint and weary, he had been driven home from Gabriel Ford's rooms. He had long known the quaint old house, ivy-covered, with its gables, which had once been red, stained to a ruddy brown—close to the Heath, yet as secluded from the outer world as though miles away from the haunts of men.

Adama Acosta had recovered from his indisposition, and the welcome which Felix received from him and his daughter was so true that it was surer medicine to his ill than any skill of physician.

Both with father and daughter he found himself in thorough sympathy in all matters literary and artistic, and, man of wide and deep culture though he was, he gained more insight and a keener enjoyment in those frequent hours at Dreamthorpe than he had acquired in all his somewhat solitary years.

But as the days went by he came more and more to avoid a subject which had once been for him full of the most vivid interest, and latterly he strove, even when alone with Acosta, to keep in abeyance all allusion to or discussion of the new movement in Israel. He saw, although not until after he had intuitively guessed, that, in his presence, the subject was distasteful to Sanpriel; yet, by some strange contradictoriness, she would not infrequently, when they walked together in the quaint old hedgerow-hidden garden, or sat in the low-roofed drawing-room which looked out upon it, introduce the theme, and expatiate upon it with the familiar ardent enthusiasm. Latterly, however, Felix's sensitive ears had caught —or so he fancied—something strained in Sanpriel's voice when she was most eloquent upon the immediate hopes of her father and herself. Once, when she had been carried away by her own ardour, and had glorified renunciation of all that the individual held most precious, if thereby the general good were to be aided, she had become conscious of the fixity of her companion's gaze, and had then all at once flushed, while such a look—surcharged for a moment with the mingled joy and pathos of surrender—came into her eyes, that Felix almost yielded to the passion which possessed him and prompted him to tell her then and there of the love which had given him new life and hope and energy. But the sudden, sharp, strident wail of her father's violin gave Sanpriel an excuse to turn abruptly, and, with a hurried word, pass into the house.

As June slowly lapsed towards its midmost, he spent many evenings, instead of afternoons, at Dreamthorpe. He liked best to arrive at the afterglow, and then to sit or walk with Sanpriel in the gradual twilight, when the flowers and even the grass emitted their rarest fragrance, and when through the stillness rippled and throbbed the voice of the blackcap or the long vibrant notes of merle and thrush. The cries of children and laughter of wayfarers upon the Heath, the barking of dogs, and occasionally the soft lowing of distant cattle, with below all the indeterminate undertone, the vague gnat-like hum borne upward from the populous leagues beyond the heights, accentuated rather than detracted from the sense of exquisite remoteness, of happy serenity and repose, of which both were at such moments conscious.

He knew that Ford sometimes came to Dreamthorpe, but he had not yet encountered him there; nor did he take heed of him at all, for, apart from Gabriel's own admission to him, he had intuitively learned that Sanpriel neither liked nor trusted the man whom her father—in his vague, inconsequent way—had come to look upon as a probable son-inlaw.

Ford, however, had several times been at The Sycamores since the night Felix had returned home; once as the guest of both Mr. and Mrs. Dane, but otherwise as the friend of Lydia. Occasionally Felix had entered the drawing-room and found them in earnest conversation, and at first he noticed how much younger and happier his wife seemed. But after a week or two had passed he noticed a growing hardness in Lydia's face, and more than once he thought he saw in her eyes a look as of dull rage. She had become strangely watchful of him; at meals, at "evenings" or "afternoons" at friends' houses, wherever they met in fact, he could not but notice the stealthy yet steady gaze of those cold grey-blue eyes of hers.

Once—and it was the first time that he had

ever known Lydia prevaricate—when he had returned late from Dreamthorpe he had noticed round the point of one of his wife's slippers a little clay, a new composite which he had that very morning obtained from Paris, and so knew that she must have been in his studio, though, in reply to his question, she denied having been there.

A little later, and while Felix was sitting in apparent absorption in a magazine, she caught sight of the clay upon her slipper, and flushed as she knew that she had betrayed herself. But her voice was harder than ever when she rose and said good-night.

What would be the result if Sanpriel and Lydia met? Felix sometimes wondered, but always with the hope that auspicious fate would keep them apart.

One day close upon midsummer he and Lydia went by special invitation to the Dilletante Club to view a number of paintings, drawings, and etchings by members. As they entered they met, just as they were about to mount the stairs, Mr. and Miss Acosta, but, to the evident surprise of the latter, Felix only bowed, as though delay were inconvenient, or in the circumstances undesirable.

Lydia, who for some time had been wont to scrutinise every one to whom her husband bowed or spoke, could not but be struck by the beauty of the girl who had just passed, nor fail to perceive the bright welcome, almost radiance, of her smile as she had recognised Felix.

"Who are these people?" she asked, and her voice had that metallic vibration in it which always set his nerves on edge.

"These? Who? Oh, they are the Acostas, father and daughter. You have probably heard Ford speak of them. Ah, there are the Elliotts, and Mrs. Warwick with them."

"Ah, so that was Sanpriel?" Lydia remarked, without heed of her husband's latest words.

There was a great crush at the "Dilletante," and to Felix's relief, further conversation with Lydia was impracticable. The exhibition was even better than usual, but also, as usual, the prevalent tone was even more "realistic" than at the *Salon*. The members might have been pure-blooded Latins, if the testimony of their works were to be considered. Scenes of torture, episodes of mental agony, martyrdom, and the like, combined with several really artistic and several unmistakably insincere, and therefore indecent, "nudities," made the walls appear a curious contrast to the suave conventionalities and general appearance of the guests of the club. It did not take long to discover that two pictures by Gabriel Ford attracted the greatest amount of attention. One was the " Found Dead " which Felix had already seen, though he noticed, with a curious sensation which he could not define, that the face had been sufficiently altered to obviate any comparisons of likeness to him ; and the other, cynically entitled " An Immortal Soul," represented the bloated corpse of a drunkard who had died by the wayside.

"How horrible !" Felix said to himself, as he turned away in disgust ; "and what folly for men like Ford to call themselves naturalists, realists ! It is only man who obtrudes death upon our notice; the very animals have a worthier instinct."

Nature, truly enough, has her decencies, and avenges their violation. When death occurs in her unusurped regions, how speedily the innumerable agencies at her command make haste to obliterate the insignia of decease !—the leaves fall and cover the stricken doe, whose flesh will incredibly soon be removed from sight and become part of the general life around ; the grasses enshroud the corpse, and ere long only a few harmless bones will remain, and these ere long will have the fruitful earth about them, or delicate mosses or lichen will recapture them from wanton ugliness.   Birth and death are her chosen secrets ; her veil of mystery should always envelop the one, her dignified reticence protect the other.

" Artists like Ford," Felix continued to himself, " are at enmity with our beneficent mother Nature. They constantly violate her dignity and despoil her of what she would fain disguise.   There is something about human death which should protect it from too realistic depicture on canvas.   No artistic representation can ever adequately convey the horror or terror, the beauty or dignity, of the final act of life ; " and it was with an uncomfortable sense of nausea, a feeling of revolt, a sensation as of having witnessed some treachery against his fellow-men, that he turned away from the much-praised canvases.

It was on the day subsequent to the exhibition at the Dilletante Club that his happy dream received a certain shock.

Anxious to remove any false impression his reticence at the club entrance may have given, and eager to see Sanpriel after the interminable interval of a day and a half, he had, early in the afternoon, made his way to Dreamthorpe.   Acosta was busy, and though his daughter was writing, she gladly put aside her manuscripts, and, as the heat was tempered by a cool breeze, suggested a stroll round the garden.

So absorbed were both during the half-hour which ensued that neither noticed, if either heard, the clang of the gate-bell.

They were close to the house when he glanced to the right with a startled look. At the window of the drawing-room stood Lydia, looking at him with an expression which he knew of old. Ford stood behind her, and Felix fancied that he saw upon his face a smile of malicious enjoyment.

The next moment Lydia stepped forth, and greeted Sanpriel with a cold politeness that had in it too much of condescension to please either Miss Acosta or her lover.

"I have so often heard of you, Miss Acosta, that I have ventured to call upon you. Our mutual friend, Mr. Ford, assured me that I might do so, and as he pressed me to come with him to-day, I willingly agreed, as you see. I was sorry not to meet you at the Dilletante Club yesterday, but my husband did not tell me in time who you were."

"You are most welcome, Mrs. Dane," Sanpriel replied gravely. With the best will to be courteous, she could not be cordial, for she instinctively disliked Lydia, and could not but resent the condescending tone of her words.

Lydia, however, quickly discovered that she had no inexperienced girl to deal with, and she soon changed her manner, and did her utmost to make herself pleasant. So successful was she that her husband was put off his guard, and was conscious almost of an affectionate glow towards her, and Sanpriel also was in great part won over; Ford alone perceived, and was amused by, the feline grace and ease wherewith polite dissimulation was practised.

Afternoon tea was served in the garden, and before Lydia made ready for departure a definite arrangement had been come to in regard to the house-boat holiday.

Felix shared the expense of a house-boat on the Thames, for the months of May, June, and July, with Richard Prendergast, the landscape-painter, and by a mutual arrangement each had the boat for six weeks, Prendergast till midsummer's-day, and Felix thence until the close of July. As in the previous summer Lydia had expressed her distaste for another experience of the kind, her husband had hoped that she would not join him on the *Lotus*. How delightful it would be if he could spend a week or two, at least, without other company than that of Sanpriel and her father! and the more he thought of the idea the more feasible it seemed. In July there were several sets of friends whom he had promised a few days on the river, and it would be much pleasanter for Lydia to go then, if she wished, when she would have acquaintances about her, and when the weather would be disagreeably hot in town. So he argued, knowing not that it was otherwise ordained.

A chance inquiry from Acosta, who had joined the small party, and at whom Lydia looked as at some strange and rather repellent species of *genus homo*, precipitated matters.

"Oh no, I have not forgotten; far from it," Felix had replied, in some confusion. "We must arrange for the trip immediately, and I know it will do you and Miss Acosta good—it is always so delightful on the river in the early summer. But you will take things as they come, Miss Acosta, won't you? For I shall have very simple fare to offer you, as my wife does not find the river climate suit her, and does not intend to try the *Lotus* again this year."

This was a diplomatic move on the part of Felix, and as such Lydia no doubt regarded it, for she immediately played her counter-check.

"Would the beginning of July be too late for you, Miss Acosta? No? Well, in that case I shall join you, so that we can all have a pleasant time of it together. And Mr. Ford, *you* will come then also, will you not? I know how fond of the

Thames you are, and I am sure a quiet week of *idlesse* will be as good for you as for any of us."

"It will give me the greatest pleasure," Ford answered lightly, and then, turning to Felix, added that he supposed there was accommodation for all, and that of course he should only join them if his advent were not to cause any inconvenience.

Felix gave him the requisite assurances, politely if not cordially, and then asked Lydia if she could not leave Hampstead earlier——a question he had no sooner asked than he regretted having done so, as it was his one hope that his wife should *not* be able to leave home ere the beginning of July. Greatly to his relief, however, she replied curtly that her, that their engagements rendered that impracticable.

Then, after some conditional arrangements and a few polite words between Lydia and Sanpriel on the subject of their new acquaintanceship, Mrs. Dane shook hands with her hosts, and declared that she must go.

"Felix, you are coming too, I suppose? My brother and his wife are to dine with us to-night, and dinner is to be an hour earlier than usual, so that they may get back to Walthamstow in good time."

Dane secretly anathematised his brother-in-law and his wife, but there was no help for it, so he had to bid farewell to the Acostas. His chagrin was not mitigated by the knowledge that Ford had remained, nor by what he had overheard the latter say—words to the effect that he wanted to have a long talk with Sanpriel, and was glad to find her disengaged. He half-suspected — what was the case — that Ford had spoken with interest to cause him uneasiness, but none the less he felt sufficiently miserable.

A few days later, however, and an event occurred which indirectly restored him to almost jubilant spirits. Lydia's aunt, Lady Margaret Trevor, suddenly announced her intention of coming to The Sycamores for a week—an annual infliction which Felix sometimes patiently endured and sometimes evaded by precipitate retreat to Paris or elsewhere. There was no love lost between him and Lady Margaret, but Lydia had a genuine liking for the hard, worldly, arrogant old woman, and, moreover, was sole heir-presumptive to her aunt's not inconsiderable fortune.

As soon as he knew that Lydia had despatched her letter of welcome, and had made her arrangements, he announced that he was going up the river for a week or so, as he could not settle to work, and felt that the advent of Lady Margaret would be as the last straw.

Some bitter words followed, but, to his relief, without allusion to the Acostas, and so he set forth gladly, and in due time communicated his new suggestion to Adama and Sanpriel, both of whom gladly agreed to take advantage of the glorious weather that had set in, and to join Felix at Pangbourne on the morrow. He smiled as he noticed how relieved both seemed when they heard that Mrs. Dane could not possibly leave Hampstead for a week or more, and that there would be no one on board the *Lotus* but their host and themselves.

He went home feeling as though he were ten years younger and life a vision of halcyon days, and spent the rest of the afternoon and evening in making arrangements for the river-trip. Lydia had gone out to dinner with some friends whom he did not know, and he was thankful to be alone.

He had commenced to work at sculpture again, and, inspired by a passage in Sanpriel's book, had so far wrought an heroic figure representing "Destiny." All the meretricious tendency that had spoiled his later work had disappeared, and though in the rough "Destiny" seemed almost too simple in its details, he well knew that it was likely to prove not only the greatest thing he had ever done, but to rank among the foremost achievements of modern sculpture. Dane was singularly free from conceit, but he had that justifiable vanity which enables a man of genius to estimate more or less aright his own work apart from the fact of its being his own.

He was sorry to leave what he had begun to work at with so much new impulse and power, but he could still carry on his efforts in miniature on board the *Lotus*—and what pleasure, he thought, in showing each touch, each modelling, to Sanpriel, and in being aided by her sympathy and appreciation!

He had scarce finished breakfast next morning, when, to his surprise, Lydia came into the room, dressed to go out.

He rose, kissed her politely, and then asked her whither she was bound so early.

"I have to meet Aunt Margaret at Victoria at 10.45, and go with her to the Gascoignes'. Mrs. Gascoigne and her daughter are going to America to join Mr. Gascoigne, and they leave London about two o'clock. Aunt Margaret and I promised to go and say good-bye to them to-day, and have early lunch with them. I promised also that you would come."

"You had no right to do so, Lydia. You know perfectly well that I never go anywhere in the first part of the day."

"Are you coming?"

"No."

"When are you going on the house-boat?"

"To-day. I'm eager to get away. I've never been so sick of London before. By the way, Lydia, you may tell Lady Margaret that I shall make a point of running up to town some day before she leaves."

"Thank you; I prefer you to deliver your prevarications yourself," his wife replied, in a tone so cold and quiet as almost to disguise the sneer that animated it. "Pray remember that I, and the Acostas, and—and—Mr. Ford are to join you a week hence. I presume you will return for a day before then? And have you left instructions about your letters? You have? Well, good-bye—but do not expect me to smooth over Aunt Margaret's displeasure. You have already offended her, and she told me she was very disappointed in you—in which sentiment she is not altogether alone."

As she finished speaking, Lydia turned and

walked from the room with that air of wounded dignity and cold superiority combined which Felix always resented so much, howsoever silently.

He contented himself, however, with a low bow, as he held the door open for his wife, and with a single quiet remark—

"Good-bye, Lydia. I know you always enjoy having your Aunt Margaret here, and I hope you will have a pleasant week."

How warm the sunshine seemed on the carpet, he thought, as he returned to the table ; and what a glow there was among the ferns in the corner stand ! A little ago the room had seemed somewhat cheerless. The canary, which had been sitting silent, had suddenly commenced to sing blithely. The urn hissed as though in emulation, and there was that happy air throughout the breakfast-room which is the supreme tonic.

He rose, crossed the room, and sat down in a long leathern arm-chair which was irradiated with sunlight, and stretched himself luxuriously. Outside, the sparrows twittered in wildest jubilation, and even that most soul-depressing of all sounds, the wail of the London milkman, rose and fell with a certain pleasant aptness.

"By Jove !" thought Felix, "it never struck me before, but the reason why I've always cursed that milkman is my own lack of imagination. Milk suggests cows,—cows suggest meadows,— meadows suggest green hedges and shady beeches, and larks, and cowslips, and blue skies, and pretty dairymaids, and curds and cream,—oh, well there, I'm getting rather mixed; but, 'pon my word, that fellow's cry to-day seems to me quite poetic, and to suit the hour and season to perfection."

But soon his pleasant languor gave way to eagerness, and having hailed a hansom—his baggage having been already taken forward—he drove off to the Great Western Station.

Delighted as he was to be again on the *Lotus,* and to see and hear about him the river he loved so well, the three or four hours of waiting slipped by very slowly. At length, however, a carriage drove up to the meeting-place near Pangbourne, and a little later his guests were on board the house-boat.

What a day-close it was, and what an evening that followed! Felix almost felt tempted to throw overboard his small model of " Destiny " in order to propitiate the too-auspicious Fates.

But at last, after hours of languorous ease, happy talk, violin music, and short, sweet breaks of song, the time came for separation. Slowly and reluctantly Sanpriel said good-night and went to her cabin, though in her eyes there was a dreamy light which was that of a new strange joy.

For a little longer Acosta and Felix sat enjoying the midsummer eve, the latter smoking and idly watching the moths as they flickered out from the beeches in whose shadow the boat lay moored, and the former intent upon some reverie of the past or future.

The sound of the low wind among the sedges and grasses, and in the beech-boughs overhead, with the soft lapping of the water and swish of the central current, made indolence inexpressibly seductive. There was a low humming, too, of gnats, as they danced in aerial mazes below and through the outspreading alder-branches, and from inland shallows came mellowly the croaking of frogs. Occasionally a thrush or blackbird sang a few notes, but only to cease immediately, as though awed by the dusk and silence. There was no moon, and the stars shone dimly through the heat-vapours that had not yet been absorbed; all save Venus, which hung low, and pulsed and flamed as though heavy with liquid fires.

When Felix lay down to sleep it was to the soothing lipse-lapse of the flowing water, while through the hollows of dreamland rose and fell

in haunting cadences the last verse of a song
of Sanpriel's, one that he knew well, having heard
her sing it again and again :—

> *" Sweet, sweet is sleep*
> *That knows no waking :*
> *Sweet the forsaking*
> *Of treasured toys we no more care to keep.*
> *Sweet, sweet is sleep !*
> *O heart within my breast,*
> *Thou shalt have rest !"*

And as he lay adream with the sound of the
flowing river in his ears, it seemed to him as
though it passed into the dull insistent monotone
of the sea—the sea that moaned in calm or swept
thunderously between the Yew-Grove and the
Sands of Ratho.

CHAPTER X.

"The halcyon days that come but once in life
Music and moonlight, and the passionate dream."

THE days that followed seemed to Felix to be almost flawless. It was true midsummer weather, seldom, save during the noon-heats, too warm for walking or rowing, and never even after dark too chill for late idling upon the deck of the *Lotus*. He thought of nothing save the present. It was enough for him to live, to enjoy. The world seemed so beautiful: his new-born genius laughed in its strength, like a tyrant willing to be flattered into indolent complaisance, but ready at a moment to reassert his sway.

As for Sanpriel, she entered heart and soul into his artistic aims and dreams. Every day they spent hours talking of what each meant or hoped to do in art and literature; and both helped each other, apart from the magnetism of love, for there is in genuine artistic communion a bond of infinite service.

Throughout the morning hours, sometimes even till late in the afternoon, Acosta kept to the cabin, which he had to himself, and worked steadily at his new cantata, the "Triumph of Israel." When he joined the others ashore, or sat with them under the awning on the *Lotus*, he was mostly silent—so silent that it was obvious he was haunted by reveries and indifferent to what he saw and heard around him. Ere long his two companions ceased to take much heed of him, and spoke as though there were none to listen to their conversation.

But in the evenings Adama would, as it were, come to life again. At dinner he talked fluently, sometimes of the great hopes he and Sanpriel had in common, oftener of music, art, and literature; and then afterwards, in the dusk, would bring forth his violin and play to his entranced hearers till he himself fell under the spell of his own music, and slowly became silent, absorbed, heedless of his surroundings. Thereafter Felix and Sanpriel would sit quietly beside each other, sometimes talking in low tones, oftener content to sit still and dream, while they watched the white and grey lights in the velvety flow of the river or the stars hanging like silver fruit among the branches of the oaks and alders, or listened to the wash of the water alongside of the *Lotus*.   Occasionally Felix would bring out his paint-box and attempt, for Sanpriel, impressionistic sketches of the scenes of evening or night : a labourer walking home at sundown, with bent head and weary gait—a clump of ancient alders—swans emerging from a backwater—an outrigger manned by stalwart young fellows in flannels—barges with lanterns like eyes and small steam yachts emitting smoke and swift spurts of flame—a late rower, with the water from his paddles dripping white or amber, as the crescent-moon shone upon the river from where it hung low in the heavens—and so forth. These Sanpriel always appropriated, and treasured, and saw in them a joy and beauty of which there was sometimes but the merest hint.   It was a happiness to him, however, to know that she laid such stress upon their possession.   She seemed to him, indeed, to grow more beautiful day by day. Deep down in those fathomless eyes of hers there was a light that evaded recognition, a light that whenever, for a moment, it became visible to him flashed like lightning along his nerves and touched the utmost springs of his passion.   Night and day, day and night, he thought of her, even when by her side, and laughing and talking most familiarly. Everything beautiful suggested some quality of hers : the waterlily in the backwater, the swan adrift upon the current, the curve and motion of the surge which a steam-barge sent athwart stream, the wind blowing across grass or the young grain, the swaying of a poplar, the song of lark or hedge-sparrow or shy goldfinch, the prolonged thrilling vibrations of the missel-thrush : in one and all he saw Sanpriel, heard the voice of Sanpriel—always, everywhere, Sanpriel, Sanpriel, Sanpriel.

As for Lydia, and Ford, and his habitual London life, they hardly entered into his thoughts at all. When, the first morning on the house-boat, he had received some letters which had worried him, including a curt and biting one from his wife, he had despatched a telegram to prevent any further letters from being forwarded to him till he should write for them ; and by the afternoon post he had written to Lydia and told her that the *Lotus* would be moving to and fro, that he wished to have an absolute rest, and that he had telegraphed home to countermand the sending of letters and packets.

As day followed day he forgot all about his promise to run up to Hampstead and see Lady Margaret, and this it was that precipitated the close of his halcyon hours. Ford had been in Paris for some days, and so had known nothing of the absence of the Acostas from Dreamthorpe, but on the day after his return he had called there, and, to his anger and chagrin, had learned whither and with whom they had gone. Resentful as he was, Lydia's anger was more imperative. That morning, a Saturday, she had sent three telegrams to different addresses along Thames-side, any one of which she felt sure would reach her husband. They were to remind him that Lady Margaret was to leave on Monday morning, and that friends were coming to dinner—whom she did not specify. But when the late afternoon came without word from Felix, and when Ford arrived with his news, strangely enough as unexpected as unwelcome, her jealous wrath could not disguise itself even from her aunt. Lady Margaret Trevor was not the woman to pour oil upon troubled waters; she preferred to cast all available oil upon smouldering flames, and watch them leap up and scorch and consume all within their reach. What lay dormant in Lydia's mind was electrified into passionate suspicion, and not even the presence of the man she loved could make her, during the long, dull dinner, gracious and seemly. She felt happier, however, after she had written to Felix, and told him how offended Lady Margaret was, and how she, Lydia, had made arrangements to join the *Lotus* party on Monday, and would be escorted by Gabriel Ford.

Felix, however, had not received any telegram. Early in the forenoon he and the Acostas had driven a long distance inland to see an old priory and its beautiful gardens, and had there spent the day. When, on his return, he found two of the messages which Lydia had despatched, it was too late even to send a reply ; and though he complaisantly reproached himself for his neglect of his aunt-in-law, he could not repress a sigh of thankfulness at having so unconsciously succeeded in evasion.

He felt instinctively, when he told the news to his guests at dinner, that it was unwelcome. Of course they could say nothing about Mrs. Dane, nor indeed discuss the matter at all ; but later on Sanpriel alluded to Ford's advent.

"I know you do not care for him : may I ask why ?" she inquired, as they sat sipping their coffee on deck, and watched the slow uprising of the yellow crescent above an eyot a few hundred yards down the river.

" Well, we have little in common, though we are both artists. We have no aims in which we share —for Ford does not care a straw about art in any other than a purely selfish way. Then as a man —to be frank, I don't trust him. My wife values his friendship, and therefore he is always welcome at The Sycamores, but he comes to see her and not me, for there is no love lost between us."

On the few occasions, latterly, when Felix had alluded to Lydia, he had noticed that Sanpriel had glanced at him, sometimes curiously, sometimes with a look whose significance he could not fathom, but always so swiftly and momentarily that he knew not whether it were voluntary or purely instinctive. And so it was when he mentioned her in connection with Ford—though the glance that searched his eyes seemed to him to endure longer than a moment.

Both Acosta and his daughter seemed depressed that evening, and their host himself felt somewhat despondent, though he scarce knew why, unless it was at the prospect of the uncongenial company which would soon be forced upon him. Sanpriel, however, was a little distraught on her father's account, for he did not seem well, and she knew that physical and mental depression generally preceded one of his brief attacks of frenzy. Fortunately, he seemed to shake off his indisposition as the evening advanced, and long ere midnight the three friends were again adrift on the tide of happiness.

As Felix and Sanpriel stood in the shadow

bidding each other good-night, he held her hand in his while he suggested a plan for the morrow.

"Let us have one quiet and perfect day, Miss Acosta, to end fittingly what has been, to me at any rate, one of the happiest weeks any mortal could desire. If your father come with us, well and good; but if he prefer to stay here and work at his cantata, let us row up the backwater and spend the day under the shade of the willows and alders."

A slight flush came into her face, but she quickly acquiesced; and then Felix let go her hand and went to his cabin triumphant and happy because she had not resented his long clasp; nay, had even, so he persuaded himself, returned his parting pressure.

The morrow, however, brought the first signs of change, and ere breakfast was over the thunder-clouds had massed themselves heavily in all directions, and a warm, large-dropping rain began to fall. Dane was weather-wise, and able conscientiously to prophesy a fine afternoon; but though the others laughed at his augury, and considered it to be but the ghost of his wish, they were ere long convinced—for about noon the rain ceased, and by three there was not a cloud in the sky, only a thin filmy mist near the horizons.

Adama had been at work most of the morning, but the electric atmosphere had affected his nerves, and, after lunch, he declared that his headache was so painful he would lie down during the afternoon, but bade his companions go off·and enjoy themselves up-stream.

The air was fresh and sweet, though the electricity which had been generating for days had not been wholly exhausted. The tall reeds and sedges glittered in vivid green, and when the sunlight flashed upon the broad flags, among which the purple iris and yellow marshmallow grew profusely, the effect was almost dazzling. With what rapture the birds twittered and sang, though no more with the fulness and frequency of the bygone love-weeks of April and May ; and how gladsome everything appeared, from the swallows swooping above the water-lilies amid-stream to the wet daisied grasses and green glades on the mainland ! Even the vagrant who tramped negligently along the meadow-path on the southern bank appeared not ill-content—and to the eyes of the two spectators who watched him for a few moments, the sunlight, glowing, redundant, transmutive as an alchemist's wand, seemed to ennoble his soiled humanity.

In the sheer pleasure of movement, they preferred for a time the open stream, but at last Felix grew tired of rowing, and both felt the heat, which, being damper than of late, was the less endurable. He therefore oared the boat round, let it drift for a while, and then, when the upper reach of the backwater was gained, guided it in below the sweeping boughs of the alders—so wide and dense-foliaged just there that the retreat they hid was secure from all casual boaters.

The coolness and shade were welcome after the glare of the flashing water and the hot whiteness of the underspaces of the sky, and erewhile an exquisite nook was reached, where the pool was blue as a turquoise except where covered with water-lilies or overhung by green branches, which made the depths reflect intricate black shadows shot through and through with lines and dappled spaces of fluent emerald.

A beech threw its lowest bough half-way across, and to its stalwart girth Felix fastened the boat.

For a time they talked upon all manner of things bearing upon their two arts, but gradually, though he would fain have avoided so perilous a theme, the conversation turned upon the hopes of Israel, and the great part the nation might yet play in the world's history.

"There are so few who realise what we are," urged Sanpriel eagerly, in reply to a question. "We are the torch-bearers of the moderns. Do you know what one of our foremost contemporary poets, Emma Lazarus, has said? Here are her words: 'Every student of the Hebrew language is aware that we have in the conjugation of our verbs a mode known as the *intensive voice*, which, by means of an almost imperceptible modification of vowel-points, intensifies the meaning of the primitive root. A similar significance seems to attach to the Jews themselves in connection with the people among whom they dwell. They are the intensive form of any nationality whose language and customs they adopt.' Is not that well put?"

"It is; and it is surely true. Who is Miss Lazarus?"

"Ah, you must read her poems: she is dead now, but her words will live. Such poems as 'The Crowing of the Red Cock,' 'The Banner of the Jew,' and 'Rosh-Hashanah' are like life-blood to us weary and famished children of Israel. Ah, my friend, we are yet going to lead you to a hope greater than any that has yet dawned upon humanity. Will you let me recite to you two little prose-poems by Emma

Lazarus? One, called 'The Test,' embodies that terrible quality which makes our people so misunderstood; the other, called 'The Sower,' will remind you what we *are*. Here is 'The Test':—

'*Daylong I brooded upon the Passion of Israel.*
I saw him bound to the wheel, nailed to the cross, cut off
by the sword, burned at the stake, tossed into the seas.
And always the patient, resolute, martyr face arose in
silent rebuke and defiance.
A Prophet . . . a Poet . . . a placid-browed Sage . . .
these I saw, with princes and people in their train:
the monumental dead and the standard-bearers of the
future.
And suddenly I heard a burst of mocking laughter, and
turning, I beheld the shuffling gait, the ignominious
features, the sordid mask of the son of the Ghetto.'

But here is the reverse side, 'The Sower':—

'*Over a boundless plain went a man, carrying seed.*
His face was blackened by sun and rugged from tempest,
scarred and distorted by pain. Naked to the loins,
his back was ridged with furrows, his breast was
ploughed with stripes.
From his hand dropped the fecund seed.
And behold, there started from the soil a blade, a sheaf,
a springing trunk, a myriad-branching, cloud-aspir-
ing tree. Its arms touched the ends of the horizon,
the heavens were darkened with its shadow.
It bare blossoms of gold and blossoms of blood, fruitage
of health and fruitage of poison; birds sang amid
its foliage, and a serpent was coiled about its stem.
Under its branches a divinely beautiful man, crowned with
thorns, was nailed to a cross.

> *And the tree put forth treacherous boughs to strangle the Sower : his flesh was bruised and torn, but cunningly he disentangled the murderous knot and passed to the eastward.*
>
> *Again there dropped from his hand the fecund seed.*
>
> *And behold, again there started from the soil a blade, a sheaf, a springing trunk, a myriad-branching, cloud-aspiring tree. Crescent-shaped like little emerald moons were the leaves : it bare blossoms of silver and blossoms of blood, fruitage of health and fruitage of poison ; birds sang amid its foliage and a serpent was coiled about its stem.*
>
> *Under its branches a turbaned, mighty-limbed Prophet brandished a drawn sword.*
>
> *And behold this tree likewise puts forth perfidious arms to strangle the Sower : but cunningly he disentangles the murderous knot and passes on.*
>
> *Lo, his hands are not empty of grain, the strength of his arm is not spent.*
>
> *What germ hast thou saved for the future, O miraculous Husbandman ? Tell me, thou Planter of Christhood and Islam : tell me, thou seed-bearing Israel.'"*

"They are certainly beautiful and pregnant lines. But it seems to me the Sower might also be taken as representative of the Spirit of Humanity."

"You can so take it if you will ; just as *we* adopt the name of 'Children of To-morrow,' although Siwäarmill is not a Jew, nor writes for Jews, but means his words for all who suffer and live acutely."

"Whenever I hear that phrase, I think of the lines of Omar Khayyám :—

'Alike for those who for To-day prepare,
And those that after some To-morrow stare,
    A muezzín from the Tower of Darkness cries,
"Fools, your Reward is neither Here nor There."' "

"Ah, how sad he is, the beautiful old Persian poet!" Sanpriel exclaimed; "how sad despite all his bantering and *abandon!* One can often hear the sigh beneath his laughter! After all, what has collective modern pessimism to add to—

'Oh threats of Hell and Hopes of Paradise!
One thing at least is certain—*This* Life flies:
    One thing is certain and the rest is Lies;
The Flower that once has blown for ever dies'?"

"Ay, and their terrible complement or commentary, a few quatrains farther on, Miss Acosta; do you remember?—

'I sent my Soul through the Invisible,
Some letter of that After-life to spell:
    And by-and-by my Soul returned to me,
And answered, "I Myself am Heav'n and Hell:"

Heaven's but the Vision of fulfill'd Desire,
And Hell the Shadow from a Soul on fire.'"

"I remember well; I do not think you could quote the first line of a single quatrain in the 'Rubáiyát' that I could not at once follow up with the proper sequence. The quatrains I have oftenest thought of sadly are these four:—

' Ah, my Belovèd, fill the Cup that clears
  To-day of past Regret and future Fears :
    To-morrow !—why, To-morrow I may be
  Myself with Yesterday's Seven Thousand Years.

  For some we loved, the loveliest and the best
  That from his vintage rolling Time hath prest,
    Have drunk their Cup a Round or two before,
  And one by one crept silently to rest.

  And we that now make merry in the Room
  They left, and Summer dresses in new bloom,
    Ourselves must we beneath the Couch of Earth
  Descend—ourselves to make a Couch—for whom ?

  Ah, make the most of what we yet may spend,
  Before we too into the Dust descend ;
    Dust into Dust, and under Dust, to lie,
  Sans Wine, *sans* Song, *sans* Singer—*and sans* End !' "

While Sanpriel was repeating the lines one of
the earlier quatrains came into Felix's mind, and
when she had finished he added in a low voice,
but in a tone that betrayed the true significance
of the words—

  " ' A Book of Verses underneath the Bough,
    A Jug of Wine, a Loaf of Bread—and Thou
      Beside me singing in the Wilderness—
    Oh, wilderness were Paradise enow !' "

A slight flush came into Sanpriel's face, but she
took no notice of the quotation, and immediately
asked some questions about other Persian poets
whose works have been translated.

But the spell of Omar's lines had settled upon them, and after a time they became silent, and each fell into a reverie which was all the sweeter for the presence of the other, though no words were said nor even glances interchanged.

Sanpriel sat leaning back against the stern-cushions, idly playing with a water-lily she had plucked, with her eyes dreamily fixed upon the green perspectives of the backwater; Felix leaned over the side and looked down into the still shallows, and watched the water-beetles and minnows darting to and fro, and shadow-birds flitting among the shadow-branches. As often happens when emotion is high-wrought, a certain reaction had set in with him. It seemed to him that Sanpriel was hopelessly removed from his love; that to Lydia he would have to forfeit all that he held most dear; that the previous TO-DAY on which Omar laid such stress was slipping away from him, all unused and unenjoyed—and he repeated another of the Persian's couplets :—

> " The Wine of Life keeps oozing drop by drop,
> The Leaves of Life keep falling one by one,"

with a sad feeling as if they had been written of himself. Slowly, however, his thoughts drifted into other channels, and as he became more lost in happy reveries of work and love he grew almost oblivious of Sanpriel's presence. So quiet were they that the swallows sometimes swooped close above them and the water-hens swam close by. A kingfisher, resplendent in purple and glowing azure, forgot his coyness and flashed backward and forward at intervals, and the ousels seemed no shyer than the sharded green beetles and wall-flower-moths and large, white, flickering butterflies which flew hither and thither, like blossoms and leaflets blown abroad.

But when the sun, setting low by the river-reaches, sent a flood of golden light through the alders so that it fell upon the backwater and made its silent surface all agleam, Sanpriel stirred and gave a low laugh.

"We must be going back to the *Lotus* now, Mr. Dane. But though we have been so silent, I have had such a happy afternoon : it has been a Day of Rest indeed. But I have left my father alone long enough—and, besides, there is a slight chill here now."

He was about to urge a little longer stay, and words of still stronger pleading would have followed them, but almost as she spoke there was a loud splashing, and the next moment a four-oared boat, with two or three girls in the stern-sheets, entered the backwater, and was lightly moored by the young fellow in the bow to an impendent willow.

So there was nothing for it but to row *Lotus*-ward, and Felix managed to control his chagrin at the interlopers, and laugh and chat as blithely as though he knew nought of the overtrue songs of Omar and other prophets of To-day and mockers of To-morrow.

But so radiant was the sundown, so peaceful the afterglow, that both yielded to the happy quiescence of nature, and Adama Acosta vaguely wondered, as he looked at them, how it was that youth and happiness, potent though these are, could so irradiate human faces with the light as of an assured and serene joy.

The evening was not less happy, though no different from those which had preceded it. Acosta played melody after melody, and Sanpriel, too tired to sing, as she said, at last yielded, and sang again the song of her own, wedded to her father's music, which Felix knew so well. For some unfathomable reason, however, it now pained him to hear it, and he could barely restrain the tears from his eyes when the singer's voice ceased in one long, tender vibration. Perhaps it was the emotion that she put into it, or the subtle pathos of the cadences to which it was set, or something in the exquisite hush of the gloaming, violet-hued, dewy, scarce yet star-litten.

> *Sweet, sweet is life*
> *That knows no sorrow :*
> *O golden morrow,*
> *With what hid things is your bright coming rife ?*
> *Sweet, sweet is life.*
> *Can grief, can pain be where*
> *Joy fills the air ?*
>
> *Sweet, sweet is sleep*
> *That knows no waking :*
> *Sweet the forsaking*
> *Of treasured toys we no more care to keep.*
> *Sweet, sweet is sleep !*
> *O heart within my breast,*
> *Thou shalt have rest !*

But when he lay down in his berth and, for a long while, vainly strove to induce sleep, it was not Sanpriel's song that haunted him. For he had now consciously cast off his past from him, he had now in spirit divorced himself utterly from Lydia and his wedded life, and found that the Hour of Repentance had no meaning, no reality for him. It was of Omar's quatrain that he thought :—

> " Come, fill the Cup, and in the fire of Spring
> Your Winter-garment of Repentance fling :
> The Bird of Time has but a little way
> To flutter—and the Bird is on the Wing."

CHAPTER XI.

MONDAY was dull and heavy. There was neither wind nor rain, though the clouds hung low, and the upper edges of those in the west were fringed and, in places, deeply serrated. Along the river-reaches the mists hung, or dispersed slowly in their smoke-like vapours. The water, grey and lustreless, flowed monotonously, though the swirling of the surface-currents, and the force of under-eddies caused it to take on a certain serpentine grace.

No one felt very much inclined for pleasure-seeking, so by common consent the morning was devoted to correspondence and such work as might be feasible. But either letter-writing was uncongenial and work impossible, or else the atmospheric pressure was accountable, for ere long all three found themselves on the deck of the *Lotus*, and each with the same excuse of laziness. About noon the small steam-cutter for which Felix had arranged duly arrived, and took the house-boat in tow up-stream.   Motion was delightful on that still day, and the spirits of all on board the *Lotus* rapidly rose; and by the time, late in the after-noon, that King's Ferry was reached, they, or Sanpriel and Felix at any rate, had become almost happy again.

It was at King's Ferry that the new-comers were to arrive—the hour and place having been altered from those originally fixed upon.   Felix disembarked about four o'clock, and walked, about a mile, to the little station—but whether he had been late in starting, or had loitered by the way, he did not arrive in time to meet Lydia and Ford as the train came into the station.   Neither was the fly that Lydia had ordered by telegram in attendance, and so both time and temper were lost ere arrangements were made for the transference of the baggage.   At no time was Mrs. Dane fond of walking, and in the country she detested it.   It did not improve matters that the road was rough and, despite the yester thunder-showers, dusty, and that the atmosphere was hot and almost stifling.   In the heavy air the gnats and midges seemed to multiply each moment, and the pinging noise of the wasps among the vervain and loose-strife, or as they clung to the purple scabious-tufts, was unpleasantly strident and added to the sense of heat-weariness. Even the small blue butterflies, sprites of perpetual motion, fluttered weakly among the blooms of the elder and bryony; and there was a vicious twang in the darting to and fro of the brown dragon-flies over the bladder-campions and limp knapweeds.

They seemed to have very little to say to each other, Felix and Lydia and Ford, as they tramped along the road to King's Ferry. To Dane it appeared as though the midsummer glory were over, the autumn come before her date; and surely, he thought, there must be more than twenty-four hours between the cool, sweet summer's afternoon in the backwater and that, hot and dusty, wherein he now walked anything but blithely.

To his immense relief, however, Lydia recovered from or disguised her irritation as soon as she boarded the *Lotus.* If she was not cordial to Sanpriel, who greeted her with friendly welcome, she was neither rude nor supercilious, and she became almost friendly when she found that her own stern-cabin, that which she had occupied the previous summer, had been reserved for her. A frown, however, crossed her face when she learned that, of the two adjoining cabins, separate though both entered by the same outer door, one, that astern, was occupied by her husband, and the other by Sanpriel. But it soon became evident that she had not come to make open war. By many a covert sneer or unnecessary interference she let it be seen that she was mistress of the *Lotus*, but otherwise she made herself almost agreeable to Miss Acosta; as for Adama, she disliked him, but was polite in her manner.

Altogether the dreaded Monday night passed more pleasantly than Felix had dared to anticipate, and though he sorely missed the happy evenings of the past week, he felt by no means ill-content as he took a last turn upon the deck of the house-boat with Ford, and smoked in silence.

He knew that his companion hated him, but he had never yet broached the subject of the quicksand episode, except on the first occasion when he had met Gabriel after the studio episode on the night of his return from Grantley. He had then referred meaningly to the loss of the mare and to the extraordinary disappearance of the warning-board, but his remarks had been taken with such mingled indifference and conventionally polite attention that he had been staggered. In any case, he had realised, no good was to be gained by the reopening of a dubious subject. He should have

demanded an explanation at the time he saw Ford
in his studio, or, if his fainting attack rendered that
impossible, then immediately afterward ; but since
the opportunity had gone by, he felt that it was
wisest to let it appear as though he suspected
nothing, or, at least, as though any suspicions he
might have entertained had been assuaged.

But as he walked the deck of the *Lotus* in
the solitary company of the man whom he disliked
and distrusted, and who, he was well aware, hated
him, he was on the point of breaking his resolution
and demanding a satisfactory explanation.   If,
he thought, he could force Ford into a position
wherefrom he could not emerge without betraying
himself somehow, that individual would perforce
have to leave.   The temptation was great, but,
rather from the idea that the opportunity was not
altogether suitable than from any fear of con-
sequences, he decided to preserve his reticence,
at any rate for a time.

The next few days passed pleasantly enough.
The weather improved, though there was some
rain every day, and the atmosphere was dull and
close.   Notwithstanding Lydia's efforts to prevent
separation, it again and again happened that Felix
and Sanpriel got away together, sometimes for an
hour or so at a time, either ashore or in the small

boat, and even on the *Lotus* they were not altogether deprived of intervals of uninterrupted communion.

By Thursday evening the house-boat had drifted down-stream as far as Windsor, but by this time it was evident to all that a break-up in the party must soon occur. Adama Acosta's growing absence of mind had become unpleasantly obvious, and there were other signs of mental trouble which made Sanpriel anxious on account of her father. Lydia had become strangely taciturn, and to her husband's eyes there was a look in her face which he almost feared, though he could not fathom it. Ford, again, was at all times ill at ease, however suave and attentive he might be in demeanour: sometimes he sought Sanpriel's company, and sometimes Lydia's, though latterly he absented himself more and more from either, save when they were together; at all times, however, he avoided the company of Felix. As for the latter himself, he could not but be conscious of the growing strain, the gathering electricity—but he looked only for the ordinary dull and commonplace conclusion, and now indeed rather wearied for it. On the *Lotus* he could never depend upon privacy with Sanpriel; in Hampstead he could at any time walk over to Dreamthorpe with the practical certainty of finding her at home. Lydia worried him unspeakably, not so much by her acts or words as by what these often implied; her very personality affected him unpleasantly, though he did his best to disguise this fact from himself, and, when disguise was useless, to overcome it. Thus it came about, by common agreement, that the holiday would come to an end on Saturday, unless the weather improved, in which case it might be prolonged till Monday or Tuesday.

But on Friday afternoon there seemed little likelihood of a change for the better. The atmosphere was even closer and heavier than it had been of late, and the physical depression which all experienced rendered the prospect of a break-up one actually of relief.

All day, Felix noticed, Lydia had been in a perturbed and nervous state. The sight of him and Sanpriel together, seated, or fishing, or walking to and fro, seemed to exasperate her. Her voice was sharp and bitter, and the lines in her cold, handsome face had deepened. He had been puzzled to account for the change, save on the ground that the strain which each experienced was proving insupportable to his wife; but a remark from Sanpriel in part at least explained the cause.

" I fear that Mr. Ford is making dispeace between your wife and yourself, Mr. Dane—indeed, also between her and me. I have twice lately accidentally overheard something he said to her, and in each instance it was untruthful, but at the same time credited by her. Perhaps I have no right to make the suggestion, but will you not leave me and take Mrs. Dane a row, or sit beside her? She is all alone, you see, at present; and as she is neither reading nor working, I fear that she is ill-content."

Felix was unwilling, but he felt that Sanpriel was right; and in any case he could not have refused her request.

But whether owing to the electric state of the atmosphere and the doubled transmission of sound, or whether she guessed the true origin of his motive, Lydia rose as her husband approached, and with a contemptuous glance at him, and another of evil import at Sanpriel, passed along the deck and down the stairs which led to the saloon. A moment or two later he heard her cabin-door loudly slammed and the lock turn.

He went back to Sanpriel's side, and ere long they were again in earnest conversation, after the first constraint consequent upon Lydia's action had passed away—so absorbed, indeed, did they become that they did not hear the small boat glide up alongside the *Lotus*, nor were they conscious of the nearness of Ford, as he stood up and maintained the boat in position by means of the lower loop-rope. He listened for some time, with a contemptuous sneer on his lips and an evil, furtive look in his eyes, but without eagerness, till he overheard Felix urge his companion to come on deck, after the others had gone to their cabins, for a last talk about his sculpture and her new book—in case the holiday should come to an end on the morrow.

Before Sanpriel could reply, Felix, with an expression of scornful anger which he could not control, caught sight of Ford.

"You put me in mind of the man Mr. Acosta told us about last night, Mr. Ford—the man who was never overheard, though often unexpectedly seen."

The sneering tone was too obvious to be overlooked, and Ford showed plainly that he both understood and resented the remark. For the first time he allowed his ill-will to become visible, and he scowled as he replied that he had just that moment glided alongside, and had been about to hail Miss Acosta when Dane spoke. By the time, however, that he had secured the boat and come on deck his manner had again completely changed, and he appeared anxious to be, or at least to seem, on good terms with his host.

After dinner, Acosta remained but a short time in the open air. The nervous headache from which he had been suffering for days had grown worse instead of better, and he seemed quite unable to maintain any sequent conversation. After he had departed the others sat quietly for a time, though Sanpriel and the two men ere long drifted into conversation.

Felix had gone to the saloon to fetch another cigar, when, as he turned to go on deck again, he was met by Lydia. He saw that she had come to intercept him, and was half-startled, half-curious at the set look in her face. When she spoke, however, it was in her usual slow, hard voice.

"Felix, I suppose you won't object to a change of cabins for to-night? I have told Roberts to transfer the sheets and so forth from my room to yours, and from yours to mine."

"Why? Your cabin is surely the more comfortable of the two?"

"Possibly; but I cannot sleep in it. I think I should sleep better in a smaller one."

"As you wish the change, Lydia, of course I am willing to oblige you. Has Roberts already seen to it? Yes? Well, I'll go at once to the stern-cabin, as I left my cigar-case in my boating-flannels."

Lydia turned without a word and went on deck again. What could her real motive be? he wondered, as he groped about for his cigar-case. She had never before complained of sleeplessness, and there had been something in the tone of her words which made him dubious as to her sincerity.

Having found the cigar-case, he recrossed the saloon, and as he passed the steward's pantry stooped to pick up a key that he descried on the deerskin outside. He recognised it as Roberts' skeleton-key for the opening of all the outer and inner doors of the private cabins when the guest-keys should be lost, mislaid, or not forthcoming when the berths had to be remade and the cabins tidied. As the steward was not there, he placed the key in his pocket, meaning to return it to Roberts in the morning, or when he next saw him, and then went on deck.

There was a brief vision of moonrise, but after a few minutes of veiled light the mist, or opaque undercloud, blotted it and the few visible stars from view. As the night deepened, silence fell upon the small party. The two men smoked, and occasionally Felix made a remark, but latterly he too ceased all attempt at conversation. Sanpriel lay back in a wicker-chair, and seemed deep in reverie —not an unhappy one, her companion thought, as he noted the faint smile that haunted her mouth— and Lydia sat on a side-seat, and looked straight astern, as though she descried something steadily advancing through the darkness.

A barge sailed past, hay-laden, with three or four large red and green lanterns; a man at the bow stood with a long pole, and as the helmsman listened for his comrade's directing cries he whistled a popular tune. Soon the barge became shadowy, and then its bulk merged altogether into the gloom, though, for a time, there were one or two bright lights upon the water, as the lower reaches caught the reflections from the lanterns, and the thin shrill whistling was borne backward by some wandering eddy of air.

Then again silence. A little later came a splashing sound of oars, and a four-oared boat went by. In a blithe tenor voice the "stroke" was singing, and a fragment of his song came to those on board the *Lotus* :—

> *Love in my heart; oh, heart of me, heart of me !*
> *Love is my tyrant, Love is supreme.*
> *What if it passeth, oh, heart of me, heart of me !*
> *Love is a phantom, and Life is a dream !*

What if it passeth, oh, heart of me, heart of me !
What if it . . . . heart of me . . . me !

and the song died away in the distance.

Privet-hawk and other moths fluttered by, some with jarring sound, others, like the flickering ghost-moth, in spectral silence.   The frogs in the shallows and inland pools croaked incessantly, and once and again a barn-owl swooped past, with its whirring cry.   There was no other sound, save the flow of the water, which, though the night was windless, seemed every now and again to surge more rapidly and to swirl along in fiercer eddies.

Sanpriel was the first to make a move.

"I think I shall bid good-night," she said to Mrs. Dane, as she slowly rose and gathered her light Shetland shawl about her.

The latter turned and looked at the speaker, but did not reply, nor did she seem to be aware of Miss Acosta's outstretched hand.

" Good-night, Mrs. Dane.   Are you coming below, or are you going to stay on deck for a while ? "

Lydia shortly answered " Good-night," and then turned and looked steadily astern again ; but a minute or two later she rose, and, having shaken hands silently with Ford and her husband, followed Sanpriel below.

A low laugh from his companion roused Felix's resentment. He did not wish Ford to remain long on deck, and for this and other reasons he thought the opportunity would be a good one on which to refer to what had happened at Grantley.

"You seem amused at something, Mr. Ford?" When alone with him, Felix invariably adopted a formal address, though before the others he dropped the "Mr." when he spoke to or of Ford at all, which was seldom. "If so, I am sorry to have to demand your attention to another matter. You remember the day you and the Acostas left Grantley?"

"Yes."

"Will you explain to me what you did with the letter that Miss Acosta wrote to me and left in the library?"

"Why do you ask *me*?" His voice had a cold steely ring in it, and he had half-risen from his reclining attitude and thrown his nearly finished cigar overboard.

"Because you returned to the library and took the letter from the place where Miss Acosta had left it for me."

Ford hesitated for a few moments. He knew that his companion had doubtless found out from

Sanpriel herself about a letter having been written and left for him, but, he thought, the rest must be surmise, and an effort at "bluffing" him.

"What do you mean?"

"I mean what I say—that you appropriated the letter which Miss Acosta left for me."

"I did not."

"You are a liar, Gabriel Ford." Felix spoke quietly, but in a tone of contemptuous disbelief.

Ford sprang to his feet, and seemed about to reply in great anger, but his companion calmly beckoned to him to be seated again.

"Sit down again, pray. I have one or two other questions to ask you. What did you do with that letter?"

Suddenly a wave of reckless indifference came over him. He realised that Dane was about to force him into a corner, and as he was not altogether undesirous of a quarrel, he thought he might as well meet the accusations—so far, at any rate—with cynical frankness.

"The letter? Well, my good friend, by the same kind of mistake as you made when you opened Mrs. Dane's letter to me, I opened Miss Acosta's to *you;* but not until afterwards, for, thinking it was a letter of my own, I put it in my pocket, and there found it some three days later. It was a mere line to mention that she and her father were returning to London—and so I forgot all about it. Very sorry, I am sure. Delightful place, Grantley, is it not?"

"That also is false. Will you now tell me what your object was in asking me to meet you at Ratho quicksand?"

"Well, really, my motives were rather complex. Perhaps I hoped you might ride into the quicksand, and perhaps I didn't; perhaps I wished you out of the way at the time when the Acostas were leaving; perhaps I wished—well, my dear Mr. Dane, I hardly know all *what* I wished."

"You wished to murder me?"

"Evidence rather shaky, eh?" Ford spoke in a sneering tone, and leant forward, so that unwittingly he brought his face into the light of the lamp that hung from the awning.

"Yes, if unsupported. But you rode to Ratho early in the morning and removed the warning that Sir Arthur Crane had placed there."

"That is a lie. I was not within a mile of Ratho."

"It is not a lie. The head-groom noticed that in your horse's hoofs there was a peculiar blackish clay which is found absolutely nowhere save at the margins of the quicksand.   The proof, therefore, of your having been there is incontrovertible."

Felix saw a look of baffled fury, with something of momentary fear in it, come into Ford's face ; but when the latter spoke it was without a change in his mocking tone.

"Did he really ?   Well, it is possible, in my absence of mind, that I may have ridden as far as the quicksand, but I saw no notice-board."

"So it amounts to this, Gabriel Ford : you tried to inveigle me into a quicksand—you certainly deceived me in an ungentlemanly manner, even according to your own version—and you stole a letter that was addressed to me.   You are a liar and a scoundrel."

To his surprise, Ford sat quite still and did not say a word.

"I repeat, you are a liar and a scoundrel.   I should have spoken to you earlier about this, but as long as you were my wife's guest I could not well do so.   As our party is going to break up to-morrow, I take the opportunity of letting you know what I think of you.   In these circumstances you cannot be surprised when I add that henceforth I forbid you my studio—I do not say my house, for if my wife care to see you or any of her friends, I have neither the right nor the wish to interfere—

and, in a word, decline the honour of further acquaintance so far as I am concerned."

When Felix had finished he lit another cigar, and quietly resumed smoking as though he had concluded the most ordinary conversation.

His companion sat looking at him with an evil glitter in his eyes. At last he rose.

"Good-night, Felix Dane. You have the king of trumps, but I hold the ace—and I have the other honours in my hand;" and with a sneering laugh he rose, lounged across the deck, and then went below.

What did Ford's enigmatic farewell mean, he pondered: was it a threat, or a mere idle assertion of imaginary vantage? He rose, threw away the cigar he had just lighted, and walked slowly to and fro.

How still and dark the night was! Not a thing was visible ten yards away from the *Lotus*, and even the water was but faintly illumed, save where the house-boat lanterns sent serpentine trails of light across the flood.

How was it that Sanpriel did not come on deck as she had promised? Was she unwell? Or had she fallen asleep? Or did she fear a *tête-à-tête* in that dark and seductive silence?

He became nervously impatient, and at last

stepped softly down the ladder and into the saloon.

The outer door of the central port-cabins was closed. Should he open it, he pondered, and tap gently at Sanpriel's door?—though if he did so would Lydia not overhear the summons?

While he was hesitating, he distinctly heard a slight rustle. This decided him—for it came from the inner side of the door. He gently turned the handle of the latter, which, however, remained fast. It was locked, and from the inside. What did it mean? Had Lydia—but just then he remembered the steward's skeleton-key which he had picked up and placed in his pocket, and with a swift gesture brought it forth, applied it to the lock, and noise-lessly opened the door.

He was startled, as Sanpriel stepped forward, to see how white she was, and he even fancied that she was trembling.

" What is it ? Has anything alarmed you ? " he asked in a low tone.

" I will tell you on deck. I want to get away —to get into the air."

Mechanically he relocked the door, and followed her on deck.

" Why are you so white? Has anything frightened you ? " he asked again, as soon as they were alone

—though Sanpriel would not sit down, but leant against the taffrail.

"Perhaps it is foolish of me ; but when I said good-night to Mrs. Dane as we parted at our cabin-doors she gave me such a strange look. I heard her go in and lock her door. A little later I left my cabin and crossed the saloon to say good-night to my father, but as he was asleep I went back. Quarter of an hour or so afterwards I heard a rustle and then the clicking of a lock. Thrice since then I have tried to get out, but each time I found the outer-door locked, and no key visible anywhere. It made me nervous. I am glad you came."

It was quite clear to Felix that Lydia had sus-pected—perhaps Ford had put her on her guard—that Sanpriel might go on deck again, and had taken the precaution to lock her in ; but, angry as he felt, he passed the matter lightly over, and ere long his companion seemed to have recovered her composure.

They talked in voices instinctively hushed—partly of their plans for work, partly of when they should meet in Hampstead, partly of the happy week they had spent.

"To me the happiest week of my life," added Felix in a low vibrating tone that betrayed the deep emotion which otherwise he with difficulty controlled.

He had drawn a little closer to her. Her dress touched him—and he was conscious of it through every nerve. Without conscious thought he lifted his hand and it met hers—clasped it—held it—drew it towards his lips—and the next moment he was covering it with passionate kisses.

"*Sanpriel!*"

It was the first time he had addressed her by her own name. He felt the tremor of her hand.

"Sanpriel—Sanpriel—I love you! Oh, my darling—my darling!"

She did not utter a word, but he knew that she was yielding; ah, so slightly, but still yielding. Suddenly he leaned forward, still holding her hand in his firm clasp, and kissed her: the next moment his arms were round her, and his lips pressed against hers.

In the joy, the mad intoxication of the moment, he heard nothing, saw nothing. The whole world was lost to him. It was one throb of rapture. Her lips, her eyes, close to his face, her heart beating against his—the sweet, turbulent, unspeakable passion of love regnant in both—it was the height and crown of life—nay, it was the quintessence of life, the one immortal moment that is dropped into every cup of mortal years.

"Speak one word, my darling! Tell me, Sanpriel, tell me that you love me! Ah, I know it, I feel it—but only tell it me, dear—whisper it—I dare scarce believe it. Oh, Sanpriel, Sanpriel, my heart's delight, my beautiful one, how I love you!"

He kissed her passionately again, and felt her lips touching his in return, but ere the whisper came for which his soul yearned she had repelled him and was looking out beyond him with a fixed and terrified stare.

"What is it, Sanpriel? What is it, my darling?"

"Look, what is *that?*"

He turned, and a superstitious thrill for a moment unnerved him, as he descried, a few feet away, a shadowy figure, wherefrom two eyes literally shone. They were like some feline animal's, palely luminous, save that they did not wax and wane.

But even as he looked he made out the outlines of a face, white, rigid, tense, as of one from the dead.

A low cry caught his ear, and Sanpriel stumbled against him and fell in a swoon at his feet. Indifferent now to aught else, he knelt beside her and lifted her head, and as he kissed her lips and chafed her hands he pleaded with her to open her eyes and speak to him, as though across the gulf of unconsciousness she could hear his loving summons.

He had no thought of calling any one, but he remembered that a fire-bucket stood near the gangway, filled with water. He turned, reached towards it, and plunged his handkerchief therein, and therewith moistened Sanpriel's lips and laved her forehead.

Ah, was that not a sigh ?—yes, another, and yet another ! " Thank God, she's coming to," he muttered, and again he pressed his lips to hers and whispered lovingly.

What was that hoarse hissing sound close behind him ? He started, stumbled, and then sprang to his feet, but when he looked round he could descry nothing, no one. Stop ! what was that yonder—a blackness amidst the darkness, that moved, that glided, that disappeared ! Should he follow ? No, he would not leave Sanpriel. Besides—he knew now who the phantom was; below all its concentrated fury he had recognised the voice which had uttered that hoarse hissing cry—" *Curse you !*"

It was Lydia : she had followed them, overheard all, no doubt—he thought. Well, no matter now. But what of Sanpriel? He must shield her.

Even while he pondered what to do, Sanpriel opened her eyes, passed her hand once or twice across her forehead, then with a low sobbing cry staggered to her feet.

"Hush, dear! You are all right now. Do not be frightened."

"But what was *it?*"

"Nothing. It was an owl, or cat perhaps; an animal's eyes, at any rate."

"No—no—Felix—I saw a face, white and terrible. I—I—think it was Lydia's, your wife's!"

Even in his agitation and fear for her, his heart beat faster when he heard her call him by his name—the name of all names in the world now.

"Whatever it was, you are safe with me, Sanpriel."

"Oh, I must go below now, at once, at once! Let me go, dear! Yes, yes, I love you, but let me go. No—no—no—I cannot go back to sleep *there*—near *her!* But I'll get some things from my cabin and then sit up with my father."

"Hush, Sanpriel dear, don't be foolish. You need have no fear. Lock your cabin-door and fall asleep. You really saw nothing; there was nothing there. I must have seen it if there were. Your nerves are overwrought."

To his surprise and happiness she believed him, and gave a great sigh of relief.

"Ah, well, I suppose you are right. I am foolish and hysterical. Good-night—Felix!"

As she spoke she leaned up, lightly kissed his cheek, and before he could intercept her had glided forward and disappeared down the companion-ladder.

He followed, but just in time to hear her cabin-door close and the lock click.

There was no one in the saloon, and all the cabin-doors were closed; he could see that at a glance by the light of the pendent lamp which burned low, but clearly enough.

With a long sigh of excitement, he put out the lamp and went to his cabin, that which Lydia had occupied till that evening, and two or three hours ago had interchanged for his.

Strange that after such an experience he should have slept at all, but in less than an hour, slumber, deep and profound, had come to him. To him only, the chief actor in the drama, came rest and forgetfulness.

For a long time Lydia lay in her berth as

though she were a dead woman—motionless, soundless, and with wide-staring eyes. The one passion of which she was capable—a mad, overwhelming jealousy—had taken possession of her. She neither thought of nor cared for any other thing. There was room only for hate; hate of Felix, hate of Sanpriel. But at last she thought of Gabriel: ah, she muttered, he not only loved her, but also hated her husband. The thought drew her lover closer to her heart; her eyes closed wearily; and gradually she dozed off into broken sleep.

Lydia never dreamed, but the emotions she had experienced must have excited her brain. Half-awake—for she wondered at her fancies, and at the naturalness of everything around her, the coverlet on her berth, the window-sofa she could just dimly descry, the small square curtained window—she dreamed that there was a sound at her door, just a faint, uncertain, almost inaudible sound, and that a minute or so later a shadowy shape outlined itself in the darkness. Who could it be, so stealthy, so silent, apparently so motionless? She gave a sigh of weariness and turned her head. Surely, she thought, she must now be awake; nay, she knew she was; but she would not look out into the dark room again, nor imagine fantasmal

figures.   Again, a sound—low, but audible.   No
—no—she repeated—she was becoming nervous :
she would pay no heed to creaking boards or
straining wood-joints.   She pulled the bed-clothes
close up to her face and turned her head well into
the pillow—determined to yield to no foolish weakness of eyes or ears.   Ah, she would scold Roberts
on the morrow, she thought : had not some dust
fallen lightly upon her face, and the pillow ?   How
careless of him ! how—how—ah, sleep must be
coming, though sounds, and scenes new and
strange in aspect, yet not wholly unfamiliar, are—
what confusion and medley everywhere !—and how
close it is, how stifling !—ah, there is coolness now :
how delicious, and what sweet scents !—and how
happy she and Felix as a youth and maiden wandering through the woodlands—no, she and Gabriel
—no—she and—ah, how terrible ! she has become
blind and can see no one, nothing, can hear not a
sound, cannot cry out even—though in her dream-
agony she muttered *" Gabriel."*

What made the dream-figure start ?   Softly and
silently as any shadow it had drawn close to the
berth : then a dark arm had risen above the sleeping woman, and slowly, steadily, a thin white
powder was sprinkled upon her face and upon the
pillow beyond her nostrils.

A minute passed—two—three—and then there came from the bed a sound of sobbing breath.

Then the dark figure muttered, in a tone so low that none listening might have heard it, "*So now I've played my ace of trumps, Felix Dane—and have the game in my hands.*"

It was at this moment when another Shadow had entered the cabin—a Shadow with a chill and terrifying breath, though invisible to mortal eyes —that the dying woman muttered "*Gabriel*"—that the dark figure started.

Gabriel Ford trembled like an aspen. A cold sweat broke out on his forehead; nor could he repress a low, shuddering respiration. But suddenly he stooped and listened intently, and recovered something of his composure.

"Why did he mutter 'Gabriel'—and in *her* voice, too? Perhaps I imagined it : curse these nerves that play such tricks. I do not like to touch him : but there'll be light enough from that window—I see a gleam of moonlight."

He crossed the cabin, softly pulled back the small curtain, though his heart beat the quicker as one of the brass rings jangled. The night had cleared, though a thick white mist lay along the surface of the water. A long slow-moving finger of moonlight came in at the window and pointed at the face, white and awful, of the corpse.

"How ghastly he looks!" Ford muttered, as he stepped lightly back to look at the man who could no longer be his enemy, nor come between him and Sanpriel, between him and Lydia. Ah, if Lydia knew—with all her love, how she yet would hate him! That must never be. Good God, how he loved her, cold, and serene, and impassive though she seemed to others!

Then he stooped to look at death in the face of Felix Dane.

But sharp was the low cry, terrible his trembling agony, when, in place of the man whom he had come to kill, he saw the corpse of the woman he loved—the dead body, with the awful, staring eyes of Lydia!

He could not believe it : no, no, it was impossible. He stooped, and looked close, and put his hand upon her heart. Then he knew what deed he had done—and the soul died out of the man at that moment.

He felt it, he was conscious of the change : for the moment he no longer knew sorrow or remorse, not even a longing for the woman whom he had loved, and murdered. She was dead, and that was an end of it.   What did that white thing matter to him ?   She would be none the wiser.   It was better than to grow old—and to be preyed upon when no longer able to prey.

He stooped again and mechanically blew away the white powder that lay about her nostrils and mouth, and upon the pillow.   Then with his handkerchief he removed the faintest lingering trace.   The body showed no sign of aught save the calmest death.   The extreme blueness of the lips and of the hollows under the eyes seemed to indicate heart-disease.

There was but one other precaution to take. Once more he stooped, and blew into her nostrils : a single grain of the powder might have betrayed him, would, at any rate, arouse suspicions.   He succeeded, but his lips came in contact with those of what had been Lydia.   He shuddered, and again a wave of horror and agony overcame him. Unable to endure it longer, he turned to steal silently from the cabin, but ere he went he took one farewell glance at the woman whom he had thus terribly kissed for the last time.

Whether disturbed by his touch, or fallen so by muscular contraction, her lips now formed into a smile—but a smile of the most awful mockery. Gabriel Ford went forth knowing that he should never forget it here, nor ever hereafter, if any hereafter there were.

Then deep silence settled down upon the *Lotus* —though none knew such profound quiescence, such fathomless sleep, as Lydia Dane.

CHAPTER XII.

FELIX awoke with the thin sweet crying of the swallows close under the stern of the *Lotus*. A glance outward told him that it was a glorious morning, fresh and joyous, with a blue wind-swept sky. He fancied, however, that it was much earlier than it was, but all the more readily went, lightly clad, on deck, intending to have a sunrise swim. When he reached the deck, however, he saw that the sun had been up an hour or more, though there was no one visible save the man who represented the crew, who was far forward, and in the enjoyment of a meditative pipe.

Ere long he was in the water, and swimming vigorously against the stream. He felt light-hearted and almost joyous again, though he knew that he had the change in the weather to thank rather than actual circumstance.

As he turned and floated down-stream with the current, he noticed that neither the boat nor the small punt was alongside of the *Lotus*, but as there was no one near when he went aboard again he returned to his cabin without enquiry as to their whereabouts.

In a few minutes he was dressed and on deck once more, and hailed the "crew," which had again, pipe in mouth, made its appearance.

"Hillo, Peterson, where are the boats?"

"Mr. Ford was up early this morning, sir, and he went off in the punt; Miss Acosta went away in the boat rather less nor 'alf-an-'our before you came on deck."

"Where did they go to,—on the river, or ashore?"

"Oh, ashore, sir. Mr. Ford said as how he was goin' for a walk, but would be back in good time for breakfast; and Miss Acosta said as how she hadn't slept very well, and wanted to go for a stroll, and gather some wild-flowers. Yonder's the boat, beside the alder-stump."

"It's shallow enough for you to get over the bows and wade ashore, Peterson; so just fetch the boat, will you? I'll go and meet Miss Acosta."

A few minutes later Felix pushed off from the *Lotus*, and oared the boat ashore again. On the foot-splash he noticed a pair of small shoes and a pair of slim stockings, whereby he concluded that Sanpriel had either had to wade ashore from among the flags, or that she had feared the heavy dews among the grasses on the mainland.

He had not walked a hundred yards after disembarking ere he found that the latter surmise was correct, for then he caught sight of Sanpriel, with her dress gathered up nearly to her knees in kirtle fashion, walking slowly through the tall, dew-pearled meadow grass.

She seemed the very incarnation of summer, he thought. The sun shone all about her, making her hair glow with almost metallic lustre and her skin gleam like ivory. Over her right shoulder hung her large straw-hat, secured by broad cherry-coloured ribbons; and with both arms she upheld her dress, with its wealth of gathered campions and sweet-smelling orchises, honeysuckle and dogroses and bindweed, wild-thyme and rest-harrow, speedwell and lady's-fingers, meadow crane's-bill and yellow bedstraw, corn-cockles and scabious, harebells and marguerites, and yellow toad-flax and spearwort, and many other wild-blooms to be found in that prolific region.

As she walked bare-footed through the grass and shook the dew from the wild-rye and cow-parsley, her lover thought she might be taken for the goddess Freya. How beautiful she seemed, in her youth and grace and loveliness! her every

movement was exquisite. A coquettish breezelet
came wandering by and loosened some of the tresses
of her hair—and how they rippled and shone as
their aerial lover tossed them out and caressed
them and played with them in a manner that made
her other lover wildly envious!

Above, there was a bewildering chorus of larks, and
on the honeysuckle, dogrose, privet, bryony, and
wild-clematis sprays around the redbreasts sang
their blithe but last-o'-summer songs, while the
chaffinches piped and the blackbirds called aloud as
though midsummer days were not on the wane.

Everywhere there was nothing but joy and
freshness. In the farther meadows the cattle
lowed out of sheer content, while their fragrant
breath went up in thin whorls of steam; and
among the elms and on the low-lying lands the
rooks cawed and fluttered and wheeled and swept
as if the autumnal equinox and the fowler's gun
were impossible things, rooky legends beyond the
belief of all sensible wingsters.

"This indeed is youth—the joy of life," Felix
thought, as he stepped lightly across the dewy
thyme-set grass, and, unseen by Sanpriel, drew
close. He was almost at her side before she
turned round and saw him.

A swift blush swept across her face and a light

of surprised joy came into her eyes, and then, ere she could say a word, his arms were round her and his kisses upon her lips.

"Sanpriel, you are so beautiful that you must avoid elfin-circles—you would certainly be carried away as a fairy princess! Ah, my darling, how glad I am to meet you here! Though I fell asleep last night with the memory of your farewell kiss on my lips, I woke this morning with a dreadful fear that it was all a dream, and now—now I see you here, more beautiful than ever, I—I—but what is it, dear? You are not angry with me, are you?"

She had drawn herself up, while a look of haughty displeasure had come into her face and numbed her lover's eloquence.

"We are not alone, Mr. Dane."

Felix swung round, and stared angrily at Ford, who had suddenly stepped out from behind a huge old mid-meadow oak.

To his surprise, however, Ford seemed neither resentful nor chagrined, though it was obvious that both his companions looked upon his sudden intrusion with anything but friendly eyes.

"Good-morning, Sanpriel," and as he spoke he held out his hand in greeting. Miss Acosta, however, did not take it, but bowed coldly, and then turned her eyes riverward. He gave a momentary glance of angry astonishment, but did not attempt to force recognition.

He nodded to Felix, who stiffly acknowledged the salute, but did not speak.

"I am sorry if I am interrupting you," Ford resumed in a tone of quiet dignity and with nothing of his habitual self-assertiveness; "I came ashore for a walk, and as I was on my way back I caught sight of you two—eh—ah—gathering flowers."

Sanpriel flushed slightly, as she thought of what Gabriel must have seen and probably overheard, but she gave no sign of relenting from her attitude of contemptuous indifference.

Felix could not but feel grateful at his rival's courteous reserve, and as he could never bear resentment in face of conciliation, he changed his manner, and politely suggested that all three should now walk back together, as it would ere long be time for breakfast. Surely, he thought, Sanpriel was showing her dislike of Ford with unnecessary emphasis—unless, indeed, she had recently had good cause to make her resentful. He frowned as the idea occurred to him, but a glance at what just then took place made him feel too happy for anger against even Gabriel Ford.

As, in silence, the three had turned to go riverward, Ford had taken his place at Miss Acosta's left side ; Sanpriel, however, without ostentation, but without any effort at dissimulation, slipped from her central position and walked along to the right of Felix.

Not unwilling to render the snub less trying to his rival, he asked Ford lightly a question about which he felt really quite indifferent.

" Did you see Mrs. Dane before you left ? "

There could be no doubt about it, Felix thought, as he noticed the ghastly pallor of his companion's face, or as much of it as he could see, averted as it was—he was in ill-health, beyond question. His voice, too, so much softer than its wont, was strangely low.

" No, I did not."

Ford glanced round as he spoke, and found Sanpriel's eyes fixed upon him for a moment. Her gaze seemed to fluster him, for, with a slight access of colour and more hurried speech, he added—

" She was not up, was she, when you came ashore ? I thought she was a confirmed late-riser. Moreover, she—she—did not seem to me very well last night."

" Didn't she ? H'm, well, perhaps not," Felix admitted, as he recalled the incidents of the evening.

The rest of the walk was in silence, save when Sanpriel made some remark about the wild-flowers she loved so well, as she stooped to pick up a spray of enchanter's nightshade or millefoil, of agrimony or pungent meadow-sweet.

How absorbed and indifferent Ford seems! thought Felix, as he noticed that he made no effort at conversation, and was apparently oblivious even of Sanpriel's bewitching appearance as, bare-headed and bare-footed, she walked—a very embodiment of grace and beauty—through the sunlit dewy morning.

Having helped Sanpriel into the boat, he took the oars, and having waited till Ford sprang in as he shoved the bow off-shore, sculled swiftly toward the *Lotus.*

His gaze dwelt upon the woman he loved incessantly, but ere long he noticed an anxious look come into her eyes.

" There is my father leaning over the taffrail— but—but—he does not look well. He is so white, and seems nervous and strange : I know that look so well. I wonder if anything has gone wrong with him—perhaps he has been missing me, dear old father; wondering if I've been drowned, perhaps."

Acosta gave a solemn unsmiling response to his daughter's salute as the boat drew up alongside, and as soon as the three were on deck he asked Felix to speak with him privily for a moment.

Sanpriel watched them apprehensively, particularly when she saw her lover start and grow pale.

" My friend," Adama Acosta began, as soon as he had withdrawn from the others, " that which cometh to us all has come unto you—for there is no evasion of sore pain and sorrow for any of us. A stranger hath come hither to seek out one of us—your wife, Lydia."

In a moment Felix understood that the stranger to whom Acosta alluded was none other than Death, and that Lydia was dead.

A great fear came upon him that Death had not voluntarily come, but had been summoned—that, in a word, his wife, after what she had witnessed between Sanpriel and himself, and with the knowledge of what lay between herself and Gabriel Ford, had committed suicide.

He turned and walked slowly down the companion-ladder and into the saloon, followed by Acosta.

Stopping at Lydia's cabin-door, he looked steadfastly at his companion.

" I understand. But tell me *all;* is there anything more to tell ? "

Acosta looked surprised, but replied, " Nay, I know not ; she is gone. It must have been very sudden.   This morning, not half-an-hour ago, her maid came to me and said that she was frightened about Mrs. Dane, that she could not get any answer from her, and that the door was locked.   I called to her also, but could get no reply.   I then told the steward, and he opened it with his duplicate-key, which he had picked up from the table"——

"Yes; I left it there," Felix interrupted mechanically.

"Then the maid went in, and the next moment came out trembling and sobbing.   I entered, and saw at once what had happened.   I am something of a physician, and recognised the aspect of heart-disease.   I immediately told Roberts to send the man—Peterson is his name, I think—to the nearest village or town where a doctor could be obtained. I then relocked the room—though I was puzzled by the absence of any key in the inside—though, as I have said, the door was locked."

Felix went in alone, and closed the door behind him.   Acosta had pulled the square patch of blind across the little window, and the room was in a kind of twilight gloom; but Lydia's white face was outlined with startling distinctness.   The mocking smile had disappeared.   There was a look of great weariness upon the face, but otherwise it was calm and reposeful.

Was this his wife? he wondered: the woman with whom he had lived ten years, and who yet was scarce stranger and more far removed from him in death than she had been in life? It was pitiable. All these years, and yet to have been utter strangers to each other: to have lived with each other, to have slept side by side, to have been knit together by a hundred minor circumstances, and yet to have been wide as the poles asunder in reality. And what of all the disappointment, and new hope, and passion of jealousy? Were these things dead also? Lydia *looked* so utterly, irretrievably, irrevocably dead, that—oh! cruellest wrong of all—he could not credit her immortality. Not a wave upon the deep, not a rain-drop fallen in mid-ocean, seemed more utterly lost than she.

It was with genuine and bitter pain at his heart that he could not feel more grief for the dead woman who had been his wife; but he could not. He had no heed of Sanpriel at the moment, whatever remote consciousness lay below his concentrated thoughts; but he felt that, even if he had loved no other woman, even if he had in some degree really loved *her*, she was now so utterly dead to him that his past had died with her. If Lydia Dane was no more, neither was the old Felix Dane. He looked steadily at the white face as at that of one whom he had known in boyhood. The tears came to his eyes when the pity of it all overcame him—tears for Lydia's sake, not for his loss of her, but for her wasted years, her barren life, her sterile hopes, and cold, loveless joys. Stooping, he kissed the cold forehead, passed his hand lightly across the dull, glazed eyes, and then sat down on the low window-sofa and buried his face in his hands, as he thought—thought—thought.

Less than an hour later he was disturbed by the advent of the doctor. A few questions, a brief examination, and the latter seemed quite satisfied that syncope had been the cause of death.

When Felix went on deck again he was thankful that his guests had gone. He did not wish to see even Sanpriel—nay, he would fain have avoided her had she been on board. Even passion is chilled for a time by the breath of mortality.

Ford had left an oral message with the doctor, and Felix had a pang of sympathy with the man whose loss was really a loss, whose love had been the one cherished bloom of Lydia's life. He felt as though henceforth they might be friendly, if not friends—for he knew nothing of the fury of baffled hate and baffled hope, the cancer of an eating despair, then gnawing at the heart of Gabriel Ford.

There was a brief note from Sanpriel. In a few earnest words she said that she and her father knew he would rather be alone, and that he had their deepest sympathy. There was nothing else; no words of conventional condolence; no vain parleying with empty words.

As he sat alone that night on the deck of the *Lotus*, there came to him a great wave of regret for the life he and Lydia had led. It was not the fault of either altogether; the evil of a harsh and unnatural tyranny had ruined *their* lives, as it has ruined thousands, and will yet ruin Heaven knows how many more.

But so little was the dead woman part of him that, even in sleep, her memory—though her body lay so near him—did not haunt the chambers of his brain. When, at last, wearied with many thoughts and the dull pain that beset him, he fell into a troubled sleep, it was to dream of his strange and ominous marriage to Sanpriel in the twilit Yew-Grove at Grantley, with Adama Acosta's eyes gleaming insanely, and, behind all and through all, the monotonous boom of the sea, swelling at times in dull thunders, or crying aloud with long reverberant voice.

CHAPTER XIII.

IT would have been mockery for Felix Dane to have asserted that the month which followed the death of his wife was one of unhappiness. In no sense was it so, though the joy which he had confidently anticipated from his knowledge of Sanpriel's love for him was neither as serene nor as poignant as he had imaged forth for himself. Perhaps it was because he did not see her, and because there was an element of uncertainty in their future, even in its most roseate aspect; perhaps it was for some subtler or more complex reason.

But whatever the joy that the knowledge of her love brought to him, there was no diminution in his love for her. Every morning he thought of her with added yearning; every night she dominated more absolutely his waking and sleeping dreams. For the first week of his return to Hampstead he had not gone to Dreamthorpe; and when at last he went thither, it was to find that the Acostas were out of town, and would not be back till the late autumn.

For the most part he lived in his studio. He slept in the house, and had his breakfast there, but never entered the bedroom which had been Lydia's, nor even the drawing-room. A glance at their desolate aspect had been sufficient for him. He wished to forget Lydia, for to remember was not to know any sentimental regret, any vague longing, but to resent dull and wasted years. He blamed himself much more than her, but he did not disguise from himself the fact that she had con- sciously, as well as heedlessly, set herself against all his ideals and his loyalty to his art. She had vulgarised his life; that, he was willing to admit, might be due in part to some weakness of his own, for he had always argued that the man of genius should show his strength by holding him- self aloof from influences which he knew to be of deterioration. That they might be inevitable sig- nified little; disease, poverty, all the ills of life might be unavoidable, yet the strenuous soul would be superior to the most commonplace, the most sordid, the dreariest environment. So he argued —who had known nothing of disease or poverty. The slow wear and tear of uncongenial intimacy he *had* known—and, as he well knew, had not preserved himself intact, but had slowly deteriorated in mental and spiritual insight. Sanpriel had electrified him into a new life; it was owing to her influence that his genius was again militant, that he could look forward and not backward. When a man of genius—whatever his art be— ceases to look forward, the creative instinct in him is dead or dying—and to the true artist this is a death beside which that of the body is of little moment.

He could not recall one helpful word of Lydia's. If she had been merely unappreciative or even indifferent, it would not have mattered much; it would have made his outer life less happy, but it would not have affected his real self. But never to have uttered even the most conventional word of encouragement, never to have coldly approved anything save what was meretricious, never to have shown aught but contemptuous dislike of his worthiest efforts—*this* was to alienate her from him beyond even the redemption of death. He was not one of those natures who cast a glamour round whatever they have lost, even when formerly unvalued and perhaps despised. Neither to himself nor any one else did he pretend grief; but only to himself did he admit that Lydia had never once helped him as she had done by her death. So thus it was that he came to think less and less of his wife, and even to shun the very rooms wherewith he had so long associated her. Gradually she became but a faded memory; so little had she ever entered into his life that he never caught himself listening instinctively for the rustle of her dress or the sound of her voice. She had, for him, died the second death — that most terrible and piteous passing, where there is "no resurrection in the minds of men."

From early morning till three or four o'clock each afternoon he worked in his studio, fashioning forth his "Destiny"—a sombre and impressive figure of a woman of heroic mould, in whose regnant smile there was something ominous and terrible. Thereafter he would attend to his correspondence, and then walk the three miles or so which lay between him and his club. At the latter he read the papers and magazines, sometimes chatted with artist acquaintances, who, however, for the most part, left him alone, in the impression that the poignancy of his recent loss would still be almost unendurable—occasionally spent an hour with a friend in the smoking-room, and then, having dined, walked or drove back to Hampstead. It was not to Frognal, however, but to the

Heath itself that he drove ; and it was then that the happiest hour of the twenty-four was spent. It was his habit to walk down the lane by the side of Dreamthorpe, or stand upon the Heath beyond its gates, and imagine that he and Sanpriel were there together, that her light it was that shone from one of the rooms, that her step it was which he heard sometimes upon the gravel nigh the late-flowering laurels and ceringas. They were silent eves mostly, those July and early August vespers of his ; for even those latest songsters of summer, the white-throat, chaffinch, and green linnet, had ceased to call their music through the afterglow, and in the hazy moonlit twilight only the hawk-moth and the musk-beetle jarred the stillness with their rustling flight, or the strident locust among the wild angelica or spreading sprays of hedge-parsley. In the large and mellow affluence of the harvest-moon there was something pastoral and idyllic even on Hampstead Heath, nor was the effect ruined by the distant laughter and blent sounds from belated wayfarers or from happy couples going linked arm-in-arm and in some vague way sensitive to the charm and mystery of the August night, even when most ignorant and boorish.

One afternoon in the second week of August,

more than a month after the death of Lydia, he was standing in the garden of The Sycamores, wondering with yearning and pain at his heart when he should hear from Sanpriel. He had written, but had received no answer, and he feared that she and her father might not be at Forest Manor at all, but perhaps abroad. He had been watching a long narrow exodus of swifts, the last lingerers of their kindred, and was noting the uneasiness among the house-martins, which had begun to congregate and indulge in that tumultuous hesitancy which for some weeks precedes departure, when he caught sight of the postman, whom he at once and eagerly intercepted.

There was but one letter for him, and though it bore the Grantley postmark, was not in Sanpriel's writing. With anxious eyes he glanced through its contents, relieved to find that the Acostas were at Forest Manor, and that at last, at last, he should soon see his soul's beloved.

"Dear Mr. Dane,"—it ran,—"I am sure that you will keep your promise to us, and come and spend some weeks here. The pleasure will be on our side mostly, for we can offer you but dull entertainment, though, as I hear that you want both change and rest, perhaps that is an inducement rather than the reverse. We are almost alone, and you can be as quiet as you like. My husband, I regret to say, is laid up with rheumatic gout, and is confined to his room, but Miss Acosta and Gabriel Ford are here, and both will, I am sure, heartily welcome you. I must tell you, however, what you will be very sorry to hear, that poor Adama Acosta's head-trouble has greatly increased—in fact, he is now dependent upon others. He has no longer any frenzied attacks ; the disease shows itself in strange, brooding fancies and in complete loss of memory. He does not recollect at noon what he said or saw at breakfast, and he does not even seem to recognise any one with the exception of Sanpriel. The doctors say there is no possibility of recovery. It is very sad. I am so thankful for the latter's sake that Gabriel Ford is here. He is evidently in love with her, and in the circumstances she could hardly do better. And this brings me to another reason for your coming, dear Mr. Dane ; I want you to lend me your aid in bringing these two young people together, but, first, to act as peacemaker. I like Sanpriel, but she is very aggravating sometimes with her sentimental notions, and is quite foolishly prejudiced against Gabriel. Would you believe it—she at present, for some inscrutable reason, actually refuses to be left alone with him, and will only answer his remarks at table in monosyllables.   It is all mere contrariness, of course—but *very stupid.* I told her, only this morning, that G. F. would cer- tainly take his departure in a huff, and not give her another chance, and she *positively* looked radiant ! So, you see, you are urgently required by every one !   Do write by return and say that we may expect you at once.——Most sincerely yours,

OLIVIA CRANE."

So unutterably thankful was he at the prospect of again seeing Sanpriel, of living in the same house with her, of having daily companionship with her again, that he could not dally with even the appearance of hesitancy.

With a look so buoyant and vigorous, so joyous indeed, that he scandalised the maiden ladies who lived in the opposite house in Hurst Road, he walked to the post-office at Swiss Cottage and despatched a telegram to Lady Crane, to the effect that he should arrive at Grantley on the following after- noon.   Then he walked homeward again, and set to work with almost boyish eagerness to "put things to rights" ere what he hoped would be a long holiday.   The evening was spent in de- stroying old letters, sending cheques for outstand-

s

ing accounts, and so forth. Before he locked up his studio, however, he took a long farewell look at his unfinished " Destiny."

"She would do as she stands," he muttered. " By Jove! I've never done anything like that before. It almost frightens me. She sees everything, and is scornful of our fretful dreams and plans and vain prayers. That look she has— what unutterable things it seems to convey! I wonder what she sees for *me*,—for *us ?* "

As he spoke he walked close up to the statue and looked into the sombre face. Was it some strange accident of his touch, or but the vagary of his excited fancy, that in the relentless, inscrutable features there was a grandiose reflection of those of Lydia? He shuddered, looked at the sculptured face with a sensation akin to fear, and turned abruptly away.

But when, next morning, he found himself in the " Flying Scotsman " he forgot all about his carven " Destiny." Lydia's impassive indifference might brood upon the latter's face; *his* Destiny, not that fashioned of his hands, was brighter than the rainbow, was engirt with a light of joy such as never was upon sea or land.

As the train whirled across the sun-swept flats of Cambridge and Lincoln, his spirits rose higher and higher. He was going to Sanpriel—that was enough; for it meant so much—new hope, new energy, new life. All his past life, all wherewith Sanpriel had nothing to do, fell away from him. In its unreality it became not unpleasant to look upon, as a barren and desolate tract will seem fair when surveyed from the heights that are soon to shut it off for ever.

He had never felt so serenely hopeful before. For the first time he knew what it was to be an autocrat over circumstances. "*We*, what may we not do together?" and he smiled triumphantly as the thought flashed upon him.

At York he changed his train, and it was well on in the afternoon before he reached Grantley. The dogcart was waiting for him, but the groom was a stranger, and seemed to have but newly gone into service at Forest Manor; at any rate Felix gained but little information from him, save that Sir Arthur was still confined to his bed.

How sweet and fresh the air was, with its crispness and faint odour of brine, after the exhausted atmosphere of London! What a delight the hedges wherein the bryony berries ripened in the sun, and the honeysuckle-copses where the goldfinch sang his last thrilling summer-notes! How beautiful the fluttering of the copper butterflies among the teasels and the autumnal gentians, and the blue day-moths flickering among the wild-barley! Every object appealed to him; scarce a dandelion or dusty tansy escaped his notice. In happiness the mind becomes so alert that it observes the minutest details—not with the same unreasoning accuracy or intensity as in great grief, but with a blithe acceptation of *every* living thing.

When Grantley Rise was surmounted, and he saw again the azure stretch of ocean, heard again the deep brooding voice which had so often haunted his dreams, a sense of infinite peace and rest came upon him. Behind, the dead Lydia, and the dead past; yonder, Sanpriel, and life, and the rainbow-future.

As he passed the Yew-Grove where, all unwitting of his act, Adama Acosta had married his daughter to an alien, he looked eagerly upward, but could only descry the seared trunks of the nearer trees and the thick mass of black-green foliage.

When the dogcart drew up at the Manor there was no one visible on the stone-terrace nor at the door, save Norgate, as suavely silent as of yore.

"Yes, sir, they're all in," that individual replied in answer to a question, "except Mr. Ford, who has ridden to Fenwick to attend to some business for Sir Arthur. Lady Crane is engaged for a few minutes with Mr. Carter, the Rector, in the library, but she told me to tell you that Miss Acosta is in the drawing-room, and will give you a cup of tea."

Felix silently thanked the gods for their mercies, and made haste towards the drawing-room, fearful lest Lady Crane and the Rector might have transacted their business before he could see Sanpriel alone.

The moment he entered the room he saw nothing but Sanpriel—a tall, white figure, silent, motionless.

She was clad in soft, white, clinging stuff, where the only colour was afforded by the sash of saffron gauze-silk round her waist and falling down the front of her dress, and by the cluster of yellow tea-roses amid the little cloud of lace at her neck.

She advanced a step or two with outstretched hands, and with an eager look in her eyes that almost immediately gave way to one of longing and deep love and uttermost welcome.

" Sanpriel !"

" Felix !"

Each spake but the name of the other, yet no words could have more amply conveyed their joy. He took her hands in his and drew her towards him, and pressed upon her lips a long lingering kiss.

"My darling, my darling, it is joy unspeakable to me to see you again. Tell me that you still love me, that our separation has wrought no change."

"I *do* love you, Felix; I am no weather-vane, to be idly blown this way and that," was the grave reply, so grave in tone that her lover instinctively looked into her eyes to see what possible reserve lay hidden there as yet unexpressed.

"I have longed for you, dear, night and day. Not an evening has passed that I have not haunted Dreamthorpe like a ghost—and, indeed, I often felt like one, for nothing seemed to be real where you were not present. As I told you when I wrote to you "———

"Wrote to me? I never received any letter from you. A week ago *I* wrote to *you*—but it was not in answer to any letter of yours."

"What was it about, Sanpriel?" Felix asked eagerly, still holding and caressing her hand. "I never had·any word from you since—since—you left the *Lotus.*"

"Then there has been treachery somewhere," and an angry light came into her eyes as she spoke; but the next moment, as she looked into those of her lover and saw the very passion of joy that lived therein, she flushed with a happy smile, leant forward and kissed him, and whispered, "It was but a single word, dear; I did not even address you or sign my name. All I wrote was '*Come!*' That was more than a week ago, and you never answered it. Then I feared—well, I know not what I feared; but now our twilight has waned, Felix, and even if the new day do not bring us what our hearts crave, at least we "——

"Sanpriel, dearest, why should it not? Why should you fear that it "——

"Hush! sit down; here is Lady Crane coming," and almost as she spoke the hostess entered, with Mr. Carter following close behind.

Lady Crane was perhaps surprised to find Felix looking so unlike the ordinary widower, with an expression, indeed, of far greater content and even happiness than he had worn during his last stay at Forest Manor; and as for Mr. Carter, he looked at the new visitor with a stare of dignified reproof; but all the same it was a relief to her to have a cheerful guest, and she very wisely concluded that Dane had accepted the inevitable with the good grace characteristic of well-bred people.

Consequently he rose greatly in her estimation, and she congratulated herself on his advent.

While he was telling her something about his work, in response to a polite but uninterested question, Sanpriel rose and left the room—not to appear again till dinner-time, Lady Crane remarked, as she had gone to sit with her father and Sir Arthur.

"A melancholy couple for a young girl, Mr. Dane—the one ill with gouty rheumatism, the other silent and brooding, and heedless of everything and every one save his daughter. But you will cheer her up, I know; I declare, she seemed to me like a different girl when she left the room just now—that languor of body and manner of which I spoke to you, Mr. Carter, seems to have vanished."

Felix felt a little uncomfortable, particularly as the Rector's glassy stare was fixed upon him in a curiously scrutinising way, but he managed to divert the conversation, and, with an adaptability which amused him, to broach and discuss subjects of interest to Mr. Carter and his hostess. By the time that the dressing-gong sounded he had, indeed, quite won over the pompous but worthy Rector, who now looked upon him as a young man of parts, though too self-opinionated and sometimes heedless of the convictions of older and wiser people than himself—in other words, of James Fotheringham Carter, Rector of Grantley and Fenwick-Upper.

When he returned to the drawing-room he found that Gabriel Ford had joined Lady Crane and Mr. Carter. Much as he disliked the former, and strong as were his suspicions that it was he who was responsible for the latest miscarriage of the letters, he could not but be sensible of the curious change that had come over Ford's manner towards himself. He was not apologetic, not even noticeably conciliatory, but he seemed anxious to avoid any possible cause of friction, and, at any rate in public, to disguise his smouldering resentment. He also avoided the direct meeting of his gaze—or so it seemed to Felix—but why or wherefore, if not imaginary, was of course inexplicable.

At dinner Sanpriel was quiet and strangely reticent. Although the cluster of dark crimson roses which she wore against the breast of her primrose silk dress threw a little colour into her face, it yet was too pale for perfect health, and Felix's heart yearned over her with all the passionate tenderness of love.

It was evident to all that Ford was making special efforts to attract Miss Acosta's attention, if not her interest, but without success. Once he addressed her by name, her own name, and she did not appear to hear him; he repeated his question to "Miss Acosta," and then she gravely looked at him, and coldly replied that she did not know.

This was during the dessert, and Lady Crane seemed perturbed that her well-meant efforts were of so little avail. Suddenly an idea occurred to her.

"Mr. Dane, I remember how fond you are of the sea. Will you take these two silly young people a walk?"

"I do not feel inclined to go out to-night, Lady Crane," Sanpriel somewhat hurriedly interrupted. "I am tired and sleepy, and I want to sit with my father for a while."

"Now that's just what you ought not to do, my dear; sitting and brooding is the very worst thing for you. You need not go far—go to the Yew-Grove, for instance. Have you been there yet, Mr. Dane—I mean by night?"

"Yes, I have. But I shall be only too glad to go again if Miss Acosta will come."

A little colour had come into Sanpriel's face at Lady Crane's question, but it immediately ebbed as she was conscious of Ford's scrutinising gaze.

Knowing from experience that argument with

her hostess was useless, she agreed to the proposal, and a little later left the room to obtain a shawl as a protection against the dew, and to reassure her father about her absence.

When she returned the two young men rose and went out with her, both, though for different reasons, thankful that the long dinner was at an end.

The moon was in crescent, and the stars bright and close-set; a soft wind stirred the branches of the trees, and kept up a continuous sussurrus among the foliage, and in the undergrowth and tall grasses. The odours from the shore were pungent and delicious, and the heavy booming of ocean, while as insistent as of yore, struck so freshly and sharply upon the ear that its melancholy, the habitual note of warning that the sea never wholly loses, was as though in abeyance.

It was like a dream to Felix to be in the Yew-Grove once more. If only he could be there alone with Sanpriel, he thought longingly, or even with Adama Acosta for company! Ford spoke little, but he acted, as he knew he acted, as a deterrent to their happiness, to their conversation even.

It was a joy, however, to Felix to know that Sanpriel must inevitably be also thinking of what had happened there in the sweet spring night so memorable to them both—and once, stooping in the yew-made gloom to avoid a broken branch, he caught her hand for a moment's loving pressure, and felt her caressing response. This was enough to make even the memory of the bygone night of May a mere dream as compared with the happy reality. But her plea of weariness had been no subterfuge; tired she unmistakably was, and sorry though he was to lose her, it was Felix himself who proposed a return to the house.

She said good-night as soon as they had entered the drawing-room. She had not trusted herself to do more than glance for a moment at Felix as she took his hand, but in it there was enough for him to build many a fair dream-palace upon throughout the coming hours of absence.

As she entered the corridor wherefrom her own and Mr. Acosta's room opened off she heard a step behind her. The next moment she regretted that she had looked round, for Ford stood by her side, and she could see by his expression that he had followed her with intent, for in his pale face and rigid features she read his determination to have his say, whatsoever that might be.

" Sanpriel."

" I have told you that I am Miss Acosta to you —now and always. What do you mean by following me ? I can have nothing to say to you. Good-night."

" Stop, San—Miss Acosta. I have something to say to *you.* You love Felix Dane. Hush ! you need not protest or wax indignant. I am not blind, and I can see what is so very obvious. Not that it is any new thing ; he loved you, and you loved him, during his wife's lifetime."

She resented the sneer, but took no outward notice of it. " Have you anything else to say ? You are tiresome as well as impertinent, and . I do not choose to stand here talking to *you.*"

" Miss Acosta, I wish to ask you a question— a question to which I have a right to demand an answer : What is the reason of your extreme resentment against me ? What have I done, except to dare to love you, that is so unforgivable in your eyes ? "

As his question was unanswered save by a scornful glance, he resumed :

" I know that you consider I acted treacherously with one or more letters which you wrote to Dane, or he wrote to you—I forget which ; but all that I can say is, your suspicions are absolutely unfounded."

" I do not believe you ; and in your heart of hearts you know that I do not believe you. But

I have another reason which even you, sophist though you be, cannot explain away. You seem to forget that you recently dared to hint a shameless thing to me——to hint that the death of Lydia Dane was no accident, but the act of her husband. You shrank under my scorn at the time, and I saw the lie furtively lurking in your face, like an assassin in the twilight, and that lie it is that must for ever stand between you and me, Gabriel Ford—— yea, though we two were left alone, and my most passionate hopes, my very soul's salvation, depended upon my forgetfulness of it. It is unforgetable—— for ever unforgetable, for ever unforgivable."

There was a silence of a few moments, and then Ford, in a low, sneering tone, full of repressed malice, rage, and baffled passion, spoke again.

"What if it were no lie at all, Miss Sanpriel Acosta? What if I could prove that Mrs. Dane did not die a natural death, but was—*murdered?* Ay, and that the murderer was her husband?"

Sanpriel smiled in scorn, but with so strange an expression that he hesitated for a moment before he went on.

"There is ample circumstantial evidence : Dane's dislike of his wife, his love for you, your presence on the house-boat, Lydia's jealousy, his eagerness for freedom from her yoke! But there is further evidence. Some time ago Dane was in my rooms in my absence, and there he possessed himself of a certain poison of which I had told him when speaking of my chemical experiments. I could prove that he took some away with him."

There was no answer, and he then asked angrily if she had naught to say.

"You won't answer? Well, shall I tell you what I am going to do? I shall go back to London to-morrow, and give such information in the proper quarters as will involve the exhumation of Lydia Dane's body, and then your lover will be arrested, and, on my evidence to back the logic of facts and probabilities, he shall hang—and then there will be an end to all his fine dreams, and you will have the blood of a second victim upon your head! Do you understand? Well, there is but one way in which to save *him:* will you take it?"

"No."

"By God! you are obstinate to the last. Well, so be it. I shall denounce Felix Dane."

Sanpriel took a step forward, till her hand reached one of the corridor-bells. Then she stood for a few moments with such a look of contemptuous loathing that the man before her was unable to return her steadfast gaze.

"No," she said at last, slowly and impressively,

" no, you will not denounce any one, for you, *you,* Gabriel Ford, are the murderer of Mrs. Dane ! "

He started and looked apprehensively around, and then in a hoarse voice answered her accusation.

" You speak at random.   Beware what folly you talk.   How dare you say such a thing ? "

Suddenly she came forward, fearless now, for she knew she had entrapped him.   Her words were whispered rather than spoken aloud, but they were as trumpets of shame in the ears of the guilty man who heard them.

" Because, Gabriel Ford, I saw you stealthily leave Lydia Dane's cabin in the early morning, but while yet dark.   I did not know at the time that you were a murderer, but I know it now—I knew it the day you tried to cast the foul suspicion on another."

Ford seemed too utterly taken aback to speak, and his accuser did not spare him.

" I could not sleep, and so I left my cabin and sat beside my father, holding his hand till his headache left him and he slept.   Then I rose to go back to my own room.   It was then that I caught sight of a dark figure passing through the outer door and stealing into Mrs. Dane's cabin.   I waited, not knowing what to do.   I thought that it might perchance be Mr. Dane, returned to seek for something he had left in the room he had by some strange chance exchanged that night. But at last the moonlight came in a narrow stream into the cabin, and ere long I saw you come forth, pale and trembling like the assassin you were. It was not till we regained the *Lotus* after our walk at sunrise that I knew what you were."

Then, before he could speak or make a gesture, she stepped back and rang the bell and almost simultaneously entered her room, the bolt of which shot to, so that even if he had attempted to follow her he would have failed.

But Ford had no thought of any such attempt. He knew that he had lost the game whatever happened; henceforth Sanpriel, as well as Lydia, was dead to him. The passion of revenge might yet be his, but all he was conscious of was a dull and ruthless sense of utter and ignominious failure.

CHAPTER XV.

ALL next day Adama Acosta was so unwell that his daughter did not make her appearance, and morning, noon, and afternoon had but one interesting episode for Felix—the departure of Ford.

He did not know of the latter's intention till, having accidentally emerged from the Labyrinth just as the trap drew up at the terrace-steps, he encountered the traveller.

" I see you have your baggage with you, Mr. Ford ?   Are you going back to London ? "

" Yes, I am.   You will hear from me shortly, no doubt," Ford replied, meaningly, and with studied insolence of demeanour.   " I shall be back to-morrow or next day, at latest."   Then, suddenly leaning from the front-seat, as the coachman gave the reins a shake, he asked sneeringly if Felix were well acquainted with proverbs.

" For if you are, I should like you to ponder over one which bids you make hay while the sun shines.   It seems to me that the sun is—eh—ah

—about to set. Good-bye, Felix Dane : I don't think we shall ever forget each other."

"Is the man mad, or what ?" muttered Felix angrily, as he stared after the departing dogcart, and wondered what significance lay behind Ford's enigmatic farewell. "He is fond of Parthian shots; the only thing is, they fall rather wide of the mark. However, he's gone, and that's good news."

To his relief, Lady Crane did not associate him, or even Sanpriel, with Ford's departure; for one thing, she evidently believed the latter's assurance that he would shortly return.

Sanpriel did not appear at dinner, but she came in at dessert, and accompanied Lady Crane to the drawing-room, whither Felix followed with the least permissible loss of time.

For some time he could get no chance of unheard speech with her, but at last an opportunity occurred.

"My dear, do sing that song to me about Love. I'm sure Mr. Dane would like to hear it also : she has been singing nothing else, Mr. Dane, ever since she came here this time."

Sanpriel seemed unwontedly shy of singing, but after she had hesitatingly reminded her companion, who had joined his entreaties to those of Lady

Crane, that it was associated with the last night on board the *Lotus*—for a fragment of the song had floated to them from one of the rowers in a boat—and intuitively perceived that his whole association was with *her*, she yielded.

The music to which it was set had a peculiar lilt in it, but the passion wherewith the singer electrified it was almost all her own. Her lover listened entranced, for he knew that she was singing to him :—

> *Love in my heart : oh, heart of me, heart of me !*
> *Love is my tyrant, Love is supreme.*
> *What if he passeth, oh, heart of me, heart of me !*
> *Love is a phantom, and Life is a dream !*
>
> *What if he changeth, oh, heart of me, heart of me !*
> *Oh, can the waters be void of the wind ?*
> *What if he wendeth afar and apart from me,*
> *What if he leave me to perish behind ?*
>
> *What if he passeth, oh, heart of me, heart of me !*
> *A flame i' the dusk, a breath of Desire ?*
> *Nay, my sweet Love is the heart and the soul of me,*
> *And I am the innermost heart of his fire !*
>
> *Love in my heart : oh, heart of me, heart of me !*
> *Love is my tyrant, Love is supreme.*
> *What if he passeth, oh, heart of me, heart of me !*
> *Love is a phantom, and Life is a dream !*

Felix could not speak when the last note died

away, for as he stood beside the singer he saw the rich colour in her face and could hear the quickened breath, and though her eyes did not look up at his, he knew that in them there was the light of a serene and wondrous joy.

Lady Crane drowsily muttered her approval, and still more drowsily begged that the song might be repeated. Sanpriel, however, sang something else, and before it was finished Felix had the satisfaction of assurance that his hostess was deaf to what was going on around her.

"Sanpriel," he whispered, as, having finished her song, she played idly a fragmentary air, "will you meet me in the Yew-Grove a little later on? I have much to say to you—and the night is so glorious that you will take no harm."

"I will try, but Lady Crane likes to know that the house is shut up before she goes to bed. You go now, and I shall follow shortly if I can."

Felix slipped quietly from the room, and ere long was pacing among the yews, eagerly hoping that nothing might prevent the interview. He was so wrought to excitement that he felt as though some crucial moment were approaching— his happiness, he knew, lay in perilous balance, and a word from Sanpriel, for all that had passed, might dash it to the ground.

The night was absolutely still, save at rare intervals when the strident, rasping cry of the corncrake came from the wheat-fields and meadows beyond the avenue. Not a breath stirred in the branches, not a motion of air crept along the grass or among the tufts of fennel and gipsy-wort. Although the moon was in ample crescent, her light was intercepted by a thin fibrous veil of cloud, through which here and there a star glimmered, white and dewy, but without lustre. In the open there was sufficient light for the blurred shadows of trees and shrubs to be seen, but in the Yew-Grove the obscurity was so deep that one might have moved from tree to tree and been invisible.

A faint rustling sound was the first intimation that Felix had of Sanpriel's advent. He had expected her by the avenue, and had strained his ears to hearken to her step on the gravel ; but she had come along the grass from the end of the terrace.

" Sanpriel ! "

She heard the low passionate vibration of his voice before she descried the outline of his figure, and with a quick gesture came towards him, and the next moment was in his arms, with her head upon his breast and his kisses raining down upon her face.

"My darling, my darling—I feared you might not be able to come to me. Sanpriel, my dearest, I have so longed for you, so wearied for you, and I feared that we were never to be left alone here."

"I came because you asked me, Felix dear, but I was going to have sought you to-night at any rate—I had thought of the library, but this is better every way. Felix, how greatly do you love me?"

"How greatly do I love you, my darling? Why do you ask me? You cannot doubt me? I love you, Sanpriel, in all truth, better than life itself: I love you better than my art, than my inmost dream, than my furthermost hope! I would barter my immortality for your love here. I love you beyond words, beyond dream, beyond conjecture! You are my life, my heart, my soul! Oh! my darling, my darling, do you not know that you are *everything* to me? I never knew love till I saw you, and a strong man can love but once as I love you. I cannot tell you what you are to me, but can only utter over and over again what I have said. Love has no range of eloquence, dearest; it can but repeat the beautiful, sacred old commonplaces. If

I loved you less I could protest more variously —but, Sanpriel, *I love you,* and more than that I cannot say, for with me that means everything ! "

She too trembled with the excess of his emotion, and as he kissed her again in passionate protest, she clung to him for a moment with a sob in her throat.

" I know you love me, Felix—I know *how* you love me, for it is as I love *you.*   But—but—is your love so great that it will *understand ?* "

" What do you mean, dear ?   Tell me what is troubling you, for I feel that there is some trouble here in this loving, throbbing heart."

" Felix, you know what is the doom upon me as one of my race if I should marry you, a Christian, a Gentile ? "

" Yes—yes—I know.   But "——

" And you know what it means ?   That I should not only be excommunicated by the Rabbis, but banned by my people, and cursed as a traitor and renegade by those whom it has been my lifelong hope and ambition to serve ?   That I should be as an outcast ; but worse than any poor sinful outcast, for a woman may sink to depths of iniquity and yet be faithful to her people and reverent of Jehovah— but I, a renegade, an apostate, a traitor, a setter at naught of the Thorah, I should be accursed, and my name and family be brought to shame."

"But love—our love—Sanpriel," Felix stammered, while a great fear came into his heart, and his voice grew strained and hoarse.

"Do you set our personal love, then, above everything—above aspiration and hope and long, glorious effort? Am I to forfeit all that I have done, all that I and my father have helped to forward, so that my life may have its crown of joy—so that, even, *your* life may be made beautiful and strenuous in noble work?"

"God forgive me, Sanpriel, I am so weak. I dare not—I *cannot* give up my love—my hope. You are everything to me—religion, faith, work, aspiration, hope! If you cannot listen to me, let me go hence—but do not ask me to do what is impossible. I am weaker than you—a man always *is* weaker than a woman in divine unselfishness—and I cannot, I cannot forfeit my so sweet inheritance. Oh, Sanpriel! you love me—will you not sacrifice something for me? I know how infinitely greater yours must be than ever mine, at any time, could by any possibility have been or be—but, as God is my witness, there is nothing that I would not give up for you. Sanpriel, tell me if it be possible for me to become a Jew, if"——

"Hush! you wrong Love when you urge such a plea. Love that demands surrender of honour is but the poor piteous ghost of Love's very self. No—but, my darling, there is one way"——

With an eager cry he leant forward and strove through the gloom to see the secret of her eyes, but too overwrought was he by wild fear and wilder hope to do aught than listen tremblingly for what her next words would disclose.

"There is one way—a way of sacrifice too, but one wherein I alone shall suffer, so that it is of little import. Felix, if I marry you I shall have committed the inexcusable sin, the unforgivable treachery, and I shall have no part or lot in Israel, but be a stumbling-block and a curse where I had been a help and a hope. But—but—if I become yours none the less, and go forth with you, and live with you—voluntarily, openly, heedless of censure just or unjust—I should still be reprobated and banned, but I should not be cast out of Israel, I should not be excommunicated from my faith, I should still be allowed to work for the redemption of my people, for I should still be a daughter of Israel, though as one fallen and disgraced! Felix, Felix, do you understand? Can your love accept me thus—for thus only can our lives be wedded together?"

There was a pause of silence so deep after her passionate outcry had throbbed upon her lover's ears, so deep, so terrible — with the ominous pulse of the sea vibrating through it—that a sickening dread came upon her that the gulf she had feared had indeed opened and swallowed up the fair and beautiful love which had united them.

But Felix was tortured by no conflict of judgment, was distracted by no considerations of right or wrong, weal or ill, compromise or inexpediency; his whole soul was filled with reverent love and wonder at the nobility of the woman whom he loved. He knew well what a sacrifice she was willing to make for his sake, and never before had he realised what a flawless and divine thing is the absolutely pure and unselfish love of woman. Yet, great as the sacrifice was, he would have been the mere fool of a shallow convention if he had hesitated for a moment to accept it. Love does not only demand unqualified surrender; it imperiously claims an all-unstinted acceptance.

At last he spoke, but though scarcely above a whisper, and though no direct answer to her pleading, his words were the sweetest to Sanpriel she had yet heard from his lips—sweeter than love's first avowal, for then the conqueror had but knocked at the gates of gold ; now, irresistible and triumphant, he had entered in.

" I am not worthy of you, Sanpriel."

That was all, but it was sufficient. She nestled up close to him, and touched him with caressing hands, and kissed his down-turned face, and whispered again and again that she loved him, oh ! beyond words, beyond thought of his.

Softly through the night, still as a dream, but fragrant with earth-odours, sweet and poignant, stole the faint wind, just arisen from his sleep among the pine-boughs in the far woodlands. There was the innumerous rustling of green leaves beneath his light step, the susurrus of the fanning of his wing as he rose upward through the dewy glooms, unlit now of moon or star, save on the extreme horizon, where the pale fire of Jupiter shone without scintillation.

And loudly, imperiously, clamorously, the sea's voice called beyond the darkness of the land, now with a hoarse surf-like whisper, now with thunderous resonance, and anon with a heavy booming,—deep, mysterious, awful.

CHAPTER XVI.

—Edgar Allan Poe.

ALL next day the atmosphere grew denser and heavier. Its burning breath shrivelled the more delicate flowers, even where they drooped in the shade. Through the air, which palpitated like the blast of a furnace, nothing passed save the yellow wasps, radiating the heat, nothing broke the painful hush save the fierce drone of a hornet, or the loud, monotonous, metallic hum of the bronze-winged beetle. From the forest not an eddy of wind wandered, and the sea, though audible, had a stifled brooding sound, which made the silence of the land doubly silent.

Throughout the morning and forenoon Felix had roamed restlessly from room to room, in and out of the Labyrinth, along the terrace, down the avenue to the Yew-Grove, but always alone. Sanpriel had sent word at breakfast that she was suffering from headache, and Lady Crane had, long ere lunch, succumbed to the enervating influences of the day. In ordinary circumstances he would have been the first to have suffered, for he was exceptionally sensitive to atmospheric states, but with his heart all aglow with the delirium of passion, with his utmost being quick with an electric joy and elation such as, but a few months earlier, he had but vaguely dreamt of as possible, he could not remain quiescent. Ah, the joy of the past night! He could scarce trust himself to dwell upon his happiness, he so feared oblivion of aught save his love for Sanpriel. For her sake he must needs be on his guard, he knew, but at times it seemed impossible to him that upon every leaf was not writ his secret, that upon every wave of air was not borne the joyous rumour of it.

Towards the late afternoon the atmosphere grew somewhat cooler, but otherwise no whit less oppressive. The cloudy gloom darkened towards the eastward, but overhead and elsewhere it spread itself into one vast brazen pall.

Felix was standing by the bow-window of the library, thinking that he should go down to the dunes and watch the purple and green discolourations of the waters and the swift change when the imminent storm came, unless, indeed, it should brood itself away and come to nought, when suddenly he caught sight of Sanpriel as she crossed the avenue and entered among the yews.

She had recovered and had gone to meet him, whom, doubtless, she had seen from her window a short time before—for he had last come from the Yew-Grove—so he thought, with a thrill of joy. In a few moments he had leapt across the terrace and was in swift pursuit.

Just as he reached the yews he caught sight of her again, standing hesitatingly, as though uncertain whether to proceed or not.   Once she looked back, but did not see him as he stood close to the trunk of one of the sombre old trees, and then went on till she reached the skirt of the forest, which she entered and almost immediately became lost to view.   He might have called, but the sweet whim of dallying with his delight made him keep silent and follow swiftly after.   It is Whim that is the soul of Destiny—the irresponsible, heedless, fantastic vagary of Fate that blows into nothingness the gossamer of human circumstance and human plan.

He came up with her at last where the forest broke stragglingly towards the sand-dunes.   She heard his step when close upon her, and looked round, and then, with a radiant smile, came towards him with outstretched hands.

She had gathered a great cluster of poppies, but these she had thrown away as she advanced. Poor love is so superstitious, so swayed by omens fortunate and malign, that Felix was not foolish beyond the wont of lovers in his acceptation of the circumstance as of happy augury. Ever since he had seen her portrait in Ford's studio he had associated these blood-red poppies with her tragic family history. By that voluntary and instinctive act of hers, she, as it were, threw away all her past—and now gave herself up to him, and their new future, unregretfully, absolutely.

They felt so alone there in the forest stillness, so secret from all prying eyes, so remote from word or glance which would conflict with their great joy, that they cared not whither they wandered, nor how time fleeted the golden moments by. They loved, and were together, and alone; their heaven was about them, they, the Adam and Eve of the sole paradise which is vouchsafed to us—the sweet, radiant, wondrous Garden of To-day, that lies amidst the abysses of the soundless and viewless Dark.

But after a while, hand in hand, too happy almost for words however low and tender, they wandered onwards till they passed into the shadow of a vast oak—the outpost, the farthest sentinel, the first herald of the sea-wind to the forest beyond. There was nothing shoreward but a sloping dune, sparsely beset with long dry grass and yellow horn-poppies, and then, close by at full tide, the sea itself. The tide, however, had not been long upon the flow, and so the surf had not yet reached, would not for some time reach, the lower slope of the dune.

The lovers sat down in a mossy place engirt with far-spreading gnarled roots, glad to be still, glad to rest there together in the overwhelming happiness which had come upon them. It was of the future—that happy, golden-hued, rainbow-tinted future which seemed so assured—that each dreamed, sitting there hand clasped in hand.

The inky phalanx of cloud in the south-east had, with a motion so stealthy that it seemed motionless, crept landward, and now impended its vast overshadowing bulk far inland. Furtive flashings of light played upon the black, bulging hollows of its front, and a strange lurid light as of burnished brass widened along its bronze-hued bases. Casual gusts of a cold wind ruffled the seas, whereon a heavy swell rounded and lapsed, and the grasses shivered even when no current of air waylaid them. A few fallen leaves danced and circled fantastically, but still there was no sound save the rising moan of the sea and the thin, shrewd, crying of the wind a league waveward, like a far-off multitude of scythes.

They were now oblivious of storm or calm. In their own hearts was a passion greater than the one, deeper than the other.

"How beautiful it is, Felix, that future which lies before us!" Sanpriel whispered at last, and turned and looked at him with eyes so radiant that his heart leapt within him.

"Ah, my darling, yes! We 'children of To-morrow' have suffered and must still suffer, but what joy is ours! Oh, Sanpriel! you do not know what your love is to me. My powers have intensified tenfold: I shall achieve what no modern has yet accomplished—I feel it—I know it—in every fibre of my being! And you—you—my heart's delight—you, too, shall do nobler work than you could otherwise have done; you, too, shall sing away the pain and inspire afresh the flagging spirit of our fellows."

"Oh, it is all so beautiful, so wonderful! Can Life indeed give us such boon—Love, that is the touchstone of all miracles, can it indeed reward us thus marvellously?"

Louder and louder came the moan of the sea;

nearer and nearer the insistent crying of the wind; darker the gloom overhead. But still they heard not nor saw.

Suddenly both rose, as by a simultaneous instinct. His eyes had a strained passionate look in them, and hers darkened and then fell beneath their yearning gaze.

"Sanpriel"—and his voice was but a whisper, low, tremulous, but potent with a magic irresistible —"this is our wedding-day! Now are we man and wife. My darling! My darling!"

Louder still the moan of the sea, and the wind now was upon the margins of the land, and overhead there was a savage, soundless, rending apart and inward-rushing of livid, purpureally illumined masses of thunderous cloud.

But in a rapture that penetrated, that passed forth and engirt them as with a halo of consuming fire, the lovers were clasped in each other's arms, lips pressed against lips, heart beating wildly against heart, soul merged with soul in a passion of longing and joy that wrought them so that they were as one body and one soul.

Then it seemed as if the heavens split and swept apart. There was one vast, deafening, terror of sound, and simultaneously a sword of flame came forth, a blinding, scorching stream of white fire. A frightful crash followed, and the great oak fell all stricken and rent—the toil and glory of centuries brought low in a single moment.

And but a few feet away lay two figures, so closely knit that they seemed as one—scorched, devoured of flame, stricken black, terrible, irrecognisable, by the sword of the lightning.

And the roar of the sea drowned its inarticulate moan; and the wind shrieked as it swept with flying foam into the forest; and overhead the frightful howling and blasting of the thunder was as that of some mad creature of the Abyss let loose upon the world.

EPILOGUE.

Prolonged as was the tempest, it at the last expended its violence with strange suddenness. Ere nightfall the incessant, close-following thunders had passed away, and the crescent-moon hung in a cloudless waste of far-reaching, star-sprinkled, purple-black sky. But still the seas surged and toiled under the fierce tyranny of the wind, and all the woodlands, till far inland, groaned beneath its might.

Through the forest a lonely white-haired man

aimlessly wandered, sometimes stopping and listening intently, as though in expectancy of some voice that echoed not, sometimes playing fitfully upon the violin which he carried with the loving heed of a mother for her first-born, sometimes staring eagerly to right and left, and starting as his vision fashioned forth some wind-swayed birch into the figure of his Sanpriel, flying towards him on swift and gladsome feet.

To the tired, benumbed brain of Adama Acosta no sorrow or grief could now enter. He was happy if he had his violin in his hands and Sanpriel by his side, and he was vaguely distressed and distraught when the latter was absent; but beyond this no penalty of life could add to or thwart his peace.

He had been perturbed by the thunder, and had at last wandered forth, looking for Sanpriel, in a low voice calling her name as he went. None had observed him going out or forestward, and when once he reached the woodland he was lost to view. Vague memories of old ramblings seaward guided his way towards the dunes, and thither at last he arrived, weary and piteous with querulous longing.

When he came upon the fallen oak he stared at it in dull surprise, and would have sat down upon a great bole that lay earthward had he not caught sight of something like the figure of a man prone upon the ground a few yards away.

Slowly——because of a certain childish awe and horror at his heart——he drew nigh to the silent thing. What was it? Was it not two figures clasped close in the embrace of some mysterious, some unheard-of death? He could not think—— what was it that lay so heavily upon his brain, what weight of what incommensurable gloom? Sanpriel! He glanced swiftly and with startled eyes at what lay beside him, but the next moment his gaze wandered, and he half-turned.

"*Sanpriel!*" he cried in a tremulous, quavering voice, "*Sanpriel! Sanpriel!*"

Then again he looked round, and suddenly sank upon his knees, and broke into a passion of sobbing, dry, tearless, impotent, heart-breaking sobs.

The hollow booming of the sea and its moaning undertone was close by now, for the tide had reached inland within a yard or two of the base of the dune.

Was it something in its relentless voice, or something human-like in the crying of the wind beyond where the white crests of the waves loomed ghostly through the dusk, that touched him ?—or did he know, as an ignorant child will know, that death had defrauded him of his heart's treasure ?

Suddenly he sprang to his feet, grasped the thing that terrified him, and with unwonted strength half-lifted, half-dragged his burden down the slope, nor rested, panting and laughing strangely, till the waters greedily lapped round, seized, and with eager resilient clingings carried it seaward.

He could not see far, because of the gloom and the flying spray : but he saw the black burden he had given up to the ocean borne under and outward, and his frenzy left him quiet and trembling.

Louder and louder the sea called, but for a time he would not listen. Erewhile he started and groped wildly for his violin, and when he saw it a-glitter on the moonlit slope of the dune ran back, eagerly muttering vague sounds of joy. To and fro he walked, playing fragments of forgotten melodies, vagrant chords of incoherent music. Swifter and swifter grew the medley, and blent confusedly with the heavy fall of the waves upon the sand and the hoarse resurgence of the ebbing tide. Fierce, passionate, strident notes were borne inland by the wind—a requiem as wild and wayward as its very self.

All at once, as he stood upon the dune in the moonlight, erect, darkly-outlined, with his long white hair tossed about his head, he gave a cry, threw down his violin, and ran seaward.

With straining eyes and outstretched arms he stood for a brief space, heedless of the surf that flooded to his ankles, or of the salt spray blown into his face. Then suddenly he leapt into the waters, and fell prone with the receding wave, and was swept out on the breast of the tide.

And louder and louder the sea moaned, till the booming echoes of its thunders shook the ground far inland, and became one with the voice of the tempestuous wind.

THE END.

PRINTED BY BALLANTYNE, HANSON AND CO.
EDINBURGH AND LONDON.

A LIST OF BOOKS

PUBLISHED BY

CHATTO & WINDUS,

214, PICCADILLY, LONDON, W.

Sold by all Booksellers, or sent post-free for the published price by the Publishers.

Abbé Constantin (The). By LUDOVIC HALEVY, of the French Academy. Translated into English. With 36 Photogravure Illustrations by GOUPIL & Co., after the Drawings of Madame MADELEINE LEMAIRE. Only 250 copies of this choice book have been printed (in large quarto) for the English market, each one numbered. The price may be learned from any Bookseller.

About.—The Fellah: An Egyptian Novel. By EDMOND ABOUT. Translated by Sir RANDAL ROBERTS. Post 8vo, illustrated boards, 2s. ; cloth limp, 2s. 6d.

Adams (W. Davenport), Works by:
A Dictionary of the Drama. Being a comprehensive Guide to the Plays, Playwrights, Players, and Playhouses of the United Kingdom and America, from the Earliest to the Present Times. Crown 8vo, half-bound, 12s. 6d. [*Preparing.*
Quips and Quiddities. Selected by W. DAVENPORT ADAMS. Post 8vo, cloth limp, 2s. 6d.

Advertising, A History of, from the Earliest Times. Illustrated by Anecdotes, Curious Specimens, and Notices of Successful Advertisers. By HENRY SAMPSON. With Coloured Frontispiece and Illustrations. Crown 8vo, cloth gilt, 7s. 6d.

Agony Column (The) of "The Times," from 1800 to 1870. Edited, with an Introduction, by ALICE CLAY. Post 8vo, cloth limp, 2s. 6d.

Aidé (Hamilton), Works by:
Post 8vo, illustrated boards, 2s. each.
Carr of Carrlyon. | Confidences.

Alexander (Mrs.), Novels by:
Post 8vo, illustrated boards, 2s. each.
Maid, Wife, or Widow?
Valerie's Fate.

Allen (Grant), Works by:
Crown 8vo, cloth extra, 6s. each.
The Evolutionist at Large.
Vignettes from Nature.
Colin Clout's Calendar.

Crown 8vo, cloth extra, 6s. each ; post 8vo, illustrated boards, 2s. each.
Strange Stories. With a Frontispiece by GEORGE DU MAURIER.
The Beckoning Hand. With a Frontispiece by TOWNLEY GREEN.

Crown 8vo, cloth extra, 3s. 6d. each post 8vo, illustrated boards, 2s. each.
Philistia.
For Maimie's Sake.

Post 8vo, illustrated boards, 2s. each.
Babylon: A Romance.
In all Shades.

The Devil's Die. Crown 8vo, cloth extra, 3s. 6d.
This Mortal Coll. Three Vols., crown 8vo.

Architectural Styles, A Handbook of. Translated from the German of A. ROSENGARTEN, by W. COLLETT-SANDARS. Crown 8vo, cloth extra, with 639 Illustrations, 7s. 6d.

Arnold.—Bird Life in England
By EDWIN LESTER ARNOLD. Crown 8vo, cloth extra, 6s.

Artemus Ward:

Artemus Ward's Works: The Works of CHARLES FARRER BROWNE, better known as ARTEMUS WARD. With Portrait and Facsimile. Crown 8vo, cloth extra, 7s. 6d.

The Genial Showman: Life and Adventures of Artemus Ward. By EDWARD P. HINGSTON. With a Frontispiece. Cr. 8vo, cl. extra, 3s. 6d.

Art (The) of Amusing: A Collection of Graceful Arts, Games, Tricks, Puzzles, and Charades. By FRANK BELLEW. With 300 Illustrations. Cr. 8vo, cloth extra, 4s. 6d.

Ashton (John), Works by:

Crown 8vo, cloth extra, 7s. 6d. each.

A History of the Chap-Books of the Eighteenth Century. With nearly 400 Illustrations, engraved in facsimile of the originals.

Social Life in the Reign of Queen Anne. From Original Sources. With nearly 100 Illustrations.

Humour, Wit, and Satire of the Seventeenth Century. With nearly 100 Illustrations.

English Caricature and Satire on Napoleon the First. With 115 Illustrations.

Modern Street Ballads. With 57 Illustrations.

Bacteria.—A Synopsis of the Bacteria and Yeast Fungi and Allied Species. By W. B. GROVE, B.A. With 87 Illusts. Crown 8vo, cl. extra, 3s. 6d.

Bankers, A Handbook of London; together with Lists of Bankers from 1677. By F. G. HILTON PRICE. Crown 8vo, cloth extra, 7s. 6d.

Bardsley (Rev. C.W.), Works by:

English Surnames: Their Sources and Significations. Third Edition, revised. Crown 8vo, cl. ex., 7s. 6d.

Curiosities of Puritan Nomenclature. Second Edition. Crown 8vo, cloth extra, 6s.

Beaconsfield, Lord: A Biography. By T. P. O'CONNOR, M.P. Sixth Edition, with a New Preface. Crown 8vo, cloth extra, 5s.

Beauchamp. — Grantley Grange: A Novel. By SHELSLEY BEAUCHAMP. Post 8vo, illust. bds., 2s.

Beautiful Pictures by British Artists: A Gathering of Favourites from our Picture Galleries. All engraved on Steel in the highest style of Art. Edited, with Notices of the Artists, by SYDNEY ARMYTAGE, M.A. Imperial 4to, cloth extra, gilt and gilt edges 21s.

Bechstein. — As Pretty as Seven, and other German Stories. Collected by LUDWIG BECHSTEIN. With Additional Tales by the Brothers GRIMM, and 100 Illusts. by RICHTER. Small 4to, green and gold, 6s. 6d.; gilt edges, 7s. 6d.

Beerbohm. — Wanderings in Patagonia; or, Life among the Ostrich Hunters. By JULIUS BEERBOHM. With Illusts. Crown 8vo, cloth extra, 3s. 6d.

Belgravia for 1889.—One Shilling Monthly.—A New Serial Story, entitled Passion's Slave, by RICHARD ASHE KING, Author of "The Wearing of the Green," "A Drawn Game," &c., began in the JANUARY Number, and will be continued through the year.

*** Bound Volumes from the beginning kept in stock, cloth extra, gilt edges, 7s. 6d. each: Cases for Binding Vols., 2s. each.*

Belgravia Holiday Number, published Annually in JULY; and Belgravia Annual, published Annually in NOVEMBER. Each Complete in itself. Demy 8vo, with Illustrations, 1s. each.

Bennett (W.C., LL.D.), Works by:

Post 8vo, cloth limp, 2s. each.

A Ballad History of England

Songs for Sailors.

Besant (Walter) and James Rice, Novels by. Crown 8vo, cloth extra, 3s. 6d. each; post 8vo, illust. bds., 2s. each; cl. limp, 2s. 6d. each.

Ready-Money Mortiboy.

My Little Girl.

With Harp and Crown.

This Son of Vulcan.

The Golden Butterfly.

The Monks of Thelema.

By Celia's Arbour.

The Chaplain of the Fleet.

The Seamy Side.

The Case of Mr. Lucraft, &c.

'Twas in Trafalgar's Bay, &c.

The Ten Years' Tenant, &c.

Besant (Walter), Novels by:

Crown 8vo, cloth extra, 3s. 6d. each; post 8vo, illust. boards, 2s. each; cloth limp, 2s. 6d. each.

All Sorts and Conditions of Men: An Impossible Story. With Illustrations by FRED. BARNARD.

The Captains' Room, &c. With Frontispiece by E. J. WHEELER.

All in a Garden Fair. With 6 Illustrations by HARRY FURNISS.

Dorothy Forster. With Frontispiece by CHARLES GREEN.

Uncle Jack, and other Stories.

Children of Gibeon.

The World Went Very Well Then. With Illustrations by A. FORESTIER.

Besant (Walter), *continued—*
Herr Paulus: His Rise, his Greatness, and his Fall. With a New Preface. Cr. 8vo, cloth extra, 3s. 6d.
For Faith and Freedom. With Illustrations by A. Forestier and F. Waddy. Three Vols., crown 8vo.
Fifty Years Ago. With 137 full-page Plates and Woodcuts. Demy 8vo, cloth extra, 16s.
The Eulogy of Richard Jefferies. With Photograph Portrait. Cr. 8vo, cloth extra, 6s.
The Art of Fiction. Demy 8vo, 1s.

New Library Edition of
Besant and Rice's Novels.
The whole 12 Volumes, printed from new type on a large crown 8vo page, and handsomely bound in cloth, are now ready, price Six Shillings each.
1. Ready - Money Mortiboy. With Etched Portrait of James Rice.
2. My Little Girl.
3. With Harp and Crown.
4. This Son of Vulcan.
5. The Golden Butterfly. With Etched Portrait of Walter Besant.
6. The Monks of Thelema.
7. By Celia's Arbour.
8. The Chaplain of the Fleet.
9. The Seamy Side.
10. The Case of Mr. Lucraft, &c.
11. 'Twas in Trafalgar's Bay, &c.
12. The Ten Years' Tenant, &c.

Betham-Edwards (M.), Novels:
Felicia. Cr. 8vo, cloth extra, 3s. 6d. ; post 8vo, illust. bds., 2s.
Kitty. Post 8vo, illust. bds., 2s.

Bewick (Thomas) and his
Pupils. By Austin Dobson. With 95 Illusts. Square 8vo, cloth extra, 10s. 6d.

Birthday Books:—
The Starry Heavens: A Poetical Birthday Book. Square 8vo, handsomely bound in cloth, 2s. 6d.
The Lowell Birthday Book. With Illusts. Small 8vo, cloth extra, 4s. 6d.

Blackburn's (Henry) Art Handbooks.
Demy 8vo, Illustrated, uniform in size for binding.
Academy Notes, separate years, from 1875 to 1886, each 1s.
Academy Notes, 1889. With numerous Illustrations. 1s.
Academy Notes, 1880–84. Complete in One Volume, with about 700 Facsimile Illustrations. Cloth limp, 6s.
Academy Notes, 1885–89. Complete in One Vol., with about 600 Illustrations. Cloth limp, 7s. 6d. (*Only a few Copies for Sale.*)
Grosvenor Notes, 1877. 6d.
Grosvenor Notes, separate years, from 1878 to 1888, each 1s.

Blackburn (Henry), *continued—*
Demy 8vo, Illustrated, uniform in size for binding.
Grosvenor Notes, 1889. With numerous Illusts. 1s.
Grosvenor Notes, Vol. I., 1877–82. With upwards of 300 Illustrations. Demy 8vo, cloth limp, 6s.
Grosvenor Notes, Vol. II., 1883–87. With upwards of 300 Illustrations. Demy 8vo, cloth limp, 6s.
The New Gallery, 1888. With numerous Illustrations. 1s.
The New Gallery, 1889. With numerous Illustrations. 1s.
The English Pictures at the National Gallery. 114 Illustrations. 1s.
The Old Masters at the National Gallery. 128 Illustrations. 1s. 6d.
A Complete Illustrated Catalogue to the National Gallery. With Notes by H. Blackburn, and 242 Illusts. Demy 8vo, cloth limp, 3s.

The Paris Salon, 1889. With 300 Facsimile Sketches. 3s.

Blake (William): Etchings from
his Works. By W. B. Scott. With descriptive Text. Folio, half-bound boards, India Proofs, 21s.

Blind.—The Ascent of Man:
A Poem. By Mathilde Blind. Crown 8vo, printed on hand-made paper, cloth extra, 7s.

Bourne (H. R. Fox), Works by:
English Merchants: Memoirs in Illustration of the Progress of British Commerce. With numerous Illustrations. Cr. 8vo, cloth extra, 7s. 6d.
English Newspapers: Chapters in the History of Journalism. Two Vols., demy 8vo, cloth extra, 25s.

Bowers' (G.) Hunting Sketches:
Oblong 4to, half-bound boards, 21s. each
Canters in Crampshire.
Leaves from a Hunting Journal. Coloured in facsimile of the originals.

Boyle (Frederick), Works by:
Crown 8vo, cloth extra, 3s. 6d. each; post 8vo, illustrated boards, 2s. each.
Camp Notes: Stories of Sport and Adventure in Asia, Africa, America.
Savage Life: Adventures of a Globe-Trotter.

Chronicles of No-Man's Land. Post 8vo, illust. boards, 2s.

Brand's Observations on Popular Antiquities,
chiefly Illustrating the Origin of our Vulgar Customs, Ceremonies, and Superstitions. With the Additions of Sir Henry Ellis. Crown 8vo, with Illustrations, 7s. 6d.

Bret Harte, Works by:

Bret Harte's Collected Works. Arranged and Revised by the Author. Complete in Five Vols., crown 8vo, cloth extra, 6s. each.
  Vol. I. COMPLETE POETICAL AND DRAMATIC WORKS. With Steel Portrait, and Introduction by Author.
  Vol. II. EARLIER PAPERS—LUCK OF ROARING CAMP, and other Sketches—BOHEMIAN PAPERS — SPANISH AND AMERICAN LEGENDS.
  Vol. III. TALES OF THE ARGONAUTS—EASTERN SKETCHES.
  Vol. IV. GABRIEL CONROY.
  Vol. V. STORIES — CONDENSED NOVELS, &c.

The Select Works of Bret Harte, in Prose and Poetry. With Introductory Essay by J. M. BELLEW, Portrait of the Author, and 50 Illustrations. Crown 8vo, cloth extra, 7s. 6d.

Bret Harte's Complete Poetical Works. Author's Copyright Edition. Printed on hand-made paper and bound in buckram. Cr. 8vo, 4s. 6d.

Gabriel Conroy: A Novel. Post 8vo, illustrated boards, 2s.

An Heiress of Red Dog, and other Stories. Post 8vo, illust. boards, 2s.

The Twins of Table Mountain. Fcap. 8vo, picture cover, 1s.

Luck of Roaring Camp, and other Sketches. Post 8vo, illust. bds., 2s.

Jeff Briggs's Love Story. Fcap. 8vo, picture cover, 1s.

Flip. Post 8vo, illust. bds., 2s.; cl. 2s. 6d.

Californian Stories (including THE TWINS OF TABLE MOUNTAIN, JEFF BRIGGS'S LOVE STORY, &c.) Post 8vo, illustrated boards, 2s.

Maruja: A Novel. Post 8vo, illust. boards, 2s.; cloth limp, 2s. 6d.

The Queen of the Pirate Isle. With 28 original Drawings by KATE GREENAWAY, Reproduced in Colours by EDMUND EVANS. Sm. 4to, bds., 5s.

A Phyllis of the Sierras, &c. Post 8vo, illust. bds., 2s. cloth limp, 2s. 6d.

Brewer (Rev. Dr.), Works by:

The Reader's Handbook of Allusions, References, Plots, and Stories. Twelfth Thousand. With Appendix, containing a COMPLETE ENGLISH BIBLIOGRAPHY. Cr. 8vo, cloth 7s. 6d.

Authors and their Works, with the Dates: Being the Appendices to "The Reader's Handbook," separately printed. Cr. 8vo, cloth limp, 2s.

A Dictionary of Miracles: Imitative, Realistic, and Dogmatic. Crown 8vo, cloth extra 7s. 6d.

Brewster (Sir David), Works by:

More Worlds than One: The Creed of the Philosopher and the Hope of the Christian. With Plates. Post 8vo, cloth extra, 4s. 6d.

The Martyrs of Science: Lives of GALILEO, TYCHO BRAHE, and KEPLER. With Portraits. Post 8vo, cloth extra, 4s. 6d.

Letters on Natural Magic. A New Edition, with numerous Illustrations, and Chapters on the Being and Faculties of Man, and Additional Phenomena of Natural Magic, by J. A. SMITH. Post 8vo, cl. ex., 4s. 6d.

Brillat-Savarin.—Gastronomy as a Fine Art. By BRILLAT-SAVARIN. Translated by R. E. ANDERSON, M.A. Post 8vo, printed on laid-paper and half-bound, 2s.

Brydges. — Uncle Sam at Home. By HAROLD BRYDGES. Post 8vo, illust. boards, 2s.; cloth, 2s. 6d.

Buchanan's (Robert) Works:

Crown 8vo, cloth extra, 6s. each.

Ballads of Life, Love, and Humour. With a Frontispiece by ARTHUR HUGHES.

Selected Poems of Robert Buchanan. With a Frontispiece by T. DALZIEL.

The Earthquake; or, Six Days and a Sabbath.

The City of Dream: An Epic Poem. With Two Illusts. by P. MACNAB. Second Edition.

Robert Buchanan's Complete Poetical Works. With Steel-plate Portrait. Crown 8vo, cloth extra, 7s. 6d.

Crown 8vo, cloth extra, 3s. 6d. each; post 8vo, illust. boards, 2s. each.

The Shadow of the Sword.
A Child of Nature. With a Frontispiece.
God and the Man. With Illustrations by FRED. BARNARD.
The Martyrdom of Madeline. With Frontispiece by A. W. COOPER.
Love Me for Ever. With a Frontispiece by P. MACNAB.
Annan Water. | The New Abelard.
Foxglove Manor.
Matt: A Story of a Caravan.
The Master of the Mine.
The Heir of Linne.

Burnett (Mrs.), Novels by:

Surly Tim, and other Stories. Post 8vo, illustrated boards, 2s.

Fcap. 8vo, picture cover, 1s. each.
Kathleen Mavourneen.
Lindsay's Luck.
Pretty Polly Pemberton.

Burton (Captain).—The Book of the Sword: Being a History of the Sword and its Use in all Countries, from the Earliest Times. By RICHARD F. BURTON. With over 400 Illustrations. Square 8vo, cloth extra, 32s.

Burton (Robert):

The Anatomy of Melancholy. A New Edition, complete, corrected and enriched by Translations of the Classical Extracts. Demy 8vo, cloth extra, 7s. 6d.

Melancholy Anatomiced: Being an Abridgment, for popular use, of BURTON's ANATOMY OF MELANCHOLY. Post 8vo, cloth limp, 2s. 6d.

Byron (Lord):

Byron's Letters and Journals. With Notices of his Life. By THOMAS MOORE. Cr. 8vo, cloth extra, 7s. 6d.

Prose and Verse, Humorous, Satirical, and Sentimental, by THOMAS MOORE; with Suppressed Passages from the Memoirs of Lord Byron. Edited, with Notes and Introduction, by R. HERNE SHEPHERD. Crown 8vo, cloth extra, 7s. 6d.

Caine (T. Hall), Novels by:

Crown 8vo, cloth extra, 3s. 6d. each; post 8vo, illustrated boards, 2s. each.

The Shadow of a Crime.
A Son of Hagar.
The Deemster: A Romance of the Isle of Man.

Cameron (Commander).— The Cruise of the "Black Prince" Privateer. By V. LOVETT CAMERON, R.N., C.B. With Two Illustrations by P. MACNAB. Crown 8vo, cl. ex., 5s.; post 8vo, illustrated boards, 2s.

Cameron (Mrs. H. Lovett), Novels by:

Crown 8vo, cloth extra, 3s. 6d. each post 8vo, illustrated boards, 2s. each.

Juliet's Guardian. | Deceivers Ever.

Carlyle (Thomas):

On the Choice of Books. By THOMAS CARLYLE. With a Life of the Author by R. H. SHEPHERD. New and Revised Edition, post 8vo, cloth extra, Illustrated, 1s. 6d.

The Correspondence of Thomas Carlyle and Ralph Waldo Emerson, 1834 to 1872. Edited by CHARLES ELIOT NORTON. With Portraits. Two Vols., crown 8vo, cloth extra, 24s.

Chapman's (George) Works: Vol. I. contains the Plays complete, including the doubtful ones. Vol. II., the Poems and Minor Translations, with an Introductory Essay by ALGERNON CHARLES SWINBURNE. Vol. III., the Translations of the Iliad and Odyssey. Three Vols., crown 8vo, cloth extra, 18s.; or separately, 6s. each.

Chatto & Jackson.—A Treatise on Wood Engraving, Historical and Practical. By WM. ANDREW CHATTO and JOHN JACKSON. With an Additional Chapter by HENRY G. BOHN; and 450 fine Illustrations. A Reprint of the last Revised Edition. Large 4to, half-bound, 28s.

Chaucer:

Chaucer for Children: A Golden Key. By Mrs. H.R. HAWEIS. With Eight Coloured Pictures and numerous Woodcuts by the Author. New Ed., small 4to, cloth extra, 6s.
Chaucer for Schools. By Mrs. H. R. HAWEIS. Demy 8vo, cloth limp, 2s. 6d.

Chronicle (The) of the Coach: Charing Cross to Ilfracombe. By J. D. CHAMPLIN. With 75 Illustrations by EDWARD L. CHICHESTER. Square 8vo, cloth extra, 7s. 6d.

Clodd. — Myths and Dreams. By EDWARD CLODD, F.R.A.S., Author of "The Story of Creation," &c. Crown 8vo, cloth extra, 5s.

Cobban.—The Cure of Souls: A Story. By J. MACLAREN COBBAN. Post 8vo, illustrated boards, 2s.

Coleman (John), Works by:

Curly: An Actor's Story. Illustrated by J. C. DOLLMAN. Crown 8vo, 1s.; cloth, 1s. 6d.
Players and Playwrights I have Known. Two Vols., demy 8vo, cloth extra, 24s.

Collins (Mortimer), Novels by:
Crown 8vo, cloth extra, 3s. 6d. each; post 8vo, illustrated boards, 2s. each.
Sweet Anne Page. | Transmigration.
From Midnight to Midnight.

A Fight with Fortune. Post 8vo, illustrated boards, 2s.

Collins (Mortimer & Frances), Novels by:
Crown 8vo, cloth extra, 3s. 6d. each; post 8vo, illustrated boards, 2s. each.
Blacksmith and Scholar.
The Village Comedy.
You Play Me False.

Post 8vo, illustrated boards, 2s. each
Sweet and Twenty. | Frances.

Collins (Wilkie), Novels by :
Crown 8vo, cloth extra, 3s. 6d. each ;
post 8vo, illustrated boards, 2s. each ;
cloth limp, 2s. 6d. each.
Antonina. Illust. by Sir JOHN GILBERT.
Basil. Illustrated by Sir JOHN GIL-
BERT and J MAHONEY.
Hide and Seek. Illustrated by Sir
JOHN GILBERT and J. MAHONEY.
The Dead Secret. Illustrated by Sir
JOHN GILBERT.
Queen of Hearts. Illustrated by Sir
JOHN GILBERT.
My Miscellanies. With a Steel-plate
Portrait of WILKIE COLLINS.
The Woman in White. With Illus-
trations by Sir JOHN GILBERT and
F. A. FRASER.
The Moonstone. With Illustrations
by G. DU MAURIER and F. A. FRASER.
Man and Wife. Illust. by W. SMALL.
Poor Miss Finch. Illustrated by
G. DU MAURIER and EDWARD
HUGHES.
Miss or Mrs.? With Illustrations by
S. L. FILDES and HENRY WOODS.
The New Magdalen. Illustrated by
G. DU MAURIER and C. S. REINHARDT.
The Frozen Deep. Illustrated by
G. DU MAURIER and J. MAHONEY.
The Law and the Lady. Illustrated
by S. L. FILDES and SYDNEY HALL.
The Two Destinies.
The Haunted Hotel. Illustrated by
ARTHUR HOPKINS.
The Fallen Leaves.
Jezebel's Daughter.
The Black Robe.
Heart and Science: A Story of the
Present Time.
"I Say No."
The Evil Genius.
Little Novels.

The Legacy of Cain. Three Vols.,
crown 8vo.

Collins (C. Allston).—The Bar
Sinister: A Story. By C. ALLSTON
COLLINS. Post 8vo, illustrated bds., 2s.

Colman's Humorous Works:
" Broad Grins," " My Nightgown and
Slippers," and other Humorous Works,
Prose and Poetical, of GEORGE COL-
MAN. With Life by G. B. BUCKSTONE,
and Frontispiece by HOGARTH. Crown
8vo cloth extra, gilt, 7s. 6d.

Colquhoun.—Every Inch a Sol-
dier: A Novel. By M. J. COLQUHOUN.
Post 8vo, illustrated boards, 2s.

Convalescent Cookery: A
Family Handbook. By CATHERINE
RYAN. Crown 8vo, 1s. ; cloth, 1s. 6d.

Conway (Moncure D.), Works
by :
Demonology and Devil-Lore. Two
Vols., royal 8vo, with 65 Illusts., 28s.
A Necklace of Stories. Illustrated
by W. J. HENNESSY. Square 8vo,
cloth extra, 6s.
Pine and Palm: A Novel. Cheaper
Edition. Post 8vo, illustrated boards,
2s.   [*Shortly.*

Cook (Dutton), Novels by :
Leo. Post 8vo, illustrated boards, 2s.
Paul Foster's Daughter. Crown 8vo,
cloth extra, 3s. 6d.; post 8vo, illustrated boards, 2s.

Copyright. — A Handbook of
English and Foreign Copyright in
Literary and Dramatic Works. By
SIDNEY JERROLD. Post 8vo, cl., 2s. 6d.

Cornwall.—Popular Romances
of the West of England; or, The
Drolls, Traditions, and Superstitions
of Old Cornwall. Collected and Edited
by ROBERT HUNT, F.R.S. New and
Revised Edition, with Additions, and
Two Steel-plate Illustrations by
GEORGE CRUIKSHANK. Crown 8vo,
cloth extra, 7s. 6d.

Craddock. — The Prophet of
the Great Smoky Mountains. By
CHARLES EGBERT CRADDOCK. Post
8vo illust. bds., 2s. cloth limp, 2s. 6d.

Cruikshank (George) :
The Comic Almanack. Complete in
Two SERIES: The FIRST from 1835
to 1843; the SECOND from 1844 to
1853. A Gathering of the BEST
HUMOUR of THACKERAY, HOOD, MAY-
HEW, ALBERT SMITH, A'BECKETT,
ROBERT BROUGH, &c. With 2,000
Woodcuts and Steel Engravings by
CRUIKSHANK, HINE, LANDELLS, &c.
Crown 8vo, cloth gilt, two very thick
volumes, 7s. 6d. each.
The Life of George Cruikshank. By
BLANCHARD JERROLD, Author of
"The Life of Napoleon III.," &c.
With 84 Illustrations. New and
Cheaper Edition, enlarged, with Ad-
ditional Plates, and a very carefully
compiled Bibliography. Crown 8vo,
cloth extra, 7s. 6d.

Cumming (C. F. Gordon), Works
by :
Demy 8vo, cloth extra, 8s. 6d. each.
In the Hebrides. With Autotype Fac-
simile and numerous full-page Illusts.
In the Himalayas and on the Indian
Plains. With numerous Illusts.

Via Cornwall to Egypt. With a
Photogravure Frontispiece. Demy
8vo, cloth extra, 7s. 6d.

Cussans.—Handbook of Heraldry; with Instructions for Tracing Pedigrees and Deciphering Ancient MSS., &c. By JOHN E. CUSSANS. Entirely New and Revised Edition, illustrated with over 400 Woodcuts and Coloured Plates. Crown 8vo, cloth extra, 7s. 6d.

Cyples.—Hearts of Gold: A Novel. By WILLIAM CYPLES. Crown 8vo, cloth extra, 3s. 6d.; post 8vo, illustrated boards, 2s.

Daniel. — Merrie England in the Olden Time. By GEORGE DANIEL. With Illustrations by ROBT. CRUIKSHANK. Crown 8vo, cloth extra, 3s. 6d.

Daudet.—The Evangelist; or, Port Salvation. By ALPHONSE DAUDET. Translated by C. HARRY MELTZER. With Portrait of the Author. Crown 8vo, cloth extra, 3s. 6d.; post 8vo, illust. boards, 2s.

Davenant.—Hints for Parents on the Choice of a Profession or Trade for their Sons. By FRANCIS DAVENANT, M.A. Post 8vo, 1s.; cloth limp, 1s. 6d.

Davies (Dr. N. E.), Works by:
Crown 8vo, 1s. each; cloth limp, 1s. 6d. each.
One Thousand Medical Maxims.
Nursery Hints: A Mother's Guide.

Aids to Long Life. Crown 8vo, 2s.; cloth limp, 2s. 6d.

Davies' (Sir John) Complete Poetical Works, including Psalms I. to L. in Verse, and other hitherto Unpublished MSS., for the first time Collected and Edited, with Memorial-Introduction and Notes, by the Rev. A. B. GROSART, D.D. Two Vols., crown 8vo, cloth boards, 12s.

Daylight Land: The Adventures, Humorous and Otherwise, of Judge JOHN DOE, Tourist; CEPHAS PEPPERELL, Capitalist; Colonel GOFFE, and others, in their Excursion over Prairie and Mountain. By W. H. MURRAY. With 140 Illusts. in colours. Small 4to, cloth extra, 12s. 6d.

De Maistre —A Journey Round My Room. By XAVIER DE MAISTRE. Translated by HENRY ATTWELL. Post 8vo, cloth limp, 2s. 6d.

De Mille.—A Castle in Spain: A Novel. By JAMES DE MILLE. With a Frontispiece. Crown 8vo, cloth extra, 3s. 6d.; post 8vo, illust. bds., 2s.

Derwent (Leith), Novels by:
Crown 8vo, cloth extra, 3s. 6d. each; post 8vo, illustrated boards, 2s. each.
Our Lady of Tears. | Circe's Lovers.

Dickens (Charles), Novels by :
Post 8vo, illustrated boards, 2s. each.
Sketches by Boz. | Nicholas Nickleby
Pickwick Papers. | Oliver Twist.

The Speeches of Charles Dickens, 1841-1870. With a New Bibliography, revised and enlarged. Edited and Prefaced by RICHARD HERNE SHEPHERD. Cr. 8vo, cloth extra, 6s.—Also a SMALLER EDITION, in the *Mayfair Library*. Post 8vo, cloth limp, 2s. 6d.

About England with Dickens. By ALFRED RIMMER. With 57 Illustrations by C. A. VANDERHOOP, ALFRED RIMMER, and others. Sq. 8vo, cloth extra, 7s. 6d.

Dictionaries:

A Dictionary of Miracles: Imitative, Realistic, and Dogmatic. By the Rev. E. C. BREWER, LL.D. Crown 8vo, cloth extra, 7s. 6d.; hf.-bound, 9s.

The Reader's Handbook of Allusions, References, Plots, and Stories. By the Rev. E. C. BREWER, LL.D. With an Appendix, containing a Complete English Bibliography. Eleventh Thousand. Crown 8vo, 1,400 pages, cloth extra, 7s. 6d.

Authors and their Works, with the Dates. Being the Appendices to "The Reader's Handbook," separately printed. By the Rev. Dr BREWER. Crown 8vo, cloth limp, 2s.

A Dictionary of the Drama: Being a comprehensive Guide to the Plays, Playwrights, Players, and Playhouses of the United Kingdom and America, from the Earliest to the Present Times. By W. DAVENPORT ADAMS. A thick volume, crown 8vo, half-bound, 12s. 6d. [*In preparation.*

Familiar Short Sayings of Great Men. With Historical and Explanatory Notes. By SAMUEL A. BENT, M.A. Fifth Edition, revised and enlarged. Cr. 8vo, cloth extra, 7s. 6d.

The Slang Dictionary: Etymological, Historical, and Anecdotal. Crown 8vo, cloth extra, 6s. 6d.

Women of the Day: A Biographical Dictionary. By FRANCES HAYS. Cr. 8vo, cloth extra, 6s.

Words, Facts, and Phrases: A Dictionary of Curious, Quaint, and Out-of-the-Way Matters. By ELIEZER EDWARDS. New and Cheaper Issue Cr. 8vo, cl. ex., 7s. 6d.; hf.-bd., 9s.

Diderot.—The Paradox of Acting. Translated, with Annotations, from Diderot's "Le Paradoxe sur le Comédien," by WALTER HERRIES POLLOCK. With a Preface by HENRY IRVING. Cr. 8vo, in parchment, 4s. 6d.

Dobson (W. T.), Works by:
Post 8vo, cloth limp, 2s. 6d. each.
Literary Frivolities, Fancies, Follies, and Frolics.
Poetical Ingenuities and Eccentricities.

Donovan (Dick), Detective Stories by:
Post 8vo, illustrated boards, 2s. each; cloth limp, 2s. 6d. each.
The Man-hunter: Stories from the Note-book of a Detective.
Caught at Last!

Doran. — Memories of our Great Towns; with Anecdotic Gleanings concerning their Worthies and their Oddities. By Dr. JOHN DORAN, F.S.A. With 38 Illusts. New and Cheaper Edit. Cr. 8vo, cl. extra, 7s. 6d.

Drama, A Dictionary of the. Being a comprehensive Guide to the Plays, Playwrights, Players, and Playhouses of the United Kingdom and America, from the Earliest to the Present Times. By W. DAVENPORT ADAMS. (Uniform with BREWER'S "Reader's Handbook.") Crown 8vo, half-bound, 12s. 6d.   [*In preparation.*

Dramatists, The Old. Cr. 8vo, cl. ex., Vignette Portraits, 6s. per Vol.
Ben Jonson's Works. With Notes Critical and Explanatory, and a Biographical Memoir by WM. GIFFORD. Edit. by Col. CUNNINGHAM. 3 Vols.
Chapman's Works. Complete in Three Vols. Vol. I. contains the Plays complete, including doubtful ones; Vol. II., Poems and Minor Translations, with Introductory Essay by A. C. SWINBURNE; Vol. III., Translations of the Iliad and Odyssey.
Marlowe's Works. Including his Translations. Edited, with Notes and Introduction, by Col. CUNNINGHAM. One Vol.
Massinger's Plays. From the Text of WILLIAM GIFFORD. Edited by Col. CUNNINGHAM. One Vol.

Dyer. — The Folk-Lore of Plants. By Rev. T. F. THISELTON DYER, M.A. Crown 8vo, cloth extra, 6s.

Early English Poets. Edited, with Introductions and Annotations, by REV. A. B. GROSART, D.D. Crown 8vo, cloth boards, 8s. per Volume.
Fletcher's (Giles, B.D.) Complete Poems. One Vol.
Davies' (Sir John) Complete Poetical Works. Two Vols.
Herrick's (Robert) Complete Collected Poems. Three Vols.
Sidney's (Sir Philip) Complete Poetical Works. Three Vols.

Edgcumbe. — Zephyrus: A Holiday in Brazil and on the River Plate. By E. R. PEARCE EDGCUMBE. With 41 Illusts. Cr. 8vo, cl. extra, 5s.

Edwardes (Mrs. A.), Novels by:
A Point of Honour. Post 8vo, illustrated boards, 2s.
Archie Lovell. Crown 8vo, cloth extra, 3s. 6d.; post 8vo, illust. bds., 2s.

Eggleston.—Roxy: A Novel. By EDWARD EGGLESTON. Post 8vo, illust. boards, 2s.

Emanuel.—On Diamonds and Precious Stones: their History, Value, and Properties; with Simple Tests for ascertaining their Reality. By HARRY EMANUEL, F.R.G.S. With numerous Illustrations, tinted and plain. Crown 8vo, cloth extra, gilt, 6s.

Ewald (Alex. Charles, F.S.A.), Works by:
The Life and Times of Prince Charles Stuart, Count of Albany, commonly called the Young Pretender. From the State Papers and other Sources. New and Cheaper Edition, with a Portrait, crown 8vo, cloth extra, 7s. 6d.
Stories from the State Papers. With an Autotype Facsimile. Crown 8vo, cloth extra, 6s.
Studies Re-studied: Historical Sketches from Original Sources. Demy 8vo, cloth extra, 12s.

Englishman's House, The: A Practical Guide to all interested in Selecting or Building a House; with full Estimates of Cost, Quantities, &c. By C. J. RICHARDSON. Fourth Edition. With Coloured Frontispiece and nearly 600 Illustrations. Crown 8vo, cloth extra, 7s. 6d.

Eyes, Our: How to Preserve Them from Infancy to Old Age. By JOHN BROWNING, F.R.A.S., &c. Seventh Edition (Twelfth Thousand). With 70 Illustrations. Crown 8vo, cloth, 1s

Familiar Short Sayings of Great Men. By SAMUEL ARTHUR BENT, A.M. Fifth Edition, Revised and Enlarged. Cr. 8vo, cl. ex., 7s. 6d.

Faraday (Michael), Works by:
Post 8vo, cloth extra, 4s. 6d. each.
The Chemical History of a Candle: Lectures delivered before a Juvenile Audience at the Royal Institution. Edited by WILLIAM CROOKES, F.C.S. With numerous Illustrations.
On the Various Forces of Nature, and their Relations to each other: Lectures delivered before a Juvenile Audience at the Royal Institution. Edited by WILLIAM CROOKES, F.C.S. With numerous Illustrations.

Farrer (James Anson), Works by:
Military Manners and Customs. Crown 8vo, cloth extra, 6s.
War: Three Essays, Reprinted from "Military Manners." Crown 8vo, 1s.; cloth, 1s. 6d.

Fin-Bec.—The Cupboard Papers: Observations on the Art of Living and Dining. By FIN-BEC. Post 8vo, cloth limp, 2s. 6d.

Fireworks, The Complete Art of Making; or, The Pyrotechnist's Treasury. By THOMAS KENTISH. With 267 Illustrations. A New Edition, Revised throughout and greatly Enlarged. Crown 8vo, cloth extra, 5s.

Fitzgerald (Percy), Works by:
The World Behind the Scenes. Crown 8vo, cloth extra, 3s. 6d.
Little Essays: Passages from the Letters of CHARLES LAMB. Post 8vo, cloth limp, 2s. 6d.
A Day's Tour: A Journey through France and Belgium. With Sketches in facsimile of the Original Drawings. Crown 4to picture cover, 1s.
Fatal Zero: A Homburg Diary. Cr. 8vo, cloth extra, 3s. 6d.; post 8vo, illustrated boards, 2s.

Post 8vo, illustrated boards, 2s. each.
Bella Donna. | Never Forgotten.
The Second Mrs. Tillotson.
Seventy-five Brooke Street
Polly. | The Lady of Brantome.

Fletcher's (Giles, B.D.) Complete Poems; Christ's Victorie in Heaven, Christ's Victorie on Earth, Christ's Triumph over Death, and Minor Poems. With Memorial-Introduction and Notes by the Rev. A. B. GROSART, D.D. Cr. 8vo, cloth bds., 6s.

Fonblanque.—Filthy Lucre: A Novel. By ALBANY DE FONBLANQUE. Post 8vo, illustrated boards, 2s.

Francillon (R. E.), Novels by:
Crown 8vo, cloth extra, 3s. 6d. each; post 8vo, illust. boards, 2s. each.
One by One. | A Real Queen.
Queen Cophetua. |

Olympia. Post 8vo, illust. boards, 2s.
Esther's Glove. Fcap. 8vo, 1s.
King or Knave: A Novel. Cheaper Edition. Cr. 8vo, cloth extra, 3s. 6d.
Romances of the Law. Frontispiece by D. H. FRISTON. Cr. 8vo, cl. ex., 6s.

Frederic.—Seth's Brother's Wife: A Novel. By HAROLD FREDERIC. Post 8vo, illust. bds., 2s.

French Literature, History of. By HENRY VAN LAUN. Complete in 3 Vols., demy 8vo, cl. bds., 7s. 6d. each.

Frenzeny.—Fifty Years on the Trail: The Adventures of JOHN Y. NELSON, Scout, Guide, and Interpreter, in the Wild West. By HARRINGTON O'REILLY. With over 100 Illustrations by PAUL FRENZENY. Crown 8vo, cloth extra, 3s. 6d. [*Preparing.*

Frere.—Pandurang Hari; or, Memoirs of a Hindoo. With a Preface by Sir H. BARTLE FRERE, G.C.S.I., &c. Crown 8vo, cloth extra, 3s. 6d.; post 8vo, illustrated boards, 2s.

Friswell.—One of Two: A Novel. By HAIN FRISWELL. Post 8vo, illustrated boards, 2s.

Frost (Thomas), Works by:
Crown 8vo, cloth extra, 3s. 6d. each.
Circus Life and Circus Celebrities.
The Lives of the Conjurers.
Old Showmen and Old London Fairs.

Fry's (Herbert) Royal Guide to the London Charities, 1888-9. Showing their Name, Date of Foundation, Objects, Income, Officials, &c. Edited by JOHN LANE. Published Annually. Crown 8vo, cloth, 1s. 6d.

Gardening Books:
Post 8vo, 1s. each; cl. limp, 1s. 6d. each.
A Year's Work in Garden and Greenhouse: Practical Advice to Amateur Gardeners as to the Management of the Flower, Fruit, and Frame Garden. By GEORGE GLENNY.
Our Kitchen Garden: The Plants we Grow, and How we Cook Them. By TOM JERROLD.
Household Horticulture: A Gossip about Flowers. By TOM and JANE JERROLD. Illustrated.
The Garden that Paid the Rent. By TOM JERROLD.

My Garden Wild, and What I Grew there. By F. G. HEATH. Crown 8vo, cloth extra, 5s.; gilt edges, 6s.

Garrett.—The Capel Girls: A
Novel. By EDWARD GARRETT. Cr. 8vo,
cl. ex., 3s. 6d. ; post 8vo, illust. bds., 2s.

Gentleman's Magazine (The)
for 1889.—1s. Monthly.—In addition
to the Articles upon subjects in Literature, Science, and Art, for which this
Magazine has so high a reputation,
"Table Talk" by SYLVANUS URBAN
appears monthly.
⁎ *Bound Volumes for recent years are
kept in stock, cloth extra, price 8s. 6d.
each; Cases for binding, 2s. each.*

Gentleman's Annual (The).
Published Annually in November. In
illuminated cover. Demy 8vo, 1s.

German Popular Stories. Collected by the Brothers GRIMM, and
Translated by EDGAR TAYLOR. Edited,
with an Introduction, by JOHN RUSKIN.
With 22 Illustrations on Steel by
GEORGE CRUIKSHANK. Square 8vo,
cloth extra, 6s. 6d. ; gilt edges, 7s. 6d.

Gibbon (Charles), Novels by :
Crown 8vo, cloth extra, 3s 6d. each
post 8vo, illustrated boards, 2s. each.

Robin Gray.	In Honour Bound.
What will the World Say?	Braes of Yarrow.
Queen of the Meadow.	A Heart's Prob-lem.
The Flower of the Forest.	The Golden Shaft.
	Of High Degree.
	Loving a Dream.

Post 8vo, illustrated boards, 2s. each.
For Lack of Gold.
For the King. | In Pastures Green.
In Love and War.
By Mead and Stream.
Fancy Free. | A Hard Knot.
Heart's Delight.

Blood-Money, and other Stories. Two
Vols., crown 8vo, cloth, 12s

Gilbert (William), Novels by :
Post 8vo, illustrated boards, 2s. each.
Dr. Austin's Guests.
The Wizard of the Mountain.
James Duke, Costermonger.

Gilbert (W. S.), Original Plays
by: In Two Series, each complete in
itself, price 2s. 6d. each.

The FIRST SERIES contains—The
Wicked World—Pygmalion and Ga-
latea — Charity—The Princess—The
Palace of Truth—Trial by Jury.
The SECOND SERIES contains—Bro-
ken Hearts—Engaged—Sweethearts—
Gretchen—Dan'l Druce—Tom Cobb—
H.M.S. Pinafore—The Sorcerer—The
Pirates of Penzance.

Gilbert (W. S.). continued—
Eight Original Comic Operas. Writ-
ten by W. S. GILBERT. Containing:
The Sorcerer—H.M.S. "Pinafore"
—The Pirates of Penzance—Iolanthe
— Patience — Princess Ida — The
Mikado—Trial by Jury. Demy 8vo,
cloth limp, 2s. 6d.

Glenny.—A Year's Work in
Garden and Greenhouse: Practical
Advice to Amateur Gardeners as to
the Management of the Flower, Fruit,
and Frame Garden. By GEORGE
GLENNY. Post 8vo, 1s.; cloth, 1s. 6d.

Godwin.—Lives of the Necro-
mancers. By WILLIAM GODWIN.
Post 8vo, limp, 2s.

Golden Library, The :
Square 16mo (Tauchnitz size), cloth
limp, 2s. per Volume.
Bayard Taylor's Diversions of the
Echo Club.
Bennett's (Dr. W. C.) Ballad History
of England
Bennett's (Dr.) Songs for Sailors.
Godwin's (William) Lives of the
Necromancers.
Holmes's Autocrat of the Break-
fast Table. Introduction by SALA.
Holmes's Professor at the Break-
fast Table.
Hood's Whims and Oddities. Com-
plete. All the original Illustrations.
Jesse's (Edward) Scenes and Oc-
cupations of a Country Life.
Leigh Hunt's Essays: A Tale for a
Chimney Corner, and other Pieces.
With Portrait, and Introduction by
EDMUND OLLIER.
Mallory's (Sir Thomas) Mort
d'Arthur: The Stories of King
Arthur and of the Knights of the
Round Table. Edited by B. MONT-
GOMERIE RANKING.
Square 16mo, 2s. per Volume.
Pascal's Provincial Letters. A New
Translation, with Historical Intro-
duction and Notes, by T. M'CRIE, D.D.
Pope's Poetical Works. Complete.
Rochefoucauld's Maxims and Moral
Reflections. With Notes, and In-
troductory Essay by SAINTE-BEUVE.

Golden Treasury of Thought,
The: An ENCYCLOPÆDIA OF QUOTA-
TIONS from Writers of all Times and
Countries. Selected and Edited by
THEODORE TAYLOR. Crown 8vo, cloth
gilt and gilt edges, 7s. 6d.

Graham. — The Professor's
Wife : A Story. By LEONARD GRAHAM.
Fcap. 8vo, picture cover, 1s.

Greeks and Romans, The Life of the, Described from Antique Monuments. By ERNST GUHL and W. KONER. Translated from the Third German Edition, and Edited by Dr. F. HUEFFER. 545 Illusts. New and Cheaper Edition, large crown 8vo, cloth extra, 7s. 6d.

Greenaway (Kate) and Bret Harte.—The Queen of the Pirate Isle. By BRET HARTE. With 25 original Drawings by KATE GREEN-AWAY, Reproduced in Colours by E. EVANS. Sm. 4to, bds., 5s.

Greenwood (James), Works by:
Crown 8vo, cloth extra, 3s. 6d. each.
The Wilds of London.
Low-Life Deeps: An Account of the Strange Fish to be Found There.

Dick Temple: A Novel. Post 8vo, illustrated boards, 2s.

Gréville (Henri).—Nikanor: A Novel. From the French of HENRI GREVILLE, Author of "Dosia," &c. With 8 Illustrations. Crown 8vo, cloth extra, 6s.

Habberton (John), Author of " Helen's Babies," Novels by:
Post 8vo, illustrated boards, 2s. each; cloth limp, 2s. 6d. each.
Brueton's Bayou.
Country Luck.

Hair (The): Its Treatment in Health, Weakness, and Disease. Translated from the German of Dr. J. PINCUS. Crown 8vo, 1s.; cloth, 1s. 6d.

Hake (Dr. Thomas Gordon),
Poems by:
Crown 8vo, cloth extra, 6s. each.
New Symbols.
Legends of the Morrow.
The Serpent Play.

Maiden Ecstasy. Small 4to, cloth extra, 8s.

Hall.—Sketches of Irish Cha- racter. By Mrs. S. C. HALL. With numerous Illustrations on Steel and Wood by MACLISE, GILBERT, HARVEY, and G. CRUIKSHANK. Medium 8vo, cloth extra, gilt, 7s. 6d.

Halliday.—Every-day Papers. By ANDREW HALLIDAY. Post 8vo, illustrated boards, 2s.

Handwriting, The Philosophy of. With over 100 Facsimiles and Explanatory Text. By DON FELIX DE SALAMANCA. Post 8vo, cl. limp, 2s. 6d.

Hanky-Panky: A Collection of Very Easy Tricks, Very Difficult Tricks, White Magic, Sleight of Hand, &c. Edited by W. H. CREMER. With 200 Illusts. Crown 8vo, cloth extra, 4s. 6d.

Hardy (Lady Duffus). — Paul Wynter's Sacrifice: A Story. By Lady DUFFUS HARDY. Post 8vo, illust. bs., 2s.

Hardy (Thomas).—Under the Greenwood Tree. By THOMAS HARDY, Author of "Far from the Madding Crowd." With numerous Illustrations. Crown 8vo, cloth extra, 3s. 6d.; post 8vo, illustrated boards, 2s.

Harwood.—The Tenth Earl. By J. BERWICK HARWOOD. Post 8vo, illustrated boards, 2s.

Haweis (Mrs. H. R.), Works by:
The Art of Dress. With numerous Illustrations. Small 8vo, illustrated cover, 1s.; cloth limp, 1s. 6d.
The Art of Beauty. New and Cheaper Edition. Crown 8vo, cloth extra. Coloured Frontispiece and Illusts. 6s.
The Art of Decoration. Square 8vo, handsomely bound and profusely Illustrated, 10s. 6d.
Chaucer for Children: A Golden Key. With Eight Coloured Pictures and numerous Woodcuts. New Edition, small 4to, cloth extra, 6s.
Chaucer for Schools. Demy 8vo, cloth limp, 2s. 6d.

Haweis (Rev. H. R.).—American Humorists: WASHINGTON IRVING, OLIVER WENDELL HOLMES, JAMES RUSSELL LOWELL, ARTEMUS WARD, MARK TWAIN, and BRET HARTE. By Rev. H. R. HAWEIS, M.A. Cr. 8vo, 6s.

Hawthorne (Julian), Novels by
Crown 8vo, cloth extra, 3s. 6d. each
post 8vo, illustrated boards, 2s. each.

Garth.	Sebastian Strome
Ellice Quentin.	Dust.
Fortune's Fool.	Beatrix Randolph.
David Poindexter's Disappearance.	

Post 8vo, illustrated boards, 2s. each.

Miss Cadogna.	Love—or a Name.
Prince Saroni's Wife.	

Mrs. Gainsborough's Diamonds. Fcap. 8vo, illustrated cover, 1s.
A Dream and a Forgetting. By JULIAN HAWTHORNE. Cr. 8vo, picture cover, 1s.; cloth, 1s. 6d.
The Spectre of the Camera. Crown 8vo, cloth extra, 3s. 6d.

Hays.—Women of the Day: A
Biographical Dictionary of Notable
Contemporaries. By FRANCES HAYS.
Crown 8vo, cloth extra, 6s.

Heath (F. G.). — My Garden
Wild, and What I Grew There. By
FRANCIS GEORGE HEATH, Author of
"The Fern World," &c. Crown 8vo,
cloth extra, 5s.; cl. gilt, gilt edges, 6s.

Helps (Sir Arthur), Works by:
Post 8vo, cloth limp, 2s. 6d. each.
Animals and their Masters.
Social Pressure.

Ivan de Biron: A Novel. Crown 8vo,
cloth extra, 3s. 6d.; post 8vo, illustrated boards, 2s.

Henderson.—Agatha Page: A
Novel. By ISAAC HENDERSON. With
a Photograph Frontispiece from a
Picture by F. MOSCHELES. 2 Vols.,
crown 8vo.

Herman.—One Traveller Re-
turns: A Romance. By HENRY HER-
MAN and D. CHRISTIE MURRAY. Crown
8vo, cloth extra, 6s.

Herrick's (Robert) Hesperides,
Noble Numbers, and Complete Collected Poems. With Memorial-Introduction and Notes by the Rev. A. B.
GROSART, D.D., Steel Portrait, Index
of First Lines, and Glossarial Index,
&c. Three Vols., crown 8vo, cloth, 18s.

Hesse-Wartegg   (Chevalier
Ernst von), Works by:
Tunis: The Land and the People.
With 22 Illusts. Cr. 8vo, cl. ex., 3s. 6d.
The New South-West: Travelling
Sketches from Kansas, New Mexico,
Arizona, and Northern Mexico.
With 100 fine Illustrations and Three
Maps. Demy 8vo, cloth extra,
14s.   [*In preparation.*

Hindley (Charles), Works by:
Tavern Anecdotes and Sayings: In-
cluding the Origin of Signs, and
Reminiscences connected with
Taverns. Coffee Houses, Clubs, &c.
With Illustrations. Crown 8vo, cloth
extra, 3s. 6d.
The Life and Adventures of a Cheap
Jack. By One of the Fraternity.
Edited by CHARLES HINDLEY. Crown
8vo, cloth extra, 3s. 6d.

Hoey.—The Lover's Creed.
By Mrs. CASHEL HOEY. Post 8vo, illustrated boards, 2s.

Holmes (O. Wendell), Works by:
The Autocrat of the Breakfast-
Table. Illustrated by J. GORDON
THOMSON. Post 8vo, cloth limp,
2s. 6d.—Another Edition in smaller
type, with an Introduction by G. A.
SALA. Post 8vo, cloth limp, 2s.
The Professor at the Breakfast-
Table; with the Story of Iris. Post
8vo, cloth limp, 2s.

Holmes. — The . Science of
Voice Production and Voice Preser-
vation: A Popular Manual for the
Use of Speakers and Singers. By
GORDON HOLMES, M.D. With Illus-
trations. Crown 8vo, 1s.; cloth, 1s. 6d.

Hood (Thomas):
Hood's Choice Works, in Prose and
Verse. Including the Cream of the
COMIC ANNUALS. With Life of the
Author, Portrait, and 200 Illustra-
tions. Crown 8vo, cloth extra, 7s. 6d.
Hood's Whims and Oddities. Com-
plete. With all the original Illus-
trations. Post 8vo, cloth limp, 2s.

Hood (Tom), Works by:
From Nowhere to the North Pole:
A Noah's Arkæological Narrative.
With 25 Illustrations by W. BRUN-
TON and E. C. BARNES. Square
crown 8vo, cloth extra, gilt edges, 6s.
A Golden Heart: A Novel. Post 8vo,
illustrated boards, 2s.

Hook's (Theodore) Choice Hu-
morous Works, including his Ludi-
crous Adventures, Bons Mots, Puns and
Hoaxes. With a New Life of the
Author, Portraits, Facsimiles, and
Illusts. Cr. 8vo, cl. extra, gilt, 7s. 6d.

Hooper.—The House of Raby:
A Novel. By Mrs. GEORGE HOOPER.
Post 8vo, illustrated boards, 2s.

Horse (The) and his Rider: An
Anecdotic Medley. By "THORMANBY."
Crown 8vo, cloth extra, 6s.

Hopkins—"'Twixt Love and
Duty:" A Novel. By TIGHE HOPKINS.
Crown 8vo, cloth extra, 6s.; post 8vo,
illustrated boards, 2s.

Horne.—Orion: An Epic Poem,
in Three Books. By RICHARD HEN-
GIST HORNE. With Photographic
Portrait from a Medallion by SUM-
MERS. Tenth Edition, crown 8vo,
cloth extra, 7s.

Hunt (Mrs. Alfred), Novels by:
Crown 8vo, cloth extra, 3s. 6d. each;
post 8vo, illustrated boards, 2s. each.
Thornicroft's Model.
The Leaden Casket.
Self-Condemned.
That other Person.

Hunt.—Essays by Leigh Hunt.
A Tale for a Chimney Corner, and
other Pieces. With Portrait and Introduction by EDMUND OLLIER. Post
8vo, cloth limp, 2s.

Hydrophobia: an Account of M.
PASTEUR's System. Containing a
Translation of all his Communications
on the Subject, the Technique of his
Method, and the latest Statistical
Results. By RENAUD SUZOR, M.B.,
C.M. Edin., and M.D. Paris, Commis-
sioned by the Government of the
Colony of Mauritius to study M.
PASTEUR's new Treatment in Paris.
With 7 Illusts. Cr. 8vo, cloth extra, 6s.

Indoor Paupers. By ONE OF
THEM. Crown 8vo, 1s.; cloth, 1s. 6d.

Ingelow.—Fated to be Free : A
Novel. By JEAN INGELOW. Crown
8vo, cloth extra, 3s. 6d.; post 8vo,
illustrated boards, 2s.

Irish Wit and Humour, Songs
of. Collected and Edited by A. PER-
CEVAL GRAVES. Post 8vo, cl. limp, 2s. 6d.

James.—A Romance of the
Queen's Hounds. By CHARLES JAMES.
Post 8vo, picture cover, 1s.; cl., 1s. 6d.

Janvier.—Practical Keramics
for Students. By CATHERINE A.
JANVIER. Crown 8vo, cloth extra, 6s.

Jay (Harriett), Novels by:
Post 8vo, illustrated boards, 2s. each.
The Dark Colleen.
The Queen of Connaught.

Jefferies (Richard), Works by:
Nature near London. Crown 8vo,
cl. ex, 6s.; post 8vo, cl. limp, 2s. 6d.
The Life of the Fields. Post 8vo,
cloth limp, 2s. 6d.
The Open Air. Crown 8vo, cloth
extra, 6s.; post 8vo, cl. limp, 2s. 6d.
The Eulogy of Richard Jefferies.
By WALTER BESANT. With a Photo-
graph Portrait. Cr. 8vo, cl. ex., 6s.

Jennings (H. J.), Works by:
Curiosities of Criticism. Post 8vo,
cloth limp, 2s. 6d.
Lord Tennyson: A Biographical
Sketch. With a Photograph-Por-
trait. Crown 8vo, cloth extra, 6s.

Jerrold (Tom), Works by:
Post 8vo, 1s. each; cloth, 1s. 6d. each.
The Garden that Paid the Rent.
Household Horticulture: A Gossip
about Flowers. Illustrated.
Our Kitchen Garden: The Plants
we Grow, and How we Cook Them.

Jesse.—Scenes and Occupa-
tions of a Country Life. By EDWARD
JESSE. Post 8vo, cloth limp, 2s.

Jeux d'Esprit. Collected and
Edited by HENRY S. LEIGH. Post 8vo,
cloth limp, 2s. 6d.

"John Herring," Novels by
the Author of:
Red Spider. Crown 8vo, cloth extra,
3s. 6d.; post 8vo, illust. boards, 2s.
Eve. Crown 8vo, cloth extra, 3s. 6d.

Jones (Wm., F.S.A.), Works by:
Crown 8vo, cloth extra, 7s. 6d. each.
Finger-Ring Lore: Historical, Le-
gendary, and Anecdotal. With over
Two Hundred Illustrations.
Credulities, Past and Present; in-
cluding the Sea and Seamen, Miners,
Talismans, Word and Letter Divina-
tion, Exorcising and Blessing of
Animals, Birds, Eggs, Luck, &c.
With an Etched Frontispiece.
Crowns and Coronations: A History
of Regalia in all Times and Coun-
tries. One Hundred Illustrations.

Jonson's (Ben) Works. With
Notes Critical and Explanatory, and
a Biographical Memoir by WILLIAM
GIFFORD. Edited by Colonel CUN-
NINGHAM. Three Vols., crown 8vo,
cloth extra, 18s.; or separately, 6s. each.

Josephus, The Complete Works
of. Translated by WHISTON. Containing both "The Antiquities of the
Jews" and "The Wars of the Jews."
Two Vols., 8vo, with 52 Illustrations
and Maps, cloth extra, gilt, 14s.

Kempt.—Pencil and Palette :
Chapters on Art and Artists. By ROBERT
KEMPT. Post 8vo, cloth limp, 2s. 6d.

Kershaw.—Colonial Facts and
Fictions: Humorous Sketches. By
MARK KERSHAW. Post 8vo, illustrated
boards, 2s.; cloth, 2s. 6d.

King (R. Ashe), Novels by :
Crown 8vo, cloth extra, 3s. 6d. each;
post 8vo, illustrated boards, 2s. each.
A Drawn Game.
"The Wearing of the Green"

Kingsley (Henry), Novels by :
Oakshott Castle. Post 8vo, illustrated boards, 2s.
Number Seventeen. Crown 8vo, cloth
extra, 3s. 6d.

Knight.—The Patient's Vade
Mecum: How to get most Benefit
from Medical Advice. By WILLIAM
KNIGHT, M.R.C.S., and EDW. KNIGHT,
L.R.C.P. Cr. 8vo, 1s.; cloth, 1s. 6d.

Knights (The) of the Lion: A
Romance of the Thirteenth Century.
Edited, with an Introduction, by the
MARQUESS OF LORNE, K.T. Crown
8vo, cloth extra, 6s.

Lamb (Charles):

Lamb's Complete Works, in Prose and Verse, reprinted from the Original Editions, with many Pieces hitherto unpublished. Edited, with Notes and Introduction, by R. H. SHEPHERD. With Two Portraits and Facsimile of Page of the "Essay on Roast Pig." Cr. 8vo, cl. extra, 7s. 6d.

The Essays of Elia. Both Series complete. Post 8vo, laid paper, handsomely half-bound, 2s.

Poetry for Children, and Prince Dorus. By CHARLES LAMB. Carefully reprinted from unique copies. Small 8vo, cloth extra, 5s.

Little Essays: Sketches and Characters by CHARLES LAMB. Selected from his Letters by PERCY FITZGERALD. Post 8vo, cloth limp, 2s. 6d.

Lane's Arabian Nights.—The
Thousand and One Nights: commonly called, in England, "THE ARABIAN NIGHTS' ENTERTAINMENTS." A New Translation from the Arabic with copious Notes, by EDWARD WILLIAM LANE. Illustrated by many hundred Engravings on Wood, from Original Designs by WM. HARVEY. A New Edition, from a Copy annotated by the Translator, edited by his Nephew, EDWARD STANLEY POOLE. With a Preface by STANLEY LANE-POOLE. Three Vols., demy 8vo, cloth extra, 7s. 6d. each.

Larwood (Jacob), Works by:
The Story of the London Parks. With Illusts. Cr. 8vo, cl. ex., 3s. 6d.

Post 8vo, cloth limp, 2s. 6d. each.
Forensic Anecdotes.
Theatrical Anecdotes.

Leigh (Henry S.), Works by:
Carols of Cockayne. A New Edition, printed on fcap. 8vo, hand-made paper, and bound in buckram, 5s.
Jeux d'Esprit. Collected and Edited by HENRY S. LEIGH. Post 8vo, cloth limp, 2s. 6d.

Leys.—The Lindsays: A Ro-
mance of Scottish Life. By JOHN K. LEYS. Cheaper Edition. Post 8vo, illustrated boards, 2s.

Life in London; or, The History
of Jerry Hawthorn and Corinthian Tom. With the whole of CRUIKSHANK's Illustrations, in Colours, after the Originals. Cr. 8vo, cl. extra, 7s. 6d.

Linskill.—In Exchange for a
Soul. By MARY LINSKILL, Author of "The Haven Under the Hill," &c. Cheaper Edit. Post 8vo, illust. bds., 2s.

Linton (E. Lynn), Works by:
Post 8vo, cloth limp, 2s. 6d. each.
Witch Stories.
The True Story of Joshua Davidson.
Ourselves: Essays on Women.

Crown 8vo, cloth extra, 3s. 6d. each; post 8vo, illustrated boards, 2s. each.
Patricia Kemball.
The Atonement of Leam Dundas
The World Well Lost.
Under which Lord?
"My Love!" | Iona.
Paston Carew, Millionaire and Miser.

Post 8vo, illustrated boards, 2s. each.
With a Silken Thread.
The Rebel of the Family.

Longfellow's Poetical Works.
Carefully Reprinted from the Original Editions. With numerous fine Illustrations on Steel and Wood. Crown 8vo, cloth extra, 7s. 6d.

Long Life, Aids to: A Medical,
Dietetic, and General Guide in Health and Disease. By N. E. DAVIES, L.R.C.P. Cr. 8vo, 2s.; cl. limp, 2s. 6d.

Lucy.—Gideon Fleyce: A Novel.
By HENRY W. LUCY. Crown 8vo, cl. ex., 3s. 6d.; post 8vo, illust. bds., 2s.

Lusiad (The) of Camoens.
Translated into English Spenserian Verse by ROBERT FFRENCH DUFF. Demy 8vo, with Fourteen full-page Plates, cloth boards, 18s

Macalpine (Avery), Novels by:
Teresa Itasca, and other Stories. Crown 8vo, bound in canvas, 2s. 6d.
Broken Wings. With Illustrations by W. J. HENNESSY. Crown 8vo, cloth extra, 6s.

McCarthy (Justin H., M.P.),
Works by:
An Outline of the History of Ireland, from the Earliest Times to the Present Day. Cr. 8vo, 1s.; cloth, 1s. 6d.
Ireland since the Union: Sketches of Irish History from 1798 to 1886. Crown 8vo, cloth extra, 6s.
England under Gladstone, 1880-85. Second Edition, revised. Crown 8vo, cloth extra, 6s.
Doom! An Atlantic Episode. Crown 8vo, 1s.; cloth, 1s. 6d.
Our Sensation Novel. Edited by JUSTIN H. MCCARTHY. Crown 8vo, 1s.; cloth, 1s. 6d.
Dolly: A Sketch. Crown 8vo, picture cover, 1s.; cloth, 1s. 6d.
Hafiz in London. Choicely printed. Small 8vo, gold cloth, 3s. 6d.

McCarthy (Justin, M.P.), Works by :

A History of Our Own Times, from the Accession of Queen Victoria to the General Election of 1880. Four Vols. demy 8vo, cloth extra, 12s. each.—Also a POPULAR EDITION, in Four Vols. cr. 8vo, cl. extra, 6s. each. —And a JUBILEE EDITION, with an Appendix of Events to the end of 1886, complete in Two Vols., square 8vo, cloth extra, 7s. 6d. each.

A Short History of Our Own Times. One Vol., crown 8vo, cloth extra, 6s.

History of the Four Georges. Four Vols. demy 8vo, cloth extra, 12s. each.   [Vol. I. *now ready.*

Crown 8vo, cloth extra, 3s. 6d. each; post 8vo, illustrated boards, 2s. each.
Dear Lady Disdain.
The Waterdale Neighbours.
A Fair Saxon.
Miss Misanthrope.
Donna Quixote.
The Comet of a Season.
Maid of Athens.
Camiola: A Girl with a Fortune.

Post 8vo, illustrated boards, 2s. each.
Linley Rochford.
My Enemy's Daughter.

"The Right Honourable:" A Romance of Society and Politics. By JUSTIN McCARTHY, M.P., and Mrs. CAMPBELL-PRAED. New and Cheaper Edition, crown 8vo, cloth extra, 6s.

MacColl.— Mr. Stranger's Sealed Packet : A New Story of Adventure. By HUGH MACCOLL. Crown 8vo, cloth extra, 5s.

MacDonald.—Works of Fancy and Imagination. By GEORGE MAC-DONALD, LL.D. Ten Volumes, in handsome cloth case, 21s.— Vol. I. WITHIN AND WITHOUT. THE HIDDEN LIFE.— Vol. 2. THE DISCIPLE. THE GOSPEL WOMEN. A BOOK OF SONNETS, ORGAN SONGS.—Vol. 3. VIOLIN SONGS. SONGS OF THE DAYS AND NIGHTS. A BOOK OF DREAMS. ROADSIDE POEMS. POEMS FOR CHILDREN. Vol. 4. PARABLES. BALLADS. SCOTCH SONGS.— Vols. 5 and 6. PHANTASTES: A Faerie Romance.—Vol. 7. THE PORTENT.— Vol. 8. THE LIGHT PRINCESS. THE GIANT'S HEART. SHADOWS.— Vol. 9. CROSS PURPOSES. THE GOLDEN KEY. THE CARASOYN. LITTLE DAYLIGHT.— Vol. 10. THE CRUEL PAINTER. THE WOW O' RIVVEN. THE CASTLE. THE BROKEN SWORDS. THE GRAY WOLF. UNCLE CORNELIUS.
The Volumes are also sold separately in Grolier-pattern cloth, 2s. 6d. each.

Macdonell.—Quaker Cousins: A Novel. By AGNES MACDONELL. Crown 8vo, cloth extra, 3s. 6d. ; post 8vo, illustrated boards, 2s.

Macgregor. — Pastimes and Players. Notes on Popular Games. By ROBERT MACGREGOR. Post 8vo, cloth limp, 2s. 6d.

Mackay.—Interludes and Undertones ; or, Music at Twilight. By CHARLES MACKAY, LL.D. Crown 8vo cloth extra, 6s.

Maclise Portrait-Gallery (The) of Illustrious Literary Characters ; with Memoirs—Biographical, Critical, Bibliographical, and Anecdotal—illustrative of the Literature of the former half of the Present Century. By WILLIAM BATES, B.A. With 85 Portraits printed on an India Tint. Crown 8vo, cloth extra, 7s. 6d.

Macquoid (Mrs.), Works by :

Square 8vo, cloth extra, 7s. 6d. each.
In the Ardennes. With 50 fine Illustrations by THOMAS R. MACQUOID.
Pictures and Legends from Normandy and Brittany. With numerous Illusts. by THOMAS R. MACQUOID.
Through Normandy. With 90 Illustrations by T. R. MACQUOID.
Through Brittany. With numerous Illustrations by T. R. MACQUOID.
About Yorkshire. With 67 Illustrations by T. R. MACQUOID.

Post 8vo, illustrated boards, 2s. each.
The Evil Eye, and other Stories.
Lost Rose.

Magician's Own Book (The): Performances with Cups and Balls, Eggs Hats, Handkerchiefs, &c. All from actual Experience. Edited by W. H. CREMER. With 200 Illustrations. Crown 8vo, cloth extra, 4s. 6d.

Magic Lantern (The), and its Management : including full Practical Directions for producing the Limelight, making Oxygen Gas, and preparing Lantern Slides. By T. C. HEPWORTH. With 10 Illustrations. Crown 8vo, 1s. ; cloth, 1s. 6d.

Magna Charta. An exact Fac-simile of the Original in the British Museum, printed on fine plate paper, 3 feet by 2 feet, with Arms and Seals emblazoned in Gold and Colours, 5s.

Mallock (W. H.), Works by:
The New Republic; or, Culture, Faith and Philosophy in an English Country House. Post 8vo, cloth limp, 2s. 6d.; Cheap Edition, illustrated boards, 2s.
The New Paul and Virginia; or, Positivism on an Island. Post 8vo, cloth limp, 2s. 6d.
Poems. Small 4to, in parchment, 8s.
Is Life worth Living? Crown 8vo, cloth extra, 6s.

Mallory's (Sir Thomas) Mort d'Arthur: The Stories of King Arthur and of the Knights of the Round Table. Edited by B. MONTGOMERIE RANKING. Post 8vo, cloth limp, 2s.

Man - Hunter (The): Stories from the Note-book of a Detective. By DICK DONOVAN. Post 8vo, illustrated boards, 2s.; cloth, 2s. 6d.

Mark Twain, Works by:
The Choice Works of Mark Twain. Revised and Corrected throughout by the Author. With Life, Portrait, and numerous Illust. Cr. 8vo, cl. ex, 7s. 6d.
The Innocents Abroad; or, The New Pilgrim's Progress: Being some Account of the Steamship "Quaker City's" Pleasure Excursion to Europe and the Holy Land. With 234 Illustrations. Crown 8vo, cloth extra, 7s. 6d.—Cheap Edition (under the title of "MARK TWAIN'S PLEASURE TRIP"), post 8vo, illust. boards, 2s.
Roughing It, and The Innocents at Home. With 200 Illustrations by F. A. FRASER. Cr. 8vo, cl. ex., 7s. 6d.
The Gilded Age. By MARK TWAIN and CHARLES DUDLEY WARNER. With 212 Illustrations by T. COPPIN. Crown 8vo, cloth extra, 7s. 6d.
The Adventures of Tom Sawyer. With 111 Illustrations. Crown 8vo, cloth extra, 7s. 6d.—Cheap Edition, post 8vo, illustrated boards, 2s.
The Prince and the Pauper. With nearly 200 Illustrations. Crown 8vo, cloth extra, 7s. 6d.—Cheap Edition, post 8vo, illustrated boards, 2s.
A Tramp Abroad. With 314 Illusts. Cr. 8vo, cloth extra, 7s. 6d.—Cheap Edition, post 8vo, illust. bds., 2s.
The Stolen White Elephant, &c. Cr.8vo,cl.ex, 6s.; post 8vo,illust.bs.,2s.
Life on the Mississippi. With about 300 Original Illustrations. Crown 8vo, cloth extra, 7s. 6d.—Cheap Edition, post 8vo, illustrated boards, 2s.
The Adventures of Huckleberry Finn. With 174 Illustrations by E. W. KEMBLE. Crown 8vo, cloth extra, 7s. 6d.—Cheap Edition, post 8vo, illustrated boards, 2s.
Mark Twain's Library of Humour. With numerous Illustrations. Crown 8vo, cloth extra, 7s. 6d.

Marlowe's Works. Including his Translations. Edited, with Notes and Introductions, by Col. CUNNINGHAM. Crown 8vo, cloth extra, 6s.

Marryat (Florence), Novels by:
Crown 8vo, cloth extra. 3s. 6d. each; post 8vo, illustrated boards, 2s. each.
Open! Sesame! | Written in Fire.
Post 8vo, illustrated boards, 2s. each.
A Harvest of Wild Oats.
Fighting the Air.

Massinger's Plays. From the Text of WILLIAM GIFFORD. Edited by Col. CUNNINGHAM. Crown 8vo, cloth extra, 6s.

Masterman.—Half a Dozen Daughters: A Novel. By J. MASTERMAN. Post 8vo, illustrated boards, 2s.

Matthews.—A Secret of the Sea, &c. By BRANDER MATTHEWS. Post 8vo, illust. bds., 2s.; cloth, 2s. 6d.

Mayfair Library, The:
Post 8vo, cloth limp, 2s. 6d. per Volume.
A Journey Round My Room. By XAVIER DE MAISTRE. Translated by HENRY ATTWELL.
Quips and Quiddities. Selected by W. DAVENPORT ADAMS.
The Agony Column of "The Times," from 1800 to 1870. Edited, with an Introduction, by ALICE CLAY.
Melancholy Anatomised: A Popular Abridgment of "Burton's Anatomy of Melancholy."
The Speeches of Charles Dickens.
Literary Frivolities, Fancies, Follies, and Frolics. By W. T. DOBSON.
Poetical Ingenuities and Eccentricities. Selected and Edited by W. T. DOBSON.
The Cupboard Papers. By FIN-BEC.
Original Plays by W. S. GILBERT. FIRST SERIES. Containing: The Wicked World — Pygmalion and Galatea—Charity—The Princess—The Palace of Truth—Trial by Jury
Original Plays by W. S GILBERT. SECOND SERIES. Containing: Broken Hearts — Engaged — Sweethearts—Gretchen—Dan'l Druce—Tom Cobb—H.M.S. Pinafore — The Sorcerer —The Pirates of Penzance.
Songs of Irish Wit and Humour. Collected and Edited by A. PERCEVAL GRAVES.
Animals and their Masters. By Sir ARTHUR HELPS.
Social Pressure. By Sir A. HELPS.
Curiosities of Criticism. By HENRY J. JENNINGS.
The Autocrat of the Breakfast-Table. By OLIVER WENDELL HOLMES. Illustrated by J. GORDON THOMSON.

MAYFAIR LIBRARY, *continued*—
Pencil and Palette. By R. KEMPT.
Little Essays: Sketches and Characters. By CHAS. LAMB. Selected from his Letters by PERCY FITZGERALD.
Forensic Anecdotes; or, Humour and Curiosities of the Law and Men of Law. By JACOB LARWOOD.
Theatrical Anecdotes. By JACOB LARWOOD.   [LEIGH.
Jeux d'Esprit. Edited by HENRY S.
True History of Joshua Davidson. By E. LYNN LINTON.
Witch Stories. By E. LYNN LINTON.
Ourselves: Essays on Women. By E. LYNN LINTON.   [MACGREGOR.
Pastimes and Players. By ROBERT
The New Paul and Virginia. By W. H. MALLOCK.
New Republic. By W. H. MALLOCK.
Puck on Pegasus. By H. CHOLMONDELEY-PENNELL.
Pegasus Re-Saddled. By H. CHOLMONDELEY-PENNELL. Illustrated by GEORGE DU MAURIER.
Muses of Mayfair Edited by H. CHOLMONDELEY-PENNELL.
Thoreau: His Life and Aims. By H. A. PAGE.
Puniana. By the Hon. HUGH ROWLEY.
More Puniana. By Hon. H. ROWLEY.
The Philosophy of Handwriting. By DON FELIX DE SALAMANCA.
By Stream and Sea By WILLIAM SENIOR.
Leaves from a Naturalist's Note-Book. By Dr. ANDREW WILSON.

Mayhew.—London Characters and the Humorous Side of London Life. By HENRY MAYHEW. With numerous Illusts. Cr. 8vo, cl. extra, 3s. 6d.

Medicine, Family.—One Thousand Medical Maxims and Surgical Hints, for Infancy, Adult Life, Middle Age, and Old Age. By N. E. DAVIES, L.R.C.P. Lond. Cr. 8vo, 1s.; cl., 1s. 6d.

Menken.—Infelicia: Poems by ADAH ISAACS MENKEN. A New Edition, with a Biographical Preface, numerous Illustrations by F. E. LUMMIS and F. O. C. DARLEY, and Facsimile of a Letter from CHARLES DICKENS. Beautifully printed on small 4to ivory paper, with red border to each page, and handsomely bound. Price 7s. 6d.

Mexican Mustang (On a), through Texas, from the Gulf to the Rio Grande. A New Book of American Humour. By A. E. SWEET and J. ARMOY. KNOX, Editors of "Texas Siftings." With 265 Illusts. Cr. 8vo, cl. extra, 7s. 6d.

Middlemass (Jean), Novels by: Post 8vo, illustrated boards, 2s. each.
Touch and Go. | Mr. Dorillion.

Miller.—Physiology for the Young; or, The House of Life: Human Physiology, with its application to the Preservation of Health. For Classes and Popular Reading. With numerous Illusts. By Mrs. F. FENWICK MILLER. Small 8vo, cloth limp, 2s. 6d.

Milton (J. L.), Works by:
Sm. 8vo, 1s. each; cloth ex., 1s. 6d. each.
The Hygiene of the Skin. A Concise Set of Rules for the Management of the Skin; with Directions for Diet, Wines, Soaps, Baths, &c.
The Bath in Diseases of the Skin.
The Laws of Life, and their Relation to Diseases of the Skin.

Minto.—Was She Good or Bad? A Romance. By WILLIAM MINTO. Cr. 8vo, picture cover, 1s.; cloth, 1s. 6d

Molesworth (Mrs.), Novels by:
Hathercourt Rectory. Crown 8vo, cloth extra, 4s. 6d. ; post 8vo, illustrated boards, 2s.
That Girl in Black. Crown 8vo, picture cover, 1s.; cloth, 1s. 6d.

Moncrieff.—The Abdication; or, Time Tries All. An Historical Drama. By W. D. SCOTT-MONCRIEFF. With Seven Etchings by JOHN PETTIE, R.A., W. Q. ORCHARDSON, R.A., J. MACWHIRTER, A.R.A., COLIN HUNTER, A.R.A., R. MACBETH, A.R.A., and TOM GRAHAM, R.S.A. Large 4to, bound in buckram, 21s.

Moore (Thomas):
Byron's Letters and Journals; with Notices of his Life. By THOMAS MOORE. Cr. 8vo, cloth extra, 7s. 6d.
Prose and Verse, Humorous, Satirical, and Sentimental, by THOMAS MOORE; with Suppressed Passages from the Memoirs of Lord Byron. Edited, with Notes and Introduction, by R. HERNE SHEPHERD. With a Portrait. Cr. 8vo, cloth extra, 7s. 6d.

Murray (D. Christie), Novels by. Crown 8vo, cloth extra, 3s. 6d. each; post 8vo, illustrated boards, 2s. each.
A Life's Atonement. | A Model Father.
Joseph's Coat. | Coals of Fire.
By the Gate of the Sea.
Val Strange. | Hearts.
A Bit of Human Nature.
First Person Singular.
Cynic Fortune.
The Way of the World. Post 8vo, illustrated boards, 2s.
Old Blazer's Hero. With Three Illustrations by A. McCORMICK. Crown 8vo, cloth ex., 6s.—Cheaper Edition, post 8vo, illust. boards, 2s.
One Traveller Returns. By D. CHRISTIE MURRAY and H. HERMAN. Cr. 8vo, cl. ex., 6s.

Muddock.—Stories Weird and Wonderful. By J. E. Muddock. Post 8vo, illust. boards, 2s. ; cloth, 2s. 6d.

Novelists.—Half-Hours with the Best Novelists of the Century: Choice Readings from the finest Novels. Edited, with Critical and Biographical Notes, by H. T. Mackenzie Bell. Crown 8vo, cl. ex., 3s. 6d. [Preparing.

Nursery Hints: A Mother's Guide in Health and Disease. By N. E. Davies, L.R.C.P. Cr. 8vo, 1s. ; cl., 1s. 6d.

O'Connor.—Lord Beaconsfield: A Biography. By T. P. O'Connor, M.P. Sixth Edition, with a New Preface. Crown 8vo, cloth extra, 5s.

O'Hanlon (Alice), Novels by :
The Unforeseen. Post 8vo, illust. bds., 2s.
Chance? or Fate? 3 vols., cr. 8vo.

Ohnet.—Doctor Rameau: A Novel. By Georges Ohnet, Author of "The Ironmaster," &c. Translated by Mrs. Cashel Hoey. With 9 Illustrations by E. Bayard. Crown 8vo, cloth extra, 6s.

Oliphant (Mrs.) Novels by :
Whiteladies. With Illustrations by Arthur Hopkins and H. Woons. Crown 8vo, cloth extra, 3s. 6d. ; post 8vo, illustrated boards, 2s.
Crown 8vo, cloth extra, 4s. 6d. each. ; post 8vo, illustrated boards, 2s. each.
The Primrose Path.
The Greatest Heiress in England.

O'Reilly.—Phœbe's Fortunes : A Novel. With Illustrations by Henry Tuck. Post 8vo, illustrated boards, 2s.

O'Shaughnessy (A.), Poems by :
Songs of a Worker. Fcap. 8vo, cloth extra, 7s. 6d.
Music and Moonlight. Fcap. 8vo, cloth extra, 7s. 6d.
Lays of France. Cr. 8vo, cl. ex., 10s. 6d.

Ouida, Novels by. Crown 8vo, cloth extra, 3s. 6d. each ; post 8vo, illustrated boards, 2s. each.

Held in Bondage.	Pascarel.
Strathmore.	Signa. | Ariadne.
Chandos	In a Winter City.
Under Two Flags.	Friendship.
Cecil Castle-	Moths. | Bimbi.
maine's Gage.	Pipistrello.
Idalia.	In Maremma.
Tricotrin.	A Village Com-
Puck.	mune.
Folle Farine.	Wanda.
Two Little Wooden	Frescoes. [ine.
Shoes.	Princess Naprax-
A Dog of Flanders.	Othmar,

Ouida—continued.
Guilderoy: A Novel. 3 vols., crown 8vo. [June.
Wisdom, Wit, and Pathos, selected from the Works of Ouida by F. Sydney Morris. Sm. cr. 8vo, cl. ex., 5s. Cheaper Edition, illust. bds., 2s.

Page (H. A.), Works by :
Thoreau: His Life and Aims: A Study. With Portrait. Post 8vo, cl. limp, 2s. 6d.
Lights on the Way: Some Tales within a Tale. By the late J. H. Alexander, B.A. Edited by H. A. Page. Crown 8vo, cloth extra, 6s.
Animal Anecdotes. Arranged on a New Principle. Cr. 8vo, cl. extra, 5s.

Parliamentary Elections and Electioneering in the Old Days (A History of). Showing the State of Political Parties and Party Warfare at the Hustings and in the House of Commons from the Stuarts to Queen Victoria. Illustrated from the original Political Squibs, Lampoons, Pictorial Satires, and Popular Caricatures of the Time. By Joseph Grego, Author of "Rowlandson and his Works," "The Life of Gillray," &c. A New Edition, crown 8vo, cloth extra, with Coloured Frontispiece and 100 Illustrations, 7s. 6d. [Preparing.

Pascal's Provincial Letters. A New Translation, with Historical Introduction and Notes, by T. M'Crie, D.D. Post 8vo, cloth limp, 2s.

Patient's (The) Vade Mecum : How to get most Benefit from Medical Advice. By W. Knight, M.R.C.S., and E. Knight, L.R.C.P. Cr. 8vo, 1s. ; cl. 1/6.

Paul Ferroll :
Post 8vo, illustrated boards, 2s. each.
Paul Ferroll : A Novel.
Why Paul Ferroll Killed his Wife.

Payn (James), Novels by. Crown 8vo, cloth extra, 3s. 6d. each ; post 8vo, illustrated boards, 2s. each.
Lost Sir Massingberd.
Walter's Word.
Less Black than we're Painted.
By Proxy. | High Spirits.
Under One Roof.
A Confidential Agent.
Some Private Views.
A Grape from a Thorn.
From Exile. | The Canon's Ward.
The Talk of the Town.
Holiday Tasks. | Glow-worm Tales.

Post 8vo, illustrated boards, 2s. each.
Kit: A Memory. | Carlyon's Year.
A Perfect Treasure.
Bentinck's Tutor. | Murphy's Master.
The Best of Husbands,

PAYN (JAMES), *continued—*
Post 8vo, illustrated boards, 2s. each.
For Cash Only.
What He Cost Her. | Cecil's Tryst.
Fallen Fortunes. | Halves.
A County Family. | At Her Mercy
A Woman's Vengeance.
The Clyffards of Clyffe.
The Family Scapegrace.
The Foster Brothers.| Found Dead.
Gwendoline's Harvest.
Humorous Stories.
Like Father, Like Son.
A Marine Residence.
Married Beneath Him.
Mirk Abbey. | Not Wooed, but Won.
Two Hundred Pounds Reward.

Crown 8vo, cloth extra, 3s. 6d. each.
In Peril and Privation: Stories of
Marine Adventure Re-told. With 17
Illustrations.
The Mystery of Mirbridge. With a
Frontispiece by ARTHUR HOPKINS

Paul.—Gentle and Simple. By
MARGARET AGNES PAUL. With a
Frontispiece by HELEN PATERSON.
Cr 8vo, cloth extra, 3s. 6d.; post 8vo,
illustrated boards, 2s.

Pears.—The Present Depres-
sion in Trade: Its Causes and Reme-
dies. Being the "Pears" Prize Essays
(of One Hundred Guineas). By EDWIN
GOADBY and WILLIAM WATT. With
an Introductory Paper by Prof. LEONE
LEVI, F.S.A., F.S.S. Demy 8vo, 1s.

Pennell (H. Cholmondeley),
Works by:
Post 8vo, cloth limp, 2s. 6d. each.
Puck on Pegasus. With Illustrations.
Pegasus Re-Saddled. With Ten full-
page Illusts. by G. DU MAURIER.
The Muses of Mayfair. Vers de
Société, Selected and Edited by H.
C. PENNELL.

Phelps (E. Stuart), Works by:
Post 8vo, 1s. each; cl. limp, 1s. 6d. each.
Beyond the Gates. By the Author
of "The Gates Ajar."
An Old Maid's Paradise.
Burglars in Paradise.

Jack the Fisherman. With Twenty-
two Illustrations by C. W. REED.
Cr. 8vo, picture cover, 1s.; cl. 1s. 6d.

Pirkis (C. L.), Novels by:
Trooping with Crows. Fcap. 8vo,
picture cover, 1s.
Lady Lovelace. Post 8vo, illustrated
boards, 2s.

Plutarch's Lives of Illustrious
Men. Translated from the Greek,
with Notes Critical and Historical, and
a Life of Plutarch, by JOHN and
WILLIAM LANGHORNE. Two Vols.,
8vo, cloth extra, with Portraits, 10s. 6d.

Planché (J. R.), Works by:
The Pursuivant of Arms; or, Her-
aldry Founded upon Facts. With
Coloured Frontispiece and 200 Illus-
trations. Cr. 8vo, cloth extra, 7s. 6d.
Songs and Poems, from 1819 to 1879.
Edited, with an Introduction, by his
Daughter, Mrs. MACKARNESS. Crown
8vo, cloth extra, 6s.

Poe (Edgar Allan):—
The Choice Works, in Prose and
Poetry, of EDGAR ALLAN POE. With
an Introductory Essay by CHARLES
BAUDELAIRE, Portrait and Fac-
similes. Crown 8vo, cl. extra, 7s. 6d.
The Mystery of Marie Roget, and
other Stories. Post 8vo, illust. bds., 2s.

Pope's Poetical Works. Complete in One Vol. Post 8vo, cl. limp, 2s.

Praed (Mrs. Campbell-).—"The
Right Honourable:" A Romance of
Society and Politics. By Mrs. CAMP-
BELL-PRAED and JUSTIN McCARTHY,
M.P. Cr. 8vo, cloth extra, 6s.

Price (E. C.), Novels by:
Crown 8vo, cloth extra, 3s. 6d. each;
post 8vo, illustrated boards, 2s. each.
Valentina. | The Foreigners.
Mrs. Lancaster's Rival.

Gerald. Post 8vo, illust. boards, 2s.

Princess Olga—Radna; or, The
Great Conspiracy of 1881. By the
Princess OLGA. Cr. 8vo, cl. ex., 6s.

Proctor (Rich. A.), Works by:
Flowers of the Sky. With 55 Illusts.
Small crown 8vo, cloth extra, 3s. 6d.
Easy Star Lessons. With Star Maps
for Every Night in the Year, Draw-
ings of the Constellations, &c.
Crown 8vo, cloth extra, 6s.
Familiar Science Studies. Crown
8vo, cloth extra, 6s.
Saturn and Its System. New and
Revised Edition, with 13 Steel Plates.
Demy 8vo, cloth extra, 10s. 6d.
Mysteries of Time and Space. With
Illusts. Cr. 8vo, cloth extra, 6s.
The Universe of Suns, and other
Science Gleanings. With numerous
Illusts. Cr. 8vo, cloth extra, 6s.
Wages and Wants of Science
Workers. Crown 8vo, 1s. 6d.

Rambosson.—Popular Astro-
nomy. By J. RAMBOSSON, Laureate of
the Institute of France. Translated by
C. B. PITMAN. Crown 8vo, cloth gilt,
numerous Illusts., and a beautifully
executed Chart of Spectra, 7s. 6d.

Reade (Charles), Novels by:
Cr. 8vo, cloth extra, illustrated, 3s. 6d. each; post 8vo, illust. bds., 2s. each.

Peg Woffington. Illustrated by S. L. FILDES, A.R.A.

Christie Johnstone. Illustrated by WILLIAM SMALL.

It is Never Too Late to Mend. Illustrated by G. I. PINWELL.

The Course of True Love Never did run Smooth. Illustrated by HELEN PATERSON.

The Autobiography of a Thief; Jack of all Trades; and James Lambert. Illustrated by MATT STRETCH.

Love me Little, Love me Long. Illustrated by M. ELLEN EDWARDS.

The Double Marriage. Illust. by Sir JOHN GILBERT, R.A., and C. KEENE.

The Cloister and the Hearth. Illustrated by CHARLES KEENE.

Hard Cash. Illust. by F. W. LAWSON.

Griffith Gaunt. Illustrated by S. L. FILDES, A.R.A., and WM. SMALL.

Foul Play. Illust. by DU MAURIER.

Put Yourself in His Place. Illustrated by ROBERT BARNES.

A Terrible Temptation. Illustrated by EDW. HUGHES and A. W. CODFER.

The Wandering Heir. Illustrated by H. PATERSON, S. L. PILDES, A.R.A., C. GREEN, and H. WOODS, A.R.A.

A Simpleton. Illustrated by KATE CRAUFORD.   [COULDERY.

A Woman-Hater. Illust. by THOS.

Singleheart and Doubleface: A Matter-of-fact Romance. Illustrated by P. MACNAB.

Good Stories of Men and other Animals. Illustrated by E. A. ABBEY, PERCY MACQUOID, and JOSEPH NASH.

The Jilt, and other Stories. Illustrated by JOSEPH NASH.

Readiana. With a Steel-plate Portrait of CHARLES READE.

Bible Characters: Studies of David, Nehemiah, Jonah, Paul, &c. Fcap. 8vo, leatherette, Is.

Reader's Handbook (The) of
Allusions, References, Plots, and Stories. By the Rev. Dr. BREWER. Fifth Edition, revised throughout, with a New Appendix, containing a COMPLETE ENGLISH BIBLIOGRAPHY. Cr. 8vo, 1,400 pages, cloth extra, 7s. 6d.

Richardson. — A Ministry of
Health, and other Papers. By BENJAMIN WARD RICHARDSON, M.D., &c. Crown 8vo, cloth extra, 6s.

Riddell (Mrs. J. H.), Novels by:
Crown 8vo, cloth extra, 3s. 6d. each; post 8vo, illustrated boards, 2s. each.

Her Mother's Darling.
The Prince of Wales's Garden Party.
Waird Stories.

Post 8vo, illustrated boards, 2s. each.
The Uninhabited House.
Fairy Water.
The Mystery in Palace Gardens.

Rimmer (Alfred), Works by:
Square 8vo, cloth gilt, 7s. 6d. each.

Our Old Country Towns. With over 50 Illustrations.

Rambles Round Eton and Harrow. With 50 Illustrations.

About England with Dickens. With 58 Illustrations by ALFRED RIMMER and C. A. VANDERHOOF.

Robinson (F. W.), Novels by:
Crown 8vo, cloth extra, 3s. 6d. each; post 8vo, illustrated boards, 2s. each.

Women are Strange.
The Hands of Justice.

Robinson (Phil), Works by:
Crown 8vo, cloth extra, 7s. 6d. each.
The Poets' Birds.
The Poets' Beasts.
The Poets and Nature: Reptiles, Fishes, and Insects.   [Preparing.

Rochefoucauld's Maxims and
Moral Reflections. With Notes, and an Introductory Essay by SAINTE-BEUVE. Post 8vo, cloth limp, 2s.

Roll of Battle Abbey, The; or,
A List of the Principal Warriors who came over from Normandy with William the Conqueror, and Settled in this Country, A.D. 1066–7. With the principal Arms emblazoned in Gold and Colours. Handsomely printed, 5s.

Rowley (Hon. Hugh), Works by
Post 8vo, cloth limp, 2s. 6d. each.
Puniana: Riddles and Jokes. With numerous Illustrations.
More Puniana. Profusely Illustrated.

Runciman (James), Stories by:
Post 8vo, illustrated boards, 2s. each; cloth limp, 2s. 6d. each.
Skippers and Shellbacks.
Grace Balmaign's Sweetheart.
Schools and Scholars.

Russell (W. Clark), Works by:
Crown 8vo, cloth extra, 6s. each; post 8vo, illustrated boards, 2s. each.
Round the Galley-Fire.
In the Middle Watch.
A Voyage to the Cape.
A Book for the Hammock.

On the Fo'k'sle Head. Post 8vo, illustrated boards, 2s.
The Mystery of the "Ocean Star," &c. Crown 8vo, cloth extra, 6s.

Sala.—Gaslight and Daylight.
By GEORGE AUGUSTUS SALA. Post 8vo, illustrated boards, 2s.

Sanson.—Seven Generations
of Executioners: Memoirs of the Sanson Family (1688 to 1847). Edited by HENRY SANSON. Cr. 8vo, cl. ex. 3s 6d.

Saunders (John), Novels by:
Crown 8vo, cloth extra, 3s. 6d. each; post 8vo, illustrated boards, 2s. each.
Bound to the Wheel.
Guy Waterman. | Lion in the Path.
The Two Dreamers.

One Against the World. Post 8vo, illustrated boards, 2s.

Saunders (Katharine), Novels by. Cr. 8vo, cloth extra, 3s. 6d. each; post 8vo, illustrated boards, 2s. each.
Margaret and Elizabeth.
The High Mills.
Heart Salvage. | Sebastian.

Joan Merryweather. Post 8vo, illustrated boards, 2s.
Gideon's Rock. Crown 8vo, cloth extra, 3s. 6d.

Science-Gossip for 1889: An Illustrated Medium of Interchange for Students and Lovers of Nature. Edited by Dr. J. E. TAYLOR, F.L.S., &c. Devoted to Geology, Botany, Physiology, Chemistry, Zoology, Microscopy, Telescopy, Physiography, &c. Price 4d. Monthly; or 5s. per year, post free. Vols. I. to XIX. may be had at 7s. 6d. each; and Vols. XX. to date, at 6s. each. Cases for Binding, 1s. 6d. each.

Seguin (L. G.), Works by:
Crown 8vo, cloth extra, 6s. each.
The Country of the Passion Play, and the Highlands and Highlanders of Bavaria. With Map and 37 Illusts.
Walks in Algiers and its Surroundings. With 2 Maps and 16 Illusts.

"Secret Out" Series, The:
Cr. 8vo, cl. ex., Illusts., 4s. 6d. each.
The Secret Out: One Thousand Tricks with Cards, and other Recreations; with Entertaining Experiments in Drawing-room or "White Magic." By W. H. CREMER. 300 Illusts.
The Art of Amusing: A Collection of Graceful Arts, Games, Tricks, Puzzles, and Charades By FRANK BELLEW. With 300 Illustrations.
Hanky-Panky: Very Easy Tricks, Very Difficult Tricks, White Magic, Sleight of Hand. Edited by W. H. CREMER. With 200 Illustrations.
Magician's Own Book: Performances with Cups and Balls, Eggs, Hats, Handkerchiefs, &c. All from actual Experience. Edited by W. H. CREMER. 200 Illustrations.

Senior.—By Stream and Sea.
By W. SENIOR. Post 8vo, cl. limp, 2s. 6d.

Seven Sagas (The) of Prehistoric Man. By JAMES H. STODDART, Author of "The Village Life." Crown 8vo, cloth extra, 6s.

Shakespeare:
The First Folio Shakespeare.—MR. WILLIAM SHAKESPEARE'S Comedies, Histories, and Tragedies. Published according to the true Originall Copies London, Printed by ISAAC IAGGARD and ED. BLOUNT. 1623.—A Reproduction of the extremely rare original, in reduced facsimile, by a photographic process—ensuring the strictest accuracy in every detail. Small 8vo, half-Roxburghe, 7s. 6d.
The Lansdowne Shakespeare. Beautifully printed in red and black, in small but very clear type. With engraved facsimile of DROESHOUT'S Portrait. Post 8vo, cloth extra, 7s. 6d.
Shakespeare for Children: Tales from Shakespeare. By CHARLES and MARY LAMB. With numerous Illustrations, coloured and plain, by J. MOYR SMITH. Cr. 4to, cl. gilt, 6s.

Sharp.—Children of To-morrow: A Novel. By WILLIAM SHARP. Crown 8vo, cloth extra, 6s.

Sheridan (General).—Personal
Memoirs of General P. H. Sheridan: The Romantic Career of a Great Soldier, told in his Own Words. With 22 Portraits and other Illustrations, 27 Maps and numerous Facsimiles of Famous Letters. Two Vols. of 500 pages each, demy 8vo, cloth extra, 24s.

Shelley.—The Complete Works
In Verse and Prose of Percy Bysshe
Shelley. Edited, Prefaced and Anno-
tated by R. Herne Shepherd. Five
Vols., cr. 8vo, cloth bds., 3s. 6d. each.

Poetical Works, in Three Vols.

Vol. I. An Introduction by the Editor; The
Posthumous Fragments of Margaret Nichol-
son; Shelley's Correspondence with Stock-
dale; The Wandering Jew (the only complete
version); Queen Mab, with the Notes;
Alastor, and other Poems; Rosalind and
Helen; Prometheus Unbound; Adonais, &c.

Vol. II. Laon and Cythna (as originally published, instead of the emasculated "Revolt
of Islam"); The Cenci; Julian and Madda'o
(from Shelley's manuscript); Swellfoot the
Tyrant (from the copy in the Dyce Library
at South Kensington); The Witch of Atlas;
Epipsychidion; Hellas.

Vol. III. Posthumous Poems, published by
Mrs. Shelley in 1824 and 1839; The Masque
of Anarchy (from Shelley's manuscript); and
other Pieces not brought together in the ordinary editions.

Prose Works, in Two Vols.

Vol. 1. The Two Romances of Zastrozzi and St.
Irvyne; the Dublin and Marlow Pamphlets; A
Refutation of Deism; Letters to Leigh Hunt,
and some Minor Writings and Fragments.

Vol. II. The Essays; Letters from Abroad;
Translations and Fragments. Edited by Mrs.
Shelley, and first published in 1840, with
the addition of some Minor Pieces of great
interest and rarity, including one recently
discovered by Professor Dowden. With a
Bibliography of Shelley, and an exhaustive
Index of the Prose Works.

Sheridan:—
Sheridan's Complete Works, with
Life and Anecdotes. Including his
Dramatic Writings, printed from the
Original Editions, his Works in
Prose and Poetry, Translations,
Speeches, Jokes, Puns, &c. With a
Collection of Sheridaniana. Crown
8vo, cloth extra, gilt, with 10 full-
page Tinted Illustrations, 7s. 6d.

Sheridan's Comedies: The Rivals,
and The School for Scandal.
Edited, with an Introduction and
Notes to each Play, and a Bio-
graphical Sketch of Sheridan, by
Brander Matthews. With Decora-
tive Vignettes and 10 full-page Illusts.
Demy 8vo, half-parchment, 12s. 6d.

Sidney's (Sir Philip) Complete
Poetical Works, including all those in
"Arcadia." With Portrait, Memorial-
Introduction, Notes, &c., by the Rev.
A. B. Grosart, D.D. Three Vols.,
crown 8vo, cloth boards, 18s.

Signboards: Their History.
With Anecdotes of Famous Taverns
and Remarkable Characters. By
Jacob Larwood and John Camden
Hotten. Crown 8vo, cloth extra,
with 100 Illustrations, 7s. 6d.

Sims (George R.), Works by:
Post 8vo, illustrated boards, 2s. each;
cloth limp, 2s. 6d. each.
Rogues and Vagabonds.
The Ring o' Bells.
Mary Jane's Memoirs.
Mary Jane Married.
Tales of To-day.   [Shortly.

The Dagonet Reciter and Reader:
Being Readings and Recitations in
Prose and Verse, selected from his
own Works by G. R. Sims. Post
8vo, portrait cover, 1s.; cloth, 1s. 6d.

Sister Dora: A Biography. By
Margaret Lonsdale. Popular Edition, Revised, with additional Chapter, a New Dedication and Preface,
and Four Illustrations. Sq. 8vo, picture cover, 4d.; cloth, 6d.

Sketchley.—A Match in the
Dark. By Arthur Sketchley. Post
8vo, illustrated boards, 2s.

Slang Dictionary, The: Etymological, Historical, and Anecdotal.
Crown 8vo, cloth extra, gilt, 6s. 6d.

Smith (J. Moyr), Works by:
The Prince of Argolis: A Story of the
Old Greek Fairy Time. Small 8vo,
cloth extra, with 130 Illusts., 3s. 6d.
Tales of Old Thule. With numerous
Illustrations. Cr. 8vo, cloth gilt, 6s
The Wooing of the Water Witch.
With Illustrations. Small 8vo, 6s.

Society in London. By A
Foreign Resident. Crown 8vo, 1s.;
cloth, 1s. 6d.

Society out of Town. By A
Foreign Resident, Author of "Society in London." Crown 8vo, cloth
extra, 6s.   [Preparing.

Society in Paris: The Upper
Ten Thousand. By Count Paul Vasili.
Trans. by Raphael Ledos de Beau-
fort. Cr. 8vo, cl. ex., 6s. [Preparing.

Somerset.—Songs of Adieu.
By Lord Henry Somerset. Small
4to, Japanese parchment, 6s.

Speight (T. W.), Novels by:
The Mysteries of Heron Dyke.
With a Frontispiece by M. Ellen
Edwards. Crown 8vo, cloth extra,
3s. 6d.; post 8vo, illustrated bds., 2s.
Wife or No Wife? Cr. 8vo, picture
cover, 1s.; cloth, 1s. 6d.
A Barren Title. Crown 8vo, cl., 1s. 6d.
The Golden Hoop. Post 8vo, illust.
boards, 2s.
By Devious Ways; and A Barren
Title. Post 8vo, illust. boards, 2s.

Spalding.—Elizabethan Demonology: An Essay in Illustration of the Belief in the Existence of Devils, and the Powers possessed by Them. By T. A. SPALDING, LL.B. Cr. 8vo, cl. ex., 6s.

Spenser for Children. By M. H. TOWRY. With Illustrations by WALTER J. MORGAN. Crown 4to, with Coloured Illustrations, cloth gilt, 6s.

Staunton.—Laws and Practice of Chess. With an Analysis of the Openings. By HOWARD STAUNTON. Edited by ROBERT B. WORMALD. Small crown 8vo, cloth extra, 5s.

Stedman (E. C.), Works by:
Victorian Poets. Thirteenth Edition. Crown 8vo, cloth extra, 9s.
The Poets of America. Crown 8vo, cloth extra, 9s.

Sterndale.—The Afghan Knife: A Novel. By ROBERT ARMITAGE STERNDALE. Cr. 8vo, cloth extra, 3s. 6d.; post 8vo, illustrated boards, 2s.

Stevenson (R. Louis), Works by:
Travels with a Donkey in the Cevennes. Sixth Ed. Frontispiece by W. CRANE. Post 8vo, cl. limp, 2s. 6d.
An Inland Voyage. Third Edition. With Frontispiece by W. CRANE. Post 8vo, cloth limp, 2s. 6d.
Familiar Studies of Men and Books. 3rd Edit. Cr. 8vo, buckram extra, 6s.
New Arabian Nights. Tenth Edition. Crown 8vo, buckram extra, 6s.; post 8vo, illustrated boards, 2s.
The Silverado Squatters. With Frontispiece. Crown 8vo, buckram extra, 6s. Cheap Edition, post 8vo, picture cover, 1s.; cloth, 1s. 6d.
Prince Otto: A Romance. Sixth Edition. Crown 8vo, buckram extra, 6s.; post 8vo, illustrated boards, 2s.
The Merry Men. Second Edition. Crown 8vo, buckram extra, 6s.
Underwoods: Poems. Fourth Edit. Crown 8vo, buckram extra, 6s.
Memories and Portraits. Second Edition. Cr. 8vo, buckram extra, 6s.
Virginibus Puerisque, and other Papers. Fourth Edition. Crown 8vo, buckram extra, 6s.

St. John.—A Levantine Family. By BAYLE ST. JOHN. Post 8vo, illustrated boards, 2s.

Stoddard.—Summer Cruising in the South Seas. By CHARLES WARREN STODDARD. Illust. by WALLIS MACKAY. Crown 8vo, cl. extra, 3s. 6d.

Stories from Foreign Novelists. With Notices of their Lives and Writings. By HELEN and ALICE ZIMMERN. Frontispiece. Crown 8vo, cloth extra, 3s. 6d.; post 8vo, illust. bds., 2s.

Strange Manuscript (A) found in a Copper Cylinder. With 19 full-page Illustrations by GILBERT GAUL. Third Edition. Cr. 8vo, cl. extra, 5s.

Strange Secrets. Told by PERCY FITZGERALD, FLORENCE MARRYAT, JAMES GRANT, A. CONAN DOYLE, DUTTON COOK, and others. With 8 Illustrations by Sir JOHN GILBERT, WILLIAM SMALL, W. J. HENNESSY, &c. Crown 8vo, cloth extra, 6s.

Strutt's Sports and Pastimes of the People of England; including the Rural and Domestic Recreations, May Games, Mummeries, Shows, &c., from the Earliest Period to the Present Time. With 140 Illustrations. Edited by WM. HONE. Cr. 8vo, cl. extra, 7s. 6d.

Suburban Homes (The) of London: A Residential Guide to Favourite London Localities, their Society, Celebrities, and Associations. With Notes on their Rental, Rates, and House Accommodation. With Map of Suburban London. Cr. 8vo, cl. ex., 7s. 6d.

Swift's Choice Works, in Prose and Verse. With Memoir, Portrait, and Facsimiles of the Maps in the Original Edition of "Gulliver's Travels." Cr. 8vo, cloth extra, 7s. 6d.

Swinburne (Algernon C.), Works by:
Selections from the Poetical Works of Algernon Charles Swinburne. Fcap. 8vo, cloth extra, 6s.
Atalanta in Calydon. Crown 8vo, 6s.
Chastelard. A Tragedy. Cr. 8vo, 7s.
Poems and Ballads. FIRST SERIES. Cr. 8vo, 9s. Fcap. 8vo, same price.
Poems and Ballads. SECOND SERIES. Cr. 8vo, 9s. Fcap. 8vo, same price.
Poems and Ballads. THIRD SERIES. Crown 8vo, 7s.
Notes on Poems and Reviews. 8vo, 1s.
Songs before Sunrise. Cr. 8vo, 10s. 6d.
Bothwell: A Tragedy. Cr. 8vo, 12s. 6d.
George Chapman: An Essay. (See Vol. II. of GEO. CHAPMAN'S Works.) Crown 8vo, 6s.
Songs of Two Nations. Cr. 8vo, 6s.
Essays and Studies. Crown 8vo, 12s.
Erechtheus: A Tragedy. Cr. 8vo, 6s.
Songs of the Springtides. Cr. 8vo, 6s.
Studies in Song. Crown 8vo, 7s.
Mary Stuart: A Tragedy. Cr. 8vo, 8s.
Tristram of Lyonesse, and other Poems. Crown 8vo, 9s.
A Century of Roundels. Small 4to, 8s.
A Midsummer Holiday, and other Poems. Crown 8vo, 7s.
Marino Faliero: A Tragedy. Cr. 8vo, 6s.
A Study of Victor Hugo. Cr. 8vo, 6s.
Miscellanies. Crown 8vo, 12s.
Locrine: A Tragedy. Crown 8vo, 6s.

Symonds.—Wine, Women, and Song: Mediæval Latin Students' Songs. Now first translated into English Verse, with Essay by J. ADDINGTON SYMONDS. Small 8vo, parchment, 6s.

Syntax's (Dr.) Three Tours: In Search of the Picturesque, in Search of Consolation, and in Search of a Wife. With the whole of ROWLANDSON's droll page Illustrations in Colours and a Life of the Author by J. C. HOTTEN. Med. 8vo, cloth extra, 7s. 6d.

Taine's History of English Literature. Translated by HENRY VAN LAUN. Four Vols., small 8vo, cloth boards, 30s.—POPULAR EDITION, Two Vols., crown 8vo, cloth extra, 15s.

Taylor's (Bayard) Diversions of the Echo Club: Burlesques of Modern Writers. Post 8vo, cl. limp, 2s.

Taylor (Dr. J. E., F.L.S.), Works by. Crown 8vo, cloth ex., 7s. 6d. each.
The Sagacity and Morality of Plants: A Sketch of the Life and Conduct of the Vegetable Kingdom. Coloured Frontispiece and 100 Illust.
Our Common British Fossils, and Where to Find Them: A Handbook for Students. With 331 Illustrations.
The Playtime Naturalist. With 366 Illustrations. Crown 8vo, cl. ex., 5s.

Taylor's (Tom) Historical Dramas: "Clancarty," "Jeanne Darc," "'Twixt Axe and Crown," "The Fool's Revenge," "Arkwright's Wife," "Anne Boleyn," "Plot and Passion." One Vol., cr. 8vo, cloth extra, 7s. 6d.
*** The Plays may also be had separately, at 1s. each.

Tennyson (Lord): A Biographical Sketch. By H. J. JENNINGS. With a Photograph-Portrait. Crown 8vo, cloth extra, 6s.

Thackerayana: Notes and Anecdotes. Illustrated by Hundreds of Sketches by WILLIAM MAKEPEACE THACKERAY, depicting Humorous Incidents in his School-life, and Favourite Characters in the books of his every-day reading. With Coloured Frontispiece. Cr. 8vo, cl. extra, 7s. 6d.

Thames.—A New Pictorial History of the Thames, from its Source Downwards. A Book for all Boating Men and for all Lovers of the River. With over 300 Illusts. Post 8vo, picture cover, 1s.; cloth, 1s. 6d. *[Preparing.*

Thomas (Bertha), Novels by. Crown 8vo, cloth extra, 3s. 6d. each; post 8vo, illustrated boards, 2s. each.
Cressida. | Proud Maisie.
The Violin-Player.

Thomas (M.).—A Fight for Life: A Novel. By W. MOY THOMAS. Post 8vo, illustrated boards, 2s.

Thomson's Seasons and Castle of Indolence. With a Biographical and Critical Introduction by ALLAN CUNNINGHAM, and over 50 fine Illustrations on Steel and Wood. Crown 8vo, cloth extra, gilt edges, 7s. 6d.

Thornbury (Walter), Works by: Crown 8vo, cloth extra, 7s. 6d. each.
Haunted London. Edited by EDWARD WALFORD, M.A. With Illustrations by F. W. FAIRHOLT, F.S.A.
The Life and Correspondence of J. M. W. Turner. Founded upon Letters and Papers furnished by his Friends and fellow Academicians. With numerous Illusts. in Colours, facsimiled from Turner's Original Drawings.

Post 8vo, illustrated boards, 2s. each.
Old Stories Re-told.
Tales for the Marines.

Timbs (John), Works by: Crown 8vo, cloth extra, 7s. 6d each.
The History of Clubs and Club Life in London. With Anecdotes of its Famous Coffee-houses, Hostelries, and Taverns. With many Illusts.
English Eccentrics and Eccentricities: Stories of Wealth and Fashion, Delusions, Impostures, and Fanatic Missions, Strange Sights and Sporting Scenes, Eccentric Artists, Theatrical Folk, Men of Letters, &c. With nearly 50 Illusts

Trollope (Anthony), Novels by: Crown 8vo, cloth extra, 3s. 6d. each; post 8vo, illustrated boards, 2s. each.
The Way We Live Now.
Kept in the Dark.
Frau Frohmann. | Marion Fay.
Mr. Scarborough's Family.
The Land-Leaguers.
Post 8vo, illustrated boards, 2s. each.
The Golden Lion of Granpere.
John Caldigate. | American Senator

Trollope (Frances E.), Novels by Crown 8vo, cloth extra, 3s. 6d. each; post 8vo, illustrated boards, 2s. each.
Like Ships upon the Sea.
Mabel's Progress. | Anne Furness.

Trollope (T. A.).—Diamond Cut Diamond, and other Stories. By T. ADOLPHUS TROLLOPE. Post 8vo, illustrated boards, 2s.

Trowbridge.—Farnell's Folly: A Novel. By J. T. TROWBRIDGE. Post 8vo, illustrated boards, 2s.

Turgenieff. — Stories from Foreign Novelists. By IVAN TURGENIEFF, and others. Cr. 8vo, cloth extra, 3s. 6d.; post 8vo, illustrated boards, 2s.

Tytler (C. C. Fraser-). — Mistress Judith: A Novel. By C. C. FRASER-TYTLER. Cr. 8vo, cloth extra, 3s. 6d.; post 8vo, illust. boards, 2s.

Tytler (Sarah), Novels by:
Crown 8vo, cloth extra, 3s. 6d. each; post 8vo, illustrated boards, 2s. each.
What She Came Through.
The Bride's Pass. | Noblesse Oblige.
Saint Mungo's City. | Lady Bell.
Beauty and the Beast.
Citoyenne Jacqueline.
Buried Diamonds.
Post 8vo, illustrated boards, 2s. each.
Disappeared.
The Huguenot Family
The Blackhall Ghosts: A Novel. Crown 8vo, cl. ex., 3s. 6d.

Van Laun.— History of French Literature. By H. VAN LAUN. Three Vols., demy 8vo, cl. bds., 7s. 6d. each.

Villari. — A Double Bond: A Story. By LINDA VILLARI. Fcap. 8vo, picture cover, 1s.

Walford (Edw., M.A.), Works by:
The County Families of the United Kingdom (1889). Containing Notices of the Descent, Birth, Marriage, Education, &c., of more than 12,000 distinguished Heads of Families, their Heirs Apparent or Presumptive, the Offices they hold or have held, their Town and Country Addresses, Clubs, &c. Twenty-ninth Annual Edition. Cloth gilt, 50s.
The Shilling Peerage (1889). Containing an Alphabetical List of the House of Lords, Dates of Creation, Lists of Scotch and Irish Peers, Addresses, &c. 32mo, cloth, 1s.
The Shilling Baronetage (1889). Containing an Alphabetical List of the Baronets of the United Kingdom, short Biographical Notices, Dates of Creation, Addresses, &c. 32mo, cl., 1s.
The Shilling Knightage (1889). Containing an Alphabetical List of the Knights of the United Kingdom, short Biographical Notices, Dates of Creation, Addresses, &c. 32mo, cl., 1s.
The Shilling House of Commons (1889). Containing a List of all the Members of Parliament, their Town and Country Addresses, &c. 32mo, cloth, 1s.
The Complete Peerage, Baronetage, Knightage, and House of Commons (1889). In One Volume, royal 32mo, cloth extra, gilt edges, 5s.

Walford's (Edw.) Works, *continued*—
Haunted London. By WALTER THORNBURY. Edited by EDWARD WALFORD, M.A. With Illustrations by F. W. FAIRHOLT, F.S.A. Crown 8vo, cloth extra, 7s. 6d.

Walton and Cotton's Complete Angler; or, The Contemplative Man's Recreation; being a Discourse of Rivers, Fishponds, Fish and Fishing, written by IZAAK WALTON; and Instructions how to Angle for a Trout or Grayling in a clear Stream, by CHARLES COTTON. With Original Memoirs and Notes by Sir HARRIS NICOLAS, and 61 Copperplate Illustrations. Large crown 8vo, cloth antique, 7s. 6d.

Walt Whitman, Poems by. Selected and edited, with an Introduction, by WILLIAM M. ROSSETTI. A New Edition, with a Steel Plate Portrait. Crown 8vo, printed on hand-made paper and bound in buckram, 6s.

Wanderer's Library, The:
Crown 8vo, cloth extra, 3s. 6d. each.
Wanderings in Patagonia; or, Life among the Ostrich-Hunters. By JULIUS BEERBOHM. Illustrated.
Camp Notes: Stories of Sport and Adventure in Asia, Africa, and America. By FREDERICK BOYLE.
Savage Life. By FREDERICK BOYLE.
Merrie England in the Olden Time. By GEORGE DANIEL. With Illustrations by ROBT. CRUIKSHANK.
Circus Life and Circus Celebrities By THOMAS FROST.
The Lives of the Conjurers. By THOMAS FROST.
The Old Showmen and the Old London Fairs. By THOMAS FROST.
Low-Life Deeps. An Account of the Strange Fish to be found there. By JAMES GREENWOOD.
The Wilds of London. By JAMES GREENWOOD.
Tunis: The Land and the People. By the Chevalier de HESSE-WARTEGG. With 22 Illustrations.
The Life and Adventures of a Cheap Jack. By One of the Fraternity. Edited by CHARLES HINDLEY.
The World Behind the Scenes By PERCY FITZGERALD.
Tavern Anecdotes and Sayings: Including the Origin of Signs, and Reminiscences connected with Taverns, Coffee Houses, Clubs, &c. By CHARLES HINDLEY. With Illusts
The Genial Showman: Life and Adventures of Artemus Ward. By E. P. HINGSTON. With a Frontispiece.
The Story of the London Parks. By JACOB LARWOOD. With Illusts.
London Characters. By HENRY MAYHEW. Illustrated.

WANDERER'S LIBRARY, THE, *continued—*
Crown 8vo, cloth extra, 3s. 6d. each.
Seven Generations of Executioners: Memoirs of the Sanson Family (1688 to 1847). Edited by HENRY SANSON.
Summer Cruising in the South Seas. By C. WARREN STODDARD. Illustrated by WALLIS MACKAY

Warner.—A Roundabout Journey. By CHARLES DUDLEY WARNER, Author of "My Summer in a Garden." Crown 8vo, cloth extra, 6s.

Warrants, &c. :—
Warrant to Execute Charles I. An exact Facsimile, with the Fifty-nine Signatures, and corresponding Seals. Carefully printed on paper to imitate the Original, 22 in. by 14 in. Price 2s.
Warrant to Execute Mary Queen of Scots. An exact Facsimile, including the Signature of Queen Elizabeth, and a Facsimile of the Great Seal. Beautifully printed on paper to imitate the Original MS. Price 2s.
Magna Charta. An exact Facsimile of the Original Document in the British Museum, printed on fine plate paper, nearly 3 feet long by 2 feet wide, with the Arms and Seals emblazoned in Gold and Colours. 5s.
The Roll of Battle Abbey; or, A List of the Principal Warriors who came over from Normandy with William the Conqueror, and Settled in this Country, A.D. 1066-7. With the principal Arms emblazoned in Gold and Colours. Price 5s.

Wayfarer, The : Journal of the Society of Cyclists. Published at intervals. Price 1s. The Numbers for OCT., 1886, JAN., MAY, and OCT., 1887, and FEB., 1888, are now ready.

Weather, How to Foretell the, with the Pocket Spectroscope. By F. W. CORY, M.R.C.S. Eng., F.R.Met. Soc., &c. With 10 Illustrations. Crown 8vo, 1s. ; cloth, 1s. 6d.

Westropp.—Handbook of Pottery and Porcelain; or, History of those Arts from the Earliest Period. By HODDER M. WESTROPP. With numerous Illustrations, and a List of Marks. Crown 8vo, cloth limp, 4s. 6d.

Whist. — How to Play Solo Whist: Its Method and Principles Explained, and its Practice Demonstrated. With Illustrative Specimen Hands in red and black, and a Revised and Augmented Code of Laws. By ABRAHAM S. WILKS and CHARLES F. PARDON. Crown 8vo, cloth extra, 3s. 6d.

Whistler's (Mr.) "Ten o'Clock." Crown 8vo, hand-made and brown paper, 1s.

Williams (W. Mattieu, F.R.A.S.), Works by :
Science in Short Chapters. Crown 8vo, cloth extra, 7s. 6d.
A Simple Treatise on Heat. Crown 8vo, cloth limp, with Illusts., 2s. 6d.
The Chemistry of Cookery. Crown 8vo, cloth extra, 6s.

Wilson (Dr. Andrew, F.R.S.E.), Works by :
Chapters on Evolution: A Popular History of Darwinian and Allied Theories of Development. 3rd ed. Cr. 8vo, cl. ex., with 259 Illusts., 7s. 6d.
Leaves from a Naturalist's Note- book. Post 8vo, cloth limp, 2s. 6d.
Leisure-Time Studies, chiefly Biological. Third Edit., with New Preface. Cr. 8vo, cl. ex., with Illusts., 6s.
Studies in Life and Sense. With numerous Illusts. Cr. 8vo, cl. ex., 6s
Common Accidents, and How to Treat them. By Dr. ANDREW WILSON and others. With numerous Illusts. Cr. 8vo, 1s. ; cl. limp, 1s. 6d.

Winter (J. S.), Stories by :
Post 8vo, illustrated boards, 2s. each.
Cavalry Life. | **Regimental Legends.**

Women of the Day : A Biogra- phical Dictionary of Notable Contemporaries. By FRANCES HAYS. Crown 8vo, cloth extra, 5s.

Wood.—Sabina: A Novel. By Lady WOOD. Post 8vo, illust. bds., 2s.

Wood (H.F.), Detective Stories :
The Passenger from Scotland Yard. Crown 8vo, cloth extra, 6s.; post 8vo, illustrated boards, 2s.
The Englishman of the Rue Caïn. Crown 8vo, cloth extra, 6s.

Woolley.—Rachel Armstrong ; or, Love and Theology. By CELIA PARKER WOOLLEY. Post 8vo, illustrated boards, 2s. ; cloth, 2s. 6d.

Words, Facts, and Phrases : A Dictionary of Curious, Quaint, and Out-of-the-Way Matters. By ELIEZER EDWARDS. New and cheaper issue, cr. 8vo, cl. ex., 7s. 6d. ; half-bound, 9s.

Wright (Thomas), Works by :
Crown 8vo, cloth extra, 7s. 6d. each.
Caricature History of the Georges. (The House of Hanover.) With 400 Pictures, Caricatures, Squibs, Broadsides, Window Pictures, &c.
History of Caricature and of the Grotesque in Art, Literature, Sculpture, and Painting. Profusely Illustrated by F. W. FAIRHOLT, F.S.A.

Yates (Edmund), Novels by :
Post 8vo, illustrated boards, 2s. each.
Land at Last. | **The Forlorn Hope.**

NEW NOVELS.

Blood-Money, and other Stories. By CHARLES GIBBON. 2 Vols., crown 8vo, cloth, 12s.

A Strange Manuscript found in a Copper Cylinder. Illustrated by GILBERT GAUL. Third Edit. Cr. 8vo, 5s.

The Legacy of Cain. By WILKIE COLLINS. 3 Vols., cr. 8vo.

For Faith and Freedom. By WALTER BESANT. 3 Vols., cr. 8vo.

The Englishman of the Rue Cain. By H. F. WOOD. Crown 8vo, cloth extra, 6s.

Romances of the Law. By R. E. FRANCILLON. Cr. 8vo, cloth extra, 6s.

Strange Secrets. Told by PERCY FITZGERALD, &c. With 8 Illustrations. Crown 8vo, cloth extra, 6s.

Doctor Rameau. By GEORGES OHNET. Nine Illusts. Cr. 8vo, cloth extra, 6s.

This Mortal Coil. By GRANT ALLEN. 3 Vols., crown 8vo.

Agatha Page. By ISAAC HENDERSON. 2 Vols., crown 8vo.

Chance? or Fate? By ALICE O'HANLON. 3 vols., crown 8vo.

Children of To-morrow. By WILLIAM SHARP. Crown 8vo, cloth extra, 6s.

Nikanor. From the French of HENRI GREVILLE. With Eight Illustrations. Crown 8vo, cloth extra, 6s.

Mr. Stranger's Sealed Packet. By HUGH MacCOLL. Crown 8vo, cloth extra, 5s.

Guilderoy. By OUIDA. 3 Vols., crown 8vo. [*June.*

THE PICCADILLY NOVELS.

Popular Stories by the Best Authors. LIBRARY EDITIONS, many Illustrated, crown 8vo, cloth extra, 3s. 6d. each.

BY THE AUTHOR OF "JOHN HERRING."

Red Spider. | Eve.

BY GRANT ALLEN.

Philistia.
For Maimie' Sake.
The Devil's Die.

BY WALTER BESANT & J. RICE.

Ready-Money Mortiboy.
My Little Girl.
The Case of Mr. Lucraft.
This Son of Vulcan.
With Harp and Crown.
The Golden Butterfly.
By Celia's Arbour.
The Monks of Thelema.
'Twas in Trafalgar's Bay.
The Seamy Side.
The Ten Years' Tenant.
The Chaplain of the Fleet.

BY WALTER BESANT.

All Sorts and Conditions of Men.
The Captains' Room.
All in a Garden Fair.
Dorothy Forster. | Uncle Jack.
Children of Gibeon.
The World Went Very Well Then.
Herr Paulus.

BY ROBERT BUCHANAN.

A Child of Nature.
God and the Man.
The Shadow of the Sword.
The Martyrdom of Madeline.
Love Me for Ever.
Annan Water. | The New Abelard
Matt. | Foxglove Manor.
The Master of the Mine.
The Heir of Linne.

BY HALL CAINE.

The Shadow of a Crime.
A Son of Hagar. | The Deemster.

BY MRS. H. LOVETT CAMERON.

Juliet's Guardian. | Deceivers Ever.

BY MORTIMER COLLINS.

Sweet Anne Page. | Transmigration.
From Midnight to Midnight.

MORTIMER & FRANCES COLLINS.

Blacksmith and Scholar.
The Village Comedy.
You Play me False.

BY WILKIE COLLINS.

Antonina.
Basil.
Hide and Seek.
The Dead Secret.
Queen of Hearts.
My Miscellanies.
Woman in White.
The Moonstone.
Man and Wife.
Poor Miss Finch.
Miss or Mrs.?
New Magdalen.
The Frozen Deep.
The Law and the Lady.
The Two Destinies
Haunted Hotel.
The Fallen Leaves
Jezabel'e Daughter
The Black Robe.
Heart and Science
"I Say No."
Little Novels.
The Evil Genius.

BY DUTTON COOK.

Paul Foster's Daughter.

BY WILLIAM CYPLES.

Hearts of Gold.

BY ALPHONSE DAUDET.

The Evangelist; or, Port Salvation.

BY JAMES DE MILLE.

A Castle in Spain.

BY J. LEITH DERWENT.

Our Lady of Tears.
Circe's Lovers.

BY M. BETHAM-EDWARDS.

Felicia.

BY MRS. ANNIE EDWARDES.

Archie Lovell.

BY PERCY FITZGERALD.

Fatal Zero.

PICCADILLY NOVELS, *continued—*
BY R. E. FRANCILLON.
Queen Cophetua.
One by One.
A Real Queen.
King or Knave?
 Prefaced by Sir BARTLE FRERE.
Pandurang Hari.
BY EDWARD GARRETT.
The Capel Girls.
BY CHARLES GIBBON.
Robin Gray.
What will the World Say?
In Honour Bound.
Queen of the Meadow.
The Flower of the Forest.
A Heart's Problem.
The Braes of Yarrow.
The Golden Shaft.
Of High Degree.
Loving a Dream.
BY THOMAS HARDY.
Under the Greenwood Tree.
BY JULIAN HAWTHORNE.
Garth.
Ellice Quentin.
Sebastian Strome.
Dust.
Fortune's Fool.
Beatrix Randolph.
David Poindexter's Disappearance
The Spectre of the Camera.
BY SIR A. HELPS.
Ivan de Biron.
BY MRS. ALFRED HUNT
Thornicroft's Model.
The Leaden Casket.
Self-Condemned.
That other Person.
BY JEAN INGELOW.
Fated to be Free.
BY R. ASHE KING.
A Drawn Game.
"The Wearing of the Green."
BY HENRY KINGSLEY.
Number Seventeen.
BY E. LYNN LINTON.
Patricia Kemball.
Atonement of Leam Dundas.
The World Well Lost.
Under which Lord?
"My Love!"
Ione.
Paston Carew.
BY HENRY W. LUCY.
Gideon Fleyce.
BY JUSTIN McCARTHY.
The Waterdale Neighbours.
A Fair Saxon.
Dear Lady Disdain.
Miss Misanthrope.
Donna Quixote.
The Comet of a Season.
Maid of Athens.
Camiola.

PICCADILLY NOVELS, *continued—*
BY MRS. MACDONELL.
Quaker Cousins.
BY FLORENCE MARRYAT.
Open! Sesame! | Written in Fire
BY D. CHRISTIE MURRAY.
Life's Atonement. | Coals of Fire.
Joseph's Coat. | Val Strange.
A Model Father. | Hearts.
By the Gate of the Sea.
A Bit of Human Nature.
First Person Singular.
Cynic Fortune.
BY MRS. OLIPHANT.
Whiteladies.
BY OUIDA.
Held in Bondage. | Two Little Wooden
Strathmore. | Shoes.
Chandos. | In a Winter City
Under Two Flags. | Ariadne.
Idalia. | Friendship.
Cecil Castle- | Moths.
 maine's Gage. | Pipistrello.
Tricotrin. | A Village Com-
Puck. | mune.
Folle Farine. | Bimbi.
A Dog of Flanders | Wanda.
Pascarel. | Frescoes.
Signa. [ine. | In Maremma
Princess Naprax- | Othmar.
BY MARGARET A. PAUL.
Gentle and Simple.
BY JAMES PAYN.
Lost Sir Massing- | A Grape from a
 berd. | Thorn.
Walter's Word. | Some Private
Less Black than | Views.
 We're Painted. | The Canon's Ward.
By Proxy. | Talk of the Town.
High Spirits. | Glow-worm Tales.
Under One Roof. | In Peril and Pri-
A Confidential | vation.
 Agent. | Holiday Tasks.
From Exile. | The Mystery of
 | Mirbridge.
BY E. C. PRICE.
Valentina. | The Foreigners.
Mrs. Lancaster's Rival.
BY CHARLES READE.
It is Never Too Late to Mend.
Hard Cash. | Peg Woffington.
Christie Johnstone.
Griffith Gaunt. | Foul Play.
The Double Marriage.
Love Me Little, Love Me Long.
The Cloister and the Hearth.
The Course of True Love.
The Autobiography of a Thief.
Put Yourself in His Place.
A Terrible Temptation
The Wandering Heir. | A Simpleton.
A Woman-Hater. | Readiana.
Singleheart and Doubleface.
The Jilt.
Good Stories of Men and other
 Animals.

CHEAP POPULAR NOVELS, *continued—*
WILKIE COLLINS, *continued.*

Miss or Mrs.?	The Fallen Leaves.
New Magdalen.	Jezabel's Daughter
The Frozen Deep.	The Black Robe.
The Law and the Lady.	Heart and Science
The Two Destinies	"I Say No."
Haunted Hotel.	The Evil Genius.
	Little Novels.

BY MORTIMER COLLINS.

Sweet Anna Page.	From Midnight to Midnight.
Transmigration.	

A Fight with Fortune.

MORTIMER & FRANCES COLLINS.

Sweet and Twenty.	Frances.

Blacksmith and Scholar.
The Village Comedy.
You Play me False.

BY M. J. COLQUHOUN.
Every Inch a Soldier.

BY MONCURE D. CONWAY.
Pine and Palm.

BY DUTTON COOK.

Leo.	Paul Foster's Daughter.

BY C. EGBERT CRADDOCK.
The Prophet of the Great Smoky Mountains.

BY WILLIAM CYPLES.
Hearts of Gold.

BY ALPHONSE DAUDET.
The Evangelist; or, Port Salvation.

BY JAMES DE MILLE.
A Castle in Spain.

BY J. LEITH DERWENT.

Our Lady of Tears.	Circe's Lovers.

BY CHARLES DICKENS.

Sketches by Boz.	Oliver Twist.
Pickwick Papers.	Nicholas Nicklaby

BY DICK DONOVAN.
The Man-Hunter.
Caught at Last!

BY MRS. ANNIE EDWARDES.

Point of Honour.	Archie Lovell.

BY M. BETHAM-EDWARDS.

Felicia.	Kitty.

BY EDWARD EGGLESTON.
Roxy.

BY PERCY FITZGERALD.

Bella Donna.	Never Forgotten.
The Second Mrs. Tillotson.	
Polly.	Fatal Zero.

Seventy-five Brooke Street.
The Lady of Brantome.

BY ALBANY DE FONBLANQUE.
Filthy Lucre.

BY R. E. FRANCILLON.

Olympia.	Queen Cophetua.
One by One.	A Real Queen.

BY HAROLD FREDERIC.
Seth's Brother's Wife.
Prefaced by Sir H. BARTLE FRERE.
Pandurang Hari.

BY HAIN FRISWELL.
One of Two.

BY EDWARD GARRETT.
The Capel Girls.

CHEAP POPULAR NOVELS, *continued—*
BY CHARLES GIBBON.

Robin Gray.	The Flower of the Forest.
For Lack of Gold.	
What will the World Say?	Braes of Yarrow.
	The Golden Shaft.
In Honour Bound.	Of High Degree.
In Love and War.	Fancy Free.
For the King.	Mead and Stream.
In Pastures Green	Loving a Dream.
Queen of the Meadow.	A Hard Knot.
	Heart's Delight.
A Heart's Problem	

BY WILLIAM GILBERT.

Dr. Austin's Guests.	James Duke

The Wizard of the Mountain.

BY JAMES GREENWOOD.
Dick Temple.

BY JOHN HABBERTON.

Brueton's Bayou.	Country Luck.

BY ANDREW HALLIDAY
Every-Day Papers.

BY LADY DUFFUS HARDY.
Paul Wynter's Sacrifice.

BY THOMAS HARDY.
Under the Greenwood Tree.

BY J. BERWICK HARWOOD.
The Tenth Earl.

BY JULIAN HAWTHORNE.

Garth.	Sebastian Strome
Ellice Quentin.	Dust.
Prince Saroni's Wife.	
Fortune's Fool.	Beatrix Randolph.
Miss Cadogna.	Love—or a Name.

David Poindexter's Disappearance.

BY SIR ARTHUR HELPS.
Ivan de Biron.

BY MRS. CASHEL HOEY.
The Lover's Creed.

BY TOM HOOD.
A Golden Heart.

BY MRS. GEORGE HOOPER.
The House of Raby.

BY TIGHE HOPKINS.
'Twixt Love and Duty.

BY MRS. ALFRED HUNT.
Thornicroft's Model.
The Leaden Casket.

Self-Condemned.	That other Person

BY JEAN INGELOW.
Fated to be Free.

BY HARRIETT JAY.
The Dark Colleen.
The Queen of Connaught.

BY MARK KERSHAW.
Colonial Facts and Fictions.

BY R. ASHE KING.
A Drawn Game.
"The Wearing of the Green."

BY HENRY KINGSLEY.
Oakshott Castle

BY JOHN LEYS.
The Lindsays.

BY MARY LINSKILL.
In Exchange for a Soul.

BY E. LYNN LINTON.
Patricia Kemball.
The Atonement of Leam Dundas

CHEAP POPULAR NOVELS, *continued—*
E. LYNN LINTON, *continued—*
The World Well Lost.
Under which Lord? | Paston Carew.
With a Silken Thread.
The Rebel of the Family.
"My Love." | Ione.

BY HENRY W. LUCY.
Gideon Fleyce.

BY JUSTIN McCARTHY.
Dear Lady Disdain | Miss Misanthrope
The Waterdale Neighbours. | Donna Quixote.
My Enemy's Daughter. | The Comet of a Season.
A Fair Saxon. | Maid of Athens.
Linley Rochford. | Camiola.

BY MRS. MACDONELL.
Quaker Cousins.

BY KATHARINE S. MACQUOID.
The Evil Eye. | Lost Rose.

BY W. H. MALLOCK.
The New Republic.

BY FLORENCE MARRYAT.
Open! Sesame. | Fighting the Air.
A Harvest of Wild Oats. | Written in Fire.

BY J. MASTERMAN.
Half-a-dozen Daughters.

BY BRANDER MATTHEWS.
A Secret of the Sea.

BY JEAN MIDDLEMASS.
Touch and Go. | Mr. Dorillion.

BY MRS. MOLESWORTH.
Hathercourt Rectory.

BY J. E. MUDDOCK.
Stories Weird and Wonderful.

BY D. CHRISTIE MURRAY.
A Life's Atonement | Hearts.
A Model Father. | Way of the World.
Joseph's Coat. | A Bit of Human Nature.
Coals of Fire. | First Person Sin-
By the Gate of the Sea. | gular.
Val Strange [Sea. | Cynic Fortune.
Old Blazer's Hero. |

BY ALICE O'HANLON.
The Unforeseen.

BY MRS. OLIPHANT.
Whiteladies. | The Primrose Path.
The Greatest Heiress in England.

BY MRS. ROBERT O'REILLY.
Phœbe's Fortunes.

BY OUIDA.
Held in Bondage. | Two Little Wooden
Strathmore. | Shoes.
Chandos. | Ariadne.
Under Two Flags. | Friendship.
Idalia. | Moths.
Cecil Castle- | Pipistrello.
maine's Gage. | A Village Com-
Tricotrin. | Puck. | mune.
Folle Farine. | Bimbi. | Wanda.
A Dog of Flanders. | Frescoes.
Pascarel. | In Maremma.
Signa. [Ine. | Othmar.
Princess Naprax- | Wisdom, Wit, and
In a Winter City | Pathos.

CHEAP POPULAR NOVELS, *continued—*
BY MARGARET AGNES PAUL.
Gentle and Simple.

BY JAMES PAYN.
Lost Sir Massing- | Marine Residence.
berd. | Married Beneath
A Perfect Treasure | Him.
Bentinck's Tutor. | Mirk Abbey.
Murphy's Master. | Not Wooed, but
A County Family. | Won.
At Her Mercy. | Less Black than
A Woman's Ven- | We're Painted.
geance. | By Proxy.
Cecil's Tryst. | Under One Roof.
Clyffards of Clyffe | High Spirits.
The Family Scape- | Carlyon's Year.
grace. | A Confidential
Foster Brothers. | Agent.
Found Dead. | Some Private
Best of Husbands. | Views.
Walter's Word. | From Exile.
Halves. | A Grape from a
Fallen Fortunes. | Thorn.
What He Cost Her | For Cash Only.
Humorous Stories | Kit: A Memory.
Gwendoline's Har- | The Canon's Ward
vest. | Talk of the Town.
£200 Reward. | Holiday Tasks.
Like Father, Like | Glow-worm Tales.
Son. |

BY C. L. PIRKIS.
Lady Lovelace.

BY EDGAR A. POE.
The Mystery of Marie Roget.

BY E. C. PRICE.
Valentina. | The Foreigners
Mrs. Lancaster's Rival.
Gerald.

BY CHARLES READE.
It Is Never Too Late to Mend.
Hard Cash. | Peg Woffington.
Christie Johnstone.
Griffith Gaunt.
Put Yourself in His Place.
The Double Marriage.
Love Me Little, Love Me Long.
Foul Play.
The Cloister and the Hearth.
The Course of True Love.
Autobiography of a Thief.
A Terrible Temptation.
The Wandering Heir.
A Simpleton. | A Woman-Hater.
Readiana. | The Jilt.
Singleheart and Doubleface.
Good Stories of Men and other Animals.

BY MRS. J. H. RIDDELL.
Her Mother's Darling.
Prince of Wales's Garden Party.
Weird Stories. | Fairy Water.
The Uninhabited House.
The Mystery in Palace Gardens.

BY F. W. ROBINSON.
Women are Strange.
The Hands of Justice.

CHEAP POPULAR NOVELS, *continued—*
BY JAMES RUNCIMAN.
Skippers and Shellbacks.
Grace Balmaign's Sweetheart.
Schools and Scholars.
BY W. CLARK RUSSELL
Round the Galley Fire.
On the Fo'k'sle Head.
In the Middle Watch.
A Voyage to the Cape.
A Book for the Hammock.
BY BAYLE ST. JOHN.
A Levantine Family.
BY GEORGE AUGUSTUS SALA.
Gaslight and Daylight.
BY JOHN SAUNDERS.
Bound to the Wheel.
One Against the World.
Guy Waterman. | Two Dreamers.
The Lion in the Path.
BY KATHARINE SAUNDERS.
Joan Merryweather. | The High Mills.
Margaret and Elizabeth.
Heart Salvage. | Sebastian.
BY GEORGE R. SIMS.
Rogues and Vagabonds.
The Ring o' Bells. | Mary Jane Married.
Mary Jane's Memoirs.
Tales of To-day.
BY ARTHUR SKETCHLEY.
A Match in the Dark.
BY T. W. SPEIGHT.
The Mysteries of Heron Dyke.
The Golden Hoop. | By Devious Ways.
BY R. A. STERNDALE.
The Afghan Knife.
BY R. LOUIS STEVENSON.
New Arabian Nights. | Prince Otto.
BY BERTHA THOMAS.
Cressida. | Proud Maisie.
The Violin-Player.
BY W. MOY THOMAS.
A Fight for Life.
BY WALTER THORNBURY.
Tales for the Marines.
Old Stories Re-told.
BY T. ADOLPHUS TROLLOPE.
Diamond Cut Diamond.
BY ANTHONY TROLLOPE.
The Way We Live Now.
The American Senator.
Frau Frohmann. | Marion Fay.
Kept in the Dark.
Mr. Scarborough's Family.
The Land-Leaguers. | John Caldigate
The Golden Lion of Granpere.
By F. ELEANOR TROLLOPE.
Like Ships upon the Sea.
Anne Furness. | Mabel's Progress.
BY J. T. TROWBRIDGE.
Farnell's Folly.
BY IVAN TURGENIEFF, &c.
Stories from Foreign Novelists.
BY MARK TWAIN.
Tom Sawyer. | A Tramp Abroad.
The Stolen White Elephant.

CHEAP POPULAR NOVELS, *continued—*
MARK TWAIN, *continued.*
A Pleasure Trip on the Continent
Huckleberry Finn.   [of Europe
Life on the Mississippi.
The Prince and the Pauper.
BY C. C. FRASER-TYTLER.
Mistress Judith.
BY SARAH TYTLER.
What She Came Through.
The Bride's Pass.| Buried Diamonds
Saint Mungo's City.
Beauty and the Beast.
Lady Bell. | Noblesse Oblige.
Citoyenne Jacqueline | Disappeared
The Huguenot Family.
BY J. S. WINTER.
Cavalry Life. | Regimental Legends
BY H. F. WOOD.
The Passenger from Scotland Yard.
BY LADY WOOD.
Sabina.
BY CELIA PARKER WOOLLEY.
Rachel Armstrong; or, Love & Theology.
BY EDMUND YATES.
The Forlorn Hope. | Land at Last.
ANONYMOUS.
Paul Ferroll.
Why Paul Ferroll Killed his Wife.

POPULAR SHILLING BOOKS.
Jeff Briggs's Love Story.   By BRET
  HARTE.   [Ditto.
The Twins of Table Mountain. By
A Day's Tour. By PERCY FITZGERALD.
Mrs. Gainsborough's Diamonds. By
  JULIAN HAWTHORNE.
A Dream and a Forgetting. By ditto.
A Romance of the Queen's Hounds.
  By CHARLES JAMES.   [BURNETT.
Kathleen Mavourneen. By Mrs.
Lindsay's Luck. By Mrs. BURNETT.
Pretty Polly Pemberton. By Ditto.
Trooping with Crows. By C. L. PIRKIS
The Professor's Wife. By L. GRAHAM.
A Double Bond. By LINDA VILLARI.
Esther's Glove. By R. E. FRANCILLON.
The Garden that Paid the Rent
  By TOM JERROLD.
Curly. By JOHN COLEMAN. Illus-
  trated by J. C. DOLLMAN.
Beyond the Gates. By E. S. PHELPS
Old Maid's Paradise. By E. S. PHELPS
Burglars in Paradise. By E. S. PHELPS.
Jack the Fisherman. By E. S. PHELPS.
Doom: An Atlantic Episode. By
  JUSTIN H. MCCARTHY, M.P.
Our Sensation Novel. Edited by
  JUSTIN H. MCCARTHY, M.P.
Dolly. By ditto.   [WORTH.
That Girl in Black. By Mrs. MOLES-
Was She Good or Bad? By W. MINTO.
Bible Characters. By CHAS. READE.
The Dagonet Reciter. By G. R. SIMS.
Wife or No Wife? By T. W. SPEIGHT.
The Silverado Squatters. By R.
  LOUIS STEVENSON.

www.ingramcontent.com/pod-product-compliance
Lightning Source LLC
Chambersburg PA
CBHW031128120726
47905CB00006B/1611